# Just Around the Bend

## DIANE GREENWOOD MUIR

Cover Design Photography: Maxim M. Muir

ISBN: 1548332135
ISBN-13: 978-1548332136

*Don't miss any books in Diane Greenwood Muir's*

# Bellingwood Series

Diane publishes a new book in this series
on the 25th of March, June, September, and December.
Short stories are published in between those dates
and vignettes are written and published each month
in the newsletter.

# Journals

(Paperback only)
Find Joy – A Gratitude Journal
Books are Life – A Reading Journal
Capture Your Memories – A Journal

# Re-told Bible Stories

(Kindle only)
Abiding Love - the story of Ruth
Abiding Grace - the story of the Prodigal Son

You can find a list of all published works
at nammynools.com

# CONTENTS

# ACKNOWLEDGMENTS

I am writing this on Father's Day. Mine was a man who taught his children to be strong-willed, exercise patience, never give up, and work hard. We've all applied those virtues in different ways. Some may call me a work-aholic and I am ... because of him.

But now that I've discovered this life, I love being able to work insane hours. There is so much satisfaction in creating and I can't imagine not pouring all that I have into it. What a ride.

There are so many people who work with me through this process to ensure my books continue to get better and better. I am so grateful to each of them. It's incredible how different they are in what they see and uncover when they attack my manuscript - and in what they teach me. Thank you to: Diane Wendt, Carol Greenwood, Alice Stewart, Eileen Adickes, Fran Neff, Max Muir, Linda Baker, Linda Watson, Nancy Quist, and Judy Tew. They raise the bar for me and that means I move forward with confidence.

Though news and social media would like us to believe that the worst of life is the most important, they're wrong. The world is made up of people like those in Bellingwood. I meet them every day in the community we're building on Facebook. My readers are incredible people and I wish you could know all of them like I do. Spend time with us at facebook.com/pollygiller.

# CHAPTER ONE

Polly shifted in her seat. According to the program, there were only three more numbers. She gave a sideways glance to Henry, who smirked back at her. These long, combined music concerts were deadly. Rebecca was excited about this evening, though, and with good reason. Just before the band entered, the director recognized the outgoing eighth-graders. Rebecca and two others were singled out for their leadership. At the awards program last week, the respect Rebecca's teachers and fellow students had for her was expressed in certificates, plaques and awards. It had been a proud night for all of them. Polly hoped Sarah Heater knew what a wonderful daughter she raised.

Henry put his hand on Polly's back. She looked past him to Noah and Heath. The little boys had been squirming for a while now and she'd finally split them up. Elijah was doing his best to stay alert beside her. They were good boys, but this was a lot to ask of them. As far as Polly was concerned, it was a lot to ask of anyone.

Elijah wrapped his arm around hers and she smiled down at him just as he opened his mouth in a huge yawn.

"Only three more songs," she whispered. "You're doing great."

"I'm bored," he whispered back, louder than Polly would have liked.

His comment elicited a few giggles from the people in front of them and she patted his knee. She sat up straight and rolled her shoulders. The director raised her hands, instruments came up, and the music started.

Elijah leaned against Polly's arm and she gently pushed him back into his seat. "Sit still," she said. "You can do this."

He slouched his shoulders and set his jaw.

Polly grinned. Neither Mary nor her father let her get away with much when she was his age. She remembered sitting beside her dad in church, desperate to do what every other kid around her was doing — lying down in the pew, or leaning on a parent while attempting to sleep. Not Everett Giller's daughter. He expected her to sit quietly in her seat during the sermon. It was generally only for twenty minutes and there was no reason she couldn't behave for that amount of time. He didn't mind if she doodled on the bulletin, but there were no coloring books or other distractions. He fully intended for her to behave in quiet situations.

The only thing that had done for Polly was give her imagination plenty of time to roam.

When Elijah leaned on her again, she pushed him back into place and whispered, "Sit still. Dream about Little E and the adventures he's having."

Elijah smiled up at her and nodded.

Polly thought about all that was coming up in the next couple of weeks. They'd already been through many events this spring. Bill and Marie's return to Bellingwood from Arizona was celebrated with a huge party at the Bell House. Sylvie had asked Polly to help with Andrew's birthday celebration in April — a trip to Boone for a train ride and of course a run to the bookstore. The junior high production of *Young Sherlock* with Andrew as Commander Lestrade and Rebecca as Mrs. Butterworth was a grand success and Polly hosted a cast party. Noah and Elijah's school program had been a riot. Then Henry's grandparents and sister came into town for the family's Easter celebration. And Mother's Day was much tamer this year, which made Polly very happy.

Rebecca had wanted nothing more for her birthday than a short trip with Polly to go shopping. And by short trip, she wanted an overnight stay in a hotel. They spent Saturday shopping in the Amana Colonies and then came home after breakfast Sunday morning. Rebecca thought she'd like to do that every year.

Heath's graduation party was coming up, but Polly wasn't as concerned as she had been a few months ago.

When the initial round of rooms upstairs were finished, they moved Rebecca up first. She loved her new room. Since it faced west, she got to see the sunset every evening and chose to paint the west wall in large swaths of color — yellows, oranges, pinks, reds and purples. For now, the other three walls were off-white, but Polly gave her permission to do whatever she wanted with them. The room was big enough that she was able to have the dresser from her mother's room and an old recliner they'd had in the living room. Rebecca picked out fabric and Polly was struggling to sew a cover for the recliner, but it would be finished soon. Rebecca's easels sat beside the windows until they figured out an effective way to heat the outside studio.

Noah and Elijah were excited to have a great big room all to themselves. They liked to leave the door open so the dogs could sleep with them at night. Though Obiwan and Han preferred sleeping with Polly and Henry, one or the other could often be found curled up on one of the boys' beds. The boys chose blue for the color of their walls. Henry had built a second bed frame to match the first so each had his own place to sleep, but they asked to push them together, making one big sleeping space. As long as Noah and Elijah wanted to stick close, Polly was fine with that. The rest of their room was filling up with toys and books. Several of the bookshelves Polly's father had made were now in there, along with her old dresser and one from her father's bedroom. As the family spread out into the house, they began using up the furniture she'd accumulated. She had yet to tap into things still in the attic and garage, but the time would come.

She and Henry were the last to move into their new room and she'd only begun to decorate. They didn't spend enough time in there yet to make it a big concern. The curved wall on the northeast corner stumped her. For now, a comfortable chair and ottoman for herself and a wing chair for Henry filled that space. She really needed to focus on bringing cohesion to the room.

Their bathroom was another story. Henry had installed a large shower with multiple shower heads. It was heavenly. Some mornings she walked in and didn't want to ever come out. The whirlpool tub was a favorite of everyone and the kids were disappointed it wasn't in one of the common bathrooms.

With the front room downstairs emptied of Noah and Elijah's things, Heath and Hayden spread out again. They kept the room dividers up, giving them each a little more privacy, not that Hayden was around all that much anymore. Between school and his growing relationship with Tess, he rarely had extra time. Polly couldn't wait for summer break so they'd see him more often. Tess was staying in Ames this summer, though, so who knew how much Hayden would be around. He and Heath would soon start work on the next set of rooms to be demolished and rebuilt. They hoped to have those finished before school started in the fall so everyone would be upstairs and the downstairs rooms could be completed.

Polly needed to repaint the walls in Rebecca's old bedroom so they could move the office over from Sycamore House, but it had to wait because that room was now filled, floor to ceiling, with boxes, crates and plastic totes. Boxes of books were stacked in Polly's old bedroom, which would someday become the library. Henry planned to build shelves along the walls in there, but that project was far down the line.

With Simon Gardner's help, they found a beautiful old Steinway grand piano, but a great deal of work needed to be done on it before it could be used. Len Specek was interested in learning how to restore the piano, so for now, it was in residence at the shop. He'd been in contact with restorers around the country and this summer planned a trip to Tennessee with Andy to spend time learning different techniques.

After discussions with Jeanie Dykstra, the piano teacher, Polly and Henry had purchased a good, full-sized electronic piano and parked it in the future library. Noah and Elijah started piano lessons in late February, and so far, were willing to spend time practicing. That would change when summer started. Elijah was playing on a little league baseball team, something Noah had no interest in doing, but they'd signed him up for a soccer league.

She shook her head. Any sort of quiet life she'd envisioned for herself in rural Iowa was quickly flying out the window.

Henry bumped her arm and she automatically clapped her hands together as the director took a quick bow, before turning back and starting the next piece. All that time spent thinking and she still had to wait for the concert to end.

Elijah tugged her arm. "Little E needs to go to the bathroom."

"Can it wait?" she asked, knowing full well they'd gone to the bathroom during the intermission. He chewed on his lower lip and nodded. Polly turned to see Henry put a hand on Noah's leg. This really was asking a lot of these active little boys.

~~~

"Showers first," Polly said to the little boys when they walked in the side door. "Then come on back downstairs. We'll have ice cream."

"Me too?" Rebecca asked.

Polly chuckled. "You never take a shower at night. No, not you, too."

"Can I call Kayla, then?"

"You just saw her."

"I know. But we didn't get a chance to talk very long. Didn't you see her sitting with Korey Larrabie in the bleachers? I think he likes her."

"Just twenty minutes. When the boys come back for ice cream, I want you here, too." Polly took Rebecca's phone out of the charger and handed it to her. "Twenty minutes."

"I promise." Rebecca grabbed the phone and ran for her bedroom.

Henry held a leash out to Polly. "That was nice of you."

"She had a big night. They can wind down this way. Don't you remember talking on the phone all night to your friends?"

He just laughed. "Not what we did."

"Dad was forever telling me to get off the phone and do my homework or practice my flute or clean my room." Polly snapped a leash on Obiwan who wiggled with joy. She looked for Heath, who must have headed to his room.

They went outside and turned for the street instead of heading for the back yard.

Henry shook his head. "I wish we could let the dogs run on their own."

"Me too sometimes, but this is nice." Polly took his hand. "I enjoy walking with you."

"Things are going to be different," he said quietly.

"You mean with Rebecca in high school?"

"And Heath in college. I've gotten used to them being in the house all the time."

"Rebecca hasn't been here much these last few months. Maybe she was preparing us."

He squeezed her hand. "I haven't liked it. It feels like we're losing continuity with the family. We don't have dinner with all of us at the same time very often."

"They're growing up."

"Yeah. I don't like that. Would you make it stop?"

"Wish I could."

They turned the corner and Polly looked in at Jim Bridger's empty home. She'd discovered a gate in his back yard leading to theirs when ghost sightings held the town's attention. The man had grown marijuana in the empty lot of the old Springer House. It was curious that his house hadn't sold yet.

The home next to it was dark, in contrast to all of the other homes along the street with lights on in nearly every room. "Do you know who lives there? I never see anyone outside, but the place is kept up."

"I don't. You should ask your friend." Henry pointed at a little brown house across the street.

Pat and Albert Lynch lived in that little house. She was the busiest busybody around, but a sweet woman who genuinely cared about people. She'd introduced herself to Polly back before Polly and Henry even owned the Bell House. Though the couple spent winters in Florida, when they returned, she snagged Polly every time she could, just to chat or catch up. When Polly only had a short time to walk her dogs in the evenings, she went the other way, even though she liked Mrs. Lynch.

"She'd have all the gossip," Polly agreed. "I'm sure I'll run into her one of these days. That woman likes nothing more than telling me what's happening in the neighborhood. Funny thing, though, she's never mentioned the people who live in this house. Maybe it's empty."

"I don't think so. Every once in a while, I see a red SUV in the driveway."

"Maybe it's the owner checking up on the house."

He shrugged. "I suppose."

They stopped for Han to take care of business. Henry groaned and bent over with a plastic bag. "We need a big farm," he muttered.

"No we don't. I'm not renovating one more house for a very long time. I want to settle in and enjoy this one first."

They crossed the street and started back. "So I shouldn't tell you about this incredible deal I found on an old house not too far from Grandpa's place?"

"You mean Eliseo's house?" Polly asked.

"Yeah."

She stopped and took his arm. "You're messing with me, right?"

"Not really."

"Tell me you're messing with me. You have to be. How can we afford another house?"

"It's a really good deal. Think about it. Mark and Eliseo have the plans in place to build stables at Eliseo's. You could renovate the big old house into a bed and breakfast and advertise horseback riding as one of the activities."

"Jeff would kill me." She took a couple of paces. "How good is this deal?"

Henry laughed. "I knew I could tempt you. It's almost too good to pass up. Dad and I talked about it. He's willing to buy into it, too, so it doesn't get away."

"How much land is it on?"

"Just two acres. The farmland is owned by someone else, but this section is cut away by a creek."

Polly picked up the pace as they turned back onto Beech Street in front of Shawn Wesley's house. "When can I see it?"

"Are you sure you're interested?"

"You're telling me that I'm crazy not to be interested, right?"

"Yeah."

"Does Marie know you two are thinking about doing this?"

"Probably. Not much gets past her even though I told Dad not to say anything until I talked to you."

"We're crazy to even think like this, aren't we?"

"Maybe. We don't have to start renovating it right away. It can sit there for another couple of years. I'd make sure it was tight against the weather, but there's no rush to do anything. It's just that you never see that kind of price on something like this."

"Why is it so cheap?"

"The company that owns the farmland doesn't want anything to do with it and they can't talk anyone into buying just that little bit of land. It's perfect for the type of thing you do. Even if we tore the house down and rebuilt, it would be worth it. The creek winds around the entire lot. There are only straggly trees in there, so nothing as pretty as what's behind Sycamore House, but it's way cool. Whenever I drive by it, I think about how neat it would look with fog rising off the creek — all spooky and eerie."

"Did you just say neat?" Polly glanced up at Mona Bright's house. She'd checked on the woman several times during her recuperation from falling down her basement steps. They were never going to be friends; Mona was as closed off as anyone Polly knew, but at least they had a cordial relationship now. This summer she had to have a block party. It was killing her that she only knew these people well enough to wave at them, nothing more. Before her life got crazy busy with kids and activities, she needed time to get to know people.

"You really aren't going to give me trouble about the words I use, are you?"

"When you use ancient words like 'neat,' you bet I am." Polly led Obiwan across the street to their driveway and unclasped the leash. She and Henry deposited their goodie bags in the trash can and went inside. The dogs stood in front of the pantry door, wagging their tails.

"Yeah, yeah, I know," she said. "It's coming."

"There you are," Elijah said, coming in from the foyer. "I'm all clean. See?" He rubbed his wet little head against Polly's arm.

"Yes you are." She pulled him into a hug, then took out treats from the container. "Give one to each of the dogs, would you?"

He sat on the floor and held a treat out on either side. The dogs took their treats and chomped them to bits while Elijah giggled. "They make so much noise when they chew."

"Where's your brother?" Polly asked.

"He was putting his 'jamas on when I left. You should call him. He was looking at a book. You know how he gets."

She did. Noah was infatuated with Andrew and his love of books. If Andrew told him that he should read something, the little boy wouldn't stop until he was finished. He could barely wait until the next time Andrew was at the house so they could talk about what he'd read.

"You think he's gone to another world again?"

"Uh huh. He had that look in his eyes."

Polly smiled and patted Elijah's head. "I love you, little boy." She stepped over to the intercom and pressed the number for

Noah's bedroom. This system was one of the things she insisted on when they wired the house. There was no way she wanted to chase kids through this huge place, and yelling was unacceptable.

"Noah?" she said into the microphone. "It's time to come downstairs. We're ready to have ice cream." Polly waited a moment and spoke again. "Noah, did you hear me?"

"I'm coming," he said.

Polly pressed the number for Rebecca's room. "I'm looking for you too, Miss Thing. Time's up."

"Be right there."

"Wanna help me get out the ice cream?" Polly asked Elijah.

He ran for the refrigerator. With the freezer on the bottom, he could reach whatever they needed. "What kind?"

"Let's do vanilla with toppings. How does that sound?" Polly stepped around him to get to the bowls.

"Can we do this too?" Elijah held up a container of chocolate / chocolate chip, his eyes big and round.

Those beautiful eyes were irresistible.

"Sure. Grab a towel and take them both to the table, then run back to Heath's room and see if he wants to come out. He might be busy with homework."

"Can I use the intercom?"

"No. Go talk to him in person. Tell him how bad you want him to join us."

Elijah gave her a double-eyed blink, then tried to do it with just one eye.

"Go on," she said, laughing.

He ran down the hallway, yelling Heath's name.

"The yelling thing doesn't ever stop, does it?" Henry asked. He opened the pantry again and pushed the dogs out of the way.

"But he's so cute."

Henry re-emerged with nuts and mini chocolate chips. "Sprinkles too?"

Polly nodded. "We're celebrating."

Noah came in from the foyer, carrying his book. "I was just at a good part."

"They're all good parts, aren't they?" Polly asked.

He smiled up at her. "Kinda."

Rebecca came down the back steps and walked over to put her phone in the charger. "Kayla says Korey even talked to Stephanie tonight. He didn't even sit with his parents, just went and sat with her. She was so shocked."

"That's kind of cool," Polly said.

She tugged on Henry's sleeve and he turned to see Elijah drag Heath down the hallway into the kitchen.

"He said he had time for ice cream," Elijah announced.

Heath chuckled. "After he put his hands on my laptop screen."

"Homework's stupid. You're almost graduated," Elijah complained. "You shouldn't have to do homework."

"I know, right?" Heath patted the little boy's head. "Just one more project to turn in and I'm done."

"See?" Polly asked. "Celebrations all around."

# CHAPTER TWO

Once she finally landed in front of Sweet Beans the next morning, Polly took a deep breath. She'd had to argue with Rebecca about appropriate attire for school and neither of the little boys could find their backpacks, though they were supposed to be in cubbies on the back porch. After finally getting everyone out the door, barely on time, Polly stepped on a wet and slimy hairball and discovered Rebecca's flute on the kitchen counter. She finished getting dressed, cleaned up the cat vomit, then, on the way out to her truck with the flute, Henry called. He needed her to go to the shop to pick up some stained wood samples and then meet him halfway between Bellingwood and Webster City so he wouldn't be late for a meeting. No matter how she tried to keep things organized, chaos always reigned. She knew better than to expect anything different. Coffee was her only salvation.

"Hey, sweetie."

Polly turned to look out her open window. "Good morning. What are you doing here?"

Sal smiled. "Dropped Alexander with Mrs. Dobley for the day. I want coffee and then I need to work."

Polly opened her door and jumped down. As soon as her feet hit the ground, she looked up. It wasn't fair. Sal could get away with four inch heels in the morning in the middle of the week in Bellingwood, Iowa, even when she planned to work from home. It just wasn't fair. This morning Polly had been lucky to get her hair pulled back in a ponytail and find shoes that matched on her way out the door.

"What?" Sal asked.

"How do you always look so put together?"

"Come on," Sal said, hooking her arm through Polly's. "I'll buy you coffee and a muffin. Rough morning so far?"

"I'm not cut out for all of this activity."

"Sure you are. You just need to breathe."

"Whatever."

They walked into the coffee shop together and Sal stopped Polly. Lowering her voice, she said, "Look at this place. How cool is it?"

"Pretty cool."

Several tables were filled with women, one table with a group of five who had books open in front of them. Either a book club or a Bible study, Polly didn't know, but people were choosing to come downtown to spend time together. It was fun watching the town come alive.

"This is *my* business," Sal said in hushed tones. "Mine. I'm part of this."

"Yes you are," Polly replied with a chuckle.

They got to the front counter and Camille smiled as she finished an order for three women. They left and the next customer, Jed Louis, who ran the local feed store, stepped up. Polly barely knew him — only his name. She was rather proud of that. Surprised that he was here rather than having coffee with everyone else at the diner, she waited.

"Good morning, Mr. Louis," Camille said. "I have your order right here." She bent down and brought up two boxes.

"Thanks. Do I owe you anything else?" he asked.

"It's all taken care of," Camille responded. "Have a good day."

He smiled at Polly and Sal as they backed up to give him room to pass.

"What can I do for you two today?" Camille asked. "Your regular?"

Polly nodded. "Extra-large, please."

"That bad?"

"I shouldn't complain. I just feel the need for more caffeine. The morning pot didn't do much for me." Polly realized that she hadn't had much yet. There'd been no time to make a second pot of coffee and Hayden and Henry had emptied the first one after she poured out her first cup. No wonder she was dragging.

"Did you hear what happened last night?" Camille asked. "Everyone's talking about it."

"What?"

"A fire in Tucker's garage burned the whole thing down. Lucky it wasn't attached to the house. The car was nothing more than a burned husk."

"I didn't even hear the sirens go through town," Sal said.

Camille shrugged and put Polly's coffee on the counter, then went back to work on Sal's. "Somebody said they're calling it arson."

"They can't know that yet," Polly said. "There hasn't been enough time to investigate."

"Guess the person left the fuel can right there to burn with everything else."

"Why couldn't that have been the Tucker's fuel can?"

"It was under the car." Camille said. "I want it to be some kid that did something awful on a dare. Otherwise ..." she let her thought trail off. "Do you want a muffin?"

"Do you know the Tuckers?" Polly asked.

Camille nodded. "Herb's done some plumbing repairs here and Mina comes in every once in a while. She's a substitute teacher." She smiled. "She's full-time right now with Mrs. Santee on maternity leave. They live up on Walnut."

Polly leaned across the counter. "If they need anything, you'll let us know?"

Camille nodded and grinned. "I will. It's just a shock. They have three kids. It would have been awful if the fire had gotten to the house."

Three more people had come in behind Polly and Sal, so they moved away and walked to a booth.

"That's like the tenth fire around town," Polly said.

"I know. We're locking things up tight every night. Mark says people are worried."

"Yeah. But this is the biggest one so far. Who could be doing this?"

Sal looked up and smiled. "Joss is here and coming this way."

Polly turned to see her friend come toward them. "What's up?"

"Scoot. Scoot," Joss said waving her fingers at Polly. "I have to tell someone. When I saw your cars out front, I couldn't believe you were here. I was going to have to chase you down, you know."

"What?" Polly asked, after she scooted in, pulling her coffee with her.

"We're getting three more children."

"Whoa," Sal said. "You're what?"

"Three. We're going to foster them, but I want to adopt them. So does Nate."

"Three children? How old?"

Joss brought her hand up and touched her index finger. "Owen and Lucas are six and Lillian is four and a half."

"Another set of twins?" Polly asked.

Joss nodded. "Can you believe it? I'm so excited. When we got the call last night, I wanted to go get them right away, but we'll get them this weekend."

"From where?"

"Somewhere south of Des Moines. The poor kids have had a horrible time of it. Their father ended up in jail. He's still there and I don't know why. Their mother died last year." Joss gave her head a quick shake. "Some kind of accident, but I don't have the whole story. The kids went into foster care after living with an elderly grandmother who had to go into a nursing home. The father's ready to give up custody. There's an aunt in the picture, but she doesn't want them — has her own kids who have problems."

"Are you sure?" Sal asked. "Three more at once?"

Joss's eyes lit up with joy. "I know. It's perfect! This is exactly what I wanted. Can you imagine the fun and noise we'll have in that big house? We've been preparing for this and now it's here. I can hardly wait."

Polly put her arm around Joss's shoulders. "I'm excited for you. This is awesome. What are you going to do about the library? How can you work there with five children at home?"

"Mom's coming out next week to help. I'm not ready to give up the library yet. If I have to, I will, but Nate and I are talking about hiring a nanny. If I could find a college kid to be at the house in the afternoons and help with cleaning and cooking and laundry until I get the whole thing figured out, that would be perfect. This summer is going to be a bit of a problem, but we'll deal with it."

"What about Cooper and Sophie's babysitter?"

"I haven't talked to her yet," Joss said. "I don't know if she'll want to take care of three more, but it will be fine. It will be totally fine. I'm going to Boone this afternoon to order beds and furniture for their rooms. We won't decorate until I get to know them and find out what they like. Can you even believe it?"

"No." Polly shook her head. "I can't believe it. But I'm excited for you. And you know I'll do whatever I can to help. These kids are the right age for me."

Joss looked up at the clock on the wall. "Shoot. I can't stay. I'm picking up muffins for Nate's work. Bobby's birthday is tomorrow, but she has the day off so they're bringing in food today. Nate's in charge of muffins." She giggled. "Good thing he has me to run his errands."

She was gone in a flash, leaving Polly and Sal to stare after her.

"It's a good thing that woman has so much energy," Sal said. "I want a lot of kids, but spreading them out over many years sounds like a much better idea than bringing them into the house in big chunks. She's nuts."

Polly nodded. "When they chose not to stress out over being unable to have kids of their own, Joss lost her stop button. She always wanted a big family. That's why they built that huge house. I wonder how many kids it will take before she cries 'uncle.'"

"You have five."

"Yeah. Not so much," Polly said with a laugh. "You can hardly call Hayden a kid and Heath is practically an adult. Rebecca can at least take care of herself ..." Polly shook her head. "... most of the time. And they completely exhaust me every day. When are you and Mark planning to have the next one?"

"Whenever it happens."

Polly opened her mouth, then shut it. "You're trying now?"

"We aren't trying-trying, but whenever it happens, we're ready. We can put one more in this house and then we need to find something bigger. Until Mark gets those stables going, I'm not pushing for another house. He knows it's on the agenda, but right now we're on hold."

"So much going on," Polly said, shaking her head. "Henry talked to me last night about buying another old house north of town. He thinks we should build a bed and breakfast."

"This is Henry's idea? Not yours?"

"I know," Polly said with a laugh. "It's like some crazy low cost, so he and his dad think we'd be nuts to pass it up."

"Bellingwood never knew what was coming when you moved into town, did it?" Sal said. "A wave of your wand and all of a sudden, new businesses and opportunities pop up everywhere."

"Stop it," Polly said. "Lots of businesses have come to town without my involvement. I just happened to see a good thing with that old schoolhouse. I still can't believe it was such a good deal."

"Well, I'm happy you did even though I might not have been completely thrilled with you leaving me all alone out there on the East Coast."

Polly reached out and put her hand on top of Sal's. "I'm just glad you found your way to me. It's been a strange path, but here we are."

"Who's that?" Sal whispered, nodding toward the front door. "No, don't look," she said when Polly started to turn.

"Then how am I supposed to answer you?"

"Just wait."

JJ Roberts escorted a young woman to the front counter.

"Isn't he dating Tab?" Sal asked.

"Uh yeah. What's he doing with this chick?" Polly replied. "Maybe she has something to do with the winery. He wouldn't mess around on Tab, especially in my favorite hangout."

"Have you talked to him lately? I haven't heard much since his partners left. Sylvie has been doing a lot of baking for events on the weekends, too. Is he okay there by himself?"

Polly nodded. "I think he has every female in town helping. Stephanie's teaching him how to book events and put together his accounting software, Sylvie's baking for him, apparently Rachel is catering some of the smaller parties, and I heard that Sonya Beiderman's granddaughter is his new weekend hostess."

Sal shook her head.

"Sonya is one of the owners of the quilt shop next door," Polly said. "I haven't met her granddaughter yet."

"Tab's a patient woman."

"Hello, ladies," JJ said, coming over. "Ashley, do you know Polly Giller and Sal ..." He looked at them. "... Ogden?"

Sal nodded and put her hand out. "I don't know Ashley. It's nice to meet you."

The girl gave them a warm smile, and after shaking Sal's hand, took Polly's. "I've heard a lot about you, Miss Giller, and have been to a few events at the Sycamore House."

Polly shook it. "Nice to meet you. Are you going to work for JJ at the winery?"

"We're working on it," JJ interrupted. "I'm trying to talk Ashley into playing her guitar on Sunday afternoons this summer." He took her elbow and steered her away. "Talk to you two later."

"You'd almost think he was trying to keep her from us," Sal said. "Are we that intimidating?"

"Probably to him." Polly sat back. "When did I become old?"

"What do you mean?"

"She's a child."

"She's in her early twenties."

"I know," Polly said. "A child. She's Hayden's age. I feel like I'm old enough to be her mother."

"Well you aren't, so stop it. I have a little boy who is going to be one this summer. You and I are the same age and I won't have you getting old on me before I'm ready. Got it?"

"Yeah. Whatever. She's just starting her life and has millions of possibilities in front of her. She's naive about what the world is going to do to her and so hopeful that it will be good."

Sal's eyes grew big. "What in the hell are you talking about?"

"I don't know," Polly replied. "I think I'm overwhelmed by all that's going on. I haven't had a chance to sit and breathe since we moved into this house. Between renovations, kids growing up and the little boys moving in, I'm doing something all the time. Henry and I haven't had a minute to think, much less talk to each other about big thoughts. All we ever do is make plans for this and that and figure out who has to be where when. Do you remember when we used to stay up all night talking about books and things we were thinking about?"

"Those conversations usually involved a bottle of wine."

"No they didn't," Polly said, mildly scolding her. "We discussed things we were learning and why the world worked the way it did. Henry and I used to have those conversations, too. I miss thinking big thoughts and dreaming big dreams."

"Do you ever have those kinds of conversations with Rebecca? She seems like the kind of girl that wants to do that."

"Maybe when school is out this summer, but right now she wants to talk to Kayla and Andrew. They gossip about the kids and all of the boys that Kayla could date and who is seeing who and what teachers they're going to have next year and it's all so … teenagery."

"It seems to me that you can complain and whine about this all you want, but unless you make a change, it's your own fault."

Polly laughed. "And that's why you're my friend. You're right. I didn't get enough sleep last night and all I see ahead of me these next two weeks is insanity and chaos. Poor Hayden has finals this week and then he's done for the summer. He was so stressed out this morning before he left, I didn't know what to do."

"Is he still seeing that girl?"

"Tess? Yeah, but she's in the middle of finals too, so they decided that this week they were going to do their work and not spend time with each other. What kind of kids make those decisions?"

"Responsible kids?"

"But I can tell he doesn't like it."

"They'll figure it out. It's not up to you."

"That's two," Polly said.

"Two?"

"Two little lessons you've pushed at me today. I'll be good. I promise."

Sal laughed. "It's usually you telling me to straighten up. I kind of like this."

"Maybe having babies is good for you." Polly gave an evil laugh. "So, when is your mother coming back to see Alexander?"

"You're dreadful," Sal said. "There was no good reason for you to bring that woman up. She is threatening to come out for his first birthday. I'd like to avoid that, if possible, but I don't know that I'll be able to. I'd love for Daddy to come with her, though. I think he'd like spending time with Mark and meeting our friends. I know he'd like to meet Henry. Daddy asks about you and is thoroughly impressed with what you've managed to do here, but it's mean of you to bring up my mother in order to deflect me."

"It worked."

Sal looked up at the clock on the wall. "I've already spent too much time here this morning. I should get home and go to work. That was the reason I took Alexander to Mrs. Dobley. Are you okay?"

"I'm fine," Polly said. "This first coffee helped."

"You're having another?"

"To go this time." Polly laughed as she stood up with Sal. She grabbed up the trash from their table and walked to the front counter, depositing it on her way.

"What can I get for you?" Camille asked.

"Large black coffee to go," Polly said.

"Not enough yet?"

"Not yet. We'll hope this one does it for me."

"Good morning, Polly." Sylvie's assistant, Marta, brought out three trays and put them on the counter. "These are for the call center," she said to Camille. "Which boxes would you like me to use?"

"I'll pack them," Camille said. "I know you're busy back there."

"Thank you." Marta came around the counter and hugged Polly. "You look like you needed that. Are your kids keeping you on your toes?"

Polly allowed herself to drop into the shorter woman's hug and felt her eyes well up. "They really are and thank you, I did need a hug. How are you?"

"Oh, you know me," Marta said. "Every day is a gift so I unwrap it a little bit at a time. Don't want to miss out on all the fun." She pulled away. "Don't want to miss the moments for the day. Now I'd better hurry. We have six more big orders to finish up before lunch. What a great day."

Camille shook her head as the older woman disappeared down the hall. "She wears me out. I hope when I'm her age, I still have that much energy and great attitude." She laughed. "I should probably work on that attitude right now."

"Me too," Polly said. "Every day is a gift. I need to think about that." She took the coffee that Camille handed her and smiled, then headed for the front door. Waving at JJ and Ashley on her way past, she left and went to her truck.

# CHAPTER THREE

Lining up with the rest of the parents waiting for their kids in front of the elementary school, Polly saw the next few years of her life flash in front of her eyes. Today, she was taking the boys up to the soccer and baseball fields, and Eliseo's sister, Elva, was picking them up after practice. Sam, the oldest, played soccer with Noah. His younger sisters played on a different team and rode up with their own friends. The youngest, Matty, walked back to the Bell House with Rebecca, Kayla and Andrew to wait for his mother or Eliseo to get him. Shuffling kids back and forth was not what Polly had expected from this period of her life, but she knew that it was fortunate they lived in a small town. The trips to deliver kids where they needed to be were shorter, everyone knew everybody else, and the kids were always safe. She wasn't sure what she would do next year when Rebecca had to stay in Boone late into the evening. As excited as she was to have her daughter involved in extracurricular activities, Polly was sad at not having her around as much.

The back door of her truck flew open.

"Hi Polly!" Elijah yelled, climbing up.

"Where's everyone else?"

"They're coming. Noah had to talk to the teacher."

"About what?"

Elijah shrugged. "Dunno."

"How was your day?" She turned in the seat to see his face.

"It was okay."

"What okay? Not best-day-ever quality?"

He gave her a small smile. "No, just okay. Bentli likes Ethan Powers."

They hadn't heard a word about Bentli at home yet, but Polly assumed she was Elijah's latest heartthrob. He went through them on a regular basis. The girls never knew he was interested. He pined for them from afar and when they didn't pay attention to him, he became sad. Neither Polly nor Henry was excited about the fact that kids were paying attention to each other at all at this age, but she hoped if she gave him enough love and affection at home, things would run a normal course until he got older.

So far, Noah hadn't expressed interest in pairing off. At least she only had to deal with one boy for now.

The back door opened again and Matty Johnson climbed in, followed by his brother Sam. Noah got in the front seat.

"Hello, Matty," Polly said. "Not going home with the older kids today?"

"They had something after school," Sam replied for his brother. "Is it okay that he stays with us at practice?"

"He can stay with me," Polly said. "You'll be busy. What were you doing after school, Noah?"

Noah handed Polly an envelope. "Mrs. Wallers asked me to give this to you."

When she reached to take it away, he pulled it back. "But she told me to tell you that it's nothing bad and you aren't supposed to worry."

"Was she telling you that *you* weren't supposed to worry?" Polly asked with a smile.

Noah thought about it for a moment and smiled back. "Maybe that's what she meant." He released the envelope to her.

Polly put it on the console and watched Noah's eyes track her every movement. "Should I open it now before we get to the ball fields?"

He shrugged. "It's probably not about me anyway."

"Good. Then it will wait. We need to get you up there so you aren't late."

She drove away from the school and headed north on Elm Street, pulling into the park where the fields were located. "All of your gear is in the back of the truck," Polly said. "Be sure to watch for Mrs. Johnson. She's bringing you home."

Noah looked pointedly at the letter while the others jumped out.

"Fine," Polly said. She slit the top open and pulled out the piece of paper, then skimmed it. "This is great, Noah. Mrs. Wallers sent home a list of books you should read this summer. How about that?"

"That's awesome." He grinned at her and jumped out of the truck, running to the back to get his gear. She heard the rear gate slam shut and watched him run off to join his brother and Sam.

"Well, Matty, it's just you and me. What should we do?"

"Ice cream?"

Polly laughed. "That's not the worst idea. Do you want to go see the horses and your uncle? How about the library?"

"Uncle Eliseo. Can we?"

"Sure." Polly pulled out of the parking lot and drove south to Sycamore House. She'd spent most of the day working in the office, but hadn't been down to the barn for a few days. "Are you ready for summer vacation?"

Matty nodded. "Mama says I might get my own horse when they build the barn."

"Your very own?"

He shrugged and smiled at her, then scooted forward as far as his seatbelt would allow. "I have to share it with Gabby and Ana, but it's mostly mine. Mama says I'm good with horses like Uncle Eliseo is."

"I hear your mama is pretty good with them too," Polly said.

"Uncle Eliseo says that she misses them, but she doesn't like going to his barn. She says those big horses are too tame. Mama says she wants something wild."

Polly took a breath. Elva Johnson had lived a quiet and tame life for years, but the girl's fire was returning now that she had the freedom to be herself again. It had taken a long time for her to get past the divorce. Even though Elva's ex-husband was a decent man, he'd never really cared about his family. For someone who had as much spirit as Elva, shutting that down for a milquetoast, mundane husband and then being rejected by that same man for another woman must have been devastating.

Elva had been working at the Jefferson Street Alehouse since she moved into town last summer. Eliseo, Henry, and Mark Ogden were building the first of several barns on the large acreage Eliseo purchased from Henry's family. The plan was to begin with boarding horses, but plans for expansion with trail rides and lessons as well as more horse barns were sketched out on paper.

Mark had hoped to move to the country to have his horses nearby, but Sal nixed that idea. She wanted nothing to do with living far from the rest of civilization. Moving from Boston to Bellingwood was traumatic enough for the girl; she wasn't ready to give up neighbors and access to her friends and her favorite coffee shop. With that knowledge, Mark turned to Eliseo.

Once the weather warmed up, they started working. Old outbuildings came down first and they'd been clearing land for the last month. Polly had dropped the kids off one afternoon and found Elva running the bobcat, moving dead brush to the far end of the lot to be burned. The young woman wanted these stables to go up as badly as anyone else.

Polly pulled in between Eliseo's truck and Jason's car. Jason wanted to buy a pickup, but his mother said no. Until he was older, she felt a car was safer and less expensive.

Matty waited for Polly to open the back door of the truck, then climbed down and ran for the gate. He stood beside it until she caught up, then opened it for her and waited as she went through.

"Thank you," Polly said.

"Mama says I'm supposed to be a gentleman. I don't like it when I have to wait for my sisters, but Mama says even they deserve it."

The four Percherons, two donkeys, and three dogs were all out in the pasture. Eliseo had decided that Sylvie's dog, Padme, should come to the barn with him and learn to be around the horses. Jason brought her over every morning after dropping Andrew at school. She was still skittish around the big horses, but loved playing with her brothers.

"Uncle Seo, Uncle Seo!" Matty called out, running into the barn. "Are you here? Uncle Seo!"

Eliseo came out of the tack room. "Slow down, little man. What are you doing here?"

"Polly brought me. All the kids are busy. Can I give Tom and Huck some carrots?"

"Not now." Eliseo took his gloves off and knelt down to hug his nephew. "They've had enough today. How was school?"

"Tasha pushed Libby down on the playground and had to go to the office. Libby hurt her knee. It was all bloody. You should have seen it."

"There's apple juice in the fridge," Eliseo said.

Matty ran off into the feed room.

"I'm sorry you had to bring him down here."

Polly shook her head. "I could have taken him back to my house, but why go there when Uncle Seo's barn is filled with these awesome animals?"

His eyes twinkled. "He's my best helper. Elva is going to want to put him to work right away. He loves animals. Do you want to leave him with me? I'll text my sister that he's here."

"That's fine," Polly said with a shrug. "Jason got out of school early today?"

"Yeah. He and Scar are moving hay out back. I'm looking forward to the kids being here full-time. We have a lot of work to do this summer."

"You always have a lot of work to do." She chuckled. "How are things going out at the house?"

"Henry's pouring concrete soon if the weather holds. The boys can hardly wait to learn how to put fence in." Eliseo laughed deep down in his chest. "They're going to hate me when that's finished. I've tried to ease them into it, doing repairs and checking fence over here, but they have no idea what they're in for. I do appreciate having a ready supply of young helpers."

"I hope they don't give out on you."

He nodded. "I've built a good rapport with them. They'll be fine."

Matty came back into the alley of the barn, holding a bottle of juice. He sat down on a bench and waited for Hansel, the cat, to join him. The cat sniffed at the bottle, turned away and rolled over on his back. The little boy just looked at the cat's exposed tummy. "No way," he said. "I'm not touching that."

"Smart boy." Polly smiled. "Did you leave anything in my truck? You're staying here with Eliseo."

"Nope. No homework," Matty said.

Eliseo put his hand on Matty's head. "Tell her thank you for the ride."

Matty looked at his uncle. "I was going to. Thank you for bringing me."

"You're very welcome. Maybe I'll see you tomorrow."

Polly turned and left the barn. She stopped outside to watch the animals. They didn't notice her, so she went back to her truck. As soon as she backed out and onto the street, her phone buzzed with a text. Instead of going on, she pulled back into the parking lot and took out her phone.

*"Hey. What 'cha doing?"* Henry asked.

*"Nothing much. What's up?"*

*"Wanna look at an old farmhouse?"*

*"Are you there?"*

*"I can be if you're free."*

*"Okay. Where do I go?"*

*"Just go north out of town past the ball fields, like you're going to Eliseo's house. But don't turn on his gravel road. Keep going north and take the next road. It's the first driveway on the left."*

*"I'll be there in ten minutes or less,"* Polly replied.

*"I'll race ya."*

She laughed. It was always a competition and yet, it never was. He knew better than to think she'd race through town. That was probably one of the hardest things about being friends with local law enforcement. The last thing Polly wanted was to be stopped by one of her friends for speeding. The way their friendships worked, she'd never be able to wheedle her way out of it. They'd gladly write the ticket and then just as gladly announce it to everyone they saw.

Driving back out of the parking lot, Polly passed Stephanie and waved. Stephanie had spent the afternoon working with JJ Roberts at Secret Woods Winery.

Polly drove north again on Elm Street and slowed as she went past the ball fields. She couldn't see her kids, but still felt the need to look. Driving out of town, she wondered what in the world was up with this old farmhouse. The last thing they needed was another renovation project. Henry wasn't frivolous, though, so if he was interested, she'd take a look. As she drove, it occurred to Polly that not only would they have to renovate the house, but then find someone to live there and care for it. She didn't know anyone like that. Her friends were all living out their lives right now. What was Henry thinking?

She passed the gravel road that led to Eliseo's house. Farther on down that road was the home of Betty and Dick Mercer, Henry's aunt and uncle. It was strange for Polly to be part of an extended family. She'd grown up with nothing like that. But people in Bellingwood were connected to each other in ways Polly often didn't even realize. It always surprised her when someone told her they were cousins or even siblings. It shouldn't. These people had lived in town for scores of years.

The next gravel road, huh? Polly turned right. Slowing as she approached an overgrown copse of trees, she found the driveway and turned in. Ruts gave way to weeds as the drive passed under large branches. Well, that was certainly pretty. Hopefully she was in the right place. The drive followed the winding path of the creek for several hundred yards, coming to a circle in front of a large farmhouse. Polly tried to place where she was in the county, wondering if this was Sycamore Creek. Then she realized it couldn't be and gave her head a quick shake.

The house had a front porch that wrapped around the right side. She wasn't climbing up those steps no matter what Henry might say. The wood had rotted away, leaving holes she could see from her truck. The place looked haunted. Weather had done a number on the siding; streaks of grey and green discolored the roof, the walls, and even the posts on the porch. Shredded screens hung from windows and no one had bothered to do a thing with the yard. It was a horrific mess.

Polly drove on and stopped before taking the curve of the circle so she could peer behind the house. She couldn't tell how far back the porch went. Trees and bushes blocked most of her view, but there was a building that might have once been a greenhouse. That would be pretty cool. A garage sat at the end of a short path with a small shed attached to it. What a mess this place was. No wonder it was selling so inexpensively. Henry could tell her if the structure of the house was safe. It was attractive enough that if she could just imagine it with new windows and a rebuilt porch, it might have possibilities, but she wasn't ready for another project. Not by a long shot.

She came around the circle to face the entrance. There was no way she was getting out of her truck. This place was the perfect setting to find a dead body and she'd gone months and months without that happening. Now was not when she wanted to do it again, especially with all that she had going on in the next couple of weeks. Polly huffed a laugh. Like that made any difference. When the universe needed her to find someone so they could be put to rest, it was going to happen whether she wanted it to or not.

Lydia told Polly that Aaron had mentioned a vacation this summer if things stayed so quiet. Of course, he had plenty of other issues to deal with throughout the county, but not having murders to solve lately had been good for morale.

While she was thinking about murders, Polly wondered if Greg Parker had uncovered more about the possible serial killer from the early nineteen-hundreds. She'd given him the files that Margie Deacon put together. Andy said that Lucy brought back the box Polly dropped off and had taken several more out of the basement of the library. The boxes were always returned more organized than when they left, with detailed content lists printed and placed inside. When Greg was ready to let them know what he found, he would. At least it wasn't on Polly's plate any longer.

Henry's truck came around the last bend and pulled up in front of the house. He got out and walked across to her. Polly waited for him to get in.

"What do you think?" he asked.

"It's a wreck. Do you know anything about the structure?"

He shook his head. "Not yet. Dad and I need to come out and walk through before I know what we have to work with, but what do you think about the whole place? Isn't this beautiful?"

"It's creepy. Everything is dark and overgrown and the house looks haunted. I don't want to go near it for fear I'll find a dead body. Maybe even one that's been there for the last fifty years."

"It hasn't been that long," Henry said. "Probably only about twenty years. There was an old couple that lived here when I was in high school. Cobb was their last name. They had a big family and I guess all the kids moved away. Anyway, they were old when I knew them. He died and then she died or maybe she had to go in the nursing home; I don't really remember."

"Can you imagine trying to keep all this up by yourself at that age?" Polly asked.

"No. That would be hard. I think Dad was out here a couple of times fixing things. That's why he remembered the house."

"Did he ever bring you?"

"I'd never been here until he talked about it the other day. Then I had to drive in and see what it was."

Polly chuckled. "I can't believe squatters aren't living inside."

"They might be." Henry glanced at the house. "I suppose I shouldn't go in there alone the first time. But what do you think?

Even if we tear the house down, this land is really cool with these trees and that winding creek. Wouldn't it be a nice bed and breakfast?"

"It would. But Henry, I don't have time for this right now. At least not with the mess I've still got at our house. We're just getting ready to start on the next few rooms."

He reached across the console and took her hand. "I know that. But if we bought the place, we could at least get in and start pushing the worst of the brush back — take down the old dead trees and clean it up. Then we could better see what we have and think about whether the buildings come down or we restore them. I like the front of the house a lot. That big old wrap-around porch is cool and did you see there's an old greenhouse back there? Who knows what kind of gardens that woman planted."

"You really want this, don't you?"

Henry looked at her. "I do. The thing is, so does Dad." He lifted a shoulder. "I don't know if he wants it as much as he just wants *somebody* to want it, but he's willing to invest money." Henry smiled. "I think he's figured out that an investment with us will see a return."

"That's a lot of expectation. Are you sure?"

"Yeah, I am. Are you on board?"

"Of course I am." Polly took a deep breath. "I'm not going to be the first one to walk in that door, though. You can't make me."

"Got it."

# CHAPTER FOUR

Life in Bellingwood was pretty exciting these days. Every time Polly saw her catering van driving around town, a little thrill coursed through her. The doors on the van were open when she pulled into the driveway. Rachel must be heading out for a catering job.

When her phone rang, she was surprised to see Marie's name.

"Hi, Marie. Everything okay?"

"I don't call you enough if that's your first question for me," Marie said. "Everything's fine. I just wondered if you had any time this morning. The boys are up to something and I want to hear your take on it."

"The bed and breakfast?"

Marie laughed. "Yeah. The money pit."

"You really think it's a bad idea? Henry keeps telling me what a great deal the place is."

"Molly and I thought we ought to have a chat with you before those men get themselves in over their heads."

"Molly too, huh? This doesn't bode well for Henry and Bill. Have you seen it yet?"

"Not in years. It used to be a pretty farmhouse, but after all these years, decay has surely gotten pretty well out of hand."

Polly nodded. Marie was too smart to not know what was going on. "It's in bad shape."

"Do you think there's enough local interest to keep a bed and breakfast busy?" Marie asked.

"That's a question Jeff could answer better than me," Polly responded. "I haven't had an opportunity to talk to him about this scheme yet." She giggled. "I wanted to use the term hare-brained, but Henry and Bill don't do things without a lot of thought, do they?"

"Henry is like me. He's pretty sensible, but his father has been known to go off half-cocked when he gets excited."

"Where did this whole thing come from?" Polly asked.

"His brother-in-law," Marie replied. "Dick's been watching the place fall apart and it's just killing him. He used to mow the grounds, trying to keep the weeds and growth back, but it's gotten more and more difficult for him to find the time. He didn't tell Betty he was talking to Bill about this because he knew she'd stop him. Dick did all the work to find out how much the property was going for and then called Bill. I didn't hear about it until a few days ago. Bill was ready to put money down just to own the property. I told him we weren't going to do that and to let it go. That's when he talked to Henry. The two of them came up with the idea of a bed and breakfast."

"I see," Polly replied.

"And just because your husband is one of the most sensible people around, don't believe for a minute that he isn't easily swayed by his father. If Bill asks Henry to do something, that boy of mine will move heaven and earth to make it happen. Thank goodness Bill generally uses his power for good."

"You're hilarious," Polly said. "I could come over now. My work will still be here later."

"Are you sure? I don't want to take you away from anything important."

"It's just bills and more bills."

"Molly will be happy to see you."

Polly waved at Rachel who was wheeling a two-wheel cart loaded with totes to the van. Rachel smiled as Polly turned back around. While she was stopped at the end of the drive, Polly heard sirens. She waited for fire trucks and emergency vehicles to go past and took in a deep breath when they turned in front of Sycamore House to go south on Elm Street. Rather than wonder what it was about, she followed them, her heart racing. They drove past the barn. She continued to follow and let out a whoosh of air when they turned left into Ralph Bedford's driveway.

"Oh no," she whispered and turned right onto the gravel road just before his house. She stopped and took out her phone to call Eliseo.

"Polly?" he asked.

"I just followed fire trucks Ralph Bedford's house. Where are you?"

"I'm up at my place with Henry and Mark. I'll call Ralph. Are you going in?"

"I can," she said. "Just don't want to get in their way."

Eliseo hung up and Polly gave her head a quick shake. He wasn't thinking straight. Ralph was one of his best friends and if anything were to happen to him again, Eliseo would be devastated.

Polly turned and drove slowly up to Ralph's driveway. Firemen were already moving with a hose to a shed which was rapidly going up in flames. Polly pulled in and drove to the other side of the yard, then got out of her truck and looked around for the old man. She found him standing beside his pride and joy, a bright orange pickup truck, talking to a fireman. When she slammed her truck door, he started toward her.

"Polly, what are you doing here?" he asked.

"I saw the trucks come in. What happened?"

Ralph shook his head. "I don't know. I was working on my roses out back and thought I heard something. When I got here, I saw smoke in the shed. Since that's where I park my baby, I called 9-1-1 and then got her out as fast as I could."

"You went into the fire?" Polly asked.

"I was plenty safe, but my truck was not going up in flames today — not if I had anything to say about it."

She pointed at his truck. "Is your phone in the cab?"

Ralph patted his pockets. "Must be. Why?"

"Because Eliseo is trying to call you. He'll be worried sick." Polly's phone rang in her pocket. She took it out, swiped the call open, and handed it to Ralph after seeing that it was from Eliseo.

"Hello, bud. I'm fine," Ralph said. He listened. "Sorry 'bout that. Polly just told me. Phone's in the truck." Another pause and he said, "Yeah. My shed. Got my baby out, but everything else is going up. Don't know what happened. I don't think I left anything in there that would make a fire all by itself." After another pause, Ralph smiled. "I'll see you, then, but they're here and I'm all good. Don't worry about me. I'm a tough old coot."

He handed the phone back to her. "That man worries too much. He's got plenty of his own things, what with his sister and her kids living with him and now he's got that new girlfriend. Too many women for my taste." Ralph winked at her. "That's what I tell him, anyway. He knows better, though. It's a good thing he doesn't listen to me."

"Mr. Bedford?" A young woman approached.

"Excuse me," Ralph said. "My public awaits."

Polly shook her head at him. He took the young woman's arm as they walked back toward his truck. The flames were mostly gone, but smoke and steam rose from the rubble. She headed for her own truck, anxious to be out of the way before the fire trucks started moving again. Eliseo should be here any minute and he'd keep an eye on Ralph. She wondered what it was like for him to think about large fires like this, knowing how he'd been wounded.

She made her way back to the road and turned north to go back into town. As she passed the barn, she saw Eliseo driving toward her and slowed. He stopped beside her and rolled down his window.

"How's Ralph?" he asked.

"He's okay. A little proud of himself for getting his truck out of the shed before it went up in flames."

Eliseo nodded. "Foolish old man."

"Like you wouldn't do something like that."

"Not for a truck, I wouldn't. Wonder what happened?"

"Ralph said he heard something and when he came out front, the shed was on fire. There's talk about fires happening around town. Think we have an arsonist?"

"Mark said the same thing when I told them what happened here," Eliseo said. "I'm worried about the barn. This fire was set in broad daylight. He didn't know that Ralph wasn't inside his house watching. This was pretty bold."

"What do you want to do?"

"As soon as I know that Ralph's okay, I'll come back here. Probably want someone at the barn during the day, then I'll lock up tight at night."

"Do you want me to wait there until you're done?"

He slowly shook his head. "No, that's not right. You go on. You probably have a million things to do today. I'll hurry. Things will be fine until I'm there."

Polly chuckled. "It's really okay. I don't have anything that's desperate. Is there anything you'd like me to do while I wait for you?"

"You wanna haul some hay down?" Eliseo looked straight at her.

She hated that she couldn't tell if he was kidding.

"Sure," Polly said. "That would be good for me. I'll get right to work on it."

"Thanks." Eliseo put his hand on the gear shift and then looked back at her. "You know I'm joking, right?"

"Uh huh." Polly took her foot off the brake and drove away, knowing that what she was about to do would kill him.

She drove in and parked, then headed for the barn. The animals, sans dogs, were all outside again. After a chilly and wet spring, everybody was grateful for warmer temperatures and sunshine, especially her horses.

Tom and Huck caught sight of her first and trotted for the barn, knowing that she was an easy touch for treats. Polly went straight for the feed room. The stack of hay was low enough that she could do a little work and embarrass Eliseo. She grabbed a pair of gloves, brought down the ladder to the hay mow, climbed up and realized that they'd recently gotten in a new load. The place was full to the brim. Remembering how Eliseo laid out the hay, she started with the oldest bales and hefted them over to the slide Henry had built to make this task easier. After working for about twenty minutes, she'd built up quite a sweat and pushed hair away from her face. It had been much too long since she'd done this. Tearing out walls at the Bell House was one thing. She was abusing an entirely different set of muscles today.

When she'd tossed enough bales to fill the feed room, Polly climbed back down. She was halfway through stacking them, when she heard a sound.

"What did you do?" Eliseo asked.

"You told me you needed hay to come down. I brought hay down." She patted a stack of bales. "See. All nice and neat. Just like you like 'em."

"I was only kidding. I thought you knew that." He picked up a bale and tossed it to the top of the stack. "Why did you do this?"

She chuckled. "Because you asked me to."

"I didn't mean it."

"I know that. But it was fun to mess with you."

"You worked this hard to mess with me? It might have backfired on you."

"Yeah," Polly said. "You're not nearly chagrined or embarrassed enough. I sweated a lot for this."

He opened the refrigerator and took out a bottle of water. "You're a crazy woman. Thanks, though. I thought that I might talk to Sam Gardner about babysitting the barn during the day when I have to be gone. Is that okay with you?"

"Whatever you want," Polly said with a shrug. "I'd be glad to come over any time you need me." She rolled her shoulders. "That's going to hurt later, but it felt good to do some hard work.

With you, Jason, and his buddies, I don't feel quite as necessary as I used to."

"You're necessary to a lot of other people these days."

Huck nudged Polly's hip.

"What?" she asked, rubbing his forehead. "The boss is back. You know I can't sneak treats to you when he's around."

He nudged her hand and she scratched around his ears and neck. "How's Ralph doing?"

"He's fine. They'll be there for a while, just to make sure that nothing is left burning. That old shed had a lot of stuff in it. He's going to have a devil of a time making a list of what he lost."

Polly's phone buzzed with a text.

*"Is everything okay, sweetie? I thought you were coming right over."*

"Crap," she said out loud.

"What's wrong?"

"I'm supposed to be at Marie Sturtz's house. She's worried now. I forgot."

He grinned. "I've got this. You go on."

Polly headed for the main door of the barn. "You'll let me know if you need me to be here, won't you? I mean it. Don't not do something because you're afraid of asking for my help. I'll be furious if I find out." She slammed the door shut behind her before he could respond and ran for her truck.

*"Sorry. I'm on my way. Everything is okay. I'll tell you when I get there,"* she texted back to Marie. How had her day grown so out of control again? Things needed to slow down soon.

Polly went straight to the Sturtz's house and parked in the lot of the shop. She ran for the back door and reached up to knock. Her hand had barely connected with the door when Molly stood there ready to open it.

"You're here," Molly yelled. She opened the door and yelled again. "Polly's here!"

Marie stepped onto the back porch from the kitchen. "I'm right here, sweetheart. No yelling. You know better."

"But Polly's here."

"Yes she is and she can hear you, too."

Molly put her arms up and Polly hefted the little girl up onto her hip. She was just over two years old now and weighed enough that it wasn't quite as easy.

"What's this?" Molly asked, pulling a piece of hay from Polly's hair. "You smell funny, too."

"Do I?" Polly asked. "I smell like hay." She took the piece from Molly. "That's what this is. We put it in the stalls for the horses and they like to eat it, too."

Molly pulled Polly's hand toward her mouth.

"Oh no you don't," Polly said. "You're not a horse. Besides, it smells like Marie is making lunch. Her food is much better."

"Gilled chee," Molly said. She wriggled to be let down and Polly put her on the floor.

As soon as Molly was free, she ran back onto the porch. "Henry!" she yelled.

Polly looked at Marie. "Henry's coming for lunch?"

"He has to pick things up at the shop, so I told him to meet us here. We're going to have a family chat."

"Does he know we're having …"

"Having what?" Henry asked. He was carrying Molly in and stopped to give Polly a quick kiss on the cheek.

"Gilled chee," Molly said again. She plucked another piece of hay from Polly's hair. "Hay for horses."

Polly took it away from Molly before she could pop it in her mouth. "Maybe I need to go outside and give my head a shake."

"Why do you have hay in your hair?" Henry asked. "You been rolling around with someone I should know about?"

"Just hauling bales out of the hay mow at Sycamore House," Polly replied.

He looked perplexed. "Since when do you do that?"

"Since I wanted to mess with Eliseo, but it didn't have quite the effect I was going for."

"How was Ralph when you left him?" Henry asked.

"Better than he should have been. That old man went into the burning building to get his truck out. He said it wasn't very bad when he went in, but still."

"Burning building?" Marie asked.

"Yeah. His shed burned down," Polly said. "Apparently there have been some fires around town for the last few weeks. Eliseo and I were discussing how to keep the barn safe. I think we should keep an eye on all the buildings we own. I'll call Grey at the hotel and tell him to make sure things are locked up."

"We need to make sure the shop is locked whenever it's empty," Henry said. "Until they catch whoever is doing this, nothing's safe."

"Who would be setting fires?" Marie asked. "What's this world coming to?"

Henry shook his head. "It started out as just little fires. Some pallets in the alleys and some dumpster and trashcan fires, but they've been getting bigger."

"We need a couple more padlocks for the old garage," Polly said. "I'm not ready to lose all of the furniture that's stored out there and if it went up, Rebecca's little shed would go, too."

"I'll pick those up before I come home tonight," Henry replied.

"What can I do to help you, Marie?" Polly asked.

Marie pointed at the cupboard. "Jessie and Bill will be here just after noon. Would you set the table for six? We're having sandwiches and soup, so bowls too."

Henry put Molly down and she ran out to the living room, then he opened the cupboard door and took out plates, handing them to Polly. She went into the dining room and he followed her with bowls, setting them on the table.

"What's going on?" he whispered. "Why are we all here?"

She drew him into the small hallway between the dining room and living room. "Family meeting. I don't think Marie is on board with the bed and breakfast. She's afraid Bill buffaloed you into thinking it was a good idea. I don't know if she's wrong."

Henry rolled his eyes. "Sometimes family businesses are a pain in the butt." He leaned in and spoke quietly so Marie couldn't hear. "Are you on board with me or are you taking her side?"

"I'm not taking sides," Polly said. Since he was so close, she kissed his cheek. "If you want to do this, you know I will support you. You've never steered me wrong. If we need to convince your mother that it's a good idea and won't wreck their savings, then we'll take the time. She says Dick is the one who got Bill all excited about this because Dick is worried no one else will clean that place up. Apparently, he's been caring for it when he can."

"That's where this comes from," Henry said. "It makes more sense now." He smiled. "If Aunt Betty had been the one to come up with the idea, Mom would have been all over it. But Mom knows that when Dick gets a burr under his saddle about something, he won't let it go until it's taken care of. She's afraid he talked Dad into handling something for him. Having all of the information is helpful. Thank you." He tipped her chin up and kissed her lips. "You smell like hay."

"It's not a bad smell, is it?"

"No, it's kind of nice — all farm-girly and stuff. I like it. Maybe we should spend the evening in the hay mow. That would make for a nice date night."

Polly swatted at him. "You're horrible."

"Yes I am and don't you forget it."

Marie poked her head around the kitchen door. "If you two are finished discussing how you're going to handle this situation, you can finish setting the table."

"Sorry, Mom," Henry said.

She smiled at him. "Don't ever think your mother doesn't know what's going on. Ever."

"Yes, Ma'am."

# CHAPTER FIVE

Yawning, Polly stretched her arms and rolled her head. She sat in her truck, waiting for soccer and baseball practices to be finished. Elva had an extra shift at the Alehouse, so Polly offered to gather the kids. She'd take Sammy and his sisters to the Sycamore House barn to ride home with Eliseo and then return her own stinky boys home for showers before supper. There was nothing she loved more than the locker room smell that permeated her truck after they all piled out.

Before coming to the ballfields, Polly stopped for coffee. One day she'd be too old to drink it this late, but not today. Since she'd stopped drinking so much pop, coffee had become her drug of choice and she wasn't giving it up without a fight.

The front passenger door flew open and Elijah climbed into the cab. "Can I sit up here since the girls are riding with us?"

"Sure," Polly said. "How was practice?"

"It was good. I hit a home run."

"You did? That's terrific."

Elijah scrambled across the seats to hug her. "It wasn't my first one, you know."

"It wasn't?"

"I used to hit them all the time when I played in Chicago."

"You did, did you?"

"Everybody wanted me to play on their team. Now if I can just hit them when we play for real."

"Well, I'm proud of you anyway. Good job."

He beamed at her praise and sat in the middle right beside her, pulling his seatbelt on.

The next to arrive were Gabriela and Ana. Elijah motioned for them to sit in the back seat and they climbed up and in.

"How did you girls do today?" Polly asked.

"It was okay," Gabby replied. "We have a game on Saturday. Are you coming?"

"I don't know yet. But I'm sure Eliseo and your mom will be there."

"Mom might have to work," Ana replied. "She's always working. Sometimes at the bar, but she spends tons of time outside getting the ground ready. I can't wait for that barn to be built. Maybe then she'll play with us again."

"You should go outside with her," Elijah said.

"It's dirty." Gabby pulled a hair tie out and shook her long hair free, sending dust everywhere.

Sammy and Noah ran toward the truck, laughing and pushing at each other. They took stock of the seating arrangement, then Sammy climbed into the back seat while Noah opened the front door.

"Noah scored a goal today," Sammy said.

"So did you," Noah replied.

Sammy nodded and smiled. "Our team plays before the girls' game. Are you coming to watch on Saturday, Polly?"

Polly knew this was in her calendar. She just hadn't put it all together. "I will," she said. "I wouldn't miss it. You know that."

Noah buckled in, then leaned forward and smiled at her. "Will Henry and Rebecca come?"

"We'll see," she said. "I bet we can talk them into it."

Noah pointed at his leg. "I scraped myself but it doesn't hurt."

"You sure?" Elijah asked, poking at the abrasion.

"Stop that," Polly scolded.

"But he says it doesn't hurt," Elijah protested. He slid his hand over and poked his brother again.

Noah slapped Elijah's hand. "Stop that."

"But if it doesn't hurt, then why can't I poke your leg?"

"It hurts when you poke me," Noah said. He sat up straight and looked at Polly. "But not very much. I'm okay."

She had gone just a few blocks when she glanced at the boys. "Where are your glasses, Noah?"

His eyes grew big. "I forgot them."

"Where did you forget them?"

"They're on the bench. Can we go back?"

He'd worn glasses for several months, but had the worst time keeping track of them. Polly went around the block and headed back to the ball fields. She pulled up close to the soccer field and Noah jumped out of the truck. She watched him run toward the bench and walk around it twice. When he looked up at her and put his hands out, she shook her head and got out of the truck.

"The rest of you stay here."

"That's Coach Darby's car," Sammy said, pointing at a blue sedan.

"Thanks." Polly closed the door and waved for Noah to join her. They walked over to where Coach Darby was rearranging things in the trunk of his car, trying to fit all that he'd brought.

Noah looked up at her and she nodded for him to go ahead. He slumped his shoulders and walked as slowly as he could.

"Hi Noah," the man said when he turned around. "What's up?"

"I lost my glasses."

The coach grinned and reached into his jacket pocket. "Are these yours?" he asked, pulling them out.

"Yes sir," Noah said with great relief in his voice. "I thought I was dead. I'm always forgetting them."

"Thanks," Polly said. She put her hand on Noah's shoulder. "And I promise — he always lives through it."

"You fell pretty hard out there earlier," the coach said to Noah. "Everything okay?"

Noah stood up tall. "I'm okay. I didn't hurt myself."

Coach Darby winked at him and smiled at Polly. "You're a good player, Noah. Keep up the great work."

Polly turned them back to the truck. "It's nice that he picked up your glasses."

"I hate wearing them," Noah said.

"But you can see better when they're on, right?"

"Yeah, but ..."

"No yeah-buts. We've talked about this. The glasses stay on."

"Okay." He looked at them in his hand, glanced at Polly and made a decision, putting them on before getting back in the truck.

"One more time," Polly said. "Do you all have everything? Backpacks? Extra clothes? Glasses?"

Since there were nods all around, Polly headed south toward Sycamore House. She pulled in beside the barn, surprised not to see Eliseo's truck there. She had hoped to just drop the kids off and leave, but not without him on site.

"It doesn't look like your uncle is here," she said. "Let's go in and find out where he's gone."

"Us too?" Elijah asked hopefully.

"You too." Polly held the back door open as kids piled out, then checked the floor and seat. "Gabby, you left something," she called as the girls opened the gate.

Gabby ran back to the truck, climbed back in and picked up her shoes and backpack.

"Make sure there's nothing else left," Polly said. They'd been through this before and she didn't feel like running someone's backpack out to their house this evening.

The girl looked around. "That's everything," she said and jumped to the ground, then ran off to join her siblings.

Polly sighed and slammed the door shut, then walked around the truck and closed the doors on the other side. By the time she got inside the barn, the kids had scattered. She walked down the alley to the far end, looking inside the feed room and then into the tack room. No Eliseo. When she walked out the back door, she found her sons sitting on upturned five-gallon buckets while both donkeys nuzzled them looking for attention. Gabby and Ana had found Jason, who was coming back with an empty wheelbarrow. Sammy was standing in the middle of the pasture with Daisy, talking to her. The big horse had lowered her head so he could rub it up between her eyes.

"Where's Eliseo?" Polly asked.

"He and Matty went up to the grocery store," Jason said. "He thought they'd be back before you got here." He yelled out to Sammy. "If you talk her into walking back with you, she'd probably like a good brushing."

"Can I help brush her?" Elijah asked. He jumped up from the bucket, startling Huck.

"Slowly," Polly said. "Not today."

"Then soon?" he asked. He put his hand back out to touch Huck and the donkey relaxed again.

"You can leave the others with me," Jason said. "We'll be fine."

"Thanks." Polly put her hand on Elijah's shoulder. "Come on, boys."

When they got home, Kayla and Andrew were both gone. Rebecca was in her room upstairs and there were no cats to be found. Polly assumed they were all with her daughter. Han and Obiwan were thrilled to see her, though she'd only been gone a few hours. The boys dropped to their knees and each hugged a dog as if they hadn't seen them in days. Polly picked her way around the reunion, knowing it would only take a few minutes, time she was willing to let them have.

Heath came in while the boys played with the dogs. He looked completely exhausted.

"Are you okay?" Polly asked.

"I didn't sleep very well last night. Up late studying for my last finals. I can't believe I'm almost done."

"You really are. Your brother will be done on Friday, too."

He nodded and headed for the refrigerator. Opening the door, he stood in front of it until Polly had to ask.

"Is there something specific you're looking for?"

He glanced at her in surprise. "Oh. Sorry. I forgot what I was doing. I wanted something."

"Stand in the pantry," she said. "You might have more luck."

Heath took out a pitcher of apple juice, opened the cupboard and took down a glass. "This is what I wanted." He looked down at the two boys playing on the floor. "Do you want to play a video game before supper?"

They jumped up and Polly put her hand out. "Really? You're exhausted. Do you want a nap?" She looked at the boys. "Take the dogs into the foyer and play while I talk to Heath. One of you should go take a shower."

They looked back and forth at each other, then Elijah opened the door and called for Obiwan. The rest followed him.

"No, then I wouldn't sleep tonight." He wandered over to the table and sat down. "Do you have any idea how weird it is to think about not going to school again?"

"I do," she said. "It's pretty weird."

"I know that I have graduation and the party, but it feels like I've had thirteen years of buildup and then it's just over. No more classes or schedules to worry about. It's just done."

"Until this fall when everything changes and you will be in complete chaos," Polly said with a smile. She sat across from him.

"Yeah. I told myself I couldn't get nervous about that until the first week of August."

"But you're a little nervous now?"

He nodded. "Hay keeps telling me it's no big deal. He said he'd take me over and show me where all of my classes are and the easiest way to get to them."

"Orientation will do that, too."

"But I'd rather Hay showed me so I don't look stupid."

Polly smiled and put her hand out to take his. "You're going to be fine. I promise. I'm proud of how far you've come." She stopped. "No. I don't want to say it that way. I'm going to tell you that I'm proud of you. Just that."

"Thanks."

She sat back. "With you and Hayden having next week free, is there any place that you would like to go? Just the two of you."

"Like where?" he asked.

"I don't know. I was kind of thinking about a road trip — maybe next week before you start working here again for the summer. Where would you like to go within driving distance?"

"Like Rapid City?"

"Sure," Polly said. "Is that what you want?"

"We went when I was a little. It would be fun to see it again. Seriously? Just me and Hayden? What about everybody else?"

"You two boys should do something together before your lives explode. Think about where you'd like to go and then talk to your brother about it. If you want to camp, we can make that work. If you want to stay in hotels, you can do that. Go to Rapid City. But if you'd rather head to Kansas City or Chicago or St. Louis or the Twin Cities, all of those are in range."

"I've never been to Chicago. What would we do there?"

"If the Cubs are playing in town, you could maybe get tickets to Wrigley Field. There are lots of museums and the Aquarium. Who knows what shows and events are going on."

"Wow. I never thought about doing that," he said. "Have you ever seen the Arch?"

"St. Louis?" Polly nodded. "I've been there. It's pretty cool. Talk to your brother and come up with a plan."

Heath shook his head. "You come up with the weirdest things."

"What do you mean?"

"I don't know. It always seems like just about the time I figure I landed in this amazing family and things couldn't get any better, you come up with something new and I can't believe all over again that I live with you."

"I love you, too," Polly said and looked up when she heard the back door open.

Henry walked in, carrying two large paper bags. "I thought the kids might like something fun," he said.

"What did you get?"

"Barbecue. I stopped in Boone on the way home." He glanced around the kitchen. "I really hoped to get here before you started cooking. I should have called, but I was on the phone the whole way back with Skinner Realty."

"What now?" Heath asked. "More change orders?"

"And how." Henry put the bags on the island counter top. "I'm so glad I contracted to do the work and didn't go into partnership on these condos — I'd have to kill him. As long as he pays me, I'll do what he needs, but I'm going to ..." He stopped talking when Elijah came in from the foyer.

"Henry!" Elijah yelled and ran to him for a hug.

"How about some Mario Cart," Heath asked.

"Yes!" Elijah released Henry. "Come on. I'll load it up."

Heath followed him and said, "Let me change my clothes. I'll be there in a minute."

Elijah ran back into the kitchen. "Can I call and tell Noah to hurry and come play Mario Cart?"

Polly watched him hover at the intercom. "Sure." She walked over to Henry and wrapped her arms around his waist. "I didn't talk to you at all today and I've missed you. I hate how busy you are right now."

He kissed her lips. "Me too. It's not going to get any better. You know that, right?"

"I do. Thanks for bringing supper home. I promised macaroni and cheese, but I think this will be just as good."

"If you look in the bags, you might be surprised at what I bought," he said.

"No way."

"Of course, way. I know what those little boys like."

Rebecca walked in from the back staircase, took one look at them and said, "Will you two take that upstairs?"

"Nope," Henry said. "I love my wife and I missed her today."

"You didn't see me either. Did you miss me?"

"You bet." He broke away from Polly. "Do you want me to hug on you and kiss your cheeks?" Henry crouched and approached Rebecca, a wild gleam in his eyes, his hands outstretched.

"No!" she screamed and dashed for the other end of the table, laughing uproariously. "Don't slobber on me."

He went one way and she went the other. In a flash, he turned to chase her around the table. Rebecca ran to Polly, grabbed her waist, and tucked in behind her.

"Protect me!" Rebecca yelled.

By this time, Elijah and Heath were standing in the hallway, and Noah, with his eyes wide, stood watching from where he'd come down the back steps.

Henry took in the room and ran to Noah, grabbing him up.

Noah squealed with delight as Henry hugged him close and kissed the boy's cheek. He spun in a circle, put Noah down and stalked toward Elijah.

"Do you want a bear hug too, little boy?" Henry growled.

Elijah started to bolt, but got caught by Heath, who picked him up and held the boy in front of him. "Protect me, Elijah," Heath said.

Henry grabbed Elijah from Heath's hands and drew him in close, growling as he nuzzled the little boy's neck.

The dogs encircled Henry's legs as Elijah screamed and laughed.

Stepping over Han, Henry put Elijah back on the floor. "Anyone else?"

Heath started to walk away when Henry caught him. "You didn't think you were safe, did you?"

"What?"

Henry drew Heath into a hug. "I don't ever want you to think that hugging is just for girls and little boys. I love you."

Rebecca had come back around Polly and stood beside her. She took Polly's hand and clutched it to her heart. When Polly looked down, the tears in her own eyes were matched in Rebecca's.

"He's really cool," Rebecca said.

"Yeah he is," Polly replied, her words choking in her throat.

Heath slowly put his arms around Henry.

Elijah bounced on his feet beside the two, then dropped to the floor and drew Han into a hug. Rebecca took her hand back and walked over to Noah, extending it to the little boy. "I heard Heath say he's playing Mario Cart. Let's get the game loaded so we can all play."

Henry released Heath, who was embarrassed enough that he slunk down the hallway with Elijah hot on his trail.

"You just messed him up," Polly said.

"I don't know that I meant to do that, but once I started with the little ones, I wasn't going to let him walk away thinking he was too old for a hug from me."

"Did your Dad hug you?" Polly asked.

Henry shrugged. "Not really. Well, sometimes, but only on big occasions. With these kids, I just feel like they need more affection than I did. I knew that my parents loved me from the day they brought me home. These kids have all had their love interrupted over and over."

"You're an amazing man."

"I'm just doing the right thing. I love them." He pulled her back in for another kiss, then said, "Are you ready for our date tonight?"

"I need a shower."

"So do I, but I'm going to put these padlocks on the garage before I come upstairs."

# CHAPTER SIX

"So, what are you wearing on this hot date tonight?" Rebecca asked, putting plates out on the table. "It's been forever since you two did this."

"Will you kiss?" Elijah asked, bouncing up and down on the balls of his feet.

Polly laughed and gave him a hug. "I like kissing Henry."

"Polly and Henry, sitting in a tree. K I S S I N G." Noah startled even himself when he sang out the familiar words. He glanced to the side. "I heard that in school."

"No trees tonight, though," Polly said. "You see us kiss all the time. What's the big deal about this?"

"This is like ..." Elijah paused for effect. "A date. Like you're boyfriend and girlfriend. You know — lovey-dovey stuff."

"You're next in the shower," Polly said, pushing him toward the back stairway. "You stink."

He smelled his armpits and waved his arms around. "I stink really bad."

"Go fix it," she said. "Henry brought home a good supper for you, so don't waste time playing in the water. Got it?"

He nodded and ran up the back steps.

"Thanks for keeping an eye on things tonight," Polly said to Rebecca.

"We got this. Don't worry. You go ahead and get ready."

Polly gave her daughter a quick hug and before heading up the steps, stopped to hug Noah. She laid her face on his freshly washed hair. "You smell good, little boy. I love you."

He turned to hug her back and they stood that way for a moment. Noah didn't reach out to her like Elijah did, but whenever she put her arms around him, he acted as if he never wanted to let her go. Polly let him release the hug first and kissed his forehead.

Once they had moved upstairs, this back stairway saw much more use. Especially since the kitchen had become the gathering room for most everything. They still sat at the table for meals, but when she worked in the kitchen, the stools around the center island filled with family.

She stopped before going up the back steps and looked around the storage room. What a useless waste of space. With the mud room and pantry, she had plenty of storage off the kitchen. Her mind began spinning with ideas, the first being that they could knock out the wall between this room and the kitchen, opening it up entirely. The bathroom was a bit of an annoyance where it was, but they could live with that. If she opened this room up to the kitchen, they could add comfortable chairs or even a couch in the crook of the stairway. Since she wanted to put an open patio in the back yard for the grill, they could put doors into the back wall of the kitchen and still have plenty of room to move around.

As soon as she had the dining room put together, they would eat family meals in there, eliminating the need for the table they used right now. Snacks at the island and lounging where the table was would be a perfect setup. She needed to talk to Henry about this. Of course, nothing would happen for a while.

The first rooms Heath and Hayden were taking on this summer were their bedrooms and the bathroom upstairs. She wanted them to have more privacy. After all that had happened to them following the death of their parents, they'd been able to create a stronger relationship. It had been good for them to live together this last year, but now she had the space to give them freedom.

Polly stopped in the hallway before going into her bedroom. Elijah was in the shower, singing Pharrell's *Happy* at the top of his lungs. She had no idea where he got all of that crazy joy, but was so glad that it filled him up to the point he had to sing to let it out. She leaned on the door sill and listened as he sang, and found herself moving to the beat he'd set. When the shower turned off, Polly scooted into her own bedroom and shut the door. Elijah didn't need to know he'd had an audience. Pure joy like that didn't need extra attention.

She kicked her shoes off and stood in front of the wardrobe, trying to decide what to wear. Evenings were still cool, so a light sweater and pants would be perfect. Polly laid them out on the bed, then went into the bathroom and stripped down, tossing her clothes in the hamper. She loved her shower and loved the whirlpool tub just as much. Tonight was no time for relaxing, unless of course, she and Henry came back and used it. They hadn't done that yet. Most nights, they dropped into bed, completely exhausted from their day. Polly could hardly believe how much she was anticipating a slower pace this summer. She pulled the hair tie out, dropped it on the counter, and stepped into the shower.

Molly hadn't found all of the hay in Polly's hair, though she'd taken out a few more pieces when they sat in Marie's living room after lunch. After Henry and Bill went back to work, Polly had spent the rest of the afternoon with Molly and Marie. By the end of lunch, Marie finally agreed that the purchase price of the land north of town was ridiculously low and a good deal. She even acknowledged that it wouldn't be long before prices for land as miserable as that lot would increase as more and more people moved into the area.

Right now, growth was focused south and east of Bellingwood as commuters from Ames and Boone looked for small town life. In just a few more years, development would move north. The way the creek cut through the property made it unusable for anything other than a home, and farmland surrounded the plot, isolating it from other neighbors.

Marie had attempted retirement with her husband, but found that it suited neither of them. She wasn't sure though, that investing the money they'd set aside was the right thing to do at their age. When Bill pointed out that Polly and Henry had seen healthy returns on everything they'd invested in, she began to waver.

Polly still wanted to talk to Jeff about the idea before they sat down to negotiate a deal. He had a better sense of what types of visitors were coming into Bellingwood and whether a bed and breakfast would be profitable. She'd stop in to talk to him tomorrow. Henry and Bill were gung-ho on getting this nailed down. She wasn't sure why. They were too busy right now to take on more projects, but Henry was right. Even if they just purchased the property, it could sit there until they were ready to go to work. She chuckled. Like that would happen. It wouldn't sit very long before either she or Henry was in there cleaning out the trash and making plans for renovation. Bill mentioned that if they owned the property, that would give Dick license to clear out brush like he'd never felt he could before.

She turned off the shower and grabbed a towel before stepping onto the bath mat. That was one of those crazy little things she'd not thought about having to teach the boys. When Rebecca complained about how wet the bath mat was all the time, it occurred to Polly that the boys didn't realize they could start drying themselves while still standing inside the shower, then finish up after most of the water had dripped off them and gone down the drain. It was those types of things she worried she would never catch up on with Noah and Elijah. This being-a-mother thing was overwhelming on the best days.

Taking the robe off the hook beside the shower, Polly slid into it and wandered out into her bedroom.

"Hello there," she said to Obiwan, who was lying on the bed. "How long have you been up here waiting for me?"

He thumped his tail as she sat down beside him to brush out her hair. He put his head on her lap and the two of them looked out the windows at the back of the house. Seeing the fresh green in the trees had yet to become old for her. They'd moved into the Bell House after even the fall colors were gone. Watching it all come alive again had been glorious. Even the front lawn was beginning to look nice.

She could still tell where Liam Hoffman had dug it up as he replaced the water and sewer pipes, but in another year it would be perfect. The back yard was lush and green. Polly wanted to replace the fence this summer and plant more trees. She knew it was annoying to mow around them, but beauty wasn't always about easy, and she was having more trees.

Polly watched the door as steps approached.

"Hey there, hot stuff," she said when Henry came in. He closed the door behind him.

"Look at you, all fresh and clean. Maybe we should just lock ourselves in here tonight."

"We could do that, but you know the kids would find a way to extract us from our solitude."

He nodded. "I'll grab a quick shower and then we can leave." Smiling, he said, "It won't take you long to get ready, right?"

"Right," she said. "I was just sitting here enjoying the view with Obiwan. I can move it along." Polly rubbed Obiwan's neck and stood up. She picked up the clothes she'd laid out and followed Henry into the bathroom. "I have another idea for the kitchen."

He stopped moving in the middle of peeling off his t-shirt. "You what?"

"If you think it will work, I want to knock out the little wall between the present kitchen and the stairway. Then we can turn that into a lounge area. I want to put a set of French doors to the patio on that back wall."

"You do, do you?" He finished taking his clothes off, reached in and turned the shower on. "I need a couple of clones to keep up with you."

"It doesn't have to happen for a long time," she said. "We should probably be in the dining room first because I'll want to get rid of the table we're using now."

"I see. Anything else?"

"Well, the fence. But we've talked about that."

He glanced at the shower and back at her.

"Go," she said. "Don't think about this. We can talk later."

Henry nodded absently and walked into the shower.

Polly chuckled to herself and plugged the blow dryer in. It was much easier to tell Henry everything she was thinking about and give him time to process on it before he had to actually do something. The man didn't like surprises, especially when they required him to work. As long as he had time to plan, he was fine.

She left the bathroom before he was out of the shower and opened the shoe closet to see what shoes she wanted to wear. It was such a silly piece of furniture, but Polly had fallen in love with it. The best part was that using it encouraged her to pick her shoes up off the floor to put them away. Shoving them into the floor of a closet had been too easy and generally meant that she spent far too much time digging around for the mate to the one pair of shoes she wanted to wear.

"You look nice," Henry said.

"Thanks. It's nice to put something on other than jeans and a t-shirt. Where are we going?"

"Let's go to the Brewing Company in downtown Ames."

They'd been there once before with Sal and Mark and had fun. Polly didn't care where they went, just so they were together. But this place had wonderful fresh brewed root beer, too. She'd not been able to get enough of that.

Polly watched him put his pants on and flip through his dress shirts. It was hard to believe they were at this point in their lives. It had only been a few years, but it felt like decades of life had passed.

He turned and looked at her as he buttoned the dark green shirt he'd chosen. "Like what you see?" he asked, lifting his eyebrows.

She drew her tongue across her lips.

"That might make it difficult for us to leave."

"Sorry," she said. "I'll be good ... at least for now."

Henry walked across to her and kissed her lips. "Are you ready to go?"

"Yeah. I think everything's set downstairs. The boys are showered and Rebecca's in charge."

"Hayden sent me a text that he was staying in Ames tonight."

"Yeah," Polly said. "He's got that early exam tomorrow morning. I'll be glad when this week is over for him. Poor kid. I've never seen him this stressed before."

"Since last year about this time," Henry said with a laugh.

Obiwan followed them back downstairs and into the kitchen. Han let out a bark when he saw Henry and Polly.

"You kids have everything you need?" Henry asked.

Elijah ran over to them for another hug. "Are you going to kiss her tonight?"

"Of course I am," Henry said. He stopped Polly by taking her hand and drew her toward him. "Like this." He kissed her long and hard, eliciting an 'ewww gross' from Rebecca.

Heath laughed. "Elijah asked for it."

"No I didn't," Elijah said. "I just wondered."

"What's with all the questions about kissing?" Rebecca asked him. "Some girl trying to kiss you in school?"

"No!" he exclaimed. "I was just wondering."

"He wants to kiss Bentli," Noah said quietly.

Elijah spun on his brother. "I do not."

"Do too."

"Do not."

"That's enough, boys," Henry said. "You know how to get hold of us if you need anything. But don't need anything, okay? Call Grandma instead. You have her number, right?"

"Right," Rebecca said. "You kids go play and don't keep her out too late. She needs her sleep, you know."

Polly and Henry walked out onto the back porch and she turned to him. "Grandma?"

He shrugged. "I don't know what else to call her with them. I guess she's a grandma now."

"She'll love that."

"I really think she will."

When they got outside, she took his hand. "You brought it over."

He walked her to the passenger side of his Thunderbird and opened the door. "It felt like a T-bird kind of a night."

They were quiet while Henry drove out of town. He put his hand out and Polly took it, interlacing their fingers.

"Do you ever think about that first day you met me?" she asked, breaking the silence.

He smiled at her. "Sometimes. Why?"

"I was so naive. I look back on that girl and she had no idea what was coming at her. It's been less than five years and we have a house full of kids — a huge house full of kids. When I lived in Boston, I only had a few friends and now I have so many people in my life I can barely keep track of them all."

"And you have a business and employees ..." his voice trailed off.

"And horses and donkeys and cats, oh my," she said. "But I looked at you upstairs as you were getting dressed and it hit me how different I am now. I walked into that coffee shop in Boone and I was so frustrated with the contractors I'd already met. They only saw a stupid, naive girl who had more money than sense. No one wanted to listen to me and hear what my hopes and dreams were. Then you came in with those blueprints. You'd actually given it some thought. You didn't push me aside for the job — you treated me like I was a smart human being."

"You *are* a smart human being," he said, giving her hand a squeeze. "Just because you didn't know what you were doing with regards to construction didn't mean you weren't smart about it. That was my job."

"It still is."

"Thank goodness," he said with a laugh. "I will admit, though ..." Henry paused and took a breath.

"What?"

"I don't know if I should say it."

"After five years and all that we've been through, there's something you're afraid to say to me?"

He laughed. "I never told you, but when I walked in that day and saw you sitting there, I had a hard time concentrating."

Polly turned and batted her eyes at him. "Because I was so hot and sexy?"

"Pretty much."

She laughed out loud until she snorted. "Whatever."

"Polly, I was going to do whatever it took to win that bid. Even if you were engaged or married to someone else, I knew I had to work with you. When I found out that you were single, it was all over for me. I wanted to kiss you."

"That day?"

"Uh, yeah."

"You didn't know me."

"I understand that, but you weren't like any woman I'd ever met before. My parents despaired of me ever meeting someone and settling down, even though they never said anything."

"They wouldn't."

"I know that and I'm glad, but I just didn't care. I wasn't going to face a dreary life of waking up to someone I just tolerated day after day. I'd given up. It wasn't that important to me. If I was going to be single, I was going to enjoy my life. Then you showed up. You didn't make it easy on me, but that didn't matter."

"I was a scared fool," Polly said. "It was hard to imagine that someone as amazing as you really wanted to make a life with me." She sighed. "I'm glad I didn't make us wait any longer. Look at all we would have missed out on."

"A lifetime of renovating houses?"

"Well, that," she said with a giggle. "I think your mom is on board now with buying that house."

"That's a good thing. Dad was going to be disappointed if he couldn't be part of renovating the property. He's ready to sink his teeth into a big project."

"He's more than welcome to come over and help us at the Bell House," Polly said. "I have a list."

"I mentioned that, but I think he's a little afraid of you."

"Of me?"

"Yeah. He looks at what you've accomplished since you moved into town and it intimidates him."

"But I couldn't have achieved any of it without you ..." Polly paused for effect. "... *and* him. I didn't do any of this alone."

"No, but you're a force to be reckoned with when you get started on something. If nobody else will move forward and do the work, you'll do it yourself and that freaks out us big, protective manly types."

She laughed again. "You guys make too much out of it. I'm not afraid of working hard, but I much prefer that someone who knows what they're doing take the lead."

Henry turned onto Highway 30 heading east and they drove in silence. Polly watched cars go around them as passengers turned to stare at their car. Whenever they took the Thunderbird, they attracted attention.

"Did you hear that Joss and Nate are getting three more children?" she asked softly.

"Yeah, I saw him this afternoon at the hardware store when I picked up padlocks for the garage. He's pretty excited."

"Can you imagine having five kids all at once?" she asked.

"I don't know," he said, glancing at her. "Can I? Count, Polly. Count."

"I mean five *little* kids. That's a lot of little baby stuff at one time."

"The twins are potty trained, aren't they?"

"Cooper and Sophie?" Polly asked. "Yeah. Just. So at least she doesn't have to deal with diapers, but still. She's talking about hiring a nanny to help her out."

"If you had five kids under the age of six, wouldn't you?"

Polly sat back in her seat. Would she? "I don't know."

"I'll hire one for you, then."

"I love you," she said.

"Good." He drove into Ames and made his way downtown. Campus Town was buzzing with activity as kids either celebrated finishing a final or panicked over not be prepared enough for the next day. The city's downtown was busy, too, and Henry drove around a couple of times before finding a parking space.

Polly put her hand on the car door and he stopped her. "I know that I'm busy right now and we don't have enough time together, but I was telling you the truth about seeing you that first day. I knew then that you had to be in my life. I'm glad that we're doing this together."

She leaned toward him and waited for him to kiss her. "Me too, Henry. Me too."

# CHAPTER SEVEN

Polly sent the kids off to school the next morning and headed straight for Sycamore House. She and Henry had talked a lot about the house in the country last night. Before he and Bill moved forward, he agreed that speaking to Jeff about the viability of a bed and breakfast was important.

It surprised Polly to not see the Sycamore House van in the garage when she opened the door, but assumed Rachel had an early morning event. When she got to the office, Kristen was at her desk with a long face and Jeff's door was closed.

"What's going on?" Polly asked Kristen.

The girl sighed and pointed at Jeff's door. "You might as well let them tell you."

"Is it something bad?"

Kristen shook her head, stood up and tapped on the door, then opened it. "Polly's here."

Jeff stood up from his small conference table and beckoned for Polly to enter, then nodded at Kristen, who shut the door.

Stephanie had an arm around Rachel's shoulder while the girl sobbed into a tissue.

"What in the world is going on?" Polly asked. "Is everyone okay?"

"It's all my fault," Rachel choked out. "You should fire me right now."

"Fire you? For what?"

"Have a seat, Polly," Jeff said, pulling out a chair. "The van was burned up early this morning."

Polly felt like a lead weight had dropped in her stomach. "Was anyone in it?"

"No," he said. "Everyone is fine."

"Then the rest is just about insurance," she replied. "It's not life-ending."

"But it's my fault," Rachel said through sobs.

"It's not your fault at all," Polly said. She reached across the table and took one of Rachel's hands. "How could it be your fault? There's an arsonist in town. It's the fault of whoever that is. We can't take responsibility for their actions."

"But Eliseo talked to us all yesterday about making sure that things were locked up and last night I drove the van home because I was out at the winery for a late dinner and it was easier than making Billy pick me up. I didn't think anything of it." She shuddered and took a breath. "The fire department woke the complex up about four o'clock this morning because our van was going up in flames. I'm so sorry."

Jeff patted Rachel's back. "You didn't do anything wrong. None of us would have thought a thing of you taking the van if it had been a normal morning, would we?"

Rachel shook her head.

"And you've done this before, right?"

She nodded. "Every week for this event."

"And I knew that you did this, right?"

"Yes."

"So stop feeling sorry for yourself."

Polly shook her head and looked at Jeff. "Wow," she mouthed at him.

He shrugged.

"I have three jobs this week and four graduation parties this weekend," Rachel said. "I don't know what I'm going to do."

"Rent a van," Polly said. "It's as simple as that. We'll replace the equipment that was burned up and rent a van until we can purchase another one."

"Really?"

Polly looked at Jeff again, who nodded in agreement. "Really. As long as no one was hurt, we move forward. You can't outguess an arsonist, so don't tear yourself apart over this."

"I'll never take the van home again."

"Stop it," Jeff said. "Of course you will. It isn't like people are going to make a habit of torching the Sycamore House van."

Polly clenched up beside him.

"What?" he asked.

"You just jinxed us."

"You're kidding, right?"

"Not kidding. Don't you know you aren't supposed to say those kinds of things out loud? You're just asking for the universe to come down on you."

"Yeah. Okay. Whatever." Jeff rubbed Rachel's back again. "Do you need to call your husband and tell him that you still have a job and we aren't mad at you?"

"I should. He didn't want to go to work this morning, but they're really busy."

"Go call him," Jeff said. "Wash your face and take a deep breath. It's going to be okay."

Rachel stood and headed for the door. "Really okay?"

"Really okay," Polly said. She waited until Rachel shut the door. "He got us."

"The arsonist?" Stephanie asked.

"Yeah. I knew yesterday that somehow, he was going to get us. I'm just glad this was all there was to it. A van can be replaced. People and animals — not so much. I hope they catch him soon. This is ridiculous."

Jeff leaned back in his chair. "So, I got a call yesterday."

"About?"

"The Griffins want to use your upstairs apartment for their graduation party this weekend."

"No kidding," Polly said.

"They were going to have it at their house, but she called me when the guest list exploded — something about unexpected family coming in from out of town. What do you think?"

"If they don't mind the stairs, it's a great idea. Will they use the whole apartment?"

"Probably not. I was thinking they could use the apartment side with the kitchen, because ..." He paused and smiled at her.

"Because?"

"Because if we open it up, I have two other groups that would like to use rooms across the hall. I originally told them that we didn't have the space, but I know both of those families and if they can move the parties out of their houses, they'll grab the opportunity." He gestured back and forth between him and Stephanie. "And we can fill the place up next weekend, too. If you're okay with us using those rooms as party rooms, we can start using that apartment more often. It's icing on the cake."

"But no elevator," Polly said. "That's kind of limiting, don't you think?"

Jeff bit his lip and Stephanie sat forward. "I have a rep coming in next week to talk to us about installing an elevator."

"We weren't going to do anything until we talked to you, of course," Jeff said. "I just wanted to have the information first. But by opening the upstairs to the public, we can increase our income with very little outlay. It's been six months since you moved out. I hoped it would be safe to ask about it now."

Polly laughed. "I have enough to worry about. I'm not ready to see someone else live there, but renting it out for parties and events is a great idea." She took a breath. "So, speaking of renting it out ..."

Stephanie tapped her tablet, waking it up. "Do you need to schedule a date for something?"

"No, that's not it. I wondered what you two might think of opening a bed and breakfast."

"Here?" Jeff asked. "I'm not sure what you're asking."

"Henry and his dad are looking at a property north of where Eliseo lives. There's an old house on it and they want to bring it back to life."

"It's just never enough for you people, is it?" Jeff asked. "What kind of an investment are we looking at?"

"Initial investment is really cheap and Bill wants to be part of it. We don't have any idea yet how much renovation the house will require. It's still standing and doesn't look as if it's in terrible shape, but I haven't seen the inside yet. Right now, it looks like an old haunted house, but that's all cosmetic."

Jeff looked across at Stephanie. "What do you think?"

She chuckled. "You know what I think. We've been talking about this for a while. It's the perfect answer."

"Answer for what?"

"We get several requests a month for something like this," Stephanie said. "Right now we're able to divert them to the hotel since it's close to the winery, but it would be a perfect answer for some of our newlyweds who have their reception here and want a romantic place for their first night together.

"We also get requests from extended families who want to spend a full week together in a home away from home. How many bedrooms do you think are there?"

Polly shook her head. "I have no idea yet," she said with a laugh. "I just saw it from the outside."

"Well, when do you think you can kick this off? This fall? Winter?"

"Uh, no," Polly said, blinking in surprise. "We haven't even purchased the property and Henry's so busy right now that he won't be able to start working on it for quite a while."

"Maybe we find another contractor, then, and get this thing moving."

Polly looked up at Jeff and relaxed when she saw the smirk on his face. "I was going to have to kill you."

"I wouldn't trust anyone other than Henry with our properties," he said. "I'm no fool. Can I see the place?"

"Me too," Stephanie said.

"You guys want to see it now?"

"Yeah. We're free." Jeff turned to Stephanie. "You don't have any meetings this morning, do you?"

"Not until two o'clock. You've got that lunch, though."

He glanced at the clock up on the wall. "It's only nine o'clock. We'll be back long before that, right?"

"The house is just north of Eliseo's," Polly said. "Shouldn't take but fifteen minutes to get there and we'll just drive through. You can't see much."

"You driving?" Jeff asked.

"Sure."

"We'll meet you out back," he said. "I want to tell Kristen where we're going."

Polly nodded and stood to leave his office. "I miss working here all the time. I walk into a burned-up van and walk out to go look at a new property."

"We'll find an office downstairs for you any time you want to come back," Stephanie said.

"I know." Polly left and walked back to the kitchen.

Rachel looked up from a sauce pan at the stove. "Thanks for being so good about the van, Polly. I appreciate it."

"Rachel, there are things that you can be in control of. This isn't one of them," Polly said. "And you can't take responsibility for things out of your control. All we can do is pick up the pieces and make sure that our customers are taken care of."

"Billy told me you would be cool about it. I was pretty freaked out, though."

"Billy was right. Listen to him."

"That's what he said when I called him." Rachel smiled. "Kristen is looking for a rental van. We'll be okay."

"Yes we will." Polly left by the back door and went out to her truck. She moved Rebecca's jacket from the front seat, tossing it behind her, then turned to double check the back seat. Hauling kids around regularly led to a certain amount of mess, but they'd done a complete cleanup last weekend, so it wasn't too bad. Now, the bed of the truck was a different matter. She just kept that closed up as much as possible.

Stephanie got to the truck first and Polly waved her into the front seat.

"So I was thinking of throwing a party for Kayla and Rebecca and Andrew," Stephanie said. "You know, graduating from eighth grade and all."

Polly dropped her lower jaw open. "A party? I'm supposed to think about a party?"

"No, I am. I thought that we could invite their classmates up to Sweet Beans after school the Wednesday before school is out."

"They're done the Friday before Memorial Day, right? I'm going to the little graduation ceremony."

Stephanie nodded. "Sky said he'd work Wednesday for free. We just have to pay for the drinks."

"And maybe we can have cupcakes," Polly said. "It's a great idea. Have you talked to Camille?"

"Not yet. I wanted to ask you and Sylvie first. If you two said okay, I'd talk to Miss Bickel about putting an invitation out."

"I'm all in," Polly said. "I'm just sorry I didn't think of this before."

"Kayla asked about it the other night. At first, I told her that we'd just celebrate on our own, but she wanted to do something bigger." Stephanie smiled. "And the two of us are going to celebrate like crazy. It's hard to believe that we've made a home here. Kayla is so happy. She has friends and a future. Did you know that she wants to go to college? I have no idea how I'm going to pay for it, but my sister wants to go to college! That's such a big deal to me."

Jeff opened the back door and climbed in. "Sorry it took so long. I had a call come in. Kristen lined up a van for the next two weeks. She's reaching out to the insurance agent. He'll come by the office later this afternoon."

Polly backed out of the driveway and waited at the end of the lane for traffic to pass. "Did you finally get your apartment back to normal?" she asked Jeff.

"You mean from Mom's visit? Yeah. I'm glad she stayed at Sycamore House. Just three short visits and she had my apartment bathroom topsy-turvy." He huffed. "She called last night. It looks like this trip is going to become a regular event. My cousin accepted at Nebraska and Mom thinks it will be great fun to visit me more often. When I tried to tell her that I didn't know if we'd have room for her, she reminded me that I had a two-bedroom apartment and if that wasn't big enough, there were plenty of hotels in Ames. I'm in hell." He clutched his head with both hands.

'You love your mother and you know it," Polly said.

"I adore my mother," he responded, "as long as there are several states between us. I don't go into her house and change things around. Why does she think it's okay to come to my house and redecorate?"

"Maybe you should mess things up in her house," Stephanie said.

He laughed. "Like that would happen. She'd slap me silly."

Polly drove past Sweet Beans and looked at the building with yearning, but drove on.

"That nearly killed you," Jeff said.

"I haven't had enough coffee this morning. I started my daily buildup, but it was interrupted."

"You should have said something. We could have made you a cup," Stephanie said.

"Thanks. It will be difficult, but I'll live," Polly replied.

"There are some nice homes up here," Jeff said. "I should drive around town more often."

"Because you have so much extra time on your hands," Polly said.

"Well, I should." He swatted at her shoulder. "You be good."

As they left the city limits, Polly picked her speed up, then immediately brought it back down when she ran up on the back of an old beat-to-heck pickup truck driving slower than forty miles an hour.

"Go around him," Jeff said.

She turned to look at him. "Are you seriously backseat driving?"

"Well, what's this about? He's not even going the speed limit."

They approached the corner for Eliseo's house and the truck slowed, coming almost to a stop before turning left.

"Good heavens," Jeff said. "He shouldn't be allowed on the road."

"It's okay, Jeff. We lost what, like a minute?"

"Maybe three. You know, the world could change in three minutes."

"Let's hope not." Polly slowed to make the right turn onto the gravel road leading to the vacant property.

"See, that's how you're supposed to make a turn," he said. "No need for a complete stop. Puh-leeze."

Polly slowed again and pointed to the copse of trees on the north side of the road. "That's it, there."

"It's a very pretty entrance," Stephanie said. "Well, it would be if it were cleaned up some."

Turning into the lane, Polly drove slowly, letting them take in the entire effect of the creekside drive, then came to a stop in front of the house. "There it is."

Stephanie shivered. "You were right. It does look haunted, but that's a beautiful porch."

"It's bigger than I expected," Jeff said. "Do you think Henry will be able to rescue it?"

"If anyone can, he can," Stephanie said. "That creek is really pretty. With all of these trees, it's almost like this place is in its own little world. If you tore that shed down, you could put in picnic tables and one of those big outdoor swings." She pointed at the long front yard. "Can't you just see people playing horseshoes out front? We could advertise it as an old-fashioned hideaway with all the comforts of home."

Jeff turned on a drawl. "It kinda reminds me of old Savannah. People sittin' out on the porch drinkin' sweetea — one word, y'know — and fannin' themselves with those purty picture fans on a stick. Menfolk in their suspenders and ladies in their pretty flower dresses. Big ole dogs lazin' about in the sunshine and younguns runnin' around 'til they get too hot and need some lemonade."

"That's a pretty picture you're painting, there," Polly said. "Imagine how bad the mosquitos are going to be in the summer with that creek behind the house. And ticks? There will be millions of ticks in those trees. And snakes. I'll bet the grounds are just crawling with them."

"That's it," Jeff said. "Sell it like you mean it. Maybe we could enclose that porch with a screen. That would help, wouldn't it?"

She nodded and scratched her head. "That's not a bad idea. See it's making me itch just thinking about it."

"What's that back there?" Stephanie asked, pointing to the far side of the house.

"I think it was a greenhouse," Polly replied. "Until we clear the grounds we won't know for sure what all is on the back side of the house. So, what do you think?"

Stephanie craned her neck around to look at Jeff. "I like it. This could be a lot of fun."

He nodded. "It's more work than I thought it would be, but when it's finished, we could rent the heck out of the place. Who do you think might live here and be the hosts?"

"I haven't thought that far ahead at all," Polly said. "Someone always shows up, though."

She went on around the driveway and stopped before turning onto the road. She pointed straight ahead. "The stables will only be a mile away — right there. That's another draw."

"That's where Eliseo lives?" Jeff asked. "I've never been out here."

Polly turned left instead of heading back to the main road. The mile-long grids that these gravel roads were on made it easy to find your way around the back roads of Iowa. She drove down a mile and turned south.

When she got to Eliseo's road, she pointed left again. "Henry's aunt and uncle live down there." Turning back west, Polly drove and slowed as she approached Eliseo's house. The landscape had transformed completely from the day they found Henry's Uncle Loren in the ditch. Back then, the yard had been a mess and ramshackle outbuildings cluttered the space around the home. Now, the yard was green and lush due to Eliseo's tender loving care. Bicycles and children's toys could be found in the neat yard, but the house stood white and proud with fresh paint and new windows. The outbuildings had come down and land was cleared for the first barn to go in.

"This is a nice little house," Jeff said.

Polly nodded. "Eliseo has done a lot of work. Once Elva and her kids moved in, he worked even harder to finish cleaning up the yard. He's done a great job with it. They have plenty of room to run and play."

Movement caught her eye and she watched as a bobcat moved brush and trees to a burn pile at the far end of the lot. "That has to be Elva. She's intent on getting this ready."

"Eliseo's excited," Stephanie said. "He starts talking really fast when he tells us what his sister can do with it. He says she's better than he is with horses. I hope that's true if they're going to make the place work."

"Me too," Jeff said. "It will kill him if it doesn't."

"Hey now," Polly said. "Stop being negative. It's a great idea. She's a good hard worker and there's no reason it can't work. And they have our complete support. Right?"

"Yes, boss," Jeff said. "Of course, boss."

She chuckled. "Stop it. Are you ready to go back to work?"

"Nothing else you can show us out here?" he asked.

"I can drive you past Dick and Betty's house, but that's all I know."

"Okay. Take me back to work."

Polly drove on to the end of the gravel and stopped. "What's that?" she asked, pointing across Elm Street to the gravel road beyond.

"What's what?" Jeff asked.

Stephanie pointed. "It looks like that old guy's pickup truck. You know, the one you wanted to drive off the road?"

"It's just sitting there," Polly said. "I'm going to check it out. We still have plenty of time."

"No, no, no, no, no." Jeff whined. "This is a bad idea. We're out here in the middle of nowhere with Polly. Tell her to take me home, Stephanie. Please?"

"Hush up, weirdo," Stephanie said. "If the old man needs help, we have to help him."

# CHAPTER EIGHT

Instead of listening to Jeff's babbling in the back seat that it was a horrible idea, Polly kept driving toward the battered pickup truck. She didn't disagree, but knew they couldn't leave someone abandoned out here.

She pulled up beside the truck. "Can you see him in there?" she asked Stephanie.

"No." Stephanie unbuckled her belt and rose up to get a better angle. "I don't see anything."

"Well that's just weird," Polly said. "He left the thing right here in the middle of the road." She backed up and pulled in behind the truck, then unbuckled her seat belt. "Stay here. I want to see if he's in the ditch. This is weird."

"Don't you dare get out of the truck," Jeff said. "Maybe he's hunting something he shouldn't be hunting."

"Like what?"

"Like ditch weed or maybe he has a crop of marijuana planted in the cornfield there and he's checking on it."

"He would have pulled off." Polly pointed to a field entrance just ahead. "I'll be fine. Just keep your cell phones close in case somebody ..." She paused and slowly turned in her seat toward Jeff, then jumped at him, making both him and Stephanie yelp. "... jumps out at me."

"I'll come with you," Stephanie said.

"Really. It's okay." Polly patted Stephanie's arm. "I'm just going to make sure he's okay and then I'll call Chief Wallers to deal with the truck."

As Polly opened the door of her truck, she chuckled at Jeff's under-his-breath litany in the back seat. "Don't do it. Don't do it. Don't do it."

She walked around to the passenger side of the truck and looked into the ditch, half-expecting to find someone lying in the weeds, but there was no one there. The weeds hadn't been flattened by anyone traveling through them, either. Polly tried the handle of the door and was surprised when it opened, but she quickly slammed it shut. The cab of the truck was a mess, filled with fast food containers and coffee cups. She didn't know if they were empty, but from the smell, she guessed that the person driving this truck had been living in it and used them to hold all manner of awfulness. A shudder rippled through her body.

A poorly arranged tarp was used to cover the contents in the bed of the truck. Polly lifted an edge of the tarp. She gritted her teeth, closed her eyes, and retreated a step at the sight of a young man wedged between old pieces of lumber and a rusted tool box. A ratty old sofa with its stuffing torn from the cushions lay atop the lumber. Steeling herself, she reached in to make sure that he was truly dead. The skin was cold to her touch. Then she saw the matted blood on his scalp.

Polly glanced around to make sure that the driver of the vehicle wasn't returning while she made a familiar call.

"I'd like to say that I've missed you, but I have to admit, I'm not surprised," Aaron Merritt said when he answered. "Where are you and what have you found?"

"I'm just down the road from Eliseo's house. If you come up through Bellingwood, you can't miss us. Turn west instead of east."

"Got it. You're on Turnbull Road. Tab's already in town; she'll be there first. What have you got?"

Polly walked to the back of the truck. "It's an old beat-up truck and the driver is gone. We followed him out of town, but then I drove on north as he turned west. When I came back around and went past Eliseo's, I saw the truck just sitting here in the middle of the road."

"The dead person isn't the driver?"

"Based on where the body is stashed in the bed of the truck, I'd have to say probably not."

"Are you sure you're safe? Polly, you should get out of there."

"So if he comes back he can take off again? I don't think so."

"If he's killed one person, he probably isn't afraid to hurt you."

"Jeff and Stephanie are with me."

Aaron laughed. "I'm sorry. I shouldn't laugh. But are you trying to tell me that those two are your big protectors? I think Beryl and Andy might do just as well."

"I won't tell Jeff you said that. Do you want the license plate of the truck? I'm standing right here."

"Sure."

Polly rattled it off. "I haven't seen this truck around town before, but you never know. I miss things."

"Not much," Aaron said. "The least you can do for me is get back into your truck, so if someone threatening shows up, you can drive away. Please?"

"I will. But Jeff is already mad that I stopped to check on it. He's going to yell at me."

"Good for him. Now let me get started and people will be coming your way in a flash."

Polly put her phone back in her pocket and took a deep breath before walking to her own truck.

"Was that Chief Wallers you were talking to?" Jeff asked just as she opened the door.

"No," Polly said.

"No? Who did you call then?"

"Aaron."

"Why would you call ..." Jeff stopped. "You didn't. Tell me you did not just find a body. Why do you do this to me? I was having a perfectly normal day when I woke up this morning. First, Rachel comes into my office to tell me our van burned up and now you drive me right onto a crime scene. I'm a good boy. I swear I'm a good boy."

"In the bed of the truck?" Stephanie asked. "I thought I saw you take a step back. Was it bad?"

"Not horrible. I've seen worse." Polly turned to Jeff. "Are you okay back there?"

"This is the last damned time I am ever getting into a vehicle with you. You take me to bad places. I've never gone to bad places by myself. When Stephanie is driving, we don't go to bad places. I'll bet that if I were to get into a car with Sheriff Merritt, he wouldn't take me to bad places. But my boss? The one person I should trust? Her. Yeah, you. You take me where no one else should ever have to go. Never again."

"It's not so bad. It's a beautiful day out in the country."

He pointed at the truck in front of them. "It's a bad day for that poor person." Then Jeff grabbed her shoulder. "It wasn't the driver, was it? Do you think there is a murderer out here in the middle of nowhere? You see this in the movies. Why are we still sitting here? Get us out of here, chickee! Turn that truck on and drive."

Polly pried his fingers back from her shoulder and pushed his hand away. "We aren't leaving until law enforcement arrives. How would you feel if the murderer came back and drove off with the evidence?"

"A lot better than I do sitting here all exposed." He crossed his arms in front of him. "You do not take your employees' safety seriously enough. I'm lodging a complaint with management."

"You do that," Polly said. She reached over to touch Stephanie's arm. "Are you okay?"

Stephanie nodded. "Just thinking about that poor person. Right now their family doesn't know where they are. Maybe someone is waiting for them to come home."

"I know," Polly said quietly. "It's one of the reasons that finding someone like this doesn't freak me out as much as people think it should."

"What do you mean?"

"I mean that when I finally find them, even though it's awful that they've died, at least it's over. The family won't wonder any longer. It might not be the news they were hoping for, but I can't change that. All I can do is make sure they have some closure and put their family member to rest."

"I didn't look at it that way," Stephanie said. "I just think about how awful it is that they died."

"And it is," Polly acknowledged. "But whether or not I find them, they were going to die. This way it's over. Now all that's left is for the sheriff's department to discover who did it and why."

"You'll end up doing that, too," Jeff said. He still had his arms crossed and now he was glaring at her.

"I just do what I can to help. Why are you so grumpy?"

"Because I thought we were finally going to move past this cloud that hangs over you. People downtown finally stopped talking about Polly Giller and her amazing superpower. They were actually talking about summer events and how pretty the garden on the corner of Sycamore House looks. The other day people at the diner said something about a crime in Boone and it had nothing to do with you. It's been glorious. But can we let this be true for very long? Oh no. Not when we're in the presence of Polly Giller."

"Stop it," Stephanie said quietly.

"Stop what?"

"Stop talking about this like it's a bad thing."

"But it *is* a bad thing. Haven't you been listening?"

"You drama queen, you." Stephanie turned in her seat, her eyes flashing. "This is not about you. Grow up and quit acting like this poor guy's death is putting you out. You're being ridiculous."

Polly scooted back against the door of the cab, her eyes wide. Jeff slammed his mouth shut and looked at Stephanie in shock. "I'm sorry," he said.

"I know you are and I know this is weird to experience, but you've got to just calm down. The sheriff will be here and then we can leave, but until then, stop talking."

Stephanie turned back around and leaned forward to pop open Polly's glove compartment. When she didn't find what she was looking for, Polly lifted the lid on the console between them and offered the girl a handful of napkins as tears burst from the girl's eyes.

"Are you sure you're okay?" Polly asked.

"I'm fine. He's not, though," Stephanie said, pointing at the truck. "The poor guy didn't ask to die. It just happened. And now his life is over. No matter what he did in the past, he can't fix things. He can't apologize for what he screwed up and he can't celebrate the wonderful things that might have come his way. He's just done. There's no coming back from this."

"No there isn't," Polly said, rubbing her hand up and down Stephanie's arm. "I'm sorry you had to experience this today."

'No, I'm really fine." Stephanie dabbed at her eyes with a napkin before clenching her hands into fists and thrusting them into her lap.

"I'm sorry, Stephanie," Jeff said. He leaned forward and rubbed her shoulder. "I don't handle this kind of thing very well. Sometimes my mouth takes off without letting me know that it's getting me into trouble. I'm really sorry."

"It's okay," she said.

Polly watched tears ease down the girl's cheek and soon, Stephanie was sobbing.

"I'm so sorry. I don't know why I'm crying. I don't know this person at all. It just seems like such a waste."

Jeff opened the back door of Polly's truck, jumped out, opened Stephanie's door, and leaned in. She threw her arms around him and cried.

Everyone looked up at the sound of an approaching vehicle and Jeff stepped back, peering to see who was coming toward them. Still holding Stephanie's hand, he looked back at her and asked, "Will you forgive me?"

"It's really okay," she said. "Of course I do. I don't know why I flipped out."

"Death will do that," Polly said. "You two hang while I talk to Tab. I'll try to get us out of here as soon as possible."

Deputy Tab Hudson had driven around to stop in front of the other truck. She was walking back toward them and met Polly beside the cab of the little beat-up truck.

"So, where is it?" she asked.

Polly pointed to the other side. "In the bed under the tarp. You can't miss it. And Tab?"

"Yeah?"

"If you're mad at one of your coworkers, that's who should get the honor of going through the trash in the front seat."

Tab grinned. "What do you mean?" She put a pair of gloves on and opened the driver's side door, then slammed it shut and took a step back. "That reeks. What do people think they're doing? Have a little self-respect."

"It just hit me that my fingerprints are on the tarp as well as on the door handle of the passenger side," Polly said. "Sorry about that."

"Maybe you should start carrying these gloves in your truck," Tab said. "You know — just in case."

"You're not funny. I never think that I'm going to find a crime scene. It nearly always surprises me. As soon as I realize what it is, I call you and walk away."

Tab walked around the front of the truck, peered in at the passenger seat and shuddered.

"I did the same thing right there," Polly said. She pointed at the bed where she'd lifted the tarp and Tab picked up the edge.

"Yeah. I don't even have to touch him to tell you that he's been dead for a while. Did you see the driver?"

Polly shook her head. "No. We followed him out of town. He turned down this road, but I went on north to show Jeff and Stephanie a property that Henry is thinking about buying. We drove around so they could see where Eliseo lived." Polly stopped. "Weird. That was the first time I met you."

Tab glanced down the road. "That night when Henry's uncle was killed. Wow. So much has happened since then."

"I know. And here we are again. Anyway, I saw the truck in the middle of the road and thought we should check it out, but the driver was gone. I have no idea where he might be."

"What did that take you, a half hour?"

"Probably twenty minutes," Polly said. "We weren't up at that property very long. No more than a half hour, though."

"Did you see any other cars out here? Maybe someone picked the driver up after he abandoned the truck."

"I didn't think about that." Polly closed her eyes and thought back. Then she opened them and shook her head. "No, I don't remember another car. You could ask Jeff and Stephanie. Jeff was pretty upset about the truck driving so slowly in front of us. He might have looked around and seen something that I didn't see."

"We'll talk to them, too, but maybe we can let you get out of here right now. If they're around this afternoon, I'll stop by Sycamore House. I'd like to get this all locked down and processed. Did you just drive in and park behind the truck?"

Polly shook her head. "No. I'm sorry. We pulled up beside the truck so Stephanie could look in and see if the driver was in there. When I realized he wasn't, I backed up and parked there. Those are my tire marks."

"Got it. And there's been no other traffic since you arrived?"

"None."

Tab shut the little notebook she'd been jotting notes in and slid it into her breast pocket. A second sheriff's vehicle pulled up beside Polly's truck. Tab stepped over to greet him and then came back to Polly. "You can go on. I know where to find you if I have more questions. This place is about to get busy and I doubt you want to get caught in the middle of it."

"Thanks. Jeff and Stephanie are a little freaked out by the whole thing. I should take them back to Sycamore House."

They walked back to the truck together.

"Isn't it weird how different people react to death?" Tab asked.

"Tell me about it. My kids are completely fascinated by the

whole thing. Even though these two know that I find dead bodies, they haven't ever processed it — at least not until today."

Tab opened Polly's door and looked in. "Hi there," she said. "I'm going to let Polly get out of here. Can I stop by the office later today and ask questions about what you saw?"

Stephanie nodded. "I didn't see very much."

"I know that," Tab said. "I just need to make sure I've talked to everyone. Get all my ducks in a row."

"We'll be there," Jeff said.

"Thanks. See you later." Tab stepped back and held the door while Polly climbed in. She shut it and patted the truck's hood as she walked away, moving straight into business mode. Her shoulders stiffened and she walked a little taller. Now would not be a good time to cross that young woman.

Polly backed down the road, did her best imitation of a three-point turn, though it took a few more turns than that, and drove up to the highway leading into town.

As they drove, they passed more emergency vehicles headed north.

"How are you doing for time, Jeff?" Polly asked. She'd completely forgotten what time he said he had a meeting.

"I'm okay. Why?"

"Because I'm either going to Sweet Beans now with you two or after I drop you off."

Stephanie spoke up. "Take us back to Sycamore House, if you don't mind. I need to get some work done and I don't feel like talking to anyone right now."

Polly glanced in the rear-view mirror and saw Jeff nodding in agreement.

"Yeah," he said. "I should get my head back on business. We have coffee in the office."

"I'm sorry that I put you two through that," Polly said.

Jeff put his hand on her shoulder. "Don't apologize. I was the one being an idiot. As soon as I saw that truck, I had a bad feeling about what was coming next. I didn't want to believe it, but then all of a sudden we were in the thick of it."

"It feels different when you hear about it from someone else," Stephanie said. "I don't know how you do this. I'd be a wreck."

Polly slowed as she approached the downtown. City workers were installing signs for a four way stop. "I didn't know this was happening."

"It was decided at the last city council meeting," Jeff said. "They haven't approved stop signs for the other end of the street by the library, but it won't be long. There are more cars downtown now and after a couple of close calls, the council decided to vote for safety."

Polly chuckled. "I didn't even know you went to those meetings."

"Sometimes. Gotta keep my fingers in the pot so things don't get past me."

"You're pretty terrific. You know that, right?"

"I didn't feel terrific today. I am sorry for freaking out on you."

"Let it go," she said. "Both of you were just fine. Everybody reacts to death differently." She came to a stop across from Sycamore House. "This is why I'm the one who finds dead bodies and you aren't. Different strengths for different people, right?"

"Are you coming back into the office?" Jeff asked.

"Do you need me?"

"No, but if you aren't coming in, just drop us out front."

"Right. That's a good idea." Polly crossed the highway, drove into the lot and pulled up at the front door. "Thanks for going out with me. I promise to try my best to never let this happen again when you're in the truck."

Jeff smiled. "I don't think you'll have to worry. From now on, I drive myself."

Stephanie got out without saying another word. She gave Polly a small wave and let Jeff take her arm as they went inside.

# CHAPTER NINE

Coffee at Sweet Beans would require spending time making small talk with people and Polly didn't feel like doing that right now, so she headed home. There was an unopened bag of Mocha Java in the pantry that was just begging to be used on a day like today. She slowed while driving past the elementary school. On such a beautiful day, the playground was filled with kids. It wasn't hard to find her boys and she stopped to watch. Noah sat by himself on a bench while watching his brother and several others toss a ball back and forth. She hoped he was okay. Surely the nurse would call if there was an issue. Elijah ran over to his brother and Noah just shook his head until Elijah ran off again. It killed Polly to realize that the world destroyed the hopeful innocence of children. As she drove away, she realized that the only thing she could do for them was to make sure they had a bucket filled with love and confidence every morning.

Hayden's car was parked in the driveway when Polly got home. She had no idea why. He had an exam early this morning and spent last night in Ames with friends. She was sure he had at least one more final this week, if not two. He'd been spending his free time in the library studying this week. The chaos of his home life was too much when he needed to concentrate.

She pulled in beside his truck and went inside.

"Hayden?" she called out. When there was no answer, Polly went to the intercom and buzzed his bedroom. Still no answer. Both dogs came tearing down the back steps and leaped at her.

"Down," Polly said, pointing to the floor. Obiwan stopped and waited for her to pat his head. She knelt so she was on eye level with both of them and gave Han a hug. "Where's Hayden? Upstairs?"

He wagged his tail. She knew better than to believe he understood what she was asking, but still, a tail wag was better than nothing.

"Let's go see what's up." She stood and herded them to the stairway. They ran up ahead of her, Han tripping over two kittens cowering at their approach. Polly bent over and picked them up, cradling them in her arms. Once the kids moved upstairs, the cats had been given free rein of the house.

Polly crested the top step and headed for the sound of pounding and ripping down the hall. She stopped in the doorway to the bedroom they'd assigned to Heath and watched as Hayden tore into the plaster and lath. Sweat dripped from his bright red face. When he stopped to brush it from his eyes, he caught sight of Polly.

"Hi," he said and went back at the wall with a vengeance.

"What are you doing?" she asked.

Hayden turned and asked, "What?"

"I said, 'what are you doing'?"

"Working."

"I see that. What are you doing here today? Are you finished with finals?"

He shook his head and raised the sledge hammer again.

"Stop," Polly said, stepping into the room.

"What!" Hayden snapped.

She pursed her lips and stepped back. "Okay. What's got you all lathered up?"

"Nothing. I just want to get this started."

"Yeah," Polly said. "I'm not buying that. You do know better than to try to blow me off, right?"

"I'm fine. Everything's fine. Finals are fine. Tess is fine. What could be wrong?" He smashed the sledge hammer into the wall again.

"Good thing everything is fine," Polly said. "And good thing we have a room for you to demolish when everything is fine."

"No kidding."

"I didn't intend to have to clean this room until after Heath's party. You're going to make me work now, you know."

"Sorry." Hayden tore another piece out of the wall. He'd made good progress so far.

Polly wasn't sure if she wanted to slow him down when, at this rate, the walls would be down to studs in about three hours.

"Well, since you're fine," she said, "I'm going downstairs to make a pot of coffee. I found another body this morning and haven't had nearly enough caffeine to get me through the rest of the day." Without waiting for his response, she spun on her heels and speed-walked to the back stairs. He needed to gather his wits and come find her at this point. And he would. No matter how upset Hayden was, he was still a good kid.

She trotted down the steps and quickly put coffee on, then took a container of chocolate chip cookies out of the freezer on the back porch. Sometimes a mom just needed to be prepared.

While the coffee brewed, Polly shuffled through the pile of mail and papers that had collected on the dining room table. Most of it was junk that needed to be recycled and she set aside two graduation announcements addressed to Heath for him to open.

Hayden was starting to stress her out. He still hadn't come downstairs by the time the coffee was finished, so Polly poured herself a cup and left an empty mug beside the pot. She returned to the table and picked up a cookie. He needed to hurry or she was going to have to give up and go back to get in his face. She'd taken a second bite of the cookie when footsteps on the stairway rang out. Whew. She was glad she'd been right about him.

He came into the kitchen, looked around and said, "I'm sorry. I shouldn't have blown up like that. Did you really find a body?"

Polly nodded. "Yep. I'll tell you about it. The coffee is ready and there's a mug waiting for you. Join me."

"I really am sorry," Hayden said as he walked over to the coffee pot. "It's been a lousy couple of days."

"No worries. I can wait for you to calm down and tell me." She waited until he was headed back to the table. "You are going to talk to me, right?"

"I swore that I wasn't," he said with a half-smile. "All the way home I kept telling myself to let it go and not bother you with it."

"Instead, you came home and beat up the house. I like the way you think."

"Would you believe I was trying to get an early start?" he asked with a little bigger smile.

Polly pushed the plate of cookies across the table to him. "Have you had trouble with your exams?"

He took a breath and slowly shook his head. "I didn't do as well as I could have, but I did fine. That's not it."

"What is it, then?"

"First you tell me about the body."

"That's not fair," Polly said. "This happens to me all the time. I've never seen you so upset." And she hadn't. Hayden was the most even-tempered young man she'd ever met — even more so than Henry. Polly was also surprised that he was here today and not at Marie's house. Those two had created an especially strong bond. Marie and Molly made it a point to spend time with him every week, either meeting him in Ames or at their house for lunch. He told Marie everything. Polly knew it should bother her, but she was thrilled they'd found each other. Hayden needed the wisdom of the older woman in his life. She was much closer in age to being his mother than Polly was.

"Tell me anyway," he said. "Was it someone local?"

"I don't know that," Polly said. "I've never met him. He was in the back of an old beat-up pickup truck that someone left in the middle of the gravel road down from Eliseo's house."

"What were you doing way out there?" He chuckled. "Why am I asking you that? He needed to be found. Something was going to draw you out there."

"Actually, we followed the truck out of town, but I didn't realize what it was until later. I was showing Stephanie and Jeff a property that Bill and Henry want to buy."

"Oh," he said, nodding. "They were talking about it last week. Marie isn't too happy about it."

"She's doing better. The price is ridiculously low and I agree with Henry. Even if we tear the house down, the property is worth that price. We could put up a pretty house and turn it into a bed and breakfast." She reached out to pull the plate of cookies back. "Or I could send you out and have you demolish the inside so we can renovate it from the ground up."

"I'm really sorry," he said, hanging his head.

"Stop it. What's going on? If it isn't your exams, is it Tess?"

He looked up at her, then back down. She realized his eyes were glistening.

"What happened with Tess?"

"I don't know. She's been really distant and the other night she told me she didn't have time for me and made me go away. I don't know what's going on and she won't talk to me."

Polly took a slow, deep breath. There were times men were idiots and she was pretty certain that Hayden wasn't above that, no matter what a great guy he was. "What is her exam week like?"

"It's pretty rough. That's why I was there. I wanted to take supper over so she didn't have to think about it."

"And she was in the middle of studying?"

"But I wasn't going to take more than a few minutes. I thought if she could just take time to eat something, she'd feel rejuvenated and ready to go back after it."

"And she told you to go away."

"Yeah. When I asked what was wrong, she told me it was nothing, but she slammed the door in my face. I texted her later to ask what was wrong and she told me it was nothing again. Then she stopped responding."

"Tell me what happened yesterday."

"She had an exam at three, so I waited outside for her to be done. I didn't have to be anywhere until six o'clock for a study group. I just wanted to take her home and spend a few minutes, but she already had plans with friends from class and was mad because I hadn't checked in with her first."

"These other friends. Was she meeting with them to study for her next exam?"

"No, I think she was having supper before her eight o'clock."

"So she had two tests yesterday, with very little time in between and you presented yourself as a surprise."

"Yeah." He looked up. "That was really stupid of me, wasn't it? Like I said, I'm an idiot."

If their relationship was strong and solid, it shouldn't have been a problem, but Polly wasn't going to say that. "Tell me how Tess usually responds to tests and quizzes," Polly said.

"She gets pretty stressed out. I don't know why. She's really smart and can't ..." He paused. "She can't stand it when she doesn't get one of the top grades. It's all about the scores for her." Hayden shook his head. "I must have sounded like a desperate lover trying to get her attention when she was trying to focus." He put his hands out in supplication. "But I was just trying to be helpful. I wanted to make it easier on her — not harder. Man, I screwed up."

"Do you two usually spend time together when she studies for tests?" Polly asked.

"She gets laser-focused, but I usually know in advance that she's not going to be available. This time, it's been over a week and down deep, I knew I wouldn't see her until Friday or Saturday. Apparently, my sub-conscious didn't like that answer. What am I going to do?"

"Well," Polly said with a chuckle. "At this point, you'd better not try to talk to her until Friday. She doesn't want to think about taking care of you in the middle of her exams. When it's over, the two of you can sit down and discuss it, but until then, take hold of yourself and prepare for your own tests."

"Women are hard to understand," Hayden said. "None of you are ever the same. I figure it out for one woman and then the next one of you is completely different. Just about the time I figure out that one, I come across yet another who wants the polar opposite from a relationship."

Polly rapped on the table. "Maybe you don't apply that just to women. Relationships are hard. Every single person, whether they are male or female, needs something different from a relationship. That's part of the excitement — trying to discover what will make it work."

"Okay," he replied. "Women are hard for *me* to understand. How's that?"

"A little better," she said with a smile. "But it's more fun that way, right? You wouldn't want to be in a relationship where you didn't have to make an effort. Look at poor Henry. He's never sure what I'll come up with next."

"You do make him crazy," Hayden said.

"I hope that never ends. I want to wake up every morning wondering what new thing is going to happen and I want the same for him."

"Have you told him about this body yet?"

Polly shuddered. "Not yet, though I'd be surprised if he hasn't heard about it by now." She sat forward. "Quick change of subject. I have a question about Noah."

"What's up?"

"Does he talk to you or Heath?"

"I suppose," Hayden replied with a shrug. "Why?"

"When I drove past the school, I saw him sitting on a bench by himself during recess. Elijah was playing, but not Noah. Has he said anything about whether he's doing okay?"

"He hasn't said anything to me," Hayden responded. "Heath spends more time with them lately. But I don't think he's sad or upset about school. He seems to really like it."

"Maybe he was just taking a rest when I drove by," Polly said. "I hope that's all there is to it."

"You worry too much."

"No kidding. Sometimes it's what I do best." She pushed the cookies back at him. "Are you ready for your next exam?"

"I'm tired of studying. I know this stuff backwards and forwards. This afternoon I just want to destroy a couple of rooms and then I'll get back to it tonight."

"Backwards and forwards." Polly sighed. "I never felt like that when it came to finals. Never ever. I envy you."

"You do realize that this is mostly what Tess and me do," he said.

"Tess and I." Polly laughed at herself. "I correct everybody, don't I?"

She watched him repeat the sentence in his head a few times, working out the grammar. He finally nodded.

"What do you and Tess do?"

"We study all the time. I've never worked this hard in my life."

"If she's going to law school, this will serve her well." Polly looked at him. "Are you certain that you want to be with her through law school? If she's like this now, she's going to be a terror when those classes begin."

"I hadn't thought about that."

"The two of you might need to have a long conversation before it begins. Set out expectations on both sides."

"She doesn't even know where she wants to go yet. For all I know, she'll leave the state."

That hadn't occurred to Polly, but it made sense. Poor Hayden. This wasn't going to be easy.

Her phone buzzed on the table and she glanced at it.

"It's Henry, just a second."

"I'm going back upstairs. I've unloaded on you and had coffee," he said, standing up.

"Come back down later for lunch. I'll make sandwiches."

Polly picked up her phone and swiped the call open. "Hello?"

"What did you do?"

"About what?"

"What did you do? Things were going along so well."

"What did you hear?" she asked.

"Don't get coy with me. Do you realize whose truck that was?"

Polly frowned. "What? How do you know whose truck it was? Who did you talk to?"

"Dad called."

"How did your dad know?"

"And your van? Why didn't you call me?"

Polly shook her head. "What are you talking about?"

"Your van burning up. You didn't call and tell me about it."

"Where did you hear about that? Your dad again?"

"Yeah. He was up at the diner when Jeff got there all freaked out."

"Jeff went to the diner?"

"Yeah. He had a meeting there. But he couldn't quit babbling about the body you found out by Uncle Loren's place. What were you doing out there anyway?"

"I told you that I wanted to ask Jeff what he thought about the feasibility of a bed and breakfast. He and Stephanie wanted to see the place, so I took them to see it. Then we drove by Eliseo's place so they could see what's been going on there and then ..." Polly stopped talking.

"And then you had to go check out an abandoned pickup truck."

"You know I did. Why are you yelling at me?"

"I'm not yelling at you." Henry brought the level of his voice down. "I'm sorry. I'm not yelling at you. I'm just a little excited. It's strange to hear from my father about terrible things happening to you before you actually tell me."

"I've been busy. I got home and found Hayden upstairs ripping out the walls in the bedrooms that he and Heath will move into."

"What's he doing home? I didn't expect to see him until the end of the week."

"Yeah, well, he and Tess had a fight."

"Oh no."

"It's not a fight, I guess. She just didn't want him around. He was offended and then he got worried because they were fighting.

I'm going to tell you that she isn't even thinking about him because she's so focused on her finals. She doesn't even know that they had a fight."

"Did they have a fight or not?"

"He thinks they did. He tried to wriggle his way into her space when she was concentrating on her work. She pushed him away and it freaked him out."

"You and he talked about it?"

"Once he calmed down. When this week is all over, they'll need to have a long talk to work it out. She didn't handle it well, but I've known people like Tess. When she's in the middle of stress like this, she doesn't know how to handle it, and now is not the time to confront her. They can work it out when life is back to normal and decide whether the two of them can handle this behavior in the future."

"Law school is going to suck for Hayden."

"Yes it is. We discussed that. Now back to this pickup truck. How do you know whose it was?"

"That's Barney Loeffler's truck. He's the junk man."

"I don't know what that means."

"He picks up people's junk. That's how he makes his money. People pay him to haul away their junk. He'll recycle some of it, sell some of it and fix some of it. Was it Barney you found?"

"I have no idea," Polly replied. "I don't know who this Barney guy is. He's from Bellingwood?"

"No. I think his dad lives up in Boxholm. But he travels the whole county."

"This was a young guy. Maybe in his mid-thirties."

"That's about how old Barney is. The business used to be his dad's, but old man Loeffler can't haul stuff any longer. Bad back, bad knees. It would be too bad if Barney was gone. He was a nice guy. A little odd, but people liked him."

"Aaron probably knows who he is, right? So he shouldn't be too hard to identify?"

"Yeah. Aaron would know him. Are you okay? Dad said Jeff was kind of a mess."

"Jeff let his imagination run wild. He didn't see the body or anything. And I'm fine. Tab was the one who met us there."

"She still dating JJ?"

"Yeah, I think so."

"Now about your van. What are you doing about that?"

Polly laughed. "I don't have to do anything. Rachel and Jeff are working it out. They rented a van until they process the insurance and find a new one."

"Okay. That means everything is fine in your world? I don't have to worry about you?"

"You can worry all you want, but I'm fine."

"Then I'm going back to work. I love you."

"I love you too."

# CHAPTER TEN

"Keep away from me!" Elijah yelled, rushing in the back door. "Is Hayden here? I saw his car." He skittered away from Sammy and Noah, who were chasing him. Matty followed them in with Rebecca, Andrew, and Kayla.

"He's upstairs," Polly said.

Elijah grabbed Noah's wrist. "Come on. Let's go see him."

The two boys stopped and Elijah ran back to grab Sam Johnson's hand. "Come on. Let's see what Hayden's doing."

Polly turned to look at Rebecca, who shrugged.

"No soccer or baseball tonight?"

"Some girls soccer match is going on, I guess," Rebecca said. "Sam's mother asked if he could come here with Noah and Elijah because he'd get bored watching his sisters." She put her hand on Matty's back. "I told her that it was okay. Do you care?"

"I guess not," Polly said. "Next time, text me, though."

"Yeah, I was going to, but she had to leave really fast and then I had all of these little kids around me."

Thundering steps down the back stairway announced the arrival of the older boys.

"Hayden's going to go out back with us. Come on, Matty," Elijah said. "We're going to play with Hayden. He's the best."

"Would you put the dogs on their leads?" Polly asked Rebecca. "They'd like to be out there with you."

She really needed to finish the fencing this summer. Tying her dogs up was no fun, but for now, at least it let them be outside with the kids.

"Balls in the garage?" Hayden asked.

She nodded. "Thanks. You don't have to do this, you know."

"It will be good for me." He smiled. "Just look at those faces. How can a person be upset when they're around that much happiness?"

"I know."

The decibel level decreased significantly when the kids and dogs all left the house. Polly went into the pantry to get lemonade mix and another pitcher. When she came back through the door, Andrew was sitting at the island.

"You don't want to be outside?"

"Not yet," he said. "Can I ask you a question?"

"Sure. What's up?"

He reached into the pocket of his shorts and took out a small blue velvet drawstring bag. Opening it, he poured the contents on the counter.

Polly picked up a necklace that had a single diamond hanging from it. "What's this?"

"I didn't spend very much money on it, so don't think I'm ridiculous, but it's kind of a graduation present for Rebecca. Will you be mad at me if I give it to her?"

"A diamond?"

He looked at Polly like she was an idiot. "It's her birth stone, nothing else. I thought about giving it to her for her birthday, but then she did that whole collecting canned goods for the food pantry thing. She got mad at me when I mentioned getting her a personal gift from me."

That sounded like Rebecca. She'd been adamant this year that she didn't need anything other than the trip to the Amanas —

especially when there were people who didn't have enough to eat. While Polly didn't mind not having to track down something unique for a gift, she and Henry had gone back and forth about whether to do something above and beyond. After a long discussion with Rebecca, they'd made a sizable donation in her name. It was what she wanted to do and it made her happy. Polly was proud of her daughter.

"Why are you asking me?" Polly asked.

"Because I wanted you to know that it wasn't like a promise thing or a relationship thing. Mom says we're still too young to be doing stuff like that. She wanted me to be honest with you so I didn't get Rebecca into trouble."

"Well, thank you. And I agree with your mother. You are too young to be making big, lifelong promises."

"Okay."

"But I think this is very sweet and Rebecca will like it."

She held it out and he returned it to the pouch.

"Have you been carrying this around all day?" Polly asked.

"It's been in my locker. I kept forgetting to bring it with me to ask you, and Rebecca is never not around."

Polly sat down beside him. "Can I ask you a question now?"

Andrew sat up a little straighter. "Sure. What's up?"

"It's about my boys. Are things okay with them at school?"

Andrew pursed his lips and thought. "I guess. I don't see them that much. They're in the other wing. Why?"

"You haven't heard anything?"

"No," he said, shaking his head. "Is something wrong?"

"I just saw Noah sitting on a bench today by himself while the other kids were playing at recess. I worry that they'll get picked on because they're different. He's so quiet and sensitive that he'd never say anything."

"But Elijah would, wouldn't he?"

"I don't know," Polly said. "But you haven't heard anything?"

"You should ask Rebecca. She pays more attention to that than I do." Andrew got a big grin on his face. "You're funny."

"Why?"

"Because you worry so much. You act like you let your kids be all independent and handle problems on their own, but you still worry about them all the time, don't you?"

"I worry about all of you," Polly said.

"Noah and Elijah are cool. Most of the kids really like them. You shouldn't worry." He hopped down from his seat. "Anything else I can help you with today?"

"Nope," Polly said. "Go on outside. Tell them I'll have lemonade and brownies after a while."

"Yes, ma'am."

Andrew ran for the back door and Polly went around the island to the sink. She mixed up lemonade and put the pitcher into the fridge.

She did worry too much. Even though she tried to talk herself out of it, there was no stopping her. Since the little boys arrived in Bellingwood, Polly worried that no matter how hard they tried, there would be people who couldn't accept them because of their skin color. Her worries had been proven out enough that she couldn't release them. No matter that ninety-eight percent of the community did all they could to be color-blind, the few who openly bullied anybody who was different was a sucker-punch to the heart.

When she took a bowl down to mix up the brownies, Leia jumped up on the counter.

"Every single one of you looks different on the outside," Polly said. "But the reason you don't like the kittens is because they're annoying in their love for you, not because you don't look the same, right?"

Leia rubbed on Polly's arm, then sat down, picked up her front paw and gave it a lick.

"I love you, but you can bathe on the floor, not on the counter." Polly picked the cat up and snuggled her head before putting Leia on the floor. Without missing a beat, Leia licked down her front leg, then rolled so she could clean her belly.

Polly's phone buzzed and she turned to look at it on the island.

"Hey Jeff," she said. "Are you doing any better?"

"I'm fine. I don't know how you do what you do, so I'm glad it's you and not me."

"I'm sorry that you were involved this morning."

"The funny thing is that I wasn't involved, so I should apologize to you for going off the deep end. But that's not why I'm calling. I have a big delivery here for you."

"You have a what? I haven't ordered anything."

"Yeah. It's from a Celine Delancy."

Joey's mother. Polly hadn't thought about that woman in a very long time. She couldn't imagine what would be coming to her. But of course, the only address they had for Polly was Sycamore House. Thank goodness.

"Uhhh."

"The UPS driver says that he can bring it over to the house if you don't want it here. He came in to ask it before unloading it."

"Um, okay. I guess. Something big?"

"No. I said that wrong. It's a bunch of boxes." Jeff paused. "Fifteen boxes and they're pretty heavy."

"He doesn't mind changing the delivery location?"

"Not if you don't want them here."

"If he'll bring them over, send him."

"Got it. You're going to tell me what's in the boxes?"

"Sure." Polly's heart raced in her chest. What in the world would Celine Delancy be sending to her? The last thing Polly wanted to do was call the woman to find out. Why wouldn't she have asked first?

Polly realized Jeff had hung up. She put the phone back down on the counter. "Focus, Giller. You were making brownies. Kids want brownies." Then it hit her that Sam was here. He'd come to visit often enough that she'd done research on brownies he could eat with his diabetes. It took a little more effort, but she generally had the necessary ingredients. Just as Polly scraped the last bit of brownie mix into the pan, she heard the UPS truck drive in.

Polly went into the foyer. Earlier this year she had been worried about clearing this room for Heath's graduation party. Boxes and furniture had slowly moved into other rooms in the house, mostly because her entire family knew how stressed she was over the mess. Now there were smaller rooms filled with boxes and furniture, but at least when it came time for this party to happen, she could have it without falling apart. The foyer really was beautiful.

She opened the front door as the UPS guy put a box on his two-wheel cart. Beckoning to him, she waited as he brought it up onto the porch.

"Right in here?" he asked.

"This will do."

"I'm going to have a few more loads. Stack it all right here?" He aimed to where she was pointing.

"Yeah. Thanks."

With the next load, he brought a smaller package and put it into Polly's hands. While he went back for the next, she set her jaw. This was much too stressful. She went back into the kitchen, grabbed her phone and a sharp knife and got back to the foyer just as the driver unloaded another stack of boxes.

"Just one more load," he said.

Polly took cash from her wallet and pressed it into his hand. "Thank you for bringing this over. I appreciate the extra run."

"Unloading these boxes once is more than enough," he replied. "And besides, as long as packages travel across the country, I have a good job. Thanks."

She slit the smaller package open and took an envelope off the top. Setting it aside, she lifted a carefully wrapped package out from among bubble wrap and unwrapped it, then took in a breath. She was holding a very expensive first edition of Nathaniel Hawthorne's *Scarlet Letter*. That meant the next book down was probably a signed edition of Dickens's *Oliver Twist*. She'd seen these on Joey's library shelves. He bought them for her, hoping that when they were married she would appreciate them. Polly didn't want to dig any further. She held a small fortune in her hands and knew there had to be more in there.

The UPS driver came in with one more stack. "That's it."

"Thank you for doing this," Polly said.

"These are heavy boxes."

"I think they're all books."

"That's a lot of books. Do you have a place for them?"

"Not yet, but I will."

He smiled and went back out the front door, pulling it shut behind him. Polly took the envelope and went back into the kitchen. She put the pan of brownies into the oven and turned the timer on, then sat down at the island.

"What was all that?" Rebecca asked, gasping for breath. The girl must have run in from the other end of the yard.

"I think it's books," Polly said.

Kayla and Andrew came in next.

"That was a lot of boxes. What did you order?" Kayla asked.

"I didn't order anything. Give me a minute. This should explain things." Polly brandished the white envelope.

Andrew sat down beside her. "Who's it from?"

"You aren't even going to believe it," Polly said. "Give me a minute." She slid her finger under the seal on the envelope and slid it across, then pulled out a stiff notecard with a gold 'C' embossed in one corner.

*Dear Polly Giller,*

*After much discussion with my son, his lawyers, and my husband, we have decided to acquiesce to Joey's request that you receive his library. We have closed out his home, since it appears he will never be allowed to return to the life that he lived before meeting you. As loathsome as it is to me to relinquish anything at all to you, Joey continues to insist that he loves you. I refuse to allow you to have access to our family's money, though he tried to name you as his beneficiary. I much prefer that it be given to the ducks in Boston Common. If you had chosen to become his wife, none of these terrible things would have happened to him and he would still be my sweet boy. I do blame you for everything.*

*Celine Delancy*

"Well," Polly said. "I'm not sure what to say to that."

"Who is it?" Andrew asked again.

"Joey's mother."

"Joey, as in the psycho, dragged-you-to-Boston, Joey?" he asked, his eyes huge.

"Yep, that's the one." Polly put her hand on Andrew's shoulder. "And you're going to flip out when you see what she sent. Follow me." She picked up her phone. Henry wouldn't believe this.

If there was anything that would turn Andrew into a hapless fool, it was books. This was going to be fun to watch.

They opened the doors into the foyer and Polly stopped to take a picture of the stacks of boxes beside the front door, then sent it to Henry with the message, *"Present from Joey D."*

"What's in here?" Rebecca asked.

"Books," Polly said. "Lots and lots of books."

Andrew put his hands on the top box of a stack. "Can I open it?"

"Go ahead."

"Don't let him," Rebecca said. "He'll take out three books, sit down on the floor and won't talk again for hours."

"Whatever," Andrew said. He ripped tape away from the seam and opened the flaps. "It's all hardback books," he said breathlessly. "Look at these beautiful leather books. They all match." He took two out and then two more. "They're by Charles Dickens. Do you think it's everything he wrote?"

Polly nodded. "Probably."

"I haven't read *A Tale of Two Cities* yet. Somebody told me I should wait since I'll have to read it in high school." He held it up. "Do I have to wait?"

"No," Polly said. "You can read it any time. You'll like it."

He rushed toward her, carrying five books of the set. "You have to hurry and finish your library back there. These will look so cool on shelves. Do you think there are other sets like that in those boxes?"

"Absolutely."

"Have you ever seen these before?"

"At Joey's house," she replied.

"Really? You saw his books? He liked them as much as you?"

"Yeah," she said with a smile. "And he had a lot more money than me, so he could afford expensive books."

"Is this the most expensive book he owned?"

Polly shook her head. "No it isn't, but you have to stay really calm when I show you something."

Andrew frowned at her, then his face lit up. "He sent you an expensive book? What is it?"

"I said calm." She led him back to the stacks and took down the box that held the first editions. Gently removing the Nathaniel Hawthorne book, she placed it in Andrew's hands. "That is a first edition book. Meaning that it was printed in ..."

"Eighteen fifty," Andrew gasped, having opened the cover. He spun to Rebecca and Kayla. "This book was printed in eighteen fifty!" Then Andrew sat down on the floor. "Is that ...?" He looked up at Polly.

She nodded again. "The author's signature."

"This guy just sent these books to you?" Kayla asked.

"He's going to be in jail forever," Rebecca said. "It's not like he'll ever need them again. But I can't believe they didn't sell them for the money."

"They have plenty of money," Polly said. "And Joey wanted me to have them. He bought them for me in the first place. When I broke up with him, I didn't ever think about these books again. I just needed him out of my life and no book was worth putting up with his craziness."

Kayla put her hand on a stack of boxes. "He bought these books for you?"

"No," Polly said. "He bought the book that Andrew is holding for me. There are a few other first editions in that small box. I think he bought them hoping that I'd marry him for his books. We used to visit author's homes in the Boston area." She smiled at Rebecca. "You've read *Little Women*, right?"

"Of course. A bunch of times," Rebecca said.

"I was in her family's home in Concord, just outside of Boston."

Her eyes grew wide. "I want to go there sometime."

"You will. There is so much history out there."

The foyer doors opened and Hayden came in with Noah, Elijah, Sam and Matty.

"What's going on in here?" he asked.

"Polly got a bunch of books from an old boyfriend," Andrew said. "These are the best."

When the four little boys raced over to see what he had in his hands, Polly reached down and lifted the Hawthorne book up, wrapped it back in its protective paper and returned it to the box.

"An old boyfriend?" Hayden asked.

"Yeah. I'm the keeper of the books," she said. "He's in prison."

"And he had books?"

She laughed. "It's all so convoluted."

"I took brownies out of the oven. It dinged when I came in."

"Thanks. Come on, kids. The books will be here forever. Let's have brownies."

Sam hung back and his brother tugged on Polly's hand. "He can't have brownies."

Polly smiled down at him, then at Sam. "Remember? I know how to make brownies you can eat."

"You made those?" Sam asked in shock.

"Of course I did. Whenever you're here, I'll include you in the fun."

Matty ran over, grabbed his brother's hand and dragged him through into the kitchen.

"I'm going to take a shower and head back to Ames," Hayden said. "There's another study group meeting at the library tonight. I'll be back but it might be really late."

"Just text me so I know where you are," Polly said. "And you aren't going to try to reach out to Tess, right?"

He set his jaw and shook his head. "She knows I want to talk to her and when she's free, she'll let me know."

Polly pulled him into a hug. "You are such a good kid. I'm proud of you, you know."

"For not being a jerk?"

"No. For being a great guy who is doing good work in college and being loving and kind. How's that?"

He chuckled. "It's good."

Her phone rang. "It's Henry. I sent him a picture of the boxes, so I should probably take this. I'll see you later."

As he walked across the foyer, she swiped the call open.

"You're killing me today. What is in those boxes?" Henry asked.

"Joey sent me a present."

Absolute silence.

"Did you hear me?" she asked.

"I heard you. What in the damned hell are you getting from Joey Delancy?"

"His library. His parents had it packed up and sent to me. Joey wanted me to have it. You'll have to read the friendly note his mother sent."

"She sent you a friendly note?"

"Yeah, that's an exaggeration. She blames me for him being in prison, but since he wanted me to have his library, she sent it to me anyway."

"It seems like a big library."

"There are some expensive first editions, too. I looked one of them up once and it's worth more than ten thousand dollars. And apparently Joey wanted to name me as the beneficiary in his will, but his mother would rather the ducks at the Boston Public Garden got her money."

"I see." Henry took long enough to say anything more that Polly interrupted.

"That's all you have?"

"I'm trying to decide what to say next."

"Don't say anything. We have a treasure trove of fancy books to add to our library. When Heath and Hayden have time, I'll ask them to move the boxes back to that room until we are ready to unpack them and fill the bookshelves."

"I see."

"You're not okay with this, are you?"

"I'm not *not* okay with it. I'm just stunned."

"I get that. How about you come home and we'll have a nice dinner and not talk about this tonight."

"Yeah, you've had kind of a big day. I should remember that none of this is about me."

"It's okay," Polly said. "I'm rolling with the punches. You're just getting secondhand information."

"Uh huh. Yeah. I'll be home after a while."

They ended the call and she went into the kitchen, standing in the doorway to watch the kids laugh and chatter at the table. Her life was much more entertaining now than it ever had been before. For that she was thankful.

# CHAPTER ELEVEN

Using all of the patience she possessed, Polly managed to get her kids off to school one more time without bloodshed. She needed more coffee. As soon as they were gone, she was in her truck, heading for the coffee shop. She didn't even care if she saw anyone there that she knew. All that mattered was that someone else made good coffee for her to drink, and maybe a muffin, too.

The kids were getting so excited about the end of the school year that keeping them focused in the morning was becoming impossible. Heath was finished with classes this week. How could that even be real? These kids weren't supposed to grow up so fast.

She pulled into a parking space and sent a text to Henry. *"We should send Heath and Hayden off on a road trip by themselves next week. On us. Before everything gets crazy. What do you think?"*

*"Uhh, what?"* he sent back.

*"Both of them are done with classes today. They should go be brothers together for a few days. Yes? No?"*

*"I don't care."*

Well, that was short. Polly wondered what was up. He was probably busy.

She sent back a smiley face and got out of the truck.

"Polly Giller!"

She turned to see Chief Wallers striding toward her.

"Hello there," she said. "Coming to join me for coffee? I'll buy."

He held the door open for her. "I can't stay, but I am here for coffee."

"Oh come on, not even for a few minutes?"

He shook his head. "There was another fire this morning. This guy is picking up speed."

"Where was it this time?"

"A stack of pallets behind the General Store. If one of the girls hadn't gone out for a cigarette before starting work, the fire would have spread up and down the alley. She had the presence of mind to call us and use a fire extinguisher to slow things down. I don't know how she knew not to use water, but thank goodness."

"I didn't know that," Polly said softly.

"Diesel needs to be smothered. Water will cause fuel to spread, extending the reach of the fire."

"Do you have any idea who is doing this?" Polly asked.

As they approached the counter, Skylar looked up and grinned. "Two of my favorite people. Your regulars?"

"Dark iced coffee this morning," Ken said.

"I heard about that fire," Skylar said. "Kinda scary. I wish I'd been outside. Maybe I could have seen the person in the alley. We spent the day yesterday helping the ladies next door clean up out back. Nobody is leaving anything outside right now that can be burned. Mrs. Dykstra's husband brought his pickup truck and took two loads out to the dump. Better there than here."

"I'll bet it looks great back there," Polly said.

"I know, right?" Skylar replied. "It's never been so clean. We should have things like this happen more often." When he realized what he said, Skylar turned away. "Sorry. I'm a moron."

Ken shook his head. "He's not wrong about that, though. More people are cleaning up things that burn easily. But it's surprising the things you don't see because they've always just been there."

"No ideas yet?" Polly asked.

"Not yet." He put his hand on her arm, drawing her close, so he could speak more softly. "The fuel source had red dye in it, though."

Polly frowned. "I don't know what that means."

"Red diesel is used in farm and heavy construction equipment. It isn't taxed like fuel for on-road vehicles."

"I had no idea," Polly said. "Does everyone know that?"

He laughed. "I suppose they do. Wasn't your dad a farmer?"

"Yeah, but I didn't pay attention to what he put in the tractors, and we never talked about it. I feel a little dumb."

"Not at all," Ken said.

Skylar put the two coffees down on the counter and held his hand out.

Polly looked at Ken and grinned. She took her phone wallet out, extracted a twenty-dollar bill and slapped it down in Skylar's open palm.

"I was kidding," Skylar said.

"Consider it a tip," she responded. "I hear you're going to serve our little eighth grade graduation party next week."

He waggled his eyes. "Isn't that fun? I talked to Camille and Sylvie. We're going to give each kid a free smoothie or something similar and Sylvie is making graduation cupcakes. There are only forty-three kids in the class and I doubt that all of them will come. If I need help making drinks, Stephanie can pitch in. Camille thinks this should become a new tradition for Sweet Beans, so she's at the school with Stephanie this morning to speak with the principal."

Ken touched Polly's arm. "I need to go. Thanks for buying coffee."

She nodded. It was a not-so-inside joke. The coffee shop made it quite clear that local public servants weren't allowed to pay for coffee. Since Polly owned the bakery, she never paid either. The least they could do was make sure money went into the tip jar.

"I hear you did it again," Skylar said.

"Did what?"

"You know — out on the country road."

"Oh yeah," she replied. "What did Stephanie say?"

"By the time we talked, she had calmed down. I don't know how you are so calm about that stuff. It would freak me out seeing dead people all the time."

"It's not all the time," Polly protested. "And think about it. If it wasn't me, lots of other people would have to be exposed to it."

"I suppose," he said. "It would be pretty bad if some kids were driving down the road and found that poor guy. That's an image they'd never get out of their heads."

"Exactly." She looked around. "Why aren't you in the middle of finals hell?"

"Because I worked it out so that mine all happened Monday, and one last night. The weekend was absolute hell, but at least I'm done and now it's my summertime. I'm free as a bird."

"So that means you'll be here all the time?"

He shrugged. "Here and helping with Sycamore House Catering. I might also work part time at the winery. It depends on if they need me. I talked to Mr. Roberts and he wants to wait until after Memorial Day to see what kind of crowds they get. I'll keep busy, though." He looked up as the bell on the front door jangled.

Polly turned to see who it was and waved as Tab Hudson walked in.

"I saw your truck out there," Tab said. "It seemed like a good time for coffee."

"Your regular, Deputy?" Skylar asked.

"Not today. Just black coffee. This is going to be a long day."

He poured out a mug of coffee and handed it to her.

"What's going on?" Polly asked as they walked over to a table.

"Did you hear who was in the back of that truck you found yesterday?"

"Henry said something about the truck belonging to some junk guy. Barney Loeffler? Was it him?"

Tab nodded. "Poor guy."

"Were there any clues about who drove him out there? Fingerprints? Anything like that?"

"They're still processing the truck, but so far they haven't found anything. The steering wheel and door panel had been wiped clean."

"Somebody must have seen the killer driving the truck through town," Polly said.

"But nobody looked at the driver. We're just beginning the investigation, though. How do you find that one person who might have seen the truck and realized that the driver wasn't Barney Loeffler? They might not even know what they saw. You didn't see who was driving, did you?"

Polly shook her head. "The truck was in front of me and I didn't pay any attention when it turned onto that gravel road. Jeff was yelling at me from the back seat because the guy was going so slow. I almost went around him, but then he turned."

"You know why he parked there?" Tab asked.

"No, why?"

"He ran out of gas. Who knows where he would have abandoned that truck if the tank had been full."

The bell on the front door jangled again and a very panicked Jen Dykstra ran in. "I need help," she said.

Tab jumped out of her seat. "What's wrong?"

"It's Sonya. I think she's having a heart attack. Something is really wrong."

"Have you called 9-1-1?"

Jen nodded. "But can you help me?"

Tab was already at the front door and Jen followed her. Polly didn't know whether to go next door or stay where she was. Since she couldn't sit still, she jumped out of her seat and went next door to the quilt shop. A cluster of women hovered near the checkout counter, chittering among themselves. Polly recognized Betty Sands and stepped up beside her.

"Where are they?" she asked.

Betty pointed to the back of the shop. "In the classroom. Sonya was helping Nancy with her block when she fell. I thought she was dead. Terri screamed and that brought Jen into the room. She made us all leave. I called 9-1-1. Do you think she's dead?"

Polly chuffed a laugh. "I don't know."

"But you're out here," Betty said. "Maybe that's a good sign."

"Maybe it is." Polly pointed to another room. "I'm guessing that your class is done for the morning. If you have your things, you should go. Otherwise, you'll need to move out of the way for the EMTs."

Several of the women looked at Polly as if they were deciding whether to follow her direction, but Betty herded them away from the front. Not a one of them made any movement to leave. Who would want to miss this kind of excitement?

While the women gawked, Polly made her way to the back classroom and peered in. She stood silently watching as Tab knelt beside Sonya Biederman, working to keep the woman alive. Jen looked up from where she hovered nearby.

"Anything I can do?" Polly asked.

"I don't think so," Jen said. "Did you see the ladies out front?"

"I moved them away from the door. They don't want to leave, though."

Jen gave her a wan smile. "I'd guess not. It's the most excitement some of them have seen in years."

Polly glanced toward the front as the door swung open and two EMTs came in with a gurney piled with equipment. She beckoned them to the back, then stood away from the door as they went into the classroom. They pushed tables aside and spoke in hushed tones with Tab. Jen wound her way around everything and came out into the main shop.

"I don't want to watch that," she said. "I can't believe how lucky I was that the deputy was having coffee with you."

Two women rushed to Jen's side, asking questions and trying to peer into the classroom. They were soon followed by the other women and Jen put her hand up.

"Ladies, I know that you are curious, but I'm not letting you back here."

"But *she* got to be there." One of them pointed at Polly.

Jen took a breath. "Eleanor, stop it. One doesn't necessarily lead to the other. Now I want all of you to stay out of the way. If you have your personal items with you, you should probably go on home."

"What are you planning to do about the class?" a woman asked.

Polly set her jaw. Was this really happening?

"I can't answer that right now," Jen said, exercising the patience of a saint. "I'm more concerned about Sonya's health than I am anything else. If you require a refund for the class, I'll be glad to take care of that for you tomorrow."

"That's not what I meant, but I want to finish this quilt in time for a birthday gift and ..." The woman stopped speaking and Polly realized it was because another woman had poked her friend in the ribs.

"When will we be able to get in and collect our things?" another woman asked.

"I don't know," Jen said, wilting at the onslaught of questions.

"I tell you what," Polly said, stepping forward. "Why don't you all come next door for coffee while you wait? It's on me."

"You don't have to do that." Jen turned her back to the women as she faced Polly. "We should pay for it."

"You should take care of Sonya and whatever you need to in here," Polly replied. "I'll take care of these women until we can get them out of your hair."

"I owe you." Jen gave Polly a wicked smile. "Maybe I'll let you pick out fabric for your first quilt."

"You horrible person, you." Polly pulled Jen into a quick hug. "I've got this."

Using a herding motion, Polly pushed the women to the front of the store and held the door to the coffee shop open as they went inside. How was it that women with children of their own acted like such babies in times of trouble? Once the last one was in the shop, she ran ahead to speak with Skylar.

"I'm treating these women to coffee. Run a tab and let me know what I owe you after they've ordered, okay?"

He looked confused, but nodded all the same, then turned on the charm. "Okay, ladies. What's it gonna be? When Ms. Giller says it's on her, then I say, order up. I have two hands and a pretty smile. All you have to do is tell me what you want to drink, but slowly, ladies, slowly. I might be the cutest thing you'll see all day, but I have my limits."

Polly knew that she had left the women in good hands and wandered down the hallway toward the bakery. She needed a few minutes of sanity. Marta and Sylvie were just the people to give it to her, no matter that it always looked as if they were working in complete chaos.

"Hello?" she said, poking her head in the doorway.

"Polly!" Sylvie brushed her hands on the front of her apron and came over to give Polly a hug. "What are you doing back here? Did we hear sirens out front? Tell me it wasn't a fire. Marta and I haven't been able to leave this room for the last hour. We have so much going on. Come in, come in." She patted a stool just inside the front door.

"Uhh, wow. That was a lot of words," Polly said.

"Sorry. Sky has kept us in coffee this morning." Sylvie put her hand out and giggled. "See, still steady, though. How are you doing, Marta?"

"I'm fine." Marta spoke deliberately and slowly, deepening her voice.

"Whatever. She's as wired as I am. Now tell me what's going on?"

"Sonya Biederman had a heart attack, I think," Polly said.

"Oh no." Marta turned concerned eyes to her. "But you're here and not there."

Polly pursed her lips and grinned. "Yeah. So apparently, she's still alive. The siren was the rescue squad. Luckily Deputy Hudson was having coffee with me and rushed over when Jen Dykstra came looking for help. Not that she wasn't going to get plenty of advice from the class of harpies Sonya was teaching."

"Polly," Sylvie scolded, not bothering to look up from the tray where she was piping cream filling into chocolate cupcakes.

"I'm not going to apologize. Sonya Biederman was fighting for her life, Jen was worried about her, and those women were more concerned about their damned quilt blocks than they were about what was going on. Not a one of them was going to leave the store until I offered to pay for their coffee just so they'd clear out and give everyone space. Can't afford to pay for their own damned coffee — just gonna let me do it."

Marta chuckled quietly as she bagged up loaves of bread that had been cooling.

"Are you laughing at me?" Polly asked with a grin.

"People handle stress so differently," Marta said. "You're practical. When an emergency crops up, I'll bet that in a split second, you work through lots of different scenarios in your mind. You choose the most practical one and move forward. Not everyone works that way. My friend, Dixie, was an absolute idiot in a crisis. She would literally run around in circles until someone made a decision that put her on the right path. We did our best to avoid those bad times with her. It was embarrassing to watch. I never could get her to tell me why she did that."

"My mother had to have absolute silence when she had to deal with a crisis," Sylvie said. "If we were driving and got lost, she turned the radio off and threatened me with my life if I said anything out loud — even if I knew where we were supposed to go. All I had to do was open my mouth and she would become enraged. As long as I stayed silent, she could work things out in her head. Once she finally got there, she calmed down enough to let me speak."

Marta pointed to the front. "Did you leave poor Sky out there with those women?"

Polly huffed. "He was in his element. By the time he serves them all, he'll probably have twelve phone numbers of their daughters and granddaughters."

"Only two," Skylar said, sidling in beside Polly. "But I was promised that they are beautiful and intelligent."

"You're kidding." Polly turned to look at him. "Aren't you?"

He nodded. "No phone numbers, but I did get a couple of offers." He handed her a cash register receipt. "I can't believe you bought their drinks."

Polly took her credit card out and handed it to him. "I can't either. It was the only way to get them out of the quilt shop so they wouldn't bother the EMTs. Poor Jen was at her wits end with those ladies."

"I'll take her a cupcake and some coffee after this all settles down," he said.

"Put it on my card," Polly pointed at his hand. "I'm serious."

"Okay, I will. Thanks."

"You're too nice sometimes," Sylvie said after he left.

"What good is money if I can't do nice things for people?" Polly asked.

Marta had put the loaves of bread onto a rolling cart that she pushed past Polly. When she got to the doorway, she stopped. "Is it true about you finding that Barney Loeffler fellow?"

Polly nodded. "Did you know him?"

"He picked up an old bed frame from me once. His dad was still running the business and the kid was just learning the ropes. I don't think he was the brightest bulb in the box, but he was polite and willing to do anything."

"Did he live in his truck?" Polly asked.

"I don't know. He's not from around here, but comes through pretty regular." She thought for a moment. "I guess I should say he *came* through. It's strange to think about how a person is always just there and then all of a sudden, they're gone. I didn't know him very well, but it kinda freaks me out that I'll never see him drive through town again." She shook her head and pushed the cart down the hall.

Skylar showed back up in the doorway and handed Polly her credit card and receipt. "Deputy Hudson is looking for you. Can I send her back?"

"Thanks," Polly said. "That would be great."

He walked away and soon Tab showed up. "I've never been back here," she said. "Cool."

"How's Jen doing?"

"Is that the woman who owns the store?"

Polly nodded.

"She's okay. Pretty worried about her friend. She said you didn't have to worry about the ladies any longer. She'd come over and deal with them. I can't believe you paid for their coffees."

"I had to get them out of there," Polly responded. "I'm so glad you were here to help."

Tab grinned and waved at Sylvie. "I never know what's going to happen when I'm hanging around with you. It's never boring, that's for sure."

"You're blaming Polly for this one?" Sylvie asked.

"I guess that came out wrong," Tab said. "I should be going. Need to write a report up on this and pester folks for more answers on the truck. I just need a lead. Hopefully they'll find something for me."

Sylvie came over and put a chocolate cupcake into Tab's hand. "Maybe you should take Polly with you. She's always uncovering things."

"Stop it," Polly said. "In a few minutes, I'm going back out and getting another cup of coffee. Then I'm going to work, where it's safe and quiet."

"Good luck with that," Tab said. "Trouble finds you."

# CHAPTER TWELVE

Polly put the cup of coffee down on her desk at Sycamore House. Kristen had sent her a message yesterday afternoon that there were papers she needed to sign with regards to insurance for the van that had been burned up and that she'd put some personal mail for Polly up there, too.

The insurance forms were self-explanatory so Polly signed and set them aside. She was intensely curious about the mail. Her friends had the address of the Bell House, so she wasn't surprised to find it had been postmarked from Boston.

She opened the package and recognized Joey's mother's handwriting on the face of an envelope. Something was going on out there. Maybe it was just the fact that they had finally packed up things from Joey's house, but how could there be another reason for this woman to contact Polly?

The envelope was sitting atop a second box that had been taped up and addressed to Polly. She might as well start with what was in the envelope.

The letter Polly pulled out was from Joey's mother.

*Dear Polly,*

*If you haven't received a shipment of books from my Joey's library, it should arrive any day. The box that comes with this letter contains a few other items he wanted you to have.*

*I will admit to being frustrated that he insisted on sending you such exquisite treasures after all that the two of you went through. You don't deserve the love of someone as passionate as my son as you are unable to return it, but he adores you and I cannot stop his heart from desiring even a commoner such as you.*

*Enclosed in the package is a formal request written by our lawyers to have Joey moved back to Massachusetts so that I might be able to visit him. The law firm is doing all that it can to bring this about and are in direct contact with the authorities in Iowa, but they indicated that your recommendation as the assumed injured party would go a long way toward encouraging the court system to allow this transfer.*

*All we ask is that you sign the letter that has been drafted and post it in the attached envelope.*

*I am surprised and disheartened that you have never attempted to visit my son. You know how much he needs to be reassured of the love others have for him. That he has been left alone without one whit of care for his needs is appalling to me. He gave you so much and yet you have done nothing for him in return.*

*Please consider my request.*

*With best regards,*

*Celine Delancy*

Polly couldn't even conjure enough fury to react to the woman's ridiculous words. She was as batty as her son. It was probably just as well for the old lady's peace of mind that she refused to accept the truth of who Joey was and what he'd done.

She drew out the next box and opened it. As advertised, several legal looking letters and envelopes fell out on the desk. Another hand-written letter was at the bottom of the pile and this time Polly recognized Joey's handwriting. What now?

The letter had been slit open. Polly didn't know whether they'd done that at the prison, the law firm or his mother had opened it, but certainly enough people had read it that it should be safe. She took out the note.

*My dearest Polly,*

*I know that you will never forgive me for the dreadful things I did to you. I can only tell you that I was under the spell of that horrible man who convinced me that his way was the only way to have you back in my life. I understand that now and promise that this is the last time you will ever hear from me. I've asked Father to pack all of my books and send them to you. There is no one else on earth who will treasure them as you will. If you can't accept them, I understand. Please give them to someone who will appreciate their worth as much as you and I do.*

*Along with the books, I've also asked him to send three small mementos of our time together. All I have left is memories of how you impacted my life, but I hope these items bring a smile to your face rather than concern.*

*I am not the same man who destroyed everything he touched. Much has changed for me, though I know that without constant supervision, and the medication that has finally mediated my behavior, I would soon return to that person.*

*Mother will request that you participate in the quest to return me to Massachusetts. Whether you choose to help or not, I ask your forgiveness for all that I put you through. I am satisfied to be where I am now. A move will only make it easier for my parents to see me as they will never travel to the Midwest to visit.*

*I am grateful that you are safe and that the danger I put you in has passed. Please know that I hope you are happy. I ask nothing of you but your forgiveness and if you are unable to extend that, I will understand. Thank you for being part of my life, if only for a short time.*

*Joey*

Polly sat back in her chair and re-read his letter. Was he truly sane? She grimaced. Did it matter? The only thing he asked her to do was consider his mother's request. Polly didn't care where he served his time. If his family wanted him closer, it didn't matter to her. She'd finally come to the point where nothing about Joey

Delancy stirred any feelings inside. She wasn't angry or fearful — there was nothing at all. He was simply a poor, broken man.

The first thing she did was open the letter from their lawyer. Skimming through it, she saw no reason not to, so she signed one of the copies, placed it in the envelope, sealed it and set it aside. There. Now she didn't have to think about that again.

Picking up the first small box, Polly lifted the lid off and took in a breath. Joey had purchased a gorgeous engagement ring for her. With one large emerald-cut diamond in the center, two small sapphires on either side and small diamonds on each side of the sapphires, it was quite extravagant. She couldn't believe that his mother had allowed this to come to Iowa, but after reading Joey's letter she realized that he'd asked his father to take care of it, ensuring that it would be done. Her first thought was to return this to the family, but maybe she'd talk to Henry before making that decision. If nothing else, they could re-set the stones into something else. Polly wasn't sure how to handle it.

The second box contained a small heart pendant. Diamonds and sapphires were set in the outer edge of the silver pendant, but at the bottom of the heart was a rocky coast with a lighthouse. They'd spent a wonderful weekend in Cape Cod touring the lighthouses. Joey had made a connection between how they saved men's lives and how Polly had saved his. She didn't realize he'd had this designed for her. It was just as well. Not long after that trip, they'd broken up and everything fell apart.

The third box contained something Polly never imagined she'd see again. They had stopped in to a used bookstore one cold Saturday afternoon and Polly had been immediately taken with a collection of miniature books the owner had under glass. The first book he'd pulled out for her to see was a miniature copy of the Bible printed in 1780. She had considered purchasing it just for fun, but the cost was ridiculous and she put it back. Obviously, Joey had returned for it.

These were extravagant gifts and as she thought about how she lived now, they made no sense. That was one thing Joey never understood about her, that expensive gifts like this meant nothing in the long run. The only place for these things to live was in the safe deposit box, along with those gold coins at the bank. She wouldn't put them there today. First Henry needed to see what she'd been given, but tomorrow these needed to be safely hidden away until they could decide what to do with them.

A rap on the door at the bottom of the steps was followed by Lydia's voice. "Polly, are you here?"

Polly walked over to the top of the stairs. "I am. What are you doing?"

"I'm not alone," Lydia said. "Are we bothering you?"

Glancing back at her desk, Polly realized she didn't need to sit here and fuss over the things Joey had sent to her. "I just need to clear off my desk and I'll come right down. What's going on?"

Beryl stuck her head around the corner. "Nothing much. We just felt the need to chase you down. Hurry up or we'll create chaos."

"Got it. I'll be right there." Polly went back to the desk, closed the computer and dropped the packages back in the larger box. She grabbed the paperwork for Kristen and the letter to be mailed regarding Joey. She looked at it again and put it into the box with the packages. She needed to talk to Henry before sending it off. It wasn't that she didn't trust her own decision, but he deserved to be part of whatever she did.

By the time Polly got downstairs, the women were nowhere to be found, so she went into the kitchen where Rachel and two other young women were working. She'd only met the girls once before and kind of remembered that their names were Lyndi and Peg. With the increase in weddings and events this summer, Lyndi was about to be hired full-time.

"Did Lydia and Beryl come through here?" Polly asked.

"Hi, Ms. Giller," Lyndi said, looking up from slicing a roast beef. "They went through the auditorium."

"Said something about not bothering us," Rachel said.

"How are you doing?" Polly asked. "You're okay after the fire?"

"I'm fine. I still feel guilty about having the van at the

apartment, but Jeff says there's nothing to be done about it now. I guess he's right."

"He is right. You shouldn't feel guilty about a criminal doing his evil deeds," Polly said, eliciting a giggle from Peg. "Have you replaced everything that you need?"

Rachel nodded. "I think so. Thanks for being so cool about it."

"That's me. Cool." Polly went on through the kitchen and headed for the office. She assumed that's where she would find her friends, but she needed to drop papers on Kristen's desk.

Kristen was standing in Stephanie's door when Polly walked in.

"I've signed these," Polly said. "Have you seen Lydia and Beryl? I thought they came this way."

Shaking her head, Kristen looked around. "I haven't seen them since they went up to find you. Do you want me to help look?"

"That's cool. I've got it."

"I heard those boxes were full of books," Kristen said. "Did you order those?"

Polly chuckled. "No. An old friend sent them to me. There are a lot of old books and nice treasures in the boxes. He wanted me to have them rather than put them up for sale or drop them at a used bookstore."

"It had to have been expensive to ship those all out here."

"I'm sure it was," Polly said. "But now they're here. Yay. I'll see you later." She gave Stephanie a little wave and went back out into the main hallway, wondering where Beryl and Lydia might have gone.

She headed for the front door, opened it and looked outside. Lydia's Jeep was parked in front of the building, but the two women were nowhere to be found.

"Where did you ladies go?" Polly asked out loud. She was a little surprised that Beryl didn't jump out just then. That was usually how things went. Maybe they'd gotten lost among the displays in the auditorium. Andy regularly changed out the items in the displays along the walls. They could be perusing the newest items uncovered from the crates of pop culture treasures discovered in a hidden basement room of Sycamore House during renovation.

Polly opened the door to the auditorium and looked around, fully expecting Beryl to jump out and scare her at any moment — still no friends to be found.

"Well, this is just ridiculous," Polly said and took out her phone.

*"Where did you go?"* she sent as a text to Lydia.

"We're right here, dear," Lydia said out loud, coming down the main steps.

"What are you doing up there?"

Jeff followed the two women down. "I was just talking to your friends about renting those rooms out. Mrs. Merritt is going to do some decorating in the upstairs kitchen for us and Mrs. Watson has offered to let us hang several of her paintings in the main room."

Beryl frowned at him when he used her formal married name, but then she delivered a full-blown smile to Polly. "I have several pieces that need a home for the time being. This will be a wonderful way to show them off." She patted Lydia's shoulder when they reached the main floor. "And my dear friend is going to coordinate table coverings and decorations with the paintings. Won't that be exquisite?"

"It will be wonderful," Polly said. "I'm excited to see that more of your work will be showcased in Bellingwood. I was surprised that you didn't have a gallery downtown."

"Maybe someday, dear," Lydia said.

"What are you two doing here, other than serving as Jeff's decorating lackeys?"

"Hey," Jeff said. "I just know how to access people's innate talents."

Beryl gave him a quick peck on the cheek. "You're such a good boy. Polly doesn't pay you nearly enough, does she?"

He rolled his eyes and shook his head. "Not nearly. You'd think after all she puts me through I would deserve so much more, but no, it's only a pittance."

"Shoo," Polly said. "Go work for your pittance or I'll reduce it to a smidgen."

"Let me know your ideas," Jeff said to Lydia. "I look forward to working with you." He grinned at Polly as he walked into the office.

"I can't believe he's hiring you," Polly said. "How fun is that?"

"It's a little intimidating," Lydia responded. "If it weren't for the fact that I have so much fun and he's pretty encouraging, I wouldn't do it. Aaron says I should give it a shot." She rolled her eyes. "As if I don't already have enough to keep me busy."

"But this is creative," Beryl said. "It's good for you. For once you are doing something that you love and not just coddling the entire town of Bellingwood."

"Is that why you two came up here today?" Polly asked.

Beryl hooked her arm through Polly's. "No way. We came to see you. We're lonely for your face."

"You just saw my face last week."

"I can get lonely in a week. What about you, Lydia? Aren't you lonely for Polly's glowing personality and pretty face?"

"More than I can even describe."

"And besides," Beryl said, "we want to hear all about your discovery of that Barney Loeffler. The poor young man didn't have an easy life as it was. Then to end up dead in the back of his own truck only to be found by our local Grim Reaper on an old country road? How horrible."

"Thanks for the love," Polly said.

"Aaron told us that the reason you were out on that back road was because your husband is looking at another property. A bed and breakfast?" Lydia asked.

Polly nodded. "Yeah. It's out there beyond where Eliseo lives."

Beryl propelled both women toward the front door. "We're driving out there right now. I want to see this place. I'm having trouble picturing it."

Lydia smiled at Polly. "Are you sure you didn't have plans? Because after you show us where it is, I thought we might have lunch. If we go to the diner, I could convince Andy to join us."

"What's she doing?" Polly asked.

"Working at the library." Lydia giggled. "She's taking on full-time work with Joss getting three new little ones — at least for the next few weeks while that poor girl tries to figure out how to incorporate those kiddos into her household. Isn't it fun?"

"I didn't even think about that." Polly held back, waiting for Beryl to get into the front seat of the Jeep. When Beryl stood beside her, Polly chuckled. "Is this a standoff? You should sit up front so you can see. I've already been there a couple of times."

Beryl nodded and climbed in, then pulled her seat up so Polly had more leg room.

Once they were in and Lydia headed north, Beryl unbuckled her seatbelt and turned to look at Polly.

"What are you doing, crazy lady?" Lydia asked. "Put your seatbelt back on. Aaron will beat you and arrest me."

"That man wouldn't hurt me," Beryl said. "I wanted to talk to Polly."

"Put it on," Polly said. "What did you want to talk to me about?"

"Nothing important. I told you. I missed your face. If I'm going to talk to you, I want to talk to your face."

Polly chuckled, opened her phone, took a quick selfie and then sent it off as a text.

When Beryl's phone dinged, she jumped. "What is it?"

"Check your messages," Polly said.

Beryl started laughing. "You're a little smartie-pants, you are. Now I'll never have to miss your face. Are you going to tell us what's in that box you're carrying around?"

Polly had forgotten about Joey and his family for just a few minutes. She knew that it was situational and immediate, but right now it felt like she would never be finished with him. How this one man could still be so pervasive in her life, she didn't understand. It was never anything more than a short-term relationship and yet, he was still there.

"Polly?" Lydia asked.

"Yeah?"

"What 'cha thinking about?"

"Oh. The box. It's from Joey."

Beryl swerved in her seat. "From who?"

"Yeah, Joey. The guy who tried more than once to ruin my life." Polly put the box on the seat beside her. "I'll tell you all about it at lunch when I can watch your reactions. You won't even believe what he's done. It's not bad and it's not threatening. At least I don't think so. But that isn't to say it's not weird."

"You gotta promise you'll tell us everything," Beryl said.

"I do."

Lydia pointed to the left. "Is that the gravel road where you found the truck?"

"Yes." Polly had a thought. "Would you mind turning there. I want to see what's at the other end."

"Just farmhouses and more roads," Lydia said.

"Would you go down there anyway?"

Lydia slowed and made the turn. "What are you looking for?"

"I'll know if I see it," Polly replied. "If I'm right, we'll have to call your husband."

"Not another body," Beryl moaned.

Polly laughed. "Nope. But it might explain why they were out here. Tab told me the truck ran out of gas. I think it was going somewhere specific. We might not find it on this road, but I'm sure it's out here."

Lydia drove along and slowed at the next intersection. "Straight or turn?" she asked.

"Straight for another mile." Polly sat forward. "It has to be here."

"What in the world are you looking for?" Beryl asked. "It's only farmland as far as the eye can see."

Polly pointed ahead to a copse of trees. "There. Slow down. What do you see?"

The two women in the front seat peered at the lot where she was pointing.

"Nothing," Beryl said. "It's just an old farmstead."

"Uh huh. What else?"

"Everything in there is broken down."

"Exactly. This is where they were going to dump that truck. No one would have thought anything about another broken down old piece of junk. I remember the first time I came across one of these old farms where people had been dumping their old vehicles for years. It seemed like such a waste of good land. Why wouldn't you just turn your junker in when you got a new one?"

Lydia came to a stop. "There's an old school bus giving way to nature in the background there and look at that old trailer. The roof is all caved in. You'd think someone would be out here scavenging the metal."

"They probably haven't found this place yet," Polly said. "It will happen. But I'd almost guarantee this is where the murderer planned to put that truck." She frowned. "Pull in, Lydia. We should call Aaron and tell him what we found."

Lydia pulled into the driveway and Polly got out of the Jeep.

"What are you doing?" Beryl asked, after rolling her window down.

"This utility trailer isn't in the same state of decay as a lot of the other stuff," Polly said. "That's kind of weird." She kept walking toward it, brushing flies away as she approached it. "Somebody dumped this thing here. It's still in pretty good shape, but the couch and chair look like they've seen better days."

"Walk away right now," Beryl yelled. "You know what's coming."

Polly barely heard her friend's words as she looked over the wall of the trailer and saw why there were so many flies. "Have you called Aaron?" she yelled back.

Beryl flung her hands in the air and turned to say something to Lydia while Polly walked back to the Jeep. "You didn't tell me that we were going on a Polly-adventure today."

"Sorry about that," Polly said.

Lydia handed her phone back to Polly. "It's ringing. You talk to him."

"Hello there, sweet wife of mine," Aaron said.

"She's my shill," Polly replied.

"What are you doing on my wife's phone? Is this more bad news?"

"I found where they were going to bring Barney Loeffler's truck. That's the good news."

"And the bad news?"

"I can pretty much guarantee that this is where they were bringing his truck."

"Sit still. Tab and I will be there soon." Polly started to hand the phone back to Lydia when she heard him bark.

"What?" she asked.

"If you see anyone — anyone at all — coming toward you, get the hell out of there. Do you hear me? I don't want my wife or my wife's friends to be caught up in this. Am I clear?"

"All clear, boss," Polly said. "We'll see you soon." She handed the phone back to Lydia. "We're supposed to clear out if anyone other than your husband or a deputy shows up."

"Ooh," Beryl said, clapping her hands. "Now we're having fun."

# CHAPTER THIRTEEN

"I'll be right back to take your orders." Lucy put menus on their table. "What can I get for you to drink?"

"Scotch. Tall and neat," Beryl said.

"If I could do that, we'd make a lot more money," Lucy replied. "Have you had a rough morning?"

Beryl pointed at Polly. "Traveling the back roads of Bellingwood with that one. Does that tell you anything?"

Lucy turned. "I'm afraid it does. Anyone we know?"

"I couldn't tell you," Polly said. She shuddered. "I can't think about it or this will be a very short lunch."

"I'm sorry, then," Lucy said with a smile. "Are you okay?"

Polly nodded. "I really am, but maybe no pork tenderloin today. Something like a salad. Anything else might sit in there doing bad things to me." She grimaced at Beryl, Lydia and Andy. "The sad thing is that I really wanted a tenderloin, but I don't think I could eat one now."

Lucy took their orders and left, then returned with a pot of coffee and glasses of water. "If you want anything else, just let me know."

After she left the second time, Polly turned to Andy. "They said you're going to work full-time for a few weeks. That's awesome."

"It's something I can do for Joss," Andy said. "It's much easier now that school is out. We have volunteers that come in and do summer programs with the kids and Joss is lining up high school kids to come in, too. She's so excited about these children."

"I need to see if she has time to go out for lunch before this all happens," Polly said. "She sprang it on us the other day and I haven't gotten any other information."

"Her mother is coming in next week. Even if the new little ones don't know her well, at least Sophie and Cooper will have their grandmother around to give them extra attention while everyone acclimates to each other." Andy looked around the table. "Isn't it time to tell me what happened this morning? Did you really find another body?"

Beryl gave her head a quick shake. "I knew as soon as this girl got out of the Jeep that we were in trouble. What was she thinking?"

"She was just doing her job," Lydia said.

"That's no job," Beryl retorted. "It's insanity — that's what it is." She patted Polly's arm. "And she's such a pretty little thing."

"What?" Polly asked with a laugh. "What does that have to do with anything?"

"If I were going to paint a picture of a person who finds dead bodies, I would make her old, with straggly grey, white and black hair — maybe with a stoop — and she'd walk with a cane. You know, like the old picture of the witch from Hansel and Gretel — her. Not this pretty thirty-something young woman who takes in stray cats, dogs, and children."

"I'm just pure entertainment for you, aren't I?"

"Sometimes." Beryl tapped the box that Polly had brought in. "You were going to tell us about this. Why is Joey bothering you again?"

"It's kind of Joey," Polly said. "But it's bigger than that. The other day I got a huge shipment of books from his mother. While they're closing up his house, they packed his library and sent it to me because Joey wanted me to have it. There were some very old first editions in there. I haven't had time to go through everything yet, but from what I remember, he had a pretty wonderful collection."

"And it's yours now?" Andy asked. "Why would he send it to you?"

Polly sighed. "At some level, he still loves me. His normal life ended when he went into that care facility after kidnapping me the first time. If you think about it, I was the center of his focus. All Joey ever thought about was making a life with me. As he sees it, his things are my things." Polly took out the letter from Joey's mother and handed it to Beryl. "His mother isn't thrilled about any of it, but in the letter from Joey, it sounds like he asked his father to handle getting the books and these items to me. Mr. Delancy was a nice enough guy. He totally fades into the background because of the crazy people he lives with, but I'd almost bet that he's made of sterner stuff than anyone knows."

"This woman's bat-shit," Beryl said, passing the letter to Andy.

"Yep." Polly took out Joey's letter and handed that to her next. "Joey almost sounds normal. It's reminiscent of the man I started dating way back when. He was such a nice, caring man. I don't know what it was about me that made him insanely jealous and obsessive, but ..."

"You can't take any blame for that," Lydia said.

Polly shook her head. "You're right and I'm not — not at all. He's his own problem, not mine. But when we first met, there was nothing wrong with him — not on the surface at least. I've thought about it a lot over the last few years. I suppose there was something hovering in the background. I never completely trusted him, and honestly, I never saw myself settling down with him. It was almost a relief when he pushed me so far that I broke it off."

Beryl passed that letter on to Andy, who handed Celine's note to Lydia. "This isn't the insane ramblings of a kidnapper," she said. "He sounds reasonable."

"Yeah," Polly agreed.

"Can you forgive him like he asked?"

With a small smile, Polly nodded. "Sure. I don't have anything against him any longer. It's too much work to be angry about something in the past."

"But he hurt you so badly," Andy said. "I don't know that I could forgive him."

Polly raised her eyebrows. "I don't want to live with that kind of anger. He can't hurt me. My anger and lack of forgiveness hurts me. Joey will never know about it or feel it. I have no intention of ever seeing him or interacting with him again, so why should I hold on to those feelings? Life's too short."

"All that wisdom in such a pretty little girl," Beryl said, a wicked grin on her face.

Lydia folded both notes and handed them to Polly. "What mementos did he send to you?"

Polly took a breath. "I don't know what I'm going to do with these things. It feels wrong to accept them. Joey bought these for a woman he thought loved and adored him back. I wouldn't have accepted them from him at the time, but now what do I do? If I return them to his mother, she'll make a terrible scene about my lack of grace and forgiveness. I can't return them to Joey, and his father would insist that I keep them."

"What are they, then?" Beryl asked, motioning for Polly to open the box.

Polly took out the first box, opened it and showed it to the women. "I think this was to be my engagement ring. He knew I loved sapphires more than diamonds. And if it wasn't an engagement ring, it's a heck of a bauble."

Andy reached for the box and Polly handed it across the table.

"Wow," Andy said. "That's a lot of ring. You never saw it until today?"

Polly shook her head. "Nope, and that surprises me. He constantly spoke of our future together. Maybe he wanted to do something grand and romantic and I didn't give him the opportunity. Then I broke up with him and never saw him again until he kidnapped me. He probably would have jammed it on my finger once we got to Boston." She rolled her eyes. "Thank God for those Renaldi boys. But what am I supposed to do with that? I'll never wear it."

"You could re-set the jewels," Lydia said, accepting it from Andy.

"I suppose. Maybe I'll do something for Rebecca with it or maybe one of the boys will need an engagement ring someday. I just don't know."

Lucy came up to the table, a large tray balanced on her forearm and hand. "What a beautiful engagement ring," she said. "Unless it's for you, Beryl, aren't the rest of you happily married?"

"Not me," Beryl announced. "Not ever again as far as I'm concerned. Don't even think it." She grabbed Polly's box and moved it out of the way so Lucy could set their plates down.

"Just in case," Lucy said, putting a small plate with a chunk of breaded tenderloin beside Polly's salad. "This little piece was lonely and I thought you might want a bite of goodness."

Polly laughed. "I love you, Lucy. Thank you. That will be just enough to satisfy my craving."

"I only wish I had a miniature bun for it, but I haven't been able to convince Joe back there that sliders would be a great addition to the menu. He's more the tried-and-true type of a boss, you know. Is there anything else I can bring for you?"

The women all shook their heads and Lucy walked away.

Lydia handed the ring back to Polly, who replaced it in the box that Beryl held out to her. "What else is in there?" Lydia asked.

"The other two items are definitely mementos of our time together," Polly said. She took out the two boxes and opened them, then placed them in the middle of the table. "The pendant is from our trip to Cape Cod and the book is a Bible I saw in a bookstore."

"Is that worth something?" Beryl asked, pointing at the Bible.

"Yeah. Probably about a thousand dollars." Polly took a bite of salad and swallowed. "What do you think Henry is going to say about these things?"

"Are you worried?" Andy asked. "Is he jealous of Joey?"

Polly laughed out loud. "No." Then she stopped. "At least I don't think he is." She shook her head. "No. That's silly. I can see that he might be jealous that Joey gave me things that are worth a small fortune, but surely he knows that I don't care about the monetary value of an item. That's not what makes it important. What Henry gives me is worth so much more than its monetary value. He'd know that, right?"

"If he doesn't," Lydia said, "he doesn't know you very well. And I don't believe that to be true."

Beryl opened the ring box again. She reached across Polly and grabbed her left hand. "Joey didn't know you very well, did he?"

Polly shrugged. "What do you mean?"

"You never would have been comfortable wearing this ring. It's too flashy."

"You're right," Polly said. "I didn't think about that. I just saw a gorgeous ring, but I would have always hidden my hand." She fingered her mother's engagement ring. "Henry knew that I would want to wear my mother's ring. He didn't even have to ask. He just took it to a jeweler, had it cleaned and re-sized, then gave it to me. This ring fits me."

"Of course it does," Lydia said. "Put the other ring away for now. If I know you, something will come up and you'll find a way to make it useful. But there's no need to return it or feel guilty about keeping it. It isn't like Joey is going to ask some other girl to marry him."

"You never know," Beryl said. "There are those strange little girls who get off on marrying prisoners. How they see romance in pursuing someone who will never be available, I'll never understand, but I guess there will always be someone for everyone."

Polly squeezed a bit of ketchup, then mustard on her bite of pork tenderloin and popped it in her mouth.

Andy laughed at her. "You really are an addict for that sandwich, aren't you?"

"And I feel much better now than when I first sat down," Polly said. "I didn't think about that poor man at all." She shuddered.

"Okay, now he's back in my brain. Let's talk about Beryl hanging her paintings at Sycamore House. That's a much better topic."

~~~

"What's this?" Henry asked when he walked into the bedroom.

They'd finally gotten everyone in the house to wind down. Both Heath and Hayden were relieved to be done with finals and Hayden had received a text message from Tess, asking if he was free Saturday night.

Heath could hardly believe that he was finished with high school. He joked about not going to graduation, but the hopeful look he gave Polly and Henry was intended to see if they'd let him get away with skipping those activities. Polly had lifted her eyebrows and he shrugged in acquiescence.

Noah and Elijah were thrilled to have both boys home. There had been so much energy, Polly sent them all into the back yard to play. The soccer ball came out and soon, they'd gotten caught up in a game. She had trouble not watching, even though she was in the middle of preparing dinner.

Rebecca, Kayla, and Andrew met some of their classmates at Pizzazz for dinner. After their disastrous attempt to sneak into the Alehouse to see a band earlier in the year, they'd not lied about going out again. Rebecca was home by ten o'clock and babbled for nearly a half hour about how much fun they had. She had gossip about all her friends — none of which Polly really cared to hear. It was just more blathering, but she'd smiled and nodded. The most interesting thing was that Korey Larrabie was very interested in Kayla and made a point of sitting beside her, even when his friends were across the room at another table.

That piece of information, Polly made sure to pay attention to. With as much as Kayla had been through in her short life, Polly was on high alert when it came to Rebecca's friend. Mostly she wanted to get a feel for how Rebecca perceived the relationship. So far, there was nothing to be worried about, and Polly relaxed. Kayla was as sweet and kind as anyone Polly knew, but she had little experience with any type of relationship. Rebecca was still learning how not to abuse that naïveté; a rotten little boy might not be quite so generous.

Since it was Friday night, the kids ended up in the family room, playing video games together. Hayden promised to get them to bed at a reasonable hour. Polly didn't really care. They'd be up and moving in the morning, no matter what. She would drop the boys at their piano lesson before taking Rebecca to her art lesson with Beryl.

"Hey, you in there," Henry said, holding up the box she'd picked up at Sycamore House earlier today. "What is this?"

"Do you know the kids have a soccer game tomorrow afternoon?" Polly asked. "Are you going to be around to go with me?"

He sat in the other chair and handed her the box. "I did know about the game and I was planning to go. Why is this up here?"

"I had kind of a weird morning," Polly said. "I should probably tell you that I found another body."

"You what?" Henry stood up and paced to the doorway, closed the door, then walked back toward her. "Another one?" He strode away and then back again. "Where were … what were … who." He dropped back into the chair. "I don't even know what questions to ask anymore."

"I know. I was with Lydia and Beryl."

"That had to have been interesting."

"It's never boring," Polly agreed. "I was going to show them the property that we're buying. Then Lydia said something and it hit me where that truck had to have been going."

"You knew where it was headed?"

"Not really," she said. "I just knew that there had to be one of those farms out there where the family never got rid of all their junky cars and trucks; they just parked them forever."

He nodded.

"I figured that there was probably one of those nearby and that's where the murderer planned to dump Barney Loeffler's truck. Nobody would ever think to look for it in the midst of all the rest of the metal carcasses. Sure enough, a couple of miles down the road, we found one of those places. There's even an old school bus rotting away." She shook her head. "I still can't get over wasting good land like that, but whatever."

"Someday someone will haul everything out and reclaim it," Henry said. "You drove in and then what?"

"I was going to have Lydia call Aaron and tell him about the place. It wouldn't make any difference, I guess, but I thought he should know what was going on in my head."

Henry smiled. "We all should know what's going on in your head."

"Whatever. Anyway ..." She drew the word out. "When Lydia drove in, I saw a trailer. You know, one of those things that people haul stuff with — not an RV. Everything else was about the same level of deterioration and this thing wasn't at all. It was just a normal trailer and looked kinda out of place. That old pickup truck Barney Loeffler drove was in worse shape than this. I thought I ought to check it out."

"Of course you did."

Polly scowled at him. "Anyway. It had been there long enough that the poor guy who had been killed wasn't identifiable."

"I don't know how you don't vomit whenever you see something like that," Henry said. "I'd have just been sick."

"It's not like I stand there looking for a long time or anything. I ran like the wind to get away."

"But you can think about that and not get sick?"

"It doesn't do much for me, but I try not to think about the reality of it. That helps, but let's not talk about it any longer."

"Then we should talk about this," he said, holding out the box. "Now you just have my curiosity up."

"It's from Joey."

She could practically see the hackles on the back of Henry's neck rise. It wasn't jealousy, but he dropped right into protective mode and wasn't going to leave that anytime soon.

"What in the hell? First, he sends you books and now, what's this? Your engagement ring?"

Polly's sharp inhalation brought him up off the chair again.

"He sent you an engagement ring?" Henry paced back and forth across the room three more times, before standing over her. "Let me see it."

She took out the small box and handed it up to him.

Henry cursed under his breath, then said, "That's beautiful. You shouldn't keep it, though. Why is he sending you an engagement ring? Has he completely lost what was left of his mind?"

Taking out the two letters, she passed those to him. "The first is more crazy-talk from his mother. She convinced their lawyers to attempt to relocate Joey to Massachusetts so she can see him more often."

"Now?" Henry asked. He sat back down and opened Celine Delancy's note, shaking his head in disbelief as he read through it. "She wants to see him now? I thought you said they didn't want anything to do with him when this all started."

"Who knows what's going on in that woman's mind," Polly said. "Now read the other letter. It's from Joey."

Henry read through it, then shook his head. "That almost sounds like a sane person."

"I thought so," Polly replied. "He knows he's never getting out of prison. Now that he's figured that out, it feels like he's trying to help his parents deal with his possessions. That's why I got the books and why I have these things."

"His dad isn't a crazy man?"

She smiled. "No. He's a very nice person. Think about how unpleasant his life must be, married to a deranged bitch like Celine and a son whose mental illness took him completely into the gutter. But he keeps trying. I'm sure that he was the one who insisted on following Joey's wishes."

"What else is in there?" Henry asked, pointing to the box. "I'm almost afraid to ask."

"The other two things are a couple of mementos from the time we were together." Polly handed the box to him. "I want to put these things in the safe-deposit box at the bank for now."

Henry reached in and took out the engagement ring again. "Did you pick this out?"

Polly laughed out loud and removed the ring from its box. Slipping it on the ring finger of her right hand, she splayed her fingers. "Do you really think I'd choose something as garish as this to wear?"

He took her hand. "It's beautiful, though."

"Yes, I know that it is. But it's not me. Tell me you know that."

"Okay. You're right. It's not you at all." Henry grinned at her. "You know, sometimes I feel like a louse for not spending money on a nice engagement ring for you."

"Spending money is more important than knowing what it is that I want? Henry William Sturtz, you're a bigger moron than I thought. There is only one man in the world who has ever made an effort to understand who I am and that's you." She wriggled the ring back off her finger and thrust it at him. "Stop being dumb about this."

"I guess maybe I should get started on another big project around here instead of worrying about jewelry, huh?"

Polly waggled her eyebrows. "What'cha got for me? A fence? The back porch? Knocking that extra wall out in the kitchen? How about the garage and breezeway?"

"Maybe we should put all of your projects on slips of paper and drop them in a hat. You pull one out and that will be the first one I tackle."

"Why don't we let the summer take us where it does," Polly said. She sat up and leaned over to kiss him. "You have enough on your plate right now. My projects will happen when they do."

# CHAPTER FOURTEEN

"Stack it on top of the others." Polly pointed Noah to the plates on the counter. "Go on and change for your game," she said.

He did what she asked and ran for the back stairs.

Elijah took his plate over to the counter as well. "I love hot dogs. They're my favorite."

"I'm glad," Polly said. "Now you head upstairs. We need to get out of here soon."

Her phone, which was in the charger, rang and she put his plate on the counter before walking over. She didn't recognize the number, but since it was local, she picked it up.

"Polly Giller."

"Ms. Giller, this is Coach Darby."

"Hello there. How are you?"

"I'm fine, but I'm afraid we need to cancel today's games."

Polly sagged. Her boys would be so disappointed. They'd been chattering about this since the moment they came downstairs. "What happened?"

"There was a fire here last night. It burned down the snack shack and scorched the bleachers pretty badly. The fire department doesn't want us using the fields today. They need to investigate and want to make sure things are safe."

"Nobody was hurt?"

"It happened before we got here. One of the neighbors across the street called it in."

"Can I help and make some calls to other parents?"

"We've got this," he said. "Thanks, though."

"Let me know if you need anything."

"I will."

She hung up, put her phone back in the charging station and walked back to the dishwasher. This arsonist was like a ghost. How could one person be so invisible? After putting the rest of the dishes in the dishwasher, Polly walked over to the intercom and buzzed Noah and Elijah's room.

"Hey boys, don't bother changing your clothes. The games are canceled today."

"Aww, why?" Elijah asked.

"There was a fire at the ballfields."

"That stinks," he said. "Why would someone do that to us?"

"I don't know," Polly replied. "We'll find something else to do today, though."

"What?" Elijah asked excitedly. "Something fun?"

She smiled. That boy was never down for long. "I'll talk to Henry. Maybe he has some good ideas."

Henry and Heath had taken off before she left to drop the kids at their various lessons, promising to be back in time to go to the games. Hayden was already on his way to Ames. He could hardly wait to see Tess and wanted to pick up flowers before going to her apartment.

After her lesson with Beryl, Rebecca asked to go to Kayla's apartment. They hadn't had nearly enough time last night after dinner to talk about Korey and Kayla as a couple. Stephanie planned to pick the girls up and take them to Ames for a movie and asked if Rebecca could spend the night. Some days Polly felt as if she needed to attach GPS collars to her family so she knew where they were.

Hayden and Heath were heading to South Dakota bright and early Monday morning. It hadn't taken much to get Hayden excited about the trip. The boys decided to just get in the truck and go. They'd eat when they were hungry and pull into a hotel when they were tired. Any and all tourist traps along the way were prime targets. Once they saw Mount Rushmore and drove through the Badlands, they'd turn around and head back. Since Heath's graduation party was on Saturday, they had a deadline, but neither was worried. Hayden would make sure they were back in time. Heath's graduation was important to him.

She and Henry had sat down with Heath and Hayden a month ago to talk about their aunt and uncle. The boys had no desire to invite those two to be part of any family celebration. Polly wanted to send an announcement and Heath agreed, but there was no invitation to participate. She had invited the older couple to Hayden's graduation party last year, but there had been no response. What miserable people they must be.

Henry and Heath came in the back door, all smiles.

"What have you two been doing?"

"We got the truck ready for their trip," Henry said. "Stopped by Nate's house. He's so excited he's about to pop. They're bringing the kids home tomorrow."

"That's going to be fun. A little nuts, but fun," Polly said.

"I prefer the way we get kids." He gave her a quick kiss on the cheek. "Before we know what happens, they're here and part of our family."

"You all knew about Noah and Elijah before I did," Polly said. "I can't believe you kept it quiet for so long."

"Me either," Heath said. He started for the foyer. "I want to change my shirt before we go to the game."

"Oh. Stop," Polly said. "There aren't any games today. That stupid arsonist torched the snack shack. Canceled everything. The boys are pretty disappointed."

"What's going on with that, anyway?" Heath asked. "It's happening all over town. I can't believe nobody's caught him yet."

"Or her," Polly said. "I'm an equal-opportunity accuser."

Henry looked back and forth between the two of them. "Then what should we do with this free time?"

"I told the boys we'd come up with something. We could take them to a movie. They were envious of Rebecca getting to do that tonight with Kayla."

"That's not going to get rid of much of their pent-up energy," he said.

"Then I don't know what."

Henry grinned. "We could get bikes for them."

Polly shot him a look. "Bikes? Today?"

"Now's as good a time as any."

"I don't even know if they can ride," she said.

Heath pointed upstairs. "Ask 'em."

"If they don't know how, we can teach them," Henry said.

"But none of the rest of us have bikes to ride with them." Polly was not ready to start down this path. Giving those little boys freedom this summer scared her, even though she knew in her heart that it was the right thing to do. Her kids were all finding new ways to be independent. This parenting thing stunk.

"We'll get bikes too," Henry said. "Think how much the dogs would love going out with us."

She gritted her teeth. "I haven't been on a bicycle in years. Decades even."

"What do you think, Heath?" Henry asked. "You in?"

"Me?"

"Yes, you. Would you ride with the boys?"

"Yeah. I suppose. Maybe. Really?"

Polly was with him. This sounded crazy.

"Come on. We'll start with the little boys today. We can buy bikes for them cheap. Once we're confident that they'll stay upright, we'll get you a bike ..." he pointed at Polly, "and me a bike. When you come back from South Dakota, we'll buy a bike for you. Rebecca's going to want one, too, don't you think?"

"I doubt it," Polly said. "None of her friends ride bikes around town."

"She can be a trend-setter." Henry pressed the intercom for the boys' room. "Elijah, Noah, come downstairs. We're taking a ride."

"Where?" Elijah yelled.

"Come on down. We'll tell you when you get here."

"Do I have to go with you?" Heath asked.

Henry smiled. "There will be ice cream." He nodded. "Yes. You have to come with us. The little boys will have more fun if you're there encouraging them. Go change your clothes. We'll leave in ten minutes."

When Heath was gone, Polly turned on her husband. "Where did this idea come from?"

"Kids need bikes," he said. "If the boys are riding bikes, they can go to the ball fields on their own."

"I'm not ready for that."

"You'd better hurry up and get ready. They can't stay in this house forever."

"Yes they can," she said. "Just watch."

Henry laughed and pulled her in for a hug. "They can't cross the highway alone until they're … say … eleven and twelve. But they can ride up to the ball fields this summer, can't they?"

"If I'm riding behind them in the truck."

"I love you, Mama Giller. Bellingwood is perfectly safe. Tell me you believe that."

Noah and Elijah came into the kitchen.

"Where are we going?" Elijah asked. "Someplace fun?"

"I think so. Your mom's not so sure, though."

Polly knelt down in front of him. "Have either of you ever ridden a bicycle?"

The two boys looked at each other and then back at her, all excitement drained from their faces.

Elijah shook his head slowly. "We tried once, but the bikes were too big and we fell off. The big boys said we were too stupid to ride bikes. I don't think I can learn how."

"Yes you can," she said, standing back up. She gave Henry a small smile. "Your dad is going to teach you how to ride. If you fall, you'll get right back up and try again."

"Where are the bicycles?"

"We're going to go buy you each a bike right now. How does that sound?"

Noah's beautiful brown eyes grew into saucers. "New bikes? For us?"

"And once you learn how to ride, Polly and I will get bicycles so we can ride with you. How's that?"

Elijah jumped up and down, then wrapped his arms around Polly. "Let's go now!"

~~~

"Go, go, go, go, go," Polly yelled as Noah finally took off on his own down the sidewalk in front of the Bell House.

Elijah pushed Henry's hands away and rode after his brother, staying upright for the first time.

Polly grinned at her husband. "No competition, there."

"I know," he said with a laugh.

The front door of the small brown house across the street opened and little Rose Bright came outside.

"Hi Noah," she called.

He stopped pedaling, put his feet on the ground, and turned at the sound of her voice. "Hi, Rose!"

Her mother, Mona, came to the doorway to see what was happening outside. She waved at Polly and Henry and then went back in, only to emerge a few minutes later with a bicycle. She walked down the steps with it, handed it off to Rose, then walked across the street.

"I thought we'd give them a little time to figure out how to ride before letting Rose come out. Is this okay?"

"This is wonderful," Polly said. "How are you?"

Mona nodded and smiled. "I'm doing good." She crossed her arms in front of her and watched her daughter ride toward the two boys. "You need to be careful with those bikes. Kids around here like to take them. That's why I keep Rose's inside. Somebody stole her bike from our garage. She was so broken-hearted."

"That's awful. Who would do that?"

Mona shrugged. "Could be anybody."

The front door of the house directly across from them opened and three more kids came outside. They picked up bikes that had been abandoned on the front lawn and rode into the street, whooping and hollering.

"Tell me their names," Polly said. "Which is which?"

"The oldest boy is Jeremy," Mona said. "Keep an eye on him. He likes to get his brother and sister in trouble. All he has to do is suggest something and before they know it, they're in trouble and he's far, far away. He tried it a couple of times with Rose, but I was on to him. The girl is Julia and the youngest boy is Aiden."

Polly nodded. "Thanks. I'll try to remember. I'm terrible at names."

Henry started across the street and she realized he was going to speak with the three kids' father, who was walking out of their garage.

"Finally getting your boys on bikes," the man said, putting his hand out.

Henry took it. "Cal, I don't believe you've formally met my wife. Come on over."

Cal walked back toward Polly and put his hand out to shake hers. "Nice to meet you, ma'am. Hello Mona. How are you?"

"Fine, thank you." Mona stepped back out of the way. "How's Chris?"

"Mean and nasty," he quipped. "Too hot, too cold, too fat, too hungry, too much this, too much that. She ain't a happy woman."

Polly had seen his very pregnant wife going in and out of the house. The woman looked miserable.

"When's she due?" Polly asked.

The doc says she has another three weeks, but if this baby doesn't come soon, I'm not going to take responsibility for what that woman does."

"Can I do anything to help?"

He turned to look at Polly. "Would you mind keeping an eye on the kids right now? They'll be fine riding around, but if I could go get her some ice cream and a Sprite, I'd be her hero, especially if she didn't have to worry about the noise-makers."

"I'll drive," Henry said. "We're out of ice cream sandwiches here, too."

"Let me tell Chris where I'm going," Cal said. "If any of the kids fall down and bloody themselves, tell them to suck it up until I'm back."

Polly chuckled. "Or I'll put a band-aid on it. I have those, you know. But we'll keep them out of your house."

He strode back across the street.

Henry patted his pockets and pulled out keys. "Mona, can Rose eat ice cream with the kids?"

She gave him a confused look. "I guess."

"Is there anything she likes best?"

"Ice cream sandwiches will be fine."

He glanced at Polly, but nodded and walked over to his truck. Backing out of the driveway, he waited for Cal to come back outside.

"Where are they going?" Elijah asked, coming to a halt in front of Polly and Mona.

"Out for ice cream."

His face drooped and his lower lip stuck out. "Without us? I love ice cream."

Mona couldn't help herself and laughed out loud, something Polly hadn't really seen before. It was amazing what a smile could do for a person. The woman lit right up.

"You're adorable, sweetie," Mona said, putting her hand on Elijah's shoulder. "They're bringing ice cream back for everyone."

He turned his bike around and rode back toward the rest of the kids. "They're getting ice cream for all of us!"

"I have some lawn chairs in the garage," Polly said to Mona. "Wanna help me get them out?"

Mona looked back toward her house. "I have two."

"If you want," Polly replied. "But we have a bunch. Come on."

"Do you ever get overwhelmed with that many kids in your house all the time?"

Polly opened the side door to the garage. They didn't store much in here that she used regularly because it was so jam-packed with furniture and construction materials. It was a horrid little building, but until they were further down the road, this was what they were stuck with. She gestured around at the mess. "This is the stuff that overwhelms me. I have so many things to deal with that the kids are easy. The two oldest pretty much take care of themselves and Rebecca is growing up. I'm confident that she will continue to be an independent girl who drives me out of my mind, but we'll get through it." She handed two bag chairs to Mona and slung three others over her shoulder.

"I don't know what I'd do with that many children living with me. Sometimes Rose is more than I want to handle." Mona smiled. "But she's a pretty good girl. Life wouldn't be the same without her."

"Those rotten kids have a way of getting under our skin, don't they?"

Mona nodded. "You and your husband have a lot of fun with your kids."

"I just love them all," Polly said. "They're unique and interesting and even though they've been through a lot, they all try in their own way to live well."

Elijah rode up beside them as they set up chairs and got off his bicycle. "I'm worn out," he said. "That's a lot of work. Is one of those chairs for me?"

"You haven't used up nearly enough energy." Polly waved back toward the street. "Look at little Rose. She's still riding and she's a lot smaller than you."

"She's only a year younger than me and she's been riding bikes for a lot longer. That means she built up all her muscles."

"I see." Polly finished setting up the other chairs and sat down in one beside Mona. "So you're going to let someone younger than you be stronger than you."

He shrugged. "If she wants."

"Come on, Jah," Noah yelled as he flew past them. "We're going to race."

Mona stood up. "Be careful of cars," she said.

Noah pointed to the other end of the street. "Jeremy's watching that end. He's racing the winner back. You'll watch here, won't you?" Without waiting for a response, he took his place in the middle of the street. They'd marked the starting line with two rocks.

"Elijah!" he demanded. "Come on."

Elijah huffed and grumped. "I'm coming."

Mona giggled, "He doesn't seem happy."

"I have no idea why," Polly said. "He's usually the happiest boy in the world. He loves everything."

The kids waited for Jeremy to give a signal and raced to the finish line. Little Aiden came in last, but he didn't seem to care. Noah was second behind Julia, but he shot his hands in the air at the other end. Rose, Aiden and Elijah rode back on the sidewalk, while Jeremy, his sister, Julia, and Noah lined up for a return race. Jeremy pushed to beat his sister and Noah came in third.

"Did you see, Polly?" Noah asked, coming riding over to her. "I'm riding fast."

"You really are." She stood up as Jeremy started toward his house. "Honey, I think your dad wants you to stay outside and give your mom some quiet time. If you kids want to take your bikes into our back yard, you can play there."

He stopped and looked at her, trying to decide whether to obey a relative stranger or not. He dropped his bike in the lawn and bent over to pick up a ball.

When he saw that, Elijah's eyes brightened. "You wanna play baseball? We can do that in the back yard."

Jeremy tossed the soccer ball he was carrying into the air a couple of times. "I'd rather play soccer. Julia and Aiden will play, too. How about you, Rose?"

The little girl looked at her mother with a mixture of hope and fear.

"If they're going into the back yard," Polly said, "we'll just move the chairs. Henry and Cal will find us. Maybe I can talk Heath into coming outside, too. He'll keep an eye on Rose."

Rose's eyes grew more hopeful and Mona slowly nodded. "You have to be very careful, though."

The little girl dropped her bike on the sidewalk and took off for the back yard with the others, leaving Elijah standing there, looking forlorn.

"I'll take her bike back to the house," Mona said. "Leave my chair here and I'll carry it around when I return."

Once she was out of earshot, Polly knelt down in front of Elijah. "What is up with you? You're awfully grumpy."

"Nobody will play the games I want to play."

"You don't like riding bikes?"

"I'm not very good," he said, slouching his shoulders. "Noah is better than me and he just learned how to ride bikes today, too."

"And soccer?"

"Noah's better at that, too."

"You like being the best, don't you?"

"Duh," he said. "Doesn't everybody?"

Polly nodded and took his hand. "Yes they do. Even your brother. Maybe it's okay for him to be better at something. What do you think about that?"

"It's not fair."

"You know better than that," she said. "Now go play with your brother and let him know how awesome he is."

He started to move away. "Wait a minute," Polly said. "First, go inside and talk Heath into coming out to play with everyone. I think Rose would do better if there was a big brother around to keep an eye on her, don't you?"

"More than me?" he asked, the glint returning to his eyes.

"Maybe both of you can help her out."

Elijah pushed his bike to the side of the house and leaned it against the steps, then ran inside, calling for Heath.

Polly picked up several chairs and hitched them along as she dragged them to the back yard. When she finally got everything set up, she went inside and put the dogs on their leashes. They were ready to be outside after listening to the sounds of kids playing.

When she got back out with them, Mona had taken one of the chairs and Heath was crouched beside the house with Rose standing in front of him. He whispered to her and she ran out to stand beside Noah.

"That's the one who's graduating this year?" Mona asked.

Polly nodded, holding tight to the leashes. The dogs wanted to run and play. "But he's planning to live with us while he attends school at Iowa State. Fortunately, that means he'll be around for a while."

She turned at the sound of Henry's truck in the driveway.

"This is a really nice place for your kids to play," Mona said. "All so protected."

"Any time the kids are outside, Rose is welcome to join them. The boys would love having someone else to play with." Polly chuckled. "And now that Cal's kids have been here once, I'm guessing it won't be the last time."

Mona sat forward when Rose fell on the grass. Polly held her breath. She didn't want to tell the woman to let her little girl play hard because it was good for her, so she held her tongue.

Rose jumped up and waved to her mother, then ran to get back in the game.

"I guess she's okay," Mona said. "I hope they don't hurt her. She's just a girl."

"She's a *girl*," Polly said, with more force than she intended. "She can do anything and won't break. I'll bet Rose is tougher than you think."

Henry and Cal came into the back yard carrying two bags each.

"What did you do?" Polly asked. "Buy out the store?"

"I'm taking one of these over to Chris," Cal said. He handed the other to Henry. "Back in a few minutes."

"I'll put these in the freezer," Henry said. "Looks like the kids are having fun. How did you get Heath out here?"

"Told him he needed to keep an eye on Rose," Polly said with a smile. "Gotta press that chivalry button every once in a while."

He looped the bags on one hand and touched Mona's shoulder. "Looks like she's having fun with the big kids."

Mona gave him a stilted nod. "I hope she's okay."

"She'll be fine," he said. "Heath will keep an eye on her. It's good for them all to figure out how to play together. She can get tougher and the older kids can learn to be gentle. Seems like a perfect plan." He turned and headed inside.

"Sometimes I think Rose missed out because she doesn't have a dad," Mona said. "I baby her."

Obiwan nosed Mona's hand and she absentmindedly rubbed his head which was exactly what the dog was looking for.

"It's just been the two of us for so long, though," Mona continued.

"Did you see, Mommy? Did you see?" Rose ran toward her mother. "I made a goal!"

Mona looked up at Polly guiltily. "Good for you, baby. Are you having fun?"

"Yessss!" Rose tore back out to where the others were playing.

"I missed it," Mona said. "If I weren't so worried all the time, I would have just enjoyed watching her play."

Polly handed Obiwan's leash to Mona. "I'm going to take Han for a quick run out front. Would you keep hold of this one for me? His name is Obiwan and he will love you to death if you let him."

"Hi Obiwan," Mona said. "You're a very gorgeous dog."

Polly turned to walk Han back toward the front yard and met Henry, who was coming back out of the house.

"We seem to have gathered a crowd," he said.

"That'll teach me," Polly replied.

"What do you mean?"

"Should have gotten bikes earlier for those little boys. All we needed to do was stand around outside and we'd get to know our neighbors better. Why didn't you tell me?"

"Some things can't be taught; they must be learned," he said with a smile and took Han's leash.

Cal walked onto the driveway, carrying a chair in one hand and holding the hand of his very pregnant wife. "Chris, this is Polly and Henry. Guys, this is my wife, Chris. She thought some fresh air might be good for her."

"It's nice to meet you, Chris," Polly said. "Everybody's in the back yard. The kids are playing and Mona is watching them. You'll join us?"

"Just for a little while," Chris replied. She patted her belly and leaned a little toward Polly. "I'll need to go home and use the bathroom in no time."

Polly laughed and took the woman's other arm. "You can use ours, too. Come on. Let's get you settled. Cal says you're not due for another few weeks."

"Cal says a lot of things. The last thing he said was that we were done having kids after Aiden was born. A lot of good that did me."

# CHAPTER FIFTEEN

"Are we without Joss tonight?" Tab asked. She smiled at the waitress who put a drink in front of her.

Polly shook her head. "I haven't heard from her. Their new kiddos are coming home today and she's been crazy busy this week preparing for it. Her mom's in town and I bet she has way too many things going on."

"We're not important enough," Sal said with a mock pout.

"That's exactly it," Polly replied. She passed the basket of cheese bread to Sylvie. "What's new with everyone this week?"

"My baby is leaving junior high," Sylvie said. "What in the heck is that about? I'm not old enough …" She stopped. "Damn it. I am old enough. But wow, that went fast. He's going to be in high school next year. That hurts."

"Maybe you and Eliseo should consider having babies," Camille said. She took a quick drink from her glass and turned away from Sylvie's scowl.

Sylvie had just been about to pass the cheese bread to Camille, but snatched it back and handed it across the table to Sandy Davis. "No bread for the bad girl."

"I'm teaching two summer classes," Elise said. "I didn't think I was going to, but the dean asked and I couldn't say no. And that starts tomorrow. What in the world?"

"Were you planning to go home for summer break?" Polly asked.

Elise puffed out a small laugh. "No. I might go home for a week in August." She shook her head. "I take that back. I might go home for a *weekend* in August."

"Your parents are nice people," Camille said. "I really like them."

"And I love them very much," Elise replied. "But now Mother has it in her head that since I'm actually interacting with people and not hiding in my room, I should find a husband and start producing children for her. For her! What about for me? Why won't she think about me?"

"Because she loves you," Sylvie said. "And she knows what's best for you."

"They never let us grow up, do they?" Camille asked. "Mama was here for the day on Wednesday and by the time she left, she'd rearranged all of my dresser drawers. She chose which clothes I should pack up until next winter and then scolded me for not having brighter colors in my wardrobe. All I could think was, 'Mama, I'm not sixteen any longer. I've been dressing myself quite nicely for years.'"

Elise dropped her head, laughing. "Mother still sends clothes to me when she finds something she thinks I should wear." She tugged at the blouse she had on. "In fact, this came in a few weeks ago. I don't know when the last time was that I went shopping for myself." She shut her eyes. "I hate to admit that she even buys my nightgowns."

"Bras and panties?" Tab asked.

Elise sighed. "I wasn't going to tell you that."

"See," Camille said. "Parents don't want us to grow up."

"Benji's father insisted on being there to help us buy our first home," Sandy said. "It was so embarrassing. He wouldn't let Benji speak and my poor husband was so ticked off that his dad didn't believe he could handle it on his own. When we moved over here to Bellingwood, Benji didn't even tell his mother that we were doing it until the sale was finished."

"Same thing still with my cars," Camille said. "Mama told me that my car needed to be replaced. Then she talked to dealers in Omaha. All of a sudden, I started receiving emails. One of the salesmen got really pushy. When I asked where he'd gotten my name, he told me that Mama had called him three different times to make sure he was in contact with me." She shook her head. "I finally had to confront her, and let me tell you, that wasn't pretty. She doesn't like to be told to back off."

Polly shuddered. "I wouldn't be able to tell your mother to back off. You must have nerves of steel. That woman is scary."

"You all know that Polly's back on track, don't you?" Tab asked.

Sylvie smirked, but Sandy looked at Tab in confusion.

"Yeah," Tab said. "Two bodies this week. And guess who Sheriff Merritt has decided should be Polly's liaison to the department?"

"Is that what he's calling it now?"

"It's all I've got," Tab said. "But I think he likes the fact that we're comfortable working together."

"I knew about the guy out on the road," Sal said, "but another one?"

Tab barked a laugh. "She was trying to solve the case and only made it worse."

"Do you know who it is yet?" Polly asked.

"Not yet," Tab said, shaking her head. "There were no plates on the trailer, so we haven't been able to trace that either. But we're just getting started." She looked around the table. "And the second person she found? That time she had the sheriff's wife with her."

"No way," Sylvie said. "Tell me you didn't take Beryl too."

"Oh yeah," Polly replied. "Both of them. I was just trying to show them this old house that Henry and his dad want to buy. They think we should put a bed and breakfast in it. Jeff says it's a good idea — that what we've got going on in Bellingwood could support it. He'd know."

"Are you moving in there?" Sal asked.

"Oh lord, no," Polly replied. "I'm not ready for that. Still too many kids around."

"What you're saying is that you're going to need a nice grand-parenty couple to show up."

"I told Henry that the right people would show up when we needed them."

"Someday you're going to be wrong," Sylvie said. "You've gotten lucky with people so far."

"I screwed up a couple of early hires," Polly said. "That's when I learned to trust my gut rather than rush into things. It will work out. It always does."

"Is this that house north of Eliseo's place?" Sylvie asked. "I heard him talking to his sister about it."

"Yeah. Henry and Bill seem to think that having the stables there would be good. Close enough that guests could go riding if they wanted to. Of course, they haven't discussed that with anyone but themselves. We'll see what Elva says when she's running things."

Their pizza arrived and the waitress brought a fresh round of drinks for those whose glasses had been emptied. The quiet only lasted for a minute.

"Two this week?" Sandy asked. "I don't know how you do it. I'd be so freaked out."

"I know," Polly said, blowing on a slice of pizza to cool it. "But I've grown to accept that this is what I do. These people need to be found and so I find them." She pointed the end of her pizza at Tab. "Then I let the professionals take over and do the hard work. My job is done."

"Your job isn't done," Tab said. "Once you're involved, we all take bets on when you will find the main clue that leads to the murderer."

"You're joking," Polly said.

"Nope. It's better not to fight with fate."

"There used to be a pool at the Elevator about Polly," Sylvie said. "They took bets on the next person she'd find." When she saw the look on Polly's face, she smiled. "I think they got rid of it finally."

Sandy shook her head. "I still don't know how you do it. I couldn't bear to see a dead body."

Polly gave her a small smile. "Honestly, honey, I don't know how you do what you're doing with your little boy. You're so strong. I know that doesn't help, but I'm awfully proud of you. How's he doing?"

"Just about the time he starts to feel better, it's time for another treatment," Sandy said. "I just get up every day, tell him that I love him and will always be close by. He's such a strong, happy little boy, even through all of this. I couldn't do it for anyone else."

Tab rubbed Sandy's back. "You're a wonderful mommy."

"I'm just glad that I can spend time with you on Sundays and leave that all behind for a couple of hours," Sandy said, smiling at her friends around the table. "The social worker keeps reminding us that we need to have other outlets so that we stay emotionally healthy through this. If I didn't have you guys, I don't know what I'd do. You're my sanity."

Sal snorted. "That's not saying much. We're all a bit over-the-top nutso-wacko."

"Speak for yourself, tootsie-pop," Polly said. "I lead a normal life. I do normal things with normal people."

Sylvie tapped on Polly's shoulder and pointed at the front door. "You should look up before you speak."

Polly had to lean to the side to see around Tab, who had turned around.

"I don't know if their timing could be any more perfect," Sal said. She stood up and waved. "Henry. Boys. We're back here."

Henry, Elijah and Noah were all wearing dark sunglasses and big wide-brimmed hats that Polly had purchased for herself and Rebecca. Henry was wearing his Hawaiian shirt and khaki shorts with flip flops on his feet. The little boys had on tie-dye t-shirts that they'd made with Rebecca one night.

"What in the world?" Polly asked. "Who are these people? They're certainly not related to me."

Elijah finally caught sight of her and ran around the table to get a hug from her. "We're inc ... cons ..." He looked at Henry. "What's that word you called us?"

"Incognito," Henry said. "Nobody is supposed to recognize us since your mom is out playing with her friends."

"What are you doing here?" Polly asked.

"Getting pizza for Hayden and Heath," Elijah announced. He took his sunglasses off and attempted to climb onto Polly's lap. She let him and he reached up to whisper in her ear. "Can I have a piece of cheese bread?"

"Is Henry getting cheese bread?" she asked him.

Elijah shrugged. "I don't know."

Polly did know. There was no way Henry would order pizza without a couple of extra orders of cheese bread. Their family ate it like candy. "I'll bet you do know." She put him back on the floor and gave his bottom a push. "I'll be right back." Taking Elijah's hand, Polly returned him to Henry and Noah.

Henry slid his glasses down on his nose and looked at Polly over the top. "Hello there, ma'am — person that I don't know. How might I be of service?"

"You three are the silliest things I've ever seen," she said. She lifted Noah's glasses up to his forehead. "And you let them do this to me?"

"It was funny."

Polly kissed his cheek. "Yes it was. I thought you were helping Heath and Hayden get packed up before they leave tomorrow morning."

"We are," Noah said. "Well, Rebecca is. She made a list of what they need. We had to come get pizza and ask you where the extra toothpaste is."

"Toothpaste?" Polly looked at Henry. "Really?"

"Pizza for sure. But where is the extra stuff? I looked for it in our bathroom."

"You really drove up here to ask me about toothpaste?"

He handed his credit card to the waitress. "Didn't you hear me? We came for pizza. Still, where are the extra travel shampoos that you keep?"

Polly knelt back down and spoke to Noah. "Listen very carefully because your dad over there is bound to forget this. Everything is downstairs in the bathroom off the library. It's in the tall linen cabinet on the bottom shelf. There's a plastic basket where you should find everything those boys will need. Got it?"

Noah nodded at her with great solemnity. "I'll remember."

"Remember these two and Rebecca have to go to school tomorrow," she said to Henry. "Don't let them stay up too late."

"But Mom," Henry whined. "Heath and Hayden are leaving before they get up. Can't we stay up until they go to bed? Just to say bye?"

She shook her head and started to turn away. Then, she stopped, licked her index and third finger and quickly wiped them down the lenses of Henry's sunglasses. "Have fun tonight." Polly walked as fast as possible back to the table and darted back into her seat.

"So," Sal said. "Normal, huh?"

"I thought we were here for Sandy's sanity. Are we helping?" Polly asked.

Sandy nodded and smiled. "A lot."

Polly watched as Henry put a small box into the hands of each boy, then herded them toward the front door. He turned and gave her a quick wave as he held the door for Noah and Elijah.

"Did you hear me?" Sandy asked.

Polly gave her friends a bemused look. "Was I really that far gone? What did you ask?"

"I was asking about that junk guy you found. Mr. Loeffler?"

"Okay? Tab probably knows more about him than I do."

"What day was it that you found him?"

Tab and Polly looked at each other, both frowning in concentration.

"This week has gotten real out of hand," Polly said. "I think it was Wednesday. Why?"

Sandy turned to Tab. "How long had he been dead?"

"We haven't gotten the full report back yet, but initial thoughts are that it was about twelve hours."

Sandy nodded.

"Why?" Polly asked. "Did you see something?"

"You'll probably find two old microwaves in his truck. Joanne paid him to take hers and my old one out to the dump. He was at her house late Tuesday afternoon. He said he had one more pickup to do before he went home."

Tab sat forward. "Did he say anything more about that last pickup?"

"I don't know," Sandy said with a shrug. "We switched off a lot this week — home and the hospital. Joanne came over later to spell me while I went home and slept for a few hours. None of us heard about the death until this weekend. I'm not sure if she even put together that she saw him just before he died."

"Will she be in town tomorrow? Can I stop by and talk to her?" Tab asked.

"Yeah. We take Will back in Tuesday morning so we're in town. She'll be at her house, though. Let me send her a text to ..." Sandy paused and shook her head. "No, that will take too long and she'll never understand what I'm telling her." She stood up. "Let me call. What time is good for you?"

"Any time," Tab said. "Schedule it and I'll make it work."

Sandy walked away from the table and wandered out the front door.

"So," Polly said. "How are things with you and Mr. Roberts?"

That was all it took. Tab blushed and took a quick breath.

"Fine. I'm going over to the winery after we're done here tonight."

"Oh you are, are you?" Sylvie taunted. "Sounds like things are getting serious."

"I promised to help him clean up," Tab responded. "He had a little concert event outside on the patio late this afternoon. There was a small crowd when I left. The girl's a pretty good singer, too."

"Lauren somebody?" Polly asked. "I saw her with him the other day at the coffee shop. Isn't she Sonya Biederman's granddaughter?"

"No, Lauren's his new hostess — Ashley is the singer." Tab tapped the table in front of Polly. "And Sonya is having open heart surgery tomorrow, but I guess the doctors aren't worried about her."

"This has been a strange week," Polly said.

Sandy rushed back into the restaurant and ran to the table. Bending over, she whispered loudly. "There's a fire down the street. I've already called 9-1-1."

"Which way?" Polly asked.

"I think it might be at the elementary school," Sandy said. "It's down that way."

"The apartment building is right there," Sylvie said.

Polly jumped back to her feet. "Stephanie and Kayla!" She took out her credit card and dropped it on the table. "Bri?"

The young waitress came out from the kitchen.

"My credit card is here. Put dinner on there. I'll be back later or get the card tomorrow. There's a fire down the street."

Dylan Foster, the owner of Pizzazz, came out at Polly's frantic words. "Take your card," he said. "We'll settle up later."

Polly was at the door of the restaurant and kept going. She knew and trusted these people, but right now, she wasn't going to stop to chat.

Tab was already halfway down the block, running full-out. The girl was impressive.

Polly realized that she'd left everyone else in the restaurant. As she ran to catch up with Tab, it occurred to her that the others probably wouldn't follow. Chaos and insanity just weren't part of their lives. How they managed to get away with that, she had no idea.

The heat from the fire slowed her and she realized that the garden level apartment below Stephanie and Kayla's was on fire. Polly looked around for them, frantic in her search. She'd lost sight of Tab.

Sirens screamed down the street as Polly pushed through the gathering crowd. She wanted to yell Stephanie's name, but the noise was so loud, she knew she wouldn't be heard.

Ken Wallers and Bert Bradford arrived and then Polly saw Tab at the front door of the building as tenants poured out. Polly crossed the street — she had to find her friends.

Polly leaned and twisted, trying to see around the folks coming out of the apartment building. She nearly dropped to her knees when Kayla crossed the threshold, followed by her older sister.

When the last people came through the door, Tab asked a few questions of them. As they pointed back into the building and then out on the lawn, Polly assumed she was asking if everyone had made it out.

Flames licked the side of the building as fire trucks came to a halt; local firefighters poured out and onto the scene. Tab, Ken Wallers and Bert Bradford pushed people back and away from the building. It was all happening so fast, all Polly could do was grab Kayla's arm, startled at its soft furriness. She suddenly realized it was Kayla's cat and found she still had a smile left in her.

"What happened?" she yelled at Stephanie.

Stephanie shrugged and put her hands up.

"Do you know who lives down there?" Polly asked, pointing at the apartment still in flames.

Stephanie leaned in closely and said, "Empty. Nobody there."

Polly nodded and looked at the bag Stephanie was carrying. "You had time to pack?"

"Go bag."

Polly peered at the young woman. "What?"

"Life lessons," Stephanie yelled back. "Always ready."

That made sense. After all these two girls had been through, Stephanie knew to be prepared for anything. She'd spent too many years of her life worrying that her abusive father would find them.

The three of them stood in the middle of a crowd of faces and watched as the fire department worked to bring the fire under control. Polly glanced at Kayla, wondering how the girl was handling this. The girl stood silently, with tears streaming down her face.

"It will be okay," Polly said.

Kayla nodded and snuggled her cat close to her face.

Looking around at the stricken faces, it hit Polly that these people probably wouldn't be allowed back in their homes tonight. Maybe the families on the other side of the building would return in a day or so, but until the structure was deemed safe, nobody was living there. She took out her phone and sent Grey a text.

*"How many rooms do you have available tonight?"*

He responded immediately. *"It's a Sunday. We're pretty empty. What do you need?"*

*"Fire at the apartments behind the elementary school. Doubt people are going home."*

*"All they need is to be safe. We have rooms."*

*"Thanks. Nobody pays. Okay?"*

*"You're such a softie. Got it."*

Ken Wallers spotted her as he walked through the gathered people and came over. He put his hand out to shake Stephanie's. "You girls doing okay?"

Stephanie nodded. "At least we're safe. We're not going back in tonight, are we?"

He shook his head. "I'm sorry."

Polly stepped forward. "Stephanie, you two are coming to my house. Rebecca would be furious if Kayla was anywhere else but with her. We have plenty of room." She took Ken's arm and led him away. "Anyone who needs a place tonight can go to the hotel. I just talked to Grey and he'll be ready for them."

Ken raised his brows. "That's a big deal."

"It's really not," Polly said. "The rooms are empty and I'm not about to let people wonder where they'll put their kids to sleep tonight. I can take care of Stephanie and Kayla, but these people are scared enough right now. Just don't make it a big deal, okay? I'd rather no one know that it came from me."

"You're very generous." He took her hand. "Thanks for making this easy, though."

Tab came over to them and took Stephanie's arm. "Did you hear or see anything this evening?"

Stephanie shook her head. "We were just watching television. I didn't even know there was a fire in the building until you knocked on the door."

"Have you seen anyone going in and out of that apartment lately?

"No." Stephanie turned to her sister. "Did you see anything?"

"I don't think so." Kayla brushed tears away from her face. "I don't know."

"That's okay," Tab said, patting Kayla's arm. "You don't have to know anything. But if either of you think of something, would you call me?" She handed Stephanie a business card.

"If we can't go back inside, is it okay if we leave?"

Tab nodded and looked at Polly.

Polly returned the nod.

"Can I go around back and get my car?" Stephanie asked.

"Absolutely." Tab moved on to the next cluster of people and Polly heard her asking the same questions.

"My truck is at Pizzazz," Polly said. "If you two want to go on over to the house, I'll meet you there."

"Are you sure about this?" Stephanie asked. "I can go to the hotel."

Polly stopped. "I'd love to have you stay with us, but if you want privacy, you know more about what's available than anyone. You can stay wherever you want."

"Please, Stephanie?" Kayla begged. "Please?"

"I just don't want to put Polly out."

"You won't at all. And if it's going to take too long for you to get back into your apartment and you want to make a different decision, you can do that too."

"Please?" Kayla asked again.

"Okay. At least for tonight," Stephanie said. "Thank you, Polly."

While Polly walked back to Pizzazz, she took out her phone and called Henry.

"What's going on?" he asked.

"Fire at the apartment building by the elementary school," she said. "Stephanie and Kayla are homeless tonight. They're coming over. Would you let Rebecca know so she's prepared for them? I have to get my truck and then I'll be there."

"Did they lose the whole building?"

"I don't think so. They got the fire out pretty fast and I'm sure it was contained to the one garden apartment, but they're worried about the structure."

"Of course," he said. "Was it on Stephanie's side of the building?"

"Yeah." Polly felt her heart sink. That was too close.

"They have to stop this guy."

"I know. I'll be home soon." She found it hard to swallow. This night could have ended very differently.

Camille, Sandy and Elise were gone, but Sylvie's car was still parked beside Sal's. Polly steeled herself for the onslaught of questions, opened the door and went inside.

# CHAPTER SIXTEEN

"Some days are worse than others," Polly said. "I'm exhausted." She dropped into the chair in their bedroom. "It wasn't much of a day until I decided to go out for pizza."

Henry smiled at her. "This arsonist really escalated."

"But still they made sure it was an empty apartment. They aren't trying to kill anyone."

"Not yet," Henry said. "But what happens when they ratchet it up again?"

"Let's hope the police catch whoever is doing this before it gets worse."

Han had jumped up in the chair next to hers and reached a paw out to her. Polly rubbed his head. "You think the boys have everything they need?"

"If they need something, they can buy it," Henry responded. "They'll be fine."

"I wish tonight hadn't been so crazy so we could have enjoyed sending them off."

"I'd guess they'll be gone before you're even awake tomorrow morning."

Polly shook her head. "I'm getting up if you are. I want to say goodbye, kiss their cheeks, and hug their necks. I know this was my idea, but I can't believe they're going to be gone all week. I'm going to miss those boys."

"But you still have plenty of people living here now that Stephanie and Kayla moved in."

"I don't know how long they'll stay. I wish we had better places for guests to sleep," Polly said. "I can't believe we had to jam poor Stephanie into the library. She probably would have been better off at the hotel. At least she'd have room to move around. Henry, I can't stand all this chaos in the house. Here I thought we were moving into a large enough space that I'd have room to put anyone up. Heath and Hayden are still in the living room, the dining room is a mess, our office is jammed with boxes and furniture, and the library has even more boxes in it now that Joey's showed up. The garage is embarrassing and I can't let the dogs outside on their own yet. I want to just scream."

He sat down on the ottoman in front of her and hitched it forward, then put his hands on her thighs. "I get it. Tell me which of those you'd like to work on next and that's what we'll attack."

Polly put her hands on top of his and rubbed them up and down across his wrists. "I'm sorry. I don't mean to complain. I should never complain. You are so good about all of this and you don't have any more time in your days. It's not fair of me to come apart just because I'm frustrated. I knew what we were getting into."

"This is pretty normal behavior, you know."

"What do you mean?"

"I've never known anyone living in the midst of a remodeling project that isn't ready to come completely unglued at some point in the middle. You can't see the end and it doesn't feel as if you've done quite enough since you began. But honey, look at what you ... what the boys ... what we've all accomplished. That foyer is awesome. You not only finished it for Christmas parties, but when it filled up with junk, you moved the junk out so we could have Heath's graduation party. If you want to move everything back in there so we can finish the office and library, we'll do that and make sure to have it all cleaned out before next Christmas."

"Okay?"

"Noah and Elijah are in their own room, Polly. *Their own room.* That room is their home until they go off on their own. They've never had anything like that in their lives and you did it. You gave that to them. Rebecca not only has her own room, but she has a studio in the back yard ..."

Polly interrupted. "If she ever uses it. She loves working in that front room of hers and it's big enough for all of her things." She laughed. "That girl has a lot of things."

"And tonight, she's got her best friend sleeping in that big old room with her."

"Along with more cats than a person can count."

"I figure that's just my life from now on, thanks to you."

Polly grinned at him.

"The yard is in great shape, we have a nice front porch on the place and a nice back yard for the kids to play in. You can tie the dogs up out there for short periods of time, but we'll figure out a fence for them this summer, I promise. I can't promise anything on the garage, but we really are making good progress. Can you see that?"

She leaned forward and wrapped her arms around his neck. "I know. You're right. I'm just being whiny. I'm sorry."

"What more can I do to make whiny-Polly retreat back into your head?"

"You've already done a lot tonight. Thanks for playing with Noah and Elijah. I thought I was going to die when I saw you walk into Pizzazz."

He laughed. "That was actually Rebecca's idea. When Heath asked about pizza, she said that you wouldn't like us all traipsing in on you. Then she told me that we should be like Hollywood stars and wear sunglasses so no one would recognize us. I kind of expanded on the idea. Elijah and Noah giggled about it all the way down and all the way back."

"I can't believe you didn't see the fire."

"We didn't go home that way. I took them to the convenience store for some chocolate milk and we came back on the highway. We had just gotten inside when we heard the sirens."

"You are such a wonderful pushover with those little boys. They sure love you."

"They're good boys. They try so hard, too. I'll be glad when we finally get an adoption hearing and they're really ours. Then they will know that they're here to stay."

"I love you, Henry."

He nodded. "Is it the fence that has you concerned the most?"

"That's the thing that I can't wrap my head around. I can clear out rooms here — move boxes back and forth. I can refinish furniture this summer so that we can put the dining room together. Once Hayden and Heath are back, they'll go to work on the upstairs bedrooms and when that's finished, the living room will be my next project." She twisted her lips around. "I guess the biggest frustration is that there's nothing I can really do right now. We just need this graduation party to be finished so I can destroy the rest of the house."

"So just one more week of excruciating patience, right?"

"Right," she said with a laugh. "I'm pathetic, aren't I?"

"Maybe a little." He ducked back as she swatted at him. "But I should have paid attention much earlier when you kept talking about that fence. Until we enclose the yard, you'll worry about letting the dogs and kids run free, won't you?"

"It's so weird," she said. "I didn't worry this much when we were at Sycamore House, and over there, we were right on the highway. But both dogs grew up there and they knew what the boundaries were. When I let them outside to run here at the house, they want to take off and go like the wind." Polly nodded. "You're right, though. I didn't have Noah and Elijah to worry about when we lived at Sycamore House. I want to know that they're safe in our yard. I don't care if all the kids in the neighborhood come over to play, but unless I'm outside, I'm not comfortable having them ride their bikes in the street or run back and forth. Not yet, anyway."

"When you get more comfortable with the neighbors, a lot of that will change, don't you think?"

"I'm sure it will. I like Cal and his wife. They're nice. I can't believe that poor woman is pregnant. She looks miserable. Their other kids are a lot older."

"When it happens, it happens," he said. Then he laughed. "Bellingwood just keeps growing — one baby at a time."

"There are certainly a lot of those happening around me," Polly said. "I can't wait to hear from Joss about her new little ones."

"They're not babies."

"No, but they're new. I hope she's as happy with these three as she is with Cooper and Sophie. That woman loves kids. I wonder how many more she'll bring into their home before she's done."

"Nate's a little worried about that. She saw a story about a couple that fostered and then adopted twenty children. He's afraid that's the bar she's set for herself."

"Wow," Polly said. "I thought I wanted to fill this place up with kids who needed love. I've got nothing on her. I was thinking seven or eight and I really like the idea of having a bunch of older kids who don't need constant supervision."

"Like Rebecca and Kayla?" Henry asked. He walked over to their door and opened it. The sound of muffled laughter came down the hallway from Rebecca's room.

"Don't make me go down there and tell them to be quiet," Polly said. She stood up. "But I'm going to have to, aren't I?"

"I'll check on Noah and Elijah."

She took his hand as they walked down the hallway. He veered into the little boys' room and Polly quietly tapped on Rebecca's door. The sound inside the room quieted and Rebecca pulled the door open.

"Were we being too loud?" she asked. "I'm sorry."

"It's time to sleep," Polly said. "You still have to go to school tomorrow. It's going to be a busy week."

"We'll try."

Polly stepped into the perpetually cluttered room. "How are you doing, Kayla?"

"I'm okay. At least everybody was safe, right?"

"Right. And your things will all be there whenever you can get in. You might have to clean them because of the smoky smell and I don't know how much water got into the upstairs apartments, but all of that can be cleaned up and fixed."

"I heard them saying that we might not be able to move back in because the fire burned up that wall. What if we don't have a place to live?"

"You can live here," Rebecca said. She turned to Polly. "Right? They can move in here. We have a lot of rooms. We might have to clean one out, but we have room. Right?"

"Whatever Stephanie wants to do, we'll help her do. How's that sound?" Polly responded. "But for tonight, you're safe and it's time to go to sleep. Please don't worry, Kayla. We've got this."

~~~

"What time is it?" Polly asked, peering at Henry through one half-opened eye.

"Four-thirty. You don't have to get up, though. The boys can get out of here on their own."

She sat up and swung her legs over the edge of the bed, rubbing her eyes. "No. I'm up."

Henry laughed. "You look like you're up."

"Hey. I'm trying. Where's my robe?"

He took it off the hook and tossed it to her.

"Will they let me make breakfast?" Polly asked. "Or are they trying to leave right away?"

"I thought I'd stir up some pancakes. They aren't planning to get on the road until five or five thirty."

Polly slipped her feet into the slippers beside her bedside table and tied the robe around her. "I'll make some juice and coffee. How do you people exist at this hour?" She swatted at him in the doorway. "Or be so smiley? What in the heck is that about?"

They went down the back steps to the still-dark kitchen. Polly flipped a light on and went straight for the coffee pot. She and

Henry met each other coming and going as they collected the necessary ingredients for juice, pancakes, eggs, and bacon.

While Henry mixed pancake batter, Polly lined bacon up on a baking sheet and put it into the oven.

"What are you doing up?" Hayden walked into the kitchen, his hair still wet from the shower.

Polly turned and smiled. "I couldn't miss saying goodbye to you. You're off on an adventure."

"But we'll be back Friday night."

"I know," she said, nodding. "Let me be a mom."

He sat down at the table and bent over to slide his shoes on. "Okay, Mom, just this once."

"Is Heath awake?" Henry asked.

"Barely. He's in the shower. Glad we packed the car last night. He's not worth anything this early." He stood and walked over to the island. "What can I do to help?"

Polly pointed at the can of concentrate she'd taken out of the freezer. "Juice."

"I just want coffee," Hayden said with a snide grin.

"Good for you. Just think of it as your last chance to help with the littles this week."

Hayden grabbed up the can and after flipping through two cabinets, found the one with the juice pitcher. "I'm going to miss them even though I haven't been around much lately."

"Any time you want to call and video chat with them, they'd be thrilled," Polly said. She poured the eggs into a frying pan. "How was your weekend with Tess? Did you two figure things out?"

He took a deep breath. "I don't know. She still doesn't get it why I was so freaked out over her behavior. Who does that?"

"Does what?" Henry asked.

"Shoves her boyfriend to the side during finals week and then gets mad when he tries to be nice? It wasn't like I was asking her to marry me."

"Apparently, they didn't figure it out," Henry said, elbowing Polly's arm.

"It wasn't great," Hayden said. "I really thought she'd apologize at least a little bit and when I wanted to talk about how we could handle this better in the future, she told me that it wasn't ever going to change. When she had to focus, everything else was unimportant — even me."

"Law school is going to be hell on your relationship," Polly said. "There's really not ever a time that she won't have to focus. Either that or she fails. It sounds like she doesn't have much balance when it comes to her schoolwork."

"She tells me I knew that going in," Hayden said. "But how was I supposed to know when she said that she really focuses when it's necessary, everything else is set aside? That's not normal." He put the pitcher into the refrigerator and turned back to them. "Is it?"

Polly didn't want to say anything. The words that would come out of her mouth would be filled with negativity. This entire thing had sent the hackles on the back of her neck rising, even if she had tried to justify it to Hayden.

Much to her surprise, Henry was the one who spoke up. "It's not normal, Hayden. You don't deserve that type of behavior from a girl. If she has to do her own thing, that's up to her and more power to her. Everyone has to find their own way, but you don't have to feel like you've done something wrong." He paused and looked at Hayden. "Unless you've not told us the whole story."

The look on Hayden's face told Polly right away that he was as stymied by things as they were.

"Maybe it's good that you're leaving for a few days," Polly said. "Give both of you some time and space. Tess probably needs to be a little further away from her finals. Do you think?"

Hayden nodded. "I suppose. I wish she would have just broken up with me. At least then I'd be able to set it all aside. I could be mad at her for treating me like crap and look for someone who won't do that."

"Someone who appreciates how terrific you are," Polly muttered into Henry's shoulder. Under her breath, she said, "Little twit."

Henry flipped more pancakes onto the plate sitting beside him while Polly scrambled the eggs.

"Why don't you get plates and silverware," she said to Hayden.

He complied and set the table. "I'm not usually like this," he said quietly. "I don't fret over relationships. They either are or they aren't. And if they aren't, I move on. I don't like being held hostage."

"Who's holding you hostage, bro?" Heath asked, coming into the kitchen. "This smells really good. I can't believe you got up, Polly."

"Look at me," she said, brandishing the spatula. "Cooking and everything."

The dogs ran to greet him and he rubbed their heads. "Have they been outside? I can do that. Is there time?"

Henry looked up after flipping more pancakes out of the pan. "That would be great. Make it a quick one. They'll want their breakfast."

"Come on, furballs," Heath said, trotting to the back porch. He jangled their leashes and both dogs clattered across the floor, coming to a stop at his feet. "We'll be back in a minute," he said, rubbing Han's head.

"He doesn't even know how bad it's going to get with girls," Hayden said.

"He's had his trouble with them," Polly replied. "He ain't so dumb."

"Yeah. But when you get older things feel so much more desperate. I'm not looking to just date girls with no hope of a future. I want to meet the right girl and make a commitment so that when we're ready we can start our lives together. How the hell long is it going to take?"

Henry stood beside Polly at the stove, his back to Hayden and started laughing. It didn't take long for him to become rather obnoxious. "Oh, Hayden," he said. "How old do you think I was when I finally got married?"

"You were waiting for Polly."

"Yeah, but I was in my thirties when she showed up and then she made me wait and wait and wait before we got married." He bumped his shoulder against hers. "I was just glad the guys down at the Elevator didn't create a pool on how long it would take for me to finally get her to agree to be my wife." He smirked at Polly. "They like their pools. They'll bet on just about anything."

"I'm just glad I'm no longer part of their games," she said. "But Hayden, please don't be in a hurry to settle down. That will only bring disaster."

"What do you mean?"

"Give yourself enough time to meet someone and get to know them. Don't rush into a relationship just because you feel the need to move that part of your life forward. What does it matter if you're single for a few more years?"

"I suppose," he said. "It just wasn't in the plan."

Henry turned around. "You have a plan?"

Hayden lifted his shoulders and gave them a cute smile. "I've already messed it up since I'm not going to be a doctor now, but I was going to find my wife and marry her while I was in med school. Once I was working in a hospital or private practice, we'd start our family. Three children — preferably two girls and a boy, but whatever we had, it would be perfect. We'd buy a nice four-bedroom house on the edge of whatever town we lived in and Uncle Heath would come over for holidays and romp with the children in the back yard."

"You do know this probably means you'll meet a great woman who's, let's say seven years older than you. You'll end up in a third-floor walkup in Manhattan and she'll already have three kids, but you'll want two or three more of your own. Right?" Polly asked. Before she completely lost control of her laughter, she bent over and took the bacon out of the oven.

Hayden laughed. "That's harsh, but it sounds like fun. When I decided not to go to med school, I tossed the plan aside. Then I met Tess and I knew she'd never want to stay at home with children. And truthfully, I'd like to meet someone who's a little more adventurous than the woman in my life plan."

"That's exactly right," Polly said. "Even if it's Tess, you need to keep adjusting that plan until it's perfect for you."

The dogs came rushing in and stopped beside their food bowls.

"Bad Polly," she said. "Didn't get breakfast ready for the boys on time." She gestured to the food they'd been putting together on the island's counter. "If you all would dish that up, I'll be right over." As she went past the hallway, she saw Stephanie peeking out of the library door. "Stephanie! Are you up? We're just putting breakfast on the table. Come. Join us."

"Are you sure?" Stephanie asked.

"Absolutely. Come on down. We've made plenty and we'll make another round when the rest of the family wakes up. Do you usually get up this early?"

Stephanie was halfway down the hall and she nodded. "Yeah. I like to get up early and have time to myself before Kayla starts moving."

"We'll let you do whatever you want," Henry said. He went back to the cupboard and took down another plate. "Coffee's in the pot and we have juice."

Han yipped and Polly turned. "Whoops. Sorry, boys. I'm on it."

# CHAPTER SEVENTEEN

"Can I please have a nap?" Polly muttered to herself while sitting in a booth at Sweet Beans. Her head in her hands, she tried to muster enough energy to drink her coffee or take a bite of the chocolate-chocolate chip muffin in front of her. People weren't meant to wake up at four-thirty in the morning, unless it was for a quick trip to the bathroom and then back to sleep. She had enough trouble waking up at six-thirty.

After Heath and Hayden left, Stephanie needed to talk. The girl hadn't slept well the night before since she was so worried about their apartment. With good reason, too, Polly discovered after listening to people talking in the coffee shop. She knew better than to believe rumors, but it sounded like bad news. The side of the apartment building that had been burned would need structural work to ensure that it was safe to live in. That wouldn't happen overnight. There was a great deal of chatter about who the arsonist might be, but so far, no one had a clue. The person was a ghost and the locations they'd chosen to burn had nothing in common. Polly couldn't make sense out of any of the craziness that was happening in Bellingwood right now. Not surprising.

She couldn't even make sense of which way was up. Sleep. She needed more sleep.

The boys were gone by five-thirty and back at five thirty-five. Heath had forgotten his charging cord. Polly didn't know when they'd call. She was trying her best not to think about them making this trip by themselves. They were big, strong, intelligent boys. But she wanted to know exactly where they were and that they were safe. Right now.

She jumped when the phone buzzed beside the plate with a text.

*"In Sioux Falls. Stopping for gas."* That came from Heath. He was such a good boy.

*"Going to do anything fun there?"* she asked back.

*"We've stopped at every historical marker on the way,"* he sent back. *"My brother is a big, dumb nerd."*

Polly giggled.

*"Going to the Corn Palace next,"* he wrote. *"You'll get pictures, I'm sure. Great Scott, what have I gotten myself into?"*

*"You love it and you know it,"* she texted. *"I can't wait for pictures. Glad you're safe. You are safe, right? You haven't hurt each other?"*

*"Not until we get to a high place where I can push him over the edge,"* Heath sent.

*"Have fun."*

"Great Scott?" Polly asked out loud. "I don't even know who he is." She put the phone back down and unwrapped the muffin, then set it back on her plate. There wasn't anything exceptionally difficult that she needed to do today, but she did need to wake up.

After the kids left for school, Polly could have gone back upstairs and taken a nap, but at that point, she wasn't tired. The boys were excited about pancakes, eggs and bacon for breakfast, a treat usually reserved for weekends. Rebecca tried to tell them that it was because Kayla had spent the night with them, but when they realized that Heath and Hayden were gone, they knew better.

Then the little boys had decided they were sad about their older brothers being gone for a week. They moped around the kitchen and took their time getting ready for school until Polly had to snap at them.

Kayla asked Polly for a large tote bag. When Polly asked why, Rebecca laughed. Kayla wanted the bag in order to begin emptying Rebecca's locker. With only a few school days left, Kayla thought it would require a load every one of those days to clean the dump out. She was excited about the chance to stay with Rebecca for as long as necessary, knowing that she would be able to attack the mess that grew on a daily basis in that room. Polly was all for that and at some very base level, wondered if she could hire Kayla to help her clean the rest of the house after the excitement of graduation was over next week.

Polly was thankful for that big, empty foyer. It was a perfect place to host a party. No one had to use any other room in the house, except maybe the bathrooms. She intended to shut as many doors as possible in the house and threaten to beat anyone who attempted to open a one of them.

"Hey, can you hold him while I get my coffee?"

Pulling her head up out of her hands, Polly was surprised to see Sal and Alexander standing at the end of her table.

"Sure," Polly said, sitting up straight. She moved her coffee and muffin further in on the table and reached up to take Alexander in her arms. It was so hard to believe he was nearly a year old. Alexander was a happy little boy.

"And who wouldn't be," Polly said to him. "You have a gorgeous, brilliant mother and a hot, rugged father. Son, you hit the jackpot."

He batted his long, black eyelashes at her when he smiled.

"Oh yeah," she said. "That's the look. You're going to knock them all dead. Boom." Polly splayed out her fingers and blew air out through the word. Then she said it again with the same actions. "Boom. They'll all fall down. One by one. Boom."

With each 'boom,' Alexander giggled at her.

"You're a little old to be flirting with my son," Sal said. She pushed a high chair to the end of the booth and reached for Alexander.

Polly let Sal take him, but put her hand on the chair. "He can sit beside me, can't he?"

"Of course," Sal said, making sure Alexander was safely strapped in. She reached into the very expensive baby bag that had taken a beating these last eleven months and pulled out a round rattle, Alexander's stuffed horse, and a soft book. "He's been good so far, but you never know." She pushed the toys toward Polly. "How was Stephanie this morning?"

"She's okay. I don't think she realizes that it's going to be a long time before they're allowed to move back in for good. I just hope they can get in and retrieve their things."

"Where will they stay?"

"I don't know," Polly said. "We offered to let them stay with us. Kayla and Rebecca would love it, but I think Stephanie is much more private than that."

Sal gestured with her head toward the front counter where Skylar was taking drink orders from a group of older women. "She could live with her boyfriend."

Polly chuckled. "If she wants to, I'm fine with that, but that doesn't sound like Stephanie."

"What's up with these damned fires?" Sal asked. "Mark was telling me that the farmers are really worried. They're afraid that no matter what measures they take to protect their things, they'll miss something and the next thing they know, it will be burned to the ground. He won't allow me to let the dogs outside in the back yard on their own either. One of us has to be with them. And we put the cars in the garage every night. He checks it before we go to bed, too. Everyone on our street is leaving all the outside lights on. This is crazy. The town is being terrorized."

"So far, the arsonist hasn't hurt anyone," Polly said. "At least there's that."

"But he's scaring people to death. That isn't very nice."

Alexander reached for the stuffed horse that Polly was holding and she handed it to him. "What are you two doing out today?"

"We have an appointment with Debbie Larson."

Polly creased her forehead. "Who?"

"Debbie Larson. The photographer? I know we're a few weeks early, but I want to get his one year photographs done so I can send them out to the family."

"You're always so together about this stuff," Polly said. "If the school didn't take pictures, I wouldn't have any formal shots of the kids."

"You really should change that this summer." Sal dug around in her bag and pulled out a business card. "Do some formal family shots, even if you do them in your back yard. That gazebo would be perfect. Think what you're missing out on. Heath just graduated from high school and you don't know how long Hayden will be around before he's married to some chick and starting his own family. You should do this every year at least."

"Yeah. I'll need someone to remind me," Polly said.

"Talk to Debbie about that. She's really organized. I'll bet she'd put a reminder in her calendar to drop you a note next year. Do it. Call her."

Polly took a picture of the business card and pushed it back across the table. "I am never going to remember to do all of the things that I'm supposed to do as a mom. How do you know about this stuff?"

Sal chuckled. "Social media is my friend. I watch all of my classmates with their perfect little families and then I pick and choose which fantastic thing I should do to make my family look good."

"You're kidding me, right?"

"Kinda. But I do pay attention to what they're doing with their kids. Some of the things are flat out ridiculous, but photos like this are a good idea. I take pictures all the time and he's changed so much since he was born, but a formal shoot would be nice to have. Give one to Mark so he can …"

Polly interrupted. "Put a framed picture on the dashboard of his truck?"

"Exactly," Sal said. "Have you heard anything from Joss yet?"

"Not yet. I hate to bother her. I figure they're living in the midst of chaos."

"We should take food over."

Polly burst out with a short laugh. "You? Take food?"

"I'd have Pizzazz deliver. But you gotta imagine she doesn't want to take time to cook this week."

"Her mother's there, though," Polly said.

"Girlfriend, you do so much for everyone in the world, with no thought other than they need it. Why are you arguing with me about taking food over?"

"Because I need more coffee. I'm sorry. I'm an idiot. I know Sophie and Cooper like macaroni and cheese. In fact, they love it. I could make up a pot of that and then take something nice for the adults. I should do that today."

"Okay, you've got today. I'll call her and find out what kind of pizza they all like and have that delivered tomorrow night. Maybe we should do a grocery run for them."

"Joss uses the on-line service. All they have to do is drive down to Boone and pick it up."

"Then I can pick it up for her. We should have talked about this last night. We've been taking care of Sandy for months now and it hasn't killed any of us." Sal grinned across the table. "You're a loser-friend, aren't you?"

"Leave me alone. I'm feak and weeble today." Polly picked up the coffee cup in front of her and realized that somehow it had become empty. She glanced at Alexander, who had fallen asleep beside her. "I want to crawl in with him. He looks so cozy."

"When I get home this afternoon, I'm emailing all of us from the Sunday night group about feeding Joss and her family this week. We can at least do that, can't we?"

"I'll cook for tonight. You've got tomorrow night. The others would each take a day, I'm sure," Polly said.

"It's a sad state of affairs when I have to take over the Polly duties of the world. You go home and take a nap so you can get your mojo back. This is embarrassing."

Polly nodded. "I should go next door and check on Sonya Biederman. I think she's having open heart surgery this morning. Maybe Jen will have heard something."

"There. That's better," Sal said. "That's the Polly I know and love. But have Skylar fill up your cup again. I think you need another jolt."

~~~

After Sal left, Polly ordered another coffee to go. She felt a bit aimless this morning and cursed herself for not remembering to bring the gift items from Joey to put in the bank's safe deposit box. That would have been a good thing to take care of today.

She drove slowly down the main street through town. She'd heard rumors that a local girl was coming home to open a bridal shop. Sure, girls got married in Bellingwood, but it was a bit surprising that someone thought this would be successful. She wondered which space the new shop would take over. The storefronts were slowly filling in. There were fewer empty shops than there had been when she moved to town. Bellingwood really was growing. Polly turned north at the end of the street and drove a couple of blocks, then found herself turning to go toward Bill and Marie's house. She wondered if Hayden had said anything to Marie about his relationship with Tess. Those two were close friends and she gave him great advice when he didn't have the courage to talk to Polly or Henry. Marie was one of those people who could draw the deepest, darkest secrets out of anyone. When she pulled into the parking lot in front of the cabinet shop, Polly saw a flash of something in the back yard. Opening her door, she heard Molly's squeals of joy. She'd almost bet that Marie had filled the little pool for Molly.

Polly got out of her truck and walked past the bin where they dumped scrap from the shop. Bill had a couple of friends who stopped by on a regular basis to gather what was available to give away as kindling next to their firewood stands. As soon as the shop created it, the stuff was used. She liked that they did that.

Just as she was about to turn toward the back yard, Polly stopped. Something was strange about the kindling box. She backed up and went back to it. It didn't smell odd and it seemed to be fine. Then she realized that it wasn't in its usual spot. She wouldn't have noticed, but it had been moved more than three feet closer to the front door, leaving a bare spot in its place. The box was only about half full, making it easy for Polly to move it. When she gave it a shove, a milk jug filled with reddish fluid tipped over.

"What in the hell?" Polly asked. She didn't touch anything and opened the front door of the shop. Thankfully, the building was quiet. It was mostly empty except for Doug Shaffer, who was turning something on the lathe.

He looked up at her, finished what he was doing and turned the machine off. "Hi, Polly."

"Hi, Doug. Is anyone around?"

He shook his head. "They all went to lunch. I brought mine today because I wanted to work on some pieces here. My wife's birthday is coming up."

She smiled at him. "Could you come here a minute?"

Doug nodded and walked toward her, then outside when she opened the door.

"Is this familiar to you?" Polly asked.

"What's the box doing this close to the door?" he asked, reaching out to push it away.

Polly stopped him and pointed at the milk jug. "Does this belong to anyone?"

"No. That's weird."

"Okay, so I'm not just misinterpreting something,"

He tilted his head when he looked at her. "Misinterpreting what?"

"Would you mind staying here while I go find Bill? Don't go back inside. Just keep an eye on this and don't touch anything."

"What's going on?" he asked.

"I'll tell you in a minute. I just need to speak with Bill."

Polly knew that she'd find Bill and Marie in the back yard with Jessie and Molly. Laughter and squeals greeted her as she turned the corner. Bill, Marie, and Jessie were seated around the pool, plates with sandwiches on tables beside them.

"Polly!" Marie jumped up. "Are you here for lunch?"

"Bill, do you have a minute? I need to ask you a question."

He pushed himself up from the chair. "What's going on, Polly? Is everything okay?"

"Yeah." She leaned around him to look at Marie. "I don't mean to be cryptic. Everything's fine. I just need Bill to look at something for me."

Marie nodded. "It's good to see you, dear. I heard from the boys. It sounds like they're ready for a fun trip. It's so nice of you to send them off on their own. It's good for them too. Before they go their separate ways, they need to make memories together."

"That's what I thought. I'm glad they were up for it," Polly said.

Bill took her elbow as they walked out of the back yard. "What's going on?" When they got to the driveway, he looked at her and then at Doug Shaffer standing beside the doorway. "Are you sure everything is okay?"

"I don't know," she said and pointed at the kindling box. "That's been moved closer to the door. Did you or someone else do that?"

"Humph," he said. "You're right. I didn't even notice that. No, there's no way we would have moved it closer. I keep trying to push it around the side, but the boys say it's in a good place right where it is. Nobody would move it by the door. That isn't a pleasant customer experience, now, is it?"

"No." Polly took him around the side and pointed at the milk jug. "Yours?"

"Hell no," he said. "What's going on here? What have you found?" It didn't take him long to assemble the information and make sense of what she was asking. "You think we were the next target, don't you?"

"We should call Chief Wallers," Polly said. She wasn't sure how to voice the thoughts in her head. The cabinet shop might be the next target, or it might only be *another* target. How many more of these setups might be out there? If the arsonist planted containers of fuel in the darkness of the night when no one was awake, they could flit in and out of a location without being noticed. All they'd have to do is splash the fuel onto whatever they wanted to burn, light it up and vanish.

Bill reached into the front pocket of his work pants and took out his phone. "I'll call the Chief. I want this out of here." He frowned. "Why would someone want to burn my place? I haven't done nobody wrong." He swiped the call open and while he waited for it to connect, he dropped it to his side. "Polly Giller, did you just save my business from going up in smoke?"

She smiled.

Bringing the phone back up to his ear, he waited and nodded, then said, "Miss Mindy, how are you? This is Bill Sturtz." She must have said something, because he smiled and nodded again. "There never seems to be enough time to do it all. Say, I need one of your boys to come over here. My smart daughter-in-law might have just found a clue to the town's arsonist and saved me having to call my insurance agent and deal with a very angry son." He listened again. "The big boss-man? I'll have Marie put coffee on. Thanks. Say hello to that Marine of yours when you talk to him the next time and tell him thanks for his service. We're proud of him."

He ended the call. "The Chief is on his way."

Doug Shaffer had been watching their interaction. "Do you need me to stay out here?" he asked.

"Go ahead, son. I know you want to finish that bowl. You're doin' nice work." Bill opened the door into the shop and held it while Doug passed through, then closed it again. "Poor kid can't afford a birthday present for his wife. I wish I could do more for him, but he's got his pride."

"That's hard for people to overcome sometimes," Polly said. "But you wouldn't know what that's about, would you?"

"You're awfully snippy in your old age — pushing on your father-in-law like that. If you weren't so spot on, I'd sic my pretty wife on you. But she'd as soon take me out." He pointed at the milk jug. "Who would do this to me? I want to know."

"It feels like it's not about you," Polly said. "These fires don't have any rhyme or reason. They're all over the place — different containers, different locations. Maybe Ken has found a pattern, but I sure don't see it."

The police chief's car came into the lot and he got out, looked around and walked over to them. Putting his hand out first to Bill and then to Polly, he stepped back to look at the kindling box with his hands on his hips. "What is this about?"

"That's why we invited you to join us," Bill said. "Thought maybe you'd want to get involved before it all went up in flames."

Ken walked around the box twice and stopped beside them again. "Who touched it?"

"I did," Polly said. "I couldn't figure out why it had been moved so close to the front door. When I pushed it, the milk jug behind it tipped over. You said the arsonist was using red diesel. That's what it is, right? I just left things as they were and went to go get Bill."

"Anyone else here?"

"Our boy, Doug Shaffer," Bill said.

"I asked him to keep an eye on it while I was talking to Bill and Marie, Polly said. "I was a little worried the arsonist might be back to light things up and didn't want that to happen once we found it."

"This is the first break we've had," Ken said. "Nice catch, Polly."

"What if this isn't the only fuel that's been planted?" she asked. "What if the arsonist plants these things in the middle of the night and then comes back to them later? All the person would need to carry was some way to light it."

Ken nodded while staring at the kindling box. "It makes sense. How do we tell people to look for this, though?" He shrugged. "If they haven't moved their flammable items inside locked buildings, they're not going to keep an eye out for this." He looked straight at Bill.

"You got me there," Bill said. "The box has always just been here. It never occurred to me that it was a potential arsonist's target."

"That's what I mean. People look past things that are familiar to them — part of their everyday existence." Ken walked to the side of the building and when he came back around, he was on the phone. He paced while talking, then ended the call, put his phone in his pocket and came back over. "We're going to have a few people show up here to take this off your hands. You okay with losing the kindling box?"

Bill grinned. "I know how to build another one."

"Good," Ken said with a laugh. "We're gonna tie up your parking lot. That okay?"

"Just point my people to the side door," Bill said. "This is all yours. No worries. I should let Marie know that it will be busy out here."

Polly put her hand out. "I'll talk to her. You direct traffic."

Bill grabbed her and pulled her into a tight hug. "I can't thank you enough for being observant today. Saved my keister. I'm telling that boy of mine to take you somewhere nice."

"He already did," Polly said. She reached up and gave Bill a quick kiss on the cheek. "I'm thankful I found it, too."

# CHAPTER EIGHTEEN

"Are things okay out there?" Marie asked, meeting Polly as she rounded the corner into the Sturtz's back yard. "Is anyone in trouble?"

Jessie was playing with Molly as the little girl sat in the pool, but kept an eye on Polly and Marie.

"No one's in trouble. I found a container of diesel fuel behind the kindling box and the box had been shoved closer to the front door."

Both women took a split second to register what Polly said. Jessie wrapped a towel around Molly and picked her up, placing the startled child into her lap.

"Mommy, no," Molly said, lunging back toward the pool.

"Molly," Jessie scolded. "You know better than that. Behave."

"But I want to play in the pool."

"I have to go back to work and Marie is going inside," Jessie said. "And you're going to be a good girl."

"No I'm not." Molly started to wail and Jessie stood up.

"I'll take her inside," Jessie said as she walked past Polly and Marie.

"Her book is in the playpen. Pillows are already there," Marie said. She led Polly to the chairs in the back yard. "Our little Molly has a strong will. It's a good thing Jessie's is stronger. I never imagined it would be, but I'm proud of her."

Polly smiled. "You've been such a good role model. Better than anything she ever had."

Marie leaned forward. "I hate to speak ill of people, but that mother of hers makes me so angry. Jessie is a sweet, wonderful girl who wants to be successful in everything she does. She knows what's wrong and what's right. All I had to do was nudge her the right way. Why that woman is so selfish, I'll never understand, but I've certainly been given a gift because of it. Now, tell me what happened out front."

"I noticed that there was something off about the kindling box," Polly said. "When I realized that it had been moved, I pushed it away from the building, thinking I'd just shove it back to where it belonged. That's when I found the fuel."

Marie rubbed her face with both palms. "Why us?"

"I don't know," Polly said. "It's hard to believe you were targeted for any reason other than that the arsonist saw an opportunity with that kindling box."

"Bill should have taken it inside."

"He says he didn't even see it."

Marie nodded. "I wonder how many more things like that go unnoticed."

"... until someone wants a target for a fire." Polly finished the thought.

"When I think of the damage — if it had gotten too far out of control, our house would have been in trouble." Marie wrapped her arms around her torso. "I can't even think about that."

"Luckily, it's been found and the police are here. Chief Wallers is hopeful they'll be able to find something since the evidence wasn't burned in a fire."

"That's good news, at least. My goodness, I'm glad you stopped by." Marie unwrapped her arms and sat forward. "Why *did* you come over?"

"I had a long conversation with Hayden this morning and wondered if he'd talked to you much about Tess."

"That silly girl doesn't know what she's losing by being so self-involved," Marie said.

Polly nodded. "I never would have thought that about her, though. I really like her."

"So do I. Hayden and I had lunch with her several times this semester. She's a perfectly nice girl." Marie grinned. "Maybe each us has a Mr. Hyde in our psyches about something. Until it presents itself, we don't even realize the urges are there."

"I hope not," Polly said. "I don't want to think about what mine might be."

"Most women turn into beasts when their children are threatened," Marie said. "But I've been proud of the way you handle yourself when things happen to yours — especially that last time Rebecca was kidnapped."

Polly shook her head. "Whose daughter is kidnapped by two separate psychos? That poor girl is going to want to escape Bellingwood just to get away from the crazies that I encounter."

"I rather think she enjoys the attention," Marie commented. "But not so much that she carries it forward. Does she ever talk about any of those experiences?"

"She's spoken of them to me several times," Polly said. "More about why they happened than fear of it happening again. She expressed a desire to understand why people need to hurt other people. We've talked about control and power. She's just trying to make sense of it."

"The girl is sensible. That's going to be good for you as she grows up. She's quite the independent thinker. Have you had any more problems with her?"

Polly sat back and relaxed. Marie was an amazing woman. Polly could tell her everything and never be concerned that it would go any further. She also knew there was never any judgment when it came to decisions that she made. If Marie disagreed, she voiced her disagreement, but in a manner that assured Polly there was no reason not to have different opinions.

"She's been too busy with things to get into much trouble." Polly chuckled. "That's disappointing because I haven't been able to assign the nasty tasks to her for punishment lately."

"Maybe summer will bring new challenges," Marie said. "When she begins to fret over attending a big new school, that stress will likely create a fresh, new monster."

Polly looked up at Marie and laughed. "You know my girl so well."

"I had one of my own," she replied. "Lonnie wasn't always the sweet young lady that she is today. Her junior high and high school years were a challenge. Not that she wasn't sweet, but that girl and I had some fights that raised the roof." Marie looked off in the distance with a smile. "Sometimes I miss those fights. They always cleared the air in a hurry. We got mad, we fought, and then we were done."

"I don't see you fighting with people, especially your daughter."

"There were some doozies. I never fought with Henry like that. He much preferred to think through a problem and talk about it. When he got angry, it wasn't readily apparent. He'd respond and all of a sudden you knew that you'd pushed him too far."

Polly thought back to the night that Henry had walked out of the back door with Rebecca's phone battery in his pocket. His tone never changed, he didn't fly off the handle, he just did what was necessary. Noah, who had been standing right beside Henry, never knew that there was a problem.

"You two don't have fights, do you?" Marie asked. She giggled and put her hand over her mouth. "That wasn't fair. I should let you have your privacy about that."

"We really don't." Polly thought about it. "I try to fight with him sometimes, but he doesn't let me get too far. It's frustrating, though. I never get to raise my voice."

"That's why I miss Lonnie," Marie said. "Sometimes we just need to let it all out."

"Do you think this thing with Hayden and Tess will fix itself or are they finished?"

Marie took a breath. "I believe he's finished. He might not realize it yet and he's going to need to talk about it a few more times before he can accept the truth of it, but she's not the right girl for him. He needs an adventurer — someone who will challenge him to dream big dreams and think big thoughts."

"That's what I want for him, too," Polly said. "A girl who is self-confident enough to live her life without him, but loving enough to want them to bring their lives together."

"That's what I wanted for Henry, you know." Marie leaned across the table and patted Polly's arm. "I didn't want to push him into a marriage with just anybody so he could produce grandbabies. I can fill my own life with children. That's not his responsibility — or Lonnie's. When he first told me about you, I wondered if you weren't the one. And now, look at him. He's doing more than I ever could have hoped. It's a lot of fun, too."

"I worry about Bill and his heart problems."

Marie gave her a little smirk. "You know what I'm going to say, don't you?"

Polly nodded. "That it's not mine to worry about. Bill sees his doctor and you make sure he takes care of himself."

"That's right. You have enough to worry about. I've been thinking ..." Marie let the sentence trail off.

"About what?"

"I would love to have Noah and Elijah spend time with us this summer. If you allowed Rebecca to stay with her friend, Kayla, or even here with us, you and Henry could sneak away for a few days, maybe even a week. Would you do that?"

"I don't know," Polly said. "Henry's so busy with work. He has jobs ramping up one after another. I hate to take him away from that. He'd just stress the entire time we were gone."

"It was just a thought. Maybe you might consider taking a long weekend. Iowa is filled with wonderful adventures."

"If we do that, we should take the kids with us. They'd love a short vacation, too."

Marie sucked in a breath. "I'm going to have to scold you. Do I need to say the words?"

"You mean that Henry and I need to have time together in order to be good parents for the rest of them?"

"Yes ... and ...?"

"And ..." Polly tried to understand where Marie was leading her.

"And you can take two long weekends this summer. Once with just Henry and then take the kids somewhere fun. Family vacations are important. If I need to speak to my son about not making you feel guilty for dragging him off on an adventure, I will, you know."

Polly nodded. "I'll talk to him, I promise. Long weekends are doable."

"Good girl. Now I should go inside and make sure that Molly lets her mother go back to work." Marie winked. "I wouldn't be at all surprised to find Jessie sound asleep in the recliner with Molly lying on her chest. She's been studying late into the night to finish up this semester. With all the excitement out at the shop, I just might let her stay that way."

~~~

It took no small amount of twisting and turning, along with waving and directions from various policemen for Polly to weave her way out of the parking lot in front of the shop, but she finally broke free.

She laughed to herself when she turned the corner. She'd not eaten lunch. Marie would have offered her a sandwich, but when everything turned upside down, it never happened. There would be a point later this afternoon when it finally hit Marie and the poor woman would be scandalized. The evil side of Polly laughed at the thought.

She turned into the driveway of Sycamore House and saw the rental van parked outside, its doors wide open. Rachel and Lyndi came out carrying totes, and placed them carefully inside. Rachel gave Polly a quick wave as she went back in. Polly parked far enough out of their way and then headed for the building, stopping to hold a door open as the girls passed through. "Can I help carry anything?" Polly asked.

"This is it," Rachel said, breathing hard. "We're running a little behind, but we should be fine."

"Where are you going?" Polly realized that the poor girl was desperately trying to get into the van, so she put her hand up. "Never mind. Have a good trip." Rachel got in the driver's side of the van and backed up, then turned to head out.

"Whoosh," Polly said. She closed the garage door and pulled the inside door shut. When she got to the kitchen, she laughed out loud. The place was a disaster. They *were* in a hurry. Rachel never left things this way. Then she saw a purse on the counter. A quick check showed that it was Rachel's.

Polly ran into the office. "Where is Rachel's catering event?" she asked, holding up the purse. "I should chase her down."

"It's just out at Secret Woods," Kristen said. "Do you want me to run that over to her?"

"I can do it," Polly replied.

"If you want." Kristen looked up. "But if I went, I could stop and get something to drink and maybe a candy bar, too."

Polly laughed and handed over the purse. "Sure."

"Do you want me to bring anything back for you?"

When Polly shook her head, Kristen knocked on Jeff's door and asked the same question, then poked her head in Stephanie's office. Polly watched Stephanie take in a long breath and then shake her head.

"I guess it's just me," Kristen said. "I'll be back in a few." With a quick wave, she ran out of the office.

"Got a minute?" Polly asked Stephanie.

"Sure. I'm having trouble focusing anyway. I can't believe that damned arsonist practically has me evicted from my home. And this place is full until after Christmas, so there's no room available. I don't want to tie up a hotel room. I know you gave people a free night there, but you can't do that forever. I just don't know what I'm going to do."

"It's for real that you can't move back in?"

"We can go in with a moving team to get everything out, but we won't be able to live there for at least a month — maybe more. Why did this happen to me?"

"You'll stay with us," Polly said. "We have plenty of room."

"No you don't, and what will I do with my stuff?"

"When do you have to move out?"

"They said they wanted people in and out next week." Stephanie looked up. "There's smoke and water damage in my living room. What am I going to do?"

Jeff came around the corner. "You could move in with me."

"Yeah — no. I'm not moving Kayla to Ames for the summer and your apartment isn't big enough for three of us."

"You'll stay with us," Polly said again. "I've been thinking about it. You can move into Hayden and Heath's room this week while they're out of town. The weekend might be messed up, but after the graduation party on Saturday, we'll empty the library back into the foyer. Kayla can stay upstairs with Rebecca until one of us decides that's a really bad idea because they are driving each other crazy. Then she can move downstairs into the office after we've cleared that room into the foyer. Your beds, dressers … everything can just be moved into those rooms. As for your living room furniture, we can send that somewhere to be cleaned …"

Stephanie put her hand up. "It's all thrift store stuff. If it needs to be put in a dumpster, I don't mind starting over."

"Okay, then we'll not worry about whatever you don't want to worry about. We'll pack your kitchen items up and label the boxes. They can be stored in the foyer with everything else until you move out. We can do this, Stephanie."

"I go back and forth between being totally freaked out and furious," Stephanie said. "How dare this person disrupt the lives of so many? And then I wonder how sad and pathetic this person must be to have to do something like this to get attention — especially negative attention."

Polly nodded. People were so broken and the world around them often suffered for it. That was one of the reasons she reached out where she could. "Will you consider moving in?"

"I don't have very many choices," Stephanie said. She looked up, surprised at her own words. "That came out wrong. You're being so generous. I just feel as if I've been backed into a corner. If I had millions of dollars, I'd buy a new house and move in there, never thinking about how to pay for everything we'll have to face over the next few months. But instead, I'm relying on you to take care of me again."

Jeff sat down in the chair beside Polly. "That's the worst of it, isn't it? You've been independent long enough that you don't like the idea of relying on us."

"Well, I don't," Stephanie said. "I didn't work this hard to have everything taken away from me."

"Nobody's taking anything away," he replied. "Stop that. You're feeling sorry for yourself. This is a blip in the continuum." He glanced at Polly. "Like my sci-fi word there? I've been practicing."

She shook her head and laughed.

"Anyway," he continued. "Next year at this time, what you'll remember most are the memories you and Kayla got to make while living with Polly and her crazy family. It's not going to be forever. You aren't dying. You aren't even hurt. You've been displaced, but only for a short time."

Stephanie lifted her upper lip on one side. "You aren't being very nice to me."

"But am I wrong?" He turned to grin at Polly. "I think she deserves this after the way she yelled at me last week."

Polly chuckled.

Jeff repeated himself. "Am I wrong?"

"No." She closed her eyes, then opened them. "I'm being a pouty little girl. Just because things aren't going my way for the short term, I lost track of what's important. I'm sorry, Polly. You are so generous and I made it unimportant." Stephanie lifted her upper lip again when she looked at Jeff. "I should apologize to you, too. I've been kind of growly around here this morning."

He nodded.

"You aren't going to yell at me about that?"

"You are allowed some measure of insanity after a fire in your complex. Will they let us in later so that we can get your clothes and other necessary things?"

Stephanie flipped up a notepad. "I have a phone number to call if no one is there when I arrive. But they'll be on site until four."

"Then we'll go over before then," Jeff said. "Do you have suitcases to carry everything you need?"

Stephanie shook her head. "Not enough."

"Then we'll take garbage bags and boxes." He turned to Polly. "Once we get things outside, maybe the kids could help. I think it would be a terrific job for Rebecca, Kayla, and Andrew, don't you? They'll be free, right?"

Polly nodded. He was right. This was a fantastic idea for those three. Then she took her phone out. "Just a sec. Let me check. I haven't been very mindful of Rebecca's schedule. It always surprises me when she isn't at home." She swiped into her calendar and didn't see anything there. In fact, there wasn't even a practice or game for the boys, either. "We can all help."

"No, not the little ones, too," Stephanie said. "I don't know what's safe and what isn't. I'd hate for them to get into anything. And five of us will be more than enough to grab what we need on this trip."

"Then next week when Hayden and Heath are in town, we'll move your furniture and kitchen out."

"I can't believe you're doing this for me. I don't deserve it."

Jeff stood up. "When will you ever understand that generosity isn't about what's deserved. It's a gift. Silly girl." He turned and winked at her before leaving the office.

"He's pretty hard on you sometimes," Polly said.

"I gave him permission. That's one of the things my counselor and I talk about — that I don't have someone in my life who holds me accountable. Your kids have you and you have Henry. Kayla has me, but I don't have anyone like that except Jeff. He doesn't usually call me out in front of people, though." Stephanie gave a weak laugh. "I guess you're family. He would never have said that to me in front of anyone else."

"Good," Polly said. "I was going to go in and kick his butt when I left here."

Stephanie sat forward. "Now that my stress is drifting away, I'm hungry. I wonder what Rachel has in the kitchen."

"I'll let you get to it," Polly said. "What time do you want the kids to be at the apartment?"

"Jeff and I will go over at three thirty. I can try to catch them at school."

"I never do this, but I'll text Rebecca to call me before she leaves the school building today. Maybe I can send them your way."

"Don't they have to walk Noah and Elijah home?"

"The boys can make it on their own. I'll make sure she knows to tell them that, too."

Polly stood as Stephanie walked past her and followed her out into the main office.

Stephanie turned and drew Polly into a hug. "You seem to keep saving my life. How will I ever repay you?"

"What would he say about that?" Polly asked, gesturing with her head toward Jeff's office.

"That repayment isn't what it's about. Kindness is its own reward." Stephanie sighed. "I need to start taking care of other people."

"That would be an incredible gift to me," Polly said.

# CHAPTER NINETEEN

Reaching for her phone, Polly stretched across the bed. It was finally Friday. She was ready for this week to be finished and hated to admit how much she missed having Heath and Hayden around. They diverted the younger boys in the evenings more than anyone realized. It had been Polly's job to read to them every night this week, and while she loved spending time with Noah and Elijah, the boys missed Hayden and Heath.

Today would be busy. This afternoon, the tables and chairs that she'd rented for tomorrow's graduation party would arrive. Rebecca and Kayla could hardly wait to start decorating. They'd dragged her to Boone to pick up streamers and table toppers, plastic plates, silverware and cups. They needed the older boys to hang graduation garland, but that could happen tomorrow.

School was out early today. Polly was certain her kids were going to make their teachers crazy all day long. The last few days it had taken a concerted effort on her part to ensure they maintained some sense of control while they were still in school. Polly could not imagine how difficult those teachers had it. Kids were ready to be done. Polly was ready for them to be done, too.

Mornings could move a little slower, bedtimes didn't have to be so rigid and schedules would ease.

Her bedroom door opened enough to get her attention and Obiwan pushed his way in, then jumped up on the bed.

"I should get up, shouldn't I?" Polly whispered into his coat. "I can sleep in on Monday."

But she knew better. Hayden and Heath were ready to tear into the other upstairs bedrooms. The sooner they finished pulling them apart, the sooner they could put them back together and move in. On Monday, they'd all head over with trucks to help Stephanie and Kayla move their things out of the apartment building. The complex had offered to put things in a storage unit for tenants who had to leave while reconstruction was being done, but for now, the girls' items would just move to the Bell House.

Stephanie had been hiding. She'd had some online coursework to finish this week and her next class began on Monday, so there wasn't any downtime for her. After supper, she escaped to Heath and Hayden's room and no one but Kayla saw her until the next morning. She and Skylar had gone out on a date after the eighth-grade graduation party Wednesday at Sweet Beans.

That was a nice success. Teachers and parents all came in to celebrate. Skylar, Camille, Marta and Sylvie decorated the room with Bellingwood's school colors — blue and gold. Sylvie made cupcakes with little blue graduation caps on them and they'd whipped up a fun punch for the kids. Sylvie used the last of the mason jars from the hoe-down four years ago at Sycamore House. There were enough for all of the kids to take one home and Stephanie had found blue and gold umbrellas to put in the drinks. The kids felt like they'd had a fun celebration.

Polly refused to cry, though she watched every other parent fight tears. Even Sylvie walked around with red-rimmed eyes. At some point this weekend, Polly knew that it would hit her, but right now, she was still in control. Henry told her that was weird since she cried at everything else. He was right. It was weird. But her kids were happy and excited about moving on. She was going enjoy it with them.

The sound of two little boys racing past her door brought Polly straight up. The last day of school was not a day for her to let the kids be late. She walked over to the bedroom door, pushed it closed and changed into her jeans and t-shirt. Polly poked her head in the bathroom to check her hair and sighed. Rather than fight it, she picked a hair tie up from the top of the television and wound it around a ponytail. Anything else was too much work.

She walked down to Rebecca's room and knocked on the door. "You two awake in there?"

Kayla opened the door. "Yeah. It's the last day! Can you believe it?"

"I can't," Polly said with a smile. She looked around the room in shock. "Can you move in forever?"

Everything was neat and tidy. Chairs were empty of clothes, dresser drawers were pushed all the way in, clothing was hung neatly on hangers in the closet and she could see the top of Rebecca's desk.

Kayla giggled. "Rebecca thinks I'm crazy. She says that it will never stay this clean, so I shouldn't even bother, but it's fun."

"There are people like you who bring order to chaos," Polly said. "I don't understand you, but at least you exist. Where is Rebecca?"

"She's in the bathroom finishing getting dressed. Is this nice enough?"

"You look wonderful," Polly said, smiling at Kayla's pretty blue dress. "Absolutely perfect for today." The school had a short graduation ceremony for the eight-graders every year. No speeches. No big production, just an opportunity for them to acknowledge the completion of this phase of their education.

Polly went down the north stairway and walked through the foyer. The girls had worked late in here last night, making favors for the tables. Black construction paper and red and white ribbons were everywhere as they cut out graduation caps to top round chocolate candies, and little plastic cups filled with more candy to put around the room. They'd been on the phone with Hayden all week and he told them where to find old photographs of Heath so they could create a memory board. He also sent back pictures of him with his brother during the trip to South Dakota, which the girls took over to Sycamore House to be printed on the color printer. The pictures that Polly had taken over the last few years were dug out and subjected to review by the two girls for use on the board.

Rebecca had been working on a painting for Heath the last few months and they'd picked it up from the framer on their last trip to Boone. For his guest book, she'd purchased a plain white notebook and personalized it for him with drawings and copies of photographs. From the day Polly asked Rebecca to help plan this party for her brother, the girl had been putting ideas into action. Heath wasn't happy with all the attention. He just wanted to be done and move to the next stage of his life. Rebecca was having none of it.

Polly opened the door to the kitchen to the smell of something wonderful baking and the sight of Stephanie in an apron, standing beside the kitchen sink.

"I made breakfast," Stephanie said. "I didn't think you'd mind. Henry is already gone. But he started the coffee."

"I certainly don't mind," Polly replied. "Thank you. What are we having?"

"Since it's the kids' last day, I thought maybe I'd make something special and you had all the ingredients here."

"That's fantastic. Do I have to wait to find out?"

Stephanie nodded. "If that's okay."

Polly looked over at the two little boys sitting at the table with glasses of apple juice in front of them. "You two are being awfully quiet."

"She said we had to wait five more minutes," Elijah said. "And then she gave us this." He held out his hand and opened it to reveal a plastic spinning top. He gave it a twist and sent it across the table to his brother, who released his own back to Elijah.

"You are not a stupid woman," Polly said with a laugh.

"The girls had a bunch of those for the tables. I took two from the pile." Stephanie grinned. "Kayla probably has them all counted out and I'm going to catch heck for it, but the boys can have some fun at breakfast, right?"

"Right." Polly poured herself a cup of coffee, brought it up to her face and took in the wonderful scent. "Have you been upstairs to see what Kayla did to Rebecca's room? I'd forgotten there was that much space in there."

"It's clean!" Elijah yelled. He jumped down to the floor to pick up a toy that had flown off the table. "Maybe she could clean our room."

"Your room is in pretty good shape," Polly said.

"We'd mess it up so she can clean it."

"If you want Kayla to come play with you in your room, you don't have to mess it up, all you have to do is ask. When this party is over tomorrow, the girls will have more time to play with the two of you boys."

Elijah ran over to Stephanie and hugged her. "Are you going to stay forever?"

Stephanie looked at Polly, at a loss as to what to say. Polly shook her head and shrugged.

"Only until the apartment is ready for us to move back in," Stephanie said.

"You shouldn't go." Elijah let her go and ran to Polly. She bent down and hugged him. "Tell her that she should stay forever."

"Stephanie and Kayla are their own family," Polly said. "They need to live in their own house. She can stay here as long as she wants, but they'll want their own place back. Someday when you grow up, you're going to want to live in your own home, too."

"No I'm not," he declared. "I want to live with you until ..." He thought about what he was going to say next, screwed up his face. "I don't want to think about that. You have to live forever."

"I'll do my best, but only if you and Noah never move out."

"We won't," Noah said softly. "I want to live with you forever, too."

"Then it's settled," Polly said. She took Elijah's hand and walked back to the table with him. Putting her coffee down on the table, she reached over and grabbed Noah up into her arms. "I know you think you're too big for this, but sometimes I just have to squeeze you and love you. Is that okay?" She peppered his face with kisses.

Polly took a step forward so Noah could put his feet on his chair, and released him. "Is that okay?"

"It's okay," he said, climbing back down.

Rebecca and Kayla came into the room and Elijah jumped up again. "Wow," he said. "You dressed up."

"Is it okay?" Rebecca spun around, her blue skirt billowing out. She wore a colorful blouse that she'd gotten last summer in New Mexico with Beryl and a white lacy vest that she'd found at a thrift store when shopping with Stephanie and Kayla.

"It's pretty," he replied. He put his hand out to take Kayla's. "You're very pretty too."

Kayla blushed and did a quick turn.

"That looks really nice," Stephanie said. "I'm glad you're wearing it today."

"Thank you," Kayla said, still blushing.

The timer on the oven went off and Stephanie opened the door, then removed a sheet pan and put it on the stove top. "I found this breakfast ring recipe on-line and thought it would make a good celebration breakfast. There's nothing in it you won't like; it's just cream cheese, sausage, eggs, cheese, and some peppers."

"Wow, you're quite the artist," Polly said. "That's gorgeous."

~~~

Polly parked outside of the elementary school and did a quick check of her makeup. She picked up her camera and got out of the truck. She saw Sylvie walking in with Stephanie and ran to catch up with them.

"Are you going to cry again?" Polly asked Sylvie.

"Shut up," Sylvie replied. "I can't believe you aren't."

"Honestly, neither can I. We'll hope I can get through this today. So far, so good, though."

"You look nice," Stephanie said. "Is Henry coming?"

"He's up by Fort Dodge somewhere. I told him I would stream video to him."

A line of younger students stood by the door and three came up to them.

The first, a girl who had to be no more than ten years old, put her arm out to Polly. "I'm Merry Hindel. We're to escort parents in," she said.

Polly took the girl's arm. "Thank you, Merry."

Merry delivered her to the second row of seats and Polly slid in, followed by Stephanie and then Sylvie.

"That was kind of cute," Stephanie said under her breath.

"Guessing the high school graduation won't be quite this intimate," Polly replied.

Sylvie leaned forward. "Are you ready for tomorrow?"

Polly nodded. "Tables are coming in. I hope they aren't early. Hayden and Heath should be back around supper. The girls have been doing a great job decorating. Knowing Rebecca, they'll stay up all night tonight just to make sure it's ready to go tomorrow."

People filled in around them. Sylvie spoke to several people she knew and Polly smiled at parents of Rebecca's classmates she'd met the last few years. It was still so hard to believe that these kids had been together for so long and would continue as a unit until they graduated from high school.

Stephanie poked Polly and pointed off to the side where Noah was sitting with his class. He gave her a small wave when she acknowledged him. Noah's class was just a short distance from Elijah, and her gregarious little boy could barely contain himself when he saw Polly wave. He jumped up and waved both hands over his head. She hoped he never lost his enthusiasm for life. He was such a good kid.

Lights went down in the auditorium and the curtains drew back on the stage, revealing the class of eighth graders. They weren't wearing robes, but did have blue graduation caps with gold tassels.

The principal, Miss Bickel, stood and welcomed everyone, then turned the ceremony over to Jan Ambleman, one of Rebecca's favorite teachers. She taught English, and this year, was also their home room teacher. She thanked parents for their involvement throughout the students' formative years and commented on what a terrific group of young people these kids were. As leaders, they would be missed. She asked people to contain their applause until the end of the ceremony, when the class would be presented to the parents.

Before cuing the music, she made a comment about how the band couldn't perform today because so many of its leading members were on stage.

Polly tried not to be overly grateful for that. While the band did quite well, a very young group of musicians struggling through Pomp and Circumstance while forty-three kids proceeded across the stage would be tiresome.

And then it began. She quickly dialed Henry's phone and turned the video camera on. He could choose to watch or not — she had no idea what he might be in the middle of doing.

When they called Kayla Anderson's name, Stephanie gripped Polly's thigh. Turning to see Stephanie's reaction, Polly was not surprised to see tears trickle from the girl's eyes. Mrs. Ambleman progressed through the class, coming to Andrew's name. He pranced up to her, shook her hand, then turned and bowed to the class before bowing to the audience. Sylvie leaned forward to look at Polly. No tears in her eyes, she simply shook her head in disbelief.

One by one, more students were called forward and then Rebecca's name was called. Polly watched her daughter proudly walk across the stage, receive the certificate, then touch it to her heart as she looked up.

Polly's eyes burned with tears. Rebecca was comfortable talking about her mother, but so far, she hadn't mentioned much about what her mother was missing.

"We got her here," Polly said under her breath. "She did most of it by herself, but so far, so good, Sarah. You would be so proud of your daughter. I know I am. There is so much more to come, but this is big."

Rebecca gave a small nod in Polly's direction and Polly lifted her hand, then brought it back to her own heart. Time was passing too quickly. This child could *not* be finished with junior high today. This had to stop.

Polly whispered to Henry that she was closing down the video. He didn't care about the rest of the students on the stage. She quit paying attention and watched Rebecca. Her face alight with excitement, Rebecca looked out over the audience and said something quietly to one of the girls beside her. The two flipped their tassels to the other side of their mortarboards. Rebecca's knees were bouncing, a sure sign of her nervous energy. She was so ready to move on, to experience all that was coming at her.

When the last student returned to his seat, Mrs. Ambleman invited Miss Bickel back to the podium to declare that this class had graduated from Bellingwood Elementary and Junior High School and was fully prepared to advance to the next adventure in their lives. When she congratulated them, the audience rose to its feet in applause with screams, hoots and hollers echoing around the room. Mrs. Ambleman gestured for the class to stand and as if on signal, all of the mortarboards went into the air and the kids hugged each other before making their way off the stage. Lights came up and Polly and her friends waited for their kids to find them.

Noah and Elijah were the first to arrive. Elijah rushed into Polly's arms and she drew Noah in as well.

"Do you need to go back to your classrooms?" she asked.

Elijah nodded effusively. "I made you a present," he said. "I have to pick that up and make sure that there's nothing left in my desk. We cleaned our classroom this morning. Will you wait for me?"

"Of course I will."

He took off running and Polly looked down at Noah. "How about you?"

"Mrs. Wallers said I could come over to you now."

Polly looked around for Noah's teacher. They managed to make eye contact. She pointed down at her son and Mrs. Wallers nodded in assent. There couldn't be much left in anyone's desk. The letter that was sent home with them last week asked parents to ensure that backpacks came to school empty every morning because the children would be bringing all of their papers and projects home throughout the week. The stack of things in the boys' cubbies was large, but they'd take time to go through that this summer.

"Congratulations," Stephanie said as Kayla came up to hug her.

"I'm awfully proud of you," Polly said, hugging Rebecca.

Rebecca bent down to hug Noah. "Was that cool?" she asked.

"You made me ..." he looked at Polly for the word.

"Proud?" Polly asked.

Noah nodded. "I told my friend that you were my sister. He didn't care."

Rebecca grinned. "Can we go to Sweet Beans and celebrate?"

Polly checked her watch. She still had an hour before the rental company was supposed to arrive, but she didn't want to cut it too close. On the other hand, a trip to Sweet Beans was never a bad idea.

"The rental company will be here soon, but we can make a quick trip." Polly touched Kayla's arm. "You're coming with us?"

Kayla looked at her sister. "Do you have to go back to work?"

"Not yet," Stephanie said with a smile. "I can walk up to the coffee shop with you."

"Walk?" Kayla asked.

Stephanie nodded. "I walked here from Sycamore House. It's a beautiful day."

Kayla looked desperately at Polly, who just laughed.

"We can all walk to the coffee shop, then come back here and I'll drive us home."

"Okay," Kayla said with a sigh. She darted away to speak with her new friend, Korey, who seemed to be waiting for her.

"Yeah, that's going to be interesting," Stephanie said quietly to Polly.

"Do you like him?" Polly asked.

"He's a nice boy. I'm just not ready for her to be passionately in love with anyone right now."

Rebecca and Andrew were standing with Sylvie, who tapped her watch. "I need to get back to work. Are you all really coming up?"

Polly nodded. "I need to wait for Elijah, but we'll be there. You go on ahead."

Rebecca started to walk away with Sylvie and Andrew, then stopped and ran back. "Thanks for coming today and thanks for letting us have a little party. This is really cool of you."

"Remember that," Polly said with a wink. "Okay?"

# CHAPTER TWENTY

"You can stay here with your friends, but I need to leave," Polly whispered to Rebecca. "The boys and I are heading home now. Come with us or you can walk home later."

She tried not to chuckle. Rebecca and Andrew wouldn't like the walk back to the Bell House, but Kayla would mightily complain.

"You wouldn't come back to get us after the table guys are gone?" Rebecca asked.

Polly just looked at her.

"Well, it's kind of a big day for us. We should get to celebrate with our friends."

Polly swallowed. "Like I said, the boys and I are leaving now. If you want to stay, you can walk home whenever you like."

"Come on, please?"

Bending over, Polly hissed into Rebecca's ear. "Are you seriously whining after all you've gotten to do these last few weeks? No. I don't have time to come back and get you. I gave you reasonable choices and now you're trying to embarrass me in public? Bad idea."

She turned to Noah and Elijah, put her best fake smile on and said, "Come on, boys. We're heading home."

They picked up their glasses, glanced at Rebecca, then ran after Polly, who held the front door open for them. Elijah skipped ahead as they headed for the parking lot of the school.

"Are you mad at Rebecca?" Elijah asked, bouncing along — first facing forward and then turning around. He stopped and pointed back toward the coffee shop. "They're coming." Running back to Rebecca, Elijah yelled, "Everybody's going to be home tonight!"

Noah took Polly's hand. "When is Heath and Hayden coming home?"

"In a few hours," Polly said, not bothering to correct him. "Hopefully they'll be here in time for supper. What shall we make for them?"

She didn't even hear Elijah's response as she saw someone dart behind an empty building. Polly turned to Rebecca, Kayla and Andrew. "Did you see that?"

"The girl?" Andrew asked.

"Yeah. Do you know who it was?"

He shook his head. "I didn't see her well enough. That hoodie covered her face."

Polly stopped, having a very bad feeling. "You kids stay here. Do not follow me. Got it?" Pushing Noah back toward Rebecca, Polly took out her phone and followed the path the girl had taken. These empty storefronts at the end of the block had been allowed to deteriorate over the years. There was talk of finding businesses to move in, but they needed to be cleaned up first. A small alley, really only a wide walkway, between the last two storefronts was filled with trash and weeds. In the space of time it took Polly to come to the other end, a fire burned hot in a pile of trash along the wall, jumping to a patch of weeds and following the trail of fuel to a stack of pallets leaning against the building. She called Mindy.

"Bellingwood Police Department," Mindy said.

"Hey Mindy, it's Polly. I need a fire squad."

"Oh no, not again. How bad is it?"

"It's just started. I think I saw the arsonist." Polly gave Mindy the address while kicking the trash apart, trying to stop the flow of the fire. The smell of diesel fuel permeated everything as Polly stamped out what she could, but the fire moved faster than she did and soon she was forced to exit at the other end of the small alley. She looked up and down for the person she'd seen previously, but saw nothing.

Sirens screamed down the street. The fire department wasn't taking any chances. Polly stepped out of the way as the first young firefighter dashed into the alley to see what they were dealing with. He called over a hose and soon foam covered the fast-growing fire. Another truck arrived, along with Chief Wallers and two other police cars. Polly waited while the chief spoke to the firemen.

"Why am I not surprised to see you here?" he asked, coming over to her. "I figured you'd be celebrating Rebecca's last day."

"We were at the coffee shop. I saw a girl run through here and it seemed strange."

"You saw someone? A girl?" he asked. "Do you know who?"

Polly shook her head. "I don't. I asked the kids if they recognized her, but she was wearing a blue hoodie."

"She?"

"It was definitely a girl. She had long brown hair, because it fluttered out of the hood when she ran. She was wearing old faded blue jeans and some kind of work boots. Those were black."

"How tall?" Ken asked, a smirk on his face.

"Maybe five-seven or five-eight."

"You could tell?"

Polly walked over to the bricks on the wall and pointed to one. "She was about that tall. At the other end of the building, there's a broken brick. I saw her pass it and then when I went past it, I saw my relationship to it."

He shook his head. "This is why Aaron loves you. Okay, so I have a girl about five-foot-seven or eight, brown hair, blue jeans, black work boots, a dark blue hoodie. That's a better description than we usually get. I wish you could have seen her face."

"I'm sorry."

He chuckled. "Don't be sorry. This is good. We've been assuming the arsonist was male, but so much for assumptions."

"Girls can be bad people, too," Polly said. "We're living in equal opportunity days, you know."

"I'm old-school."

Polly glanced up the alley and didn't see her kids. "Can I run?" she asked. "I have a rental company dropping off tables in a few minutes and five kids who are standing around on the street up there waiting for me."

Ken nodded. "Don't go through the alley. We'll be there for a while."

Polly wove in and out of the fire fighters as they moved back and forth from their trucks to the alley. When she got to Washington Street, the main street through the downtown, she looked around, but saw no one. None of her kids were there. She took out her phone to call Rebecca and realized that a text had come in.

*"We didn't know how long you'd have to be there, so we're walking home to be there before the rental truck gets here. Sorry I was bad. I'll take care of it for you if you have to be late."*

That daughter of hers was going to give her a heart attack with all the ups and downs she delivered on a regular basis. Polly smiled. When it was necessary, Rebecca always did the right thing.

She got back to the elementary school and unlocked her truck, then climbed in. Once she sat down, she stretched her legs out in front of her and rolled her neck. Only a few more days and she could completely relax. Life would soon return to normal.

Polly drove out of the parking lot and headed home, unable to make sense of the pattern this arsonist was taking. Fires big and small, and there didn't seem to be any reason for the locations she chose. What point was the girl trying to make? That she had access to fuel and liked how fire burned? But no one ever saw her near the fires. At the end of May, surely someone would notice a girl standing around wearing a hoodie.

Thinking back to the fires that she'd observed, Polly tried to recall whether there'd been such a girl at any of them. She couldn't remember, but it felt as if there were something tickling the edge of her mind. She couldn't grasp it hard enough to bring it forward, so let it go. "Stupid brain."

Polly pulled into her driveway, relieved that the rental company's truck wasn't there yet. She stepped inside the side door and shook her head at the pile of shoes on the floor of the back porch. Obiwan and Han dashed in from the foyer. The dogs had figured out that they could push those doors open with their noses. No longer would they be stopped from going wherever they wanted to go in the house.

"Has anyone taken you out yet?" Polly asked Obiwan. She didn't get a response, but assumed the answer was no since it really hadn't been that long. She went into the foyer and found Andrew and the boys sitting on the stairway.

"What are you three doing?"

"Rebecca told us we had to wait here, just in case the table people showed up." Elijah pointed at the front of the house where Rebecca's room was located. "They're changing their clothes. We have to wait to change ours."

"I see. Well, I'm going to take the dogs outside for a quick walk around the yard," Polly said.

Andrew jumped up and started down the steps. "I should do that," he said.

"Nah. It's your graduation day. I've got this. Tell Rebecca that I'll be back after a while. If she needs me, send me a text and I'll come right back." Polly went back out to the kitchen, followed closely by both dogs. She snapped their leashes on their collars, sending them both into quivers of excitement. These two were good reminders of what was truly important in life.

They stopped at the bottom of the steps, waiting for Polly to tell them which way to go.

"Oh all right," she said. "We'll walk the neighborhood." With a tug to the right, the dogs trotted for the front sidewalk. They loved the smells that they could scare up when Polly took them outside the yard. Not that there weren't millions of wonderful scents brought in to their home territory by squirrels and birds.

Polly turned the corner and looked in at the empty home that had been owned by Jim Bridger. She and Henry had once talked about buying that lot and tearing the house down, but they had plenty of space without it. It was odd to her that no one had purchased it yet. Housing was limited in Bellingwood these days.

It was even more odd that no one really knew what was going on in the house next to Mr. Bridger's. She hadn't had a chance to ask Pat Lynch about it.

Polly thought she saw someone push the front drapes together as she passed by. Who could possibly be living in there? It was dark all the time. Even now, on this beautiful day, none of the windows on the front side of the house were open. She paused to listen and didn't hear an air conditioner running. Curious.

She fished a bag out of her pants pocket and picked up Han's gift for the afternoon. "Can we go home now?" she asked.

The dogs knew she was talking to them and wagged their tails, so she crossed the street and headed for the house.

~~~

"They're here!" Elijah yelled, running for the back door.

Noah took off after his brother.

Polly felt the excitement that the little boys were able to express out loud. Her heart skipped a beat at the thought of seeing Heath and Hayden again. It had been less than five days, but the house was lonely without them. Not any quieter, but still lonely.

"Let us get in the door," she heard Heath say.

"Boys," Polly called out. She stopped at the intercom and buzzed her bedroom, where Henry was working on contracts in relative peace and quiet. "The boys are home," she said. "Dinner will be on in a half hour or so."

"Thanks," he responded.

Elijah had Hayden's hand and Heath was holding Noah's as the four entered the kitchen.

"Wow," Polly said. "I had no idea two mountain men would be returning." She hugged Hayden and brushed the beard he'd grown during the week. "That grew out nicely."

Heath's wasn't nearly as thick, but he was also working on a beard. It wasn't going to take long. She gave him a quick hug before he dropped his backpack to the floor.

As soon as it was on the floor, Elijah ran up to him for a hug. Heath knelt down. "I missed you, buddy." He reached out for Noah so he could hold onto them both. "And you, too."

"Your face is scratchy," Elijah said. "Are you keeping it?"

Heath ran his hand along the side of his face. "I don't know. It might be too warm this summer, don't you think?"

"I like it," Noah said. "When can I grow one of those?"

"Probably not for a while," Hayden commented. "Heath thought that since he was done with school, he might try something different. Mine's coming off tonight."

"Why?" Elijah asked.

"I look weird."

"You look cool."

Hayden laughed. "Well, thank you." He smiled at Polly. "Not shaving for the last couple of weeks has been kind of nice. So, where's the eighth grade graduate? She sent us pictures this afternoon of her and Andrew in their graduation hats."

"I've lost track," Polly said. "They're either upstairs or in the foyer finishing decorations for tomorrow."

"You boys want to help us take our packs to our room?" Hayden asked. "We might be able to find something fun in them for you."

Noah's eyes grew big as he looked over at Hayden. "You bought presents for us?"

"Of course we did," Hayden said, patting the boy's head. "We bought presents for everyone. Come on. You can help us sort them out."

He opened the door to the foyer, stopped and whistled. "This looks awesome. You have to see this, Heath. Come in here. You won't believe it."

His brother, who had helped Elijah pull the heavy backpack over his shoulders, walked over, then turned back to Polly. "It looks great. I can't believe this."

"I didn't do anything," Polly said. "The girls and Andrew did all the work. They'll ask you to hang some things, but otherwise, it's all them."

Heath beckoned her over. "I don't know what else they'll want us to hang."

"What?" Polly crossed the kitchen, brushing her hands on her apron. When she got to the doorway, she was surprised to find that the kids had managed to hang the "Class of 2017" banner from the top banister and then, instead of taking streamers across the ceiling, they'd woven the school colors along with white strands of lights through the balustrades. The tables had more crepe paper crisscrossing the white tablecloths and they had decorated the low windowsills with colorful streamers, white strands of lights, and the battery operated candles Polly used at Christmas. "She found all of my Christmas decorations. What a great idea."

Kayla and Rebecca opened the door at the top of the stairs and walked out. "Do you like it?" Rebecca called down.

Polly nodded and Heath went on into the room, followed closely by Elijah who was struggling mightily with the heavy pack.

"This is really nice," Heath said. "I can't believe you went to all this work for me." He walked over to a long table beside the front door, where they'd set up his photo arrays and put the guest book out. He closed the guest book and stood for a few heartbeats, staring at the work Rebecca had done. "You made this?"

Rebecca nodded and walked down the north side of the steps with Kayla. "I didn't want it to just be a boring graduation book. Look at the inside cover."

He opened the book. "That's so cool. You're really creative. Come here, Hayden. She drew a really cool frame around my graduation announcement." He peered more closely at it. "That's you," he said. "And there's Noah and Elijah."

"Everyone's in the frame," Rebecca said. "That isn't my best work. I did it really fast, but I thought that you'd like the idea that your family was part of your graduation. Look there." She pointed at the bottom of the frame.

Heath stepped back, turned to look at Polly, and ran out of the foyer to his room.

"What happened?" Kayla asked.

Hayden took a closer look at the picture and reached out to pull Rebecca into a hug. "That's so great. He just didn't want you to see him cry."

Rebecca nodded. "I knew that. I understand. But they're still part of his family. Thank you for telling me where to find that picture."

Polly had seen the drawing in progress. She'd known that having his parents as part of the family sketch would be special, but she really hadn't thought it would impact him like it did. "Do you want me to get this?" she asked Hayden.

"I should." He didn't look like he was in any hurry to head into the room, though.

"Tell you what," Polly said, rubbing his back. "I'm good with kids and tears. We won't be long."

Hayden heaved a sigh of relief. "Thanks."

"I didn't mean to make him cry," Rebecca said. "Tell him that, will you?"

"It's okay. You didn't do anything wrong," Hayden said.

Polly gave Rebecca a quick hug and went on through to the boys' room, where she found Heath sitting on his bed. "You okay?"

"I wasn't expecting that." He gave her an embarrassed laugh. "I'm glad I saw it tonight and not tomorrow. Is it bad that I don't think about them all the time anymore?"

"Not at all," Polly said. "You don't think about Hayden all the time, do you?"

"No, but I see him."

"Yeah, but you don't need to have him on your mind all the time to still know that you love him, right?"

"Well, yeah."

"And you love me and don't think about me all the time, do you?"

He shrugged.

"But then come those moments when you are overwhelmed at how much you miss them," Polly said in a low, quiet voice. "And it's all you can do not to just sob uncontrollably. You want nothing more than to be held by your mother and told how much she loves you."

Tears flowed from Heath's eyes. "Sometimes I cry a lot."

"Me too," Polly said, allowing her own tears to fall. "I miss my parents so much it hurts. But it isn't all the time. Most of the time I'm just fine and I understand how great my life is now. It would be way different if my parents were still alive. I probably wouldn't be here doing what I'm doing. I'd never have met you and your brother or gotten to know Rebecca and Henry. Everything would be different and I love how things are."

"I know that ..." he pointed at his temple. "... in my head. Don't get me wrong. I love you, but I do miss her."

"I understand," Polly said. She put her arm around his shoulders. "If I could change life for you, I would."

"But you can't." He pointed toward the foyer. "And you're the one that got me here after everything fell apart. I don't know how to say thank you for that."

"That's never necessary. I'm here for you because I love you."

Heath reached into his pocket and took out something small that had been clumsily wrapped. "I wanted to give this to you, but I don't want it to be a big deal or anything. We got other things for you and everybody, but this is just from me. I know this weekend will be crazy with all the graduation stuff, so I'm glad we have a few minutes now."

"What is it?"

He handed it to her and Polly tore the wrapping paper away from a small jewelry box. When she opened it, she smiled at the beautiful Black Hills gold ring. It was a simple design — intertwining tri-color leaves on a gold band.

She took a breath. "This is beautiful."

"There's something inscribed." He pointed at the ring.

Polly took it out and looked closely at the inside.

*"Thank you for giving me back my life. Love, Heath"*

"Oh Heath," Polly said. The tears that had flowed only moments before returned in greater measure. She threw both arms around him and for a moment, the two did nothing but hold each other and cry.

They startled apart at the sound of rapping at the door.

"Can we come in?" Hayden asked. He chuckled. "He gave it to you, didn't he? I told him he'd better do it when nobody was around or it would wreck the whole family."

"What did you get?" Elijah asked, jumping into the room.

Polly slipped the ring onto the fourth finger of her right hand. "Isn't this pretty?"

"You bought that?" Elijah asked Heath. "That's so pretty. Someday, when I'm older, I'll buy you a ring, too."

"Me too," Noah said. "You'll have lots of rings."

"Thank you, boys. Why don't you two go upstairs and clean up for dinner so Heath and Hayden can take a minute to breathe."

"But we want to stay. We haven't seen them all week," Elijah complained.

Polly was about to insist, but Hayden nodded at her. "It's okay. We can sleep at bedtime tonight. The boys can help us bring our presents to the dinner table."

"Kayla and Stephanie are here," Polly warned.

Heath grinned. "We have something for them too. It's okay."

"Great. Give me about fifteen minutes to finish dinner and we'll see you in the kitchen."

Elijah jumped up on the other side of Heath. "Can we help you unpack?"

Polly left them and went down the hallway. She tapped lightly at Stephanie's door. "Are you okay in there?"

Stephanie opened the door. "I moved some things around. There's a lot of room in here. It was just haphazard. You don't have to move the boxes out next week."

"We will anyway," Polly said. "You don't need to live in my mess. But you opened up a bunch of space." She chuckled at the rearranged boxes. Stephanie had created a flat space where she'd arranged her laptop and clock, as well as some of her toiletries. "Look how great you are. That's fantastic."

"I can't believe you're letting us stay here. And cooking all these meals? I'm never going to want to leave."

"That would be okay, too," Polly said. "Dinner is in fifteen minutes."

"Can I help you?"

"The girls will help me set the table. You rest."

# CHAPTER TWENTY-ONE

Polly knew that tomorrow would be crazy, but right now … right here, she was content. Her family was gathered around the dining room table; everyone laughing and talking.

"Did you buy anything for yourselves this week?" Henry asked the boys.

Hayden just smiled.

The little boys were wearing their cowboy hats and had pulled on their Mount Rushmore t-shirts over the shirts they'd been wearing. Right now, they were running wooden cars and trucks around on the kitchen floor.

Hayden and Heath had also purchased jackalope banks for each boy and seeded them with a few coins. Elijah announced that he was going to save money to buy his own horse someday. Noah didn't have any idea what he wanted to save for. Polly figured he'd be much more apt to actually put money into a bank and keep it than his brother.

Hayden and Heath had obviously had a great deal of fun at souvenir shops. Heath said one of his favorite places was Wall Drug. He'd never seen anything quite like it in his life. They brought back stuffed jackalopes for Stephanie, Kayla and Rebecca, announcing that no one should be without one of those to protect their treasures. There were t-shirts for everyone. The girls each received little Indian dolls. They'd found beaded Indian jewelry and purchased bracelets for Polly, Stephanie, Kayla and Rebecca.

Stephanie tried to protest that she wasn't part of the family and Hayden told her to hush. She hushed.

They gave Henry a beautiful leather wallet with a wolf painted on the front. For Polly, they found a small matching checkbook wallet. Rebecca's biggest gift was a painting of a buffalo and wolf in a standoff that had been signed. They had several pieces of literature about the artist and Rebecca was so excited to have her first piece of signed art.

When Hayden reminded her that she had many things in her room done by Beryl Watson, Rebecca brushed him off.

"None of those are framed," she said. "This is going right over my bed." Rebecca had stroked the frame a few times, as if she couldn't believe it was hers.

There were other souvenirs and trinkets scattered around the dining room table. Yes, they'd had fun.

"Can I wear my hat to the party tomorrow?" Elijah asked. He slid onto Henry's lap at the table.

"No bud, you can't," Henry replied. "Because it's a special occasion, we're letting you wear them tonight, but it's not polite to wear hats inside. They're only for outside wear."

Noah had followed his brother back to the table and looked around for a place to sit. He'd been on the other side of Rebecca while they ate dinner, but Polly could tell he didn't want to be that far from the adults. She patted her lap. He hesitated for just a moment and she opened her arms. "It's okay. You won't hurt me."

"I'm bigger than Elijah."

"Not by much. I'll be fine."

He sat crossways on her legs and put his hat on the table in front of him.

"Thanks," Polly said. "It's easier for me to see that way."

"What was your favorite site?" Henry asked. He took Elijah's hat off the boy and put it on the table beside Noah's.

Elijah didn't protest, but pulled the hat closer, so he could touch the felt.

Heath looked at Hayden. "I probably liked seeing Mount Rushmore the most. You can almost feel the bigness of America there. Like, all of the power and responsibility that comes from living in a country like this."

Rebecca looked at him in astonishment and then giggled. "That was profound."

"Well, it was a big deal." Heath flushed with embarrassment and shrugged. "That was mine."

When Polly caught her daughter's eye, she glared and Rebecca looked away. The girl couldn't help herself and glanced back at Polly, who gave her another glare.

"I didn't mean to say anything bad about it, Heath," Rebecca said. "I think it's cool that you felt like that. I've never been there."

"You should go sometime. Maybe we'll take you when we go again," Hayden said, breaking into the conversation. "It's overwhelming to see what was created out of the mountain. Those four presidents are a big part of our country's history and when you consider how the days in which they governed have impacted our history, it's ..." He grinned at her. "Profound."

"Was that *your* favorite place?" Henry asked Hayden.

"It was. We spent a lot of our day there, just soaking it in. Driving through the Black Hills was beautiful, too. I love Iowa and I love living here, but it's so awesome that we can go anywhere in this country and see these fantastic places. Heath and I were talking about where we want to go next. Maybe we'll go see some of the big cities like Chicago and New York and LA, but we want to see the Grand Canyon and hike in the Rocky Mountains and go to Salt Lake City and walk on the rocky beaches of the East Coast. Maybe we'll go surfing in California and snorkel in Hawaii. We can do it all."

Rebecca watched him with her mouth open. Heath reached over and pushed her chin up.

"Flies, you know," he said.

"I want to travel like that, too," Rebecca said, giving him a scowl. "You know Polly and Henry went to the Grand Canyon. She's got pictures. And she took pictures of all those rock formations in Utah. You should hike in there too. And if you go, you have to take me."

Henry glanced at Polly and she rolled her eyes as she shook her head.

"What?" Rebecca asked.

"We're going to have to take a big family vacation one of these summers," Polly said. "I was just talking to Marie about that."

Noah beamed at her. "Us too?"

"You're family," she said. "Of course."

"Can we go this summer?" Rebecca asked.

Henry sat forward. "Not a big vacation this summer. We need time to plan something like that. Maybe next summer, though."

"We're taking a vacation," Kayla announced. She looked at her sister. "Aren't we?"

Stephanie nodded.

"Where are you going?" Polly asked.

"We're just going to Missouri."

Hayden leaned forward to see around Kayla. "Where in Missouri?"

"St. Louis. I promised Kayla we'd see the arch someday. Then on the way back, we're going to Hannibal."

"Mark Twain's home?" Henry asked.

She smiled. "Andrew told Kayla she should read Huckleberry Finn and Tom Sawyer, so we both did this year. Then I realized how close it was. There's a cave down there that we're going to go see and everything." Stephanie shuddered. "I'm going to try not to be claustrophobic about that, but we should at least try, don't you think?"

"I think it's awesome," Polly said. "When I lived in Boston, I toured some authors' homes out there. It's inspiring to see how they lived and what kinds of things they saw every day that excited their imagination."

"We're even going to take a riverboat ride," Kayla said. "I never thought I'd get to do something like that."

"This is our first big vacation." Stephanie slumped. "I just hope that the insurance money comes through in time so I don't have to put out a bunch of money to redecorate. I can't afford to do that, too." She turned to Polly. "You know what I used to save for?"

Polly nodded. Stephanie had put aside money to be able to escape if her father ever tracked her down. Now that he was gone, she no longer worried.

"Well, I decided that Kayla and I needed to have fun together. No work, no school. Nothing but us and wherever we decided to go visit."

"Someday I want to go to Disney World," Kayla said.

"Me too," Elijah said. He turned on Polly. "There's Star Wars there, now. We should go before they take it away."

"They won't take it away," she said, laughing. "Someday. There are a lot of things to do before you boys grow up and leave us."

Noah picked up the hand she had resting on his leg. "I'm never leaving. Never, ever."

"You can stay as long as you want," Henry said. He put Elijah on the floor. "I know I ate too much, but ice cream sandwiches are in the freezer just screaming to be eaten. Anybody else?"

Elijah's hand flew into the air. "I do."

Henry looked across the group. "Why don't I ask if there is anyone here who wouldn't like to eat one?"

When nobody's hand went up, he took Elijah's in his. "You can help me carry them."

~~~

"Why were you and Mom talking about vacations?" Henry asked. He stopped as Han slowed to smell something in a yard. The sun setting in the west filled the sky with gorgeous colors.

"She said that she'd take the boys if you and I wanted to go somewhere together."

"I can't take a week off right now. I'm sorry."

Polly slowed to wait for Obiwan. "I told her that. But she insisted that we should go somewhere together, even if it's just a long weekend. What about that?"

"I could do a weekend."

"Two?"

He chuckled. "What do you mean, two?"

"What if we took one weekend for us and another weekend with the kids? Marie's right. Now that we have more kids in our life, we should show them the world."

"Neither of us are big travelers."

"But look how much conversation happened around Hayden and Heath's trip. Those two boys are ready to get on the road again. They had a blast."

"I'm glad they did. We need to kick them out into the world more often."

"And the rest of our kids need to see the world, too. Rebecca had a great time with Beryl last summer."

"So where would we take everyone?"

"A short trip. Maybe it's just to Omaha to go to the zoo for a weekend. Or maybe we could go to Kansas City or Minneapolis."

"Or some of the state parks?"

"Dear lord, you want to camp and fish? Who are you?" Polly asked.

"I don't know what I was thinking," he said. "I lost my mind. You're right, though. We should take the kids on short trips in the area. There's so much to do in Iowa."

"The boys would love going over to the Grotto in West Bend."

"Or Living History Farms in Des Moines."

Polly turned to him and grimaced. "I should just take them down there one day this summer. They'd have a ball. Why didn't I think of that?"

"Because you've been so focused on the house and school and their activities. Now that things are slowing down, you'll probably be desperate to find things to do with them."

"We should do the train in Boone again."

"I'd go on that with you."

She held her hand up. "Did you see what Heath gave me?"

"I saw it on your finger. Figured you'd tell me what it was when you were ready."

"He made me cry."

Henry laughed, catching the attention of both dogs. When they realized he wasn't talking to them, they turned back to their tasks. "That doesn't surprise me."

Polly wiggled the ring off her finger. "There's an inscription, but it's probably too dark for you to read it. He thanked me for giving him back his life."

"I love you," Henry said. He put his arm around her waist and jostled her enough to send the ring to the ground.

"Damn it," he said. "I'm sorry."

"My fault." Polly took her phone out and turned the flashlight on, scanning around the sidewalk. She'd heard it hit and bounce, but with dogs and leashes in the way, she hadn't seen where it landed.

Pushing Han out of the way, Polly patted around in the grass while shining her phone's light. Henry turned his own on and knelt beside her. Both dogs nosed around where they were when suddenly, Obiwan whined and nosed at Polly's leg.

"It's okay," Polly said. "I'll find it. It can't have gone too far."

He whined again and then barked.

"Stop it," she scolded. "Don't make this any harder. What is wrong with you?"

Then she looked up at the house in front of them. "Henry, stop."

"What's wrong?"

She gestured with her head at the house in front of her while she closed the flashlight app and dialed 9-1-1. When the call was answered, Polly gave her name and the address of the house directly across from the Lynch's home.

"What if someone is inside?" Henry asked. He pressed Han's leash into Polly's hand and ran for the front door, yelling, "Is anyone in there? Do you need help?"

Someone darted across the driveway beside the house, into the back yard of the home next door. Polly took off after the fleeting figure, both dogs running as fast as she was.

"Stop!" she yelled. "If you don't stop right now, I'll send my dogs after you and they will take you down."

The figure stopped for just a second, then turned for the open field behind the homes. With all the rain that had come this spring, planting was late and the ground, while uneven, was wide open. The farmer wasn't going to be happy with someone dashing across his soybeans.

"I said, 'STOP'!" Polly screeched. "What have you done?"

The girl — it had to be the same girl she'd seen earlier; she was wearing that hoodie pulled over her head again — was running full-out, forcing Polly to push herself harder than she had in months. She wasn't going to let this one get away. The dogs were keeping up, though Obiwan was panting hard. Polly wondered if she'd ever catch up, but she couldn't bring herself to stop.

Just when she worried that they might run all night, the girl lost her footing in the furrows and fell. She scrambled to get back up, but moaned. She half ran, half crab-walked, still trying to escape from Polly, but it was no use. Whatever had happened when she fell, she no longer had any speed. Polly and the dogs were soon on top of her.

Polly reached out and yanked on the hoodie as the girl made another attempt to stand up and run away again. The girl's balance was compromised and she dropped.

Pulling the hood back, Polly was surprised to see how young the girl was. Now that she saw her face, the girl was probably only fourteen or fifteen years old.

The girl attempted to shrug the hoodie off in a further attempt at escape, but Polly managed to grab the girl's upper arm, a move which made the girl flinch and whimper.

"You can't run any farther," Polly said. "Stop trying. Was there anyone else in the house?"

The girl gave her a look of pure venom.

"I don't know what that means. Is someone in there?"

When the girl refused to respond, Polly reached down to put her arm around the girl's waist and help her to stand. Instead, the girl dropped as dead weight onto the ground.

"Fine," Polly said with a sigh. She sat down beside the girl in the bean field and called Henry.

"Where are you?" he asked.

Sirens rang out as fire and emergency trucks came down Walnut Street to the house.

"In the field behind you. I caught the girl."

"What girl?"

Polly realized they really hadn't talked much this week at all. He had no idea what had happened uptown today. "I think she's the arsonist. She's hurt her leg — probably twisted it in the field, but she refuses to come with me, so the dogs and I are sitting here with her. When Ken arrives, would you tell him to come rescue us?"

"A girl did this?" Henry asked in amazement.

"Yeah. Did you get any response from the house? I'm afraid there's someone inside."

"Ohhhh," he breathed out. "I can't get in. The front door is too hot and the back door is locked. Maybe we can break a window. Does she know where the person is? Who the person is?"

"Will you tell me who is in the house?" Polly asked. She could see smoke and flames leaping toward the sky.

The girl sneered.

"I'm not going to get anything out of her. Just tell the firemen that there is somebody inside. I don't even know what to do with that."

"Gotta go. Are you safe?" he asked.

"Yeah. We've got this."

Even though the girl was adamant about not giving her any information about the victim inside the home, she had given up her attempts to flee and dropped to the ground in a heap, great sobs coming out of her.

Obiwan moved to sit down beside the girl's head and pushed at it with his nose.

"That's Obiwan," Polly said. "Do you have a name?"

There was no response except more sobbing.

"Have you been setting these fires in Bellingwood?" Polly didn't expect a response and didn't get it, so she sat quietly with Han in her lap. She'd been in some ridiculous situations before, but this was nuts. When her mind wandered off to wonder at the number of bushels of beans they'd destroyed, she knew things were crazy.

Her phone rang and she smiled at Ken Waller's name. "Hey, Ken."

"Henry says you've got our arsonist. Where are you?"

"I'm back behind the houses in the bean field. The girl hurt her leg, but won't let me help her up. She dropped to the ground as dead weight and I don't have the strength to carry her out. Can you help me?"

"Is she hurt so badly that I need to bring a gurney?"

"If the police come in here, do they need to bring a gurney across this field for you?" Polly asked. That elicited more sobbing, but she was pretty certain the girl shook her head in the negative. "I don't think so. Maybe just a couple of you to drag her ass out. I can hold up my phone with the light on so you can find me. Will that work?"

Ken gave a harsh chuckle. "I guess so. We're on our way. Hang up and give me a signal."

"You're a real pain, you know that?" Polly asked the girl. "I don't understand why you did any of this, but I suppose you had a good reason and I'll feel bad for being mad at you, but right now I'm furious." She turned the flashlight app back on and held her phone up in the air. "Do you see what ridiculous stuff I'm doing because you're being so rebellious? Did you think you wouldn't get caught? Well I did it — I caught you. I ran through a bean field until I was nearly out of breath and I'm an old lady. So here we are. You're sobbing into dirt, my dog is trying to take care of you and I'm jabbering like a fool, while holding my phone up in the air so the police chief can come find me." Polly took a breath. "Because you won't damned well walk out of here with me."

"Polly!" Ken yelled. He and two others were coming across the field carrying powerful flashlights.

"Back here," she shouted, waving her phone.

Han yipped and Polly realized that Henry was one of the three coming toward them. She unsnapped his leash and said, "Go get Henry. Bring him here."

The dog ran off toward the three men, barking. Polly heard Henry give a familiar click of his teeth several times and then one of the flashlights went down and came back up. Her heart rate slowed and the adrenaline that had been building up flowed away, leaving Polly's arms and legs weak.

Henry got to Polly first and reached down to help her stand. "Are you okay?"

"I ran faster than I've ever run," Polly said. "And on this ground, no less. I think she twisted her ankle, but she's not talking. Come here, Obiwan."

The dog came toward Polly as Ken Wallers and Bert Bradford grabbed the girl under her arms and lifted her upright. She attempted to drag them back down to the ground with her.

"Stop it," Polly snapped. "You're caught. Now grow up and face what you've done. You will go with these men and you will answer their questions. Now, move!"

The girl looked at her in shock and allowed Ken and Bert to stand her upright, though she flinched and whimpered when they grabbed her arms.

"Just a sec," Polly said. "I think you're hurting her. Hold her still." She unzipped the hoodie and pushed it back and off one of the girl's arms. She was only wearing a thin t-shirt and Polly winced at the bruising and blood-red welts up and down the girl's arms. "What in the world? Who did this to you?"

The girl snarled at Polly, but allowed her to pull the hoodie back up. Polly worked the zipper and drew it most of the way up the girl's front.

"If I were to look at the rest of your body, would I see the same wounds?"

Shrugging, the girl looked away.

"You don't have to say anything, but the person inside the house — did they do this to you?"

"We've got this, Polly," Ken said. "And whoever was in that house is gone. We couldn't get to them in time."

At those words, the girl seemed to brighten. She stood up a little straighter, tossed her hair back as if in defiance and allowed Ken and Bert to walk her toward the edge of the field. Polly, Henry, and the two dogs followed them.

When they crossed onto the grass behind one of the neighbor's homes, the girl looked toward the house in flames and thrust both fists into the air and shouted, "Never again!" Then she drooped and limped on with the help of the two policemen.

Polly and Henry emerged into the chaos and crossed to the other side of the street.

Pat Lynch and her husband were standing on their stoop and the woman waved at them. "Can you believe this is happening in our neighborhood?" she asked.

Polly stopped on the sidewalk. "Did you know the people who lived in that house?"

"Name was Hewitt," Pat's husband, Al, said. "They were always the quiet type. Nobody ever came outside. When we got back from Florida, I maybe saw the guy once or twice, but nothing in the last few weeks."

"I saw a red truck a couple of times," Henry said.

Pat pointed at the next house down. "That's the Thierry's son-in-law. He lives down by Burlington in a little town. He comes up sometimes to fix things in their house, but there's never any room in the driveway, so he uses this one. He's never here very long."

"What about that family?" Polly asked, pointing at the burning house to get him back to information she wanted to know.

Al looked at his wife and then back to Polly and Henry. "A feller, his wife, and I guess it was their daughter. Pretty little thing, but she didn't seem very happy. We quit seeing her go to school. What? About fifth grade or so? I asked him one day and he said that since his wife died ..." He looked at his wife again. "We didn't even know about that. But since she died, he'd sent his girl to live with her grandma in … What'd he say, Patty? Dubuque or something? It was some place over on the river. He kept to himself. Not very friendly. None of the other neighbors around here know him. Never see him unless he's coming back from the downtown with groceries. D'ya think he was inside and burned?"

Pat took in a quick breath. "Was that his daughter they brought from out back?" She looked at Polly. "You don't think he's kept her in that house all these years, do you?"

"I'd say it's likely," Polly said.

"But that might mean that …" The older woman let the sentence trail off. "I can't believe we didn't know. I believed him when he said she left town." Her face screwed up into fury. "That filthy man. I knew I didn't like him. His wife was scared to death of him. She cowered whenever he spoke to her and when we saw his little girl, she acted like a whipped puppy. I remember trying to give her some cookies one day when she came home from school. He came outside and yelled at her to come home." Pat's body shivered. "Now that I think about it, the way he touched her when she crossed the street to him wasn't right. It was possessive and jealous."

"We should have told someone," Al said, patting his wife's shoulder.

"I've never thought about people like that," she replied. "Daddies aren't supposed to hurt their daughters. They're supposed to protect them from bad people."

"He's not hurting her any longer," Henry muttered.

Polly squeezed his hand. "We should go on home. The dogs have been out a long time and the kids are probably wondering what happened to us."

"You need to bring those cute boys over someday," Pat said. "I'd like to make *them* some cookies. We don't have enough little ones coming by anymore, do we, Al?"

"No we don't, Patty. You folks take care." He leaned on the wrought iron railing as if he were going to come down the steps.

"Good night," Polly said.

Henry smiled. "Good night."

As they walked down the sidewalk, Polly said, "I wish they'd said something, too. If just one person had checked on that house."

"I don't want to think about it," he said. "That girl was a prisoner."

"Did he kill his wife?"

She felt a shudder go through Henry. "I told you I don't want to think about it. We have to let Chief Wallers take care of it now."

The rest of their family was standing on the sidewalk in front of their bushes. Elijah broke away from Rebecca and ran across the street. "I thought you two were in the fire. You never answered Rebecca's text."

"But *I* sent her a text, right?" Henry said.

Elijah put his hand on Obiwan's neck and walked along with them. "I was scared, though."

"We're okay," Polly said.

"Did someone die?"

"We don't know for sure." Henry walked past Noah and took his hand back from Polly, transferred the leash and reached out for the little boy's hand. "We'll talk about it later?"

"Can we stay and watch?" Rebecca asked, her sketchbook and pencils in hand.

"Come in when I call you, okay?" Polly said. She was exhausted and this was just the beginning of the weekend. Running her thumb across the empty finger on her right hand, she looked at the boy who had given her such a beautiful gift. It was better to be honest with him right now. "Heath?"

Henry put his hand on her arm, stopping her before she could say anything more and gave her a quick shake of his head.

"Would you take the dogs in?" she asked, smiling at her husband, wondering why he was diverting her.

Henry nodded and smiled back.

"Sure. Why don't you two boys come with me, too," Heath said, reaching for the leashes.

Stephanie and Hayden went inside with him and the little boys.

"What's up?" Polly asked.

Henry reached into his pocket and handed her the ring.

"You found it!"

"When the flashing lights filled the street, I looked down one more time and saw something glint in the grass. I hoped it was your ring, and it was."

"Thank you so much. I didn't know how I was going to tell him I lost it three hours after he gave it to me."

He kissed her cheek. "Are we going to talk about you chasing an arsonist through a bean field?"

"If I can avoid it, that would be my preference."

# CHAPTER TWENTY-TWO

"Look how amazing this is," Polly said, standing in the door between the kitchen and foyer. "You two girls have done good work today. Go upstairs and get ready. Thanks for everything."

Rebecca grabbed Kayla's hand and they tore for the back steps.

"Girls?" Polly called out.

Rebecca stopped and turned around.

"Make sure you find all of the cats. Luke and Leia can stay in my room, but the rest in yours, okay?" Stephanie and Kayla had been a little worried about bringing their kitten back into contact with its siblings, but it ended up being just fine. Well, other than the fact that there was yet one more furry beast loose in the house. For the most part, Polly was happy to have the animals in her life, but when she got busy, it was almost more than any one person could manage.

Polly looked around the kitchen. Aluminum-foil-covered pans of cheesy potatoes and green bean casserole filled her counters along with trays of cut up cold vegetables. Pitchers of punch filled her refrigerator and sherbet was in the freezer. Roasters of pulled pork were plugged in on the island. Jars of pickles, sliced onions, ketchup and mustard were already on the serving table in the foyer and bags of hamburger buns were hiding in the pantry to be pulled as needed. Henry had picked up the cake as soon as Sylvie texted Polly that it was ready, and now Polly hoped she'd not forgotten anything. They were ready.

Plans had been in motion for this afternoon since February and she was ready to implement and go. Henry only asked once why she was cooking the food herself. She'd given him a look and reminded him of the near disaster the inexperienced caterer caused at the Christmas party. Rachel and Sylvie were much too busy with catering jobs all over town and Polly knew she could handle this. All she asked for was the cake.

That was when Lydia and Andy offered to help. Those two women spent the morning in Polly's kitchen helping her put everything together. She'd been so proud of herself. Everything she needed was in the house. No last minute trips to the grocery store and no massive accidents. Polly had dreamt last night that every casserole pan slid off her counter to the floor, creating a dreadful slippery mess, but so far, so good.

While they cooked, Hayden and Heath mowed and trimmed the yard. There had been enough rainy wet days that the grass was ragged and weeds grew where they didn't belong. Today was a beautiful day; the sun shone brightly and the forecast called for near perfect temperatures in the low seventies. Noah and Elijah spent most of the morning outside with their older brothers, picking up sticks and small branches that had blown into the yard. After the graduation ceremony tomorrow, Henry promised a small bonfire in the back yard. Ingredients for s'mores were already in the pantry.

Henry, Hayden and Heath were moving the vehicles to the elementary school parking lot. They'd walk home past the house that burned last night and Polly was looking forward to hearing what they saw. It had burned late into the night.

The smell of the fire permeated the neighborhood, but that was just one of those things she'd chosen not to worry about. A man lost his life in that fire, and a girl whose life had been destroyed by him years ago sat in a cell, waiting to find out what would happen to her next.

Polly swallowed hard. She would never understand the depravity that people accepted as their reality. How a man could torture a young girl to the point that she fell apart this badly was beyond her. She glanced toward the other side of the house. Either Stephanie or Kayla could have been that girl. Rebecca rarely spoke of the men who'd been part of Sarah Heater's life. From the little bit she admitted to, Polly knew the last man had been verbally abusive, and when drunk or upset, he hurt Rebecca's mother.

There had been plenty of encounters in Polly's life with men and women who used what little power they had to abuse others. It made no sense to her. None at all, though she'd seen more than her share of it. She was thankful that her life was filled with good people.

The back door opened and Henry came inside with Han and Obiwan. He unsnapped their leashes and the dogs ran over to Polly — tails wagging, tongues lolling. She rubbed both of their heads and then reached out to pull Henry into a hug.

"I love you."

He grabbed her upper arms and pushed her back to look in her eyes. "I love you, too. What's that about?"

"Just thinking about the girl last night and the man who had power over her. I'm so thankful you are a good person." Polly leaned forward and rested her head on his chest. "I love you so much. You always make me feel safe and loved and you do that for our kids, too."

He held her tight and kissed her forehead. "Nothing else makes sense to me," he whispered into her ear.

"Where are Heath and Hayden?"

"They're coming. They stopped to talk to Bert Bradford. He's back at the house. It's all burned down, Polly. Whatever she did to set that fire, she planned to destroy everything."

"Did they find any remains yet?"

"Not yet, but they've not really started the investigation. They worked all night to make sure the houses on either side were kept safe. I think at some point, they just let this one come down. There wasn't much more they could do for it."

"I have so many questions," Polly said. "But mostly I want to know how in a small town like Bellingwood, this could go on for so long and no one knew that it was happening."

He lifted his shoulders. "I'm sure we'll start hearing more stories even today. Two news crews are there. Pat and Al were dressed in their best Sunday clothes, holding court on their front lawn. Old Al brought his rocking chair outside so he could tell anyone who would listen what he knew."

"That makes me smile."

The back door opened again and the older boys came inside.

"What a mess," Heath said. "Officer Bradford says they'll be there all day and probably tomorrow before they can start digging through the rubble."

"Did he tell you anything about the girl?"

Heath shook his head. "He wouldn't talk about her. I get it."

"The street's clogged," Hayden said. "I hope that doesn't stop people from coming to the party."

"We can't worry about that," Polly replied. "Whoever can make it will be here."

Heath gave his head a quick shake. "I wish there weren't going to be a lot of people here anyway. I hate this."

"I love you," Polly said. "You make me laugh. This is the only time you have to go through this. We're proud of you."

"You could have been proud of me at Davey's with just our family."

"There's the whole wedding reception someday," Hayden said. "That will be way worse than this. Then you'll have a pretty wife dragging you around to meet her crazy side of the family."

Heath spun and headed for the foyer, throwing his hand up to stop Hayden from saying anything more. "I'm in the shower first."

"That was mean," Henry said.

"Yeah, but it gives him something else to worry about." Hayden turned to leave.

The door leading to the back stairway crashed open. Elijah and Noah ran into the kitchen and stopped beside the table.

"Do we look good?" Elijah asked.

Polly walked over to shut the door. She'd spent all day keeping it closed so as to make sure no cats found their way into the kitchen. All of the upstairs doors were to be kept closed today. It was a chore, but they were trying.

"You two look great," Henry said. He knelt down and put out his hand. When the boys looked at it, he said, "People might try to shake your hand today. That's what this means. What do you do?"

Noah put his hand out and Henry took it.

"Grasp my hand firmly. Not too hard like you want to hurt me, but like you are strong and confident. No wimpy handshakes, okay?"

Nodding, Noah tried to strengthen his grip.

"Now sometimes people shake your hand up and down, like this." Henry showed him. "For now, you let them be in control of the shaking, okay? Especially if it is an adult."

"Yes sir," Noah said.

Henry took his hand back, shook it at his side and then put it back out. "It's nice to meet you, young man."

Noah smiled while looking at the floor and put his hand in Henry's.

Henry removed his hand. "Yeah. One more thing. You have to look people in the eye when you shake their hand. It's polite. Let's try that again." He shook his hand at his side again, then put it in front of Noah. "Nice to meet you, young man."

Noah looked up at Henry and glanced at his hand to make sure it landed in Henry's. They shook a couple of times and Noah let go.

"Very good," Henry said. He turned to Elijah. "You saw how it worked, right?"

Elijah nodded, his eyes big.

"It's nice to meet you, Elijah," Henry said, putting his hand out.

Elijah grabbed Henry's hand, beamed at him and allowed Henry to pump it twice. "Did I do it right?" he asked.

"You sure did. It's always good to learn from your brother, isn't it?"

Polly came over to them and put her hand on Noah's shoulder. "Now how are we going to keep you clean until the party? You both look so grown up."

She'd found two sweater vests, one in black and one in red. They wore white shirts under their vests and were in their good black pants. Rebecca tried to talk her into bow ties for them. Polly succumbed and purchased the ties, but decided to hold off the suffering until the graduation ceremony.

"We could sit on the front porch," Noah offered.

"Would you be able to stay off the grass?" Polly asked.

"Yes, ma'am," Elijah responded. "We'd sit in the swing and stay there."

Henry laughed. "And if a fire truck drove past with its lights flashing and sirens going?"

"We'd stay right there in the swing," Noah said firmly.

"What if two stray dogs ran into the yard?" Polly asked.

The boys looked at each other, then back at her. "We wouldn't move. We promise."

Polly hugged them to her. "You can go out on the porch. Keep an eye on things. If you feel like you have to go play, just come tell me first. I won't be upset, but I do want to know where you are."

They ran into the foyer and she clenched herself while waiting to hear the front door open and close. When that happened without the sounds of crashing table settings preceding it, Polly relaxed.

"What else can I do to help you get ready?" Henry asked her.

"Let's take the dogs upstairs with us and get dressed. I think we're set."

They waited for Obiwan and Han to enter the foyer, then herded them up the steps. Polly peered into the upstairs hallway to make sure no cats were going to bolt through before opening the door.

"You're a lot calmer about today than you were for that Christmas party," Henry said. "I expected it to be much worse since you were doing all the work."

Polly puffed air out between her lips. "That was nuts. We'd barely been in the house and I didn't know where anything was. What a crazy evening. But we pulled it off. I've had tons of time to plan this and Rebecca did all of the decorating. She has no idea how much pressure that took away from me. And besides, this is my home now. I've got this."

"Are these animals going to be okay up here?" Henry asked.

"Either one of the kids or I will come up to check on them, but they'll all just sleep. It's what they generally do this time of day anyway." She sat down on the bed, took her shoes off and rubbed one of her feet. "I'm not looking forward to heels."

Obiwan jumped up beside her, turned around three times and settled in, facing Luke and Leia, who had snuggled in on Polly's pillow.

"That looks really comfortable," Polly said.

Just as she started to lean toward the pillow, Henry grabbed her shoulders. "What are you doing?"

"It called. I was responding."

"Well stop that." He laughed out loud. "Maybe you should take a quick shower and see if that will help."

Polly yawned. "Maybe you should join me. That would help."

"You are a bad, bad woman. No tempting the good husband."

"I really just hit a wall." She yawned again. "Oh, this is a bad one. Can I please have fifteen minutes?"

Henry checked his watch. "You can have twenty. Lie down and I'll wake you up."

"You won't forget?" Polly allowed herself to drop onto the bed, pulled her legs up, and scooted back to tuck herself against Obiwan.

Henry grabbed one of the blankets draped over her chair and tossed it over her. "Shh. Sleep. I won't forget." He sat down in his chair and took out his tablet. Before Polly knew it he was shaking her awake.

"It's time to get moving," he whispered.

"Look at you, all dressed and gorgeous. You clean up nice. Is the house still standing?"

He nodded. "The girls are downstairs, keeping an eye on Noah and Elijah. Rebecca says the cats are all comfortable in her room."

Polly tossed the blanket over the top of Obiwan and sat up. "I feel so much better. Thank you."

"Will you be okay getting ready by yourself?" Henry asked with a smirk.

"Yeah," she said flatly. "I think I can manage. Are you going back downstairs?"

"I thought I'd carry one of the pulled pork roasters out to the foyer and plug it in. Rebecca seems to think we should have food ready to go when people get here."

"She's right." Polly stood up and unzipped her jeans. "I hate to think that an eighth grader is as good as me when it comes to organizing a party, but she knows what she's doing." As her pants fell to the floor and Polly reached to pull her t-shirt off, she grinned. "Do not tell her I said that. Got it?"

"Like you won't tell her anyway. I'll see you downstairs." Henry slipped out the door and pulled it shut behind him.

Han looked up when Henry left, then tucked his nose back under a paw.

"Lazy sleepy-heads," Polly said. She kicked her jeans close to the laundry basket in the corner and gave her shirt a toss. It ended up catching on the handle of her dresser and she sighed. "I'm useless."

~~~

"Can you believe they're here?" Heath asked in an undertone.

"Who?" Polly looked around to see if a local celebrity had arrived.

"All those kids from my class. I didn't even think some of them knew I existed."

"You've been going to their graduation parties, haven't you?"

"A few. But that's Jake Garfield. He's like the smartest kid at the school."

"Did you have classes with him?"

"Well, yeah."

"And you talked to him?"

"I suppose."

"So he might think you were friends."

Heath looked at her and half-closed his eyes. "You don't make this easy on me."

"No I don't," Polly said, laughing. "You're a good guy, Heath. The kids like you. When was Jake's party?"

"That was one I went to last weekend. I wasn't there very long, though."

"Go talk to him and enjoy yourself."

Heath was gone before she got the last syllable out.

Elijah ran up to her. "I had two sandwiches." He pushed his tummy out and rubbed it through the sweater vest. "I'm full."

"I bet you are. Where's your brother?"

He pointed to the stairway where Noah was sitting on the third step.

"Why is he sitting over there by himself?"

"I don't know. Should I go ask?"

"Of course you should. I'll come with you."

Elijah took her hand and pulled her across the room. Polly smiled at people who were seated at tables and clustered in groups.

"What's wrong, Noah?" he asked when they arrived at the stairway.

Noah looked at Polly in surprise. "Nothing."

"Why are you sitting here by yourself, then?" Elijah asked.

Noah stood up. "I was just tired. That's all. Talking to people makes me tired."

"Are you sure?" Polly asked.

He nodded and then his eyes lit up. "She came."

Polly turned to see who he meant and saw that Ken Wallers and his wife, Maude, had just come in the front door. "Go ahead.

Tell her how glad you are that she's here."

Noah ran off, leaving his brother standing beside Polly. "I get to be in her class next year."

"Yes you do," Polly said. "Why don't you go ask Noah to introduce you to her again. Make sure she knows that you're his brother. She really liked him."

"Do you think she'll like me, too?"

"I think she'll love you. Go on." Polly gave him a little push and he ran across the room, dodging kids and adults.

Heath had stepped up to greet Ken and Maude, shaking their hands. Even though he hated this, he was doing very well. He'd been through a lot with Ken Wallers the past few years, but the police chief refused to quit believing in him. Though Heath might never admit how important those moments had been, Polly knew that they'd changed the way he looked at life. If only more adults were aware of their impact on the kids that they encountered daily.

While Polly watched, Noah stopped in front of Maude Wallers, then put his hand out to Ken. Ken glanced around, looking for Polly. When he caught her eye, he grinned and took the little boy's hand. She couldn't hear what was said, but felt her eyes burn. Elijah slid to a halt beside his brother and put his hand out to both Ken and then to Maude. If those two couldn't steal a person's heart, there was no heart there to be taken.

She headed for the kitchen door when she saw Rebecca slip in there.

"Is everything okay?" Polly asked.

"Just getting another cheesy potato out of the oven," Rebecca said. "Those are going fast. People really like them."

"Mary used to call them funeral potatoes," Polly said. "They're popular and easy to make."

"Heath has a lot of people here. He didn't think anybody would show up."

"I'm glad they surprised him, aren't you?"

Rebecca nodded. "Andrew and Jason should be here pretty soon. They had to go to another party at Sycamore House first."

"Got it. I wondered why Andrew wasn't here."

"He wanted to come, but his mom made him do that instead."

Polly pushed the door open so Rebecca could go through. "Can I help you two with anything else?" she asked Rebecca and Kayla.

"We think we should go into catering," Kayla said.

"I don't know about that, but you could probably get jobs helping Rachel as servers next year."

"Could we?" Rebecca asked. "That would be awesome."

The two girls worked their way around the table, picking up fallen bits of vegetables and wiping up drips from the potatoes and green beans. Kayla picked up a nearly empty tray of vegetables and left for the kitchen. Polly needed to be sure the girls were well-paid for this weekend's work. They'd put a lot of effort into the party. She was grateful to have had help.

"There you are, dear," Lydia said.

"I didn't see you come in."

"I watched you disappear into the kitchen. It looks wonderful and I see you have the girls manning the table."

Polly nodded. "They're doing a good job. All I had to do was tell them how to heat the food and they were on it."

"I missed having my girls around to help once they took off for their own lives," Lydia said.

"Hello, Polly." Aaron came up to them and slipped his arm around his wife's waist. "I must thank you for taking my wife off my hands this morning. I got an extra nap in. She usually has a Saturday task list for me, but not today."

"I had the list, you just acted like you couldn't find it."

"Rats. The whole house might fall apart this week."

"You'll feel bad if it does." Lydia poked her husband's side.

"Have you gotten anywhere with that murder?" Polly asked him. "Actually, two murders?"

"No, but then you haven't had time to work on them, have you? I understand you caught the arsonist last night."

Polly nodded. "I don't know whether to be really angry with her for terrorizing the community or to feel bad for her because of what I think she was going through."

"You can do both," Lydia said. "Oh look, there's Tab and her handsome boyfriend."

Aaron growled under his breath. "Stop that. You'll embarrass her."

"I don't know what you're talking about."

Tab stopped to greet Heath and handed him a card. They spoke for a minute and then she caught Polly's eye and waved before taking JJ Roberts' arm and leading him to them.

JJ greeted everyone and handed Polly a gift bag.

"What's this?"

"We're trying a rhubarb wine. I wanted you to have a bottle."

She grinned at Lydia. "Wouldn't it be wonderful to own a winery? You always have fun hostess gifts. Thank you, JJ."

"I wouldn't let him bring a bottle to Heath," Tab said.

"But you gave him … oh never mind." JJ rolled his eyes.

"What?" Polly asked.

Tab chuckled. "I made up a get-out-of-jail free card."

Aaron laughed out loud. "You what?"

"Well. He's been around me enough to know that I'm kidding, but I also thought it wouldn't hurt that poor boy to have my number in his telephone. Things have happened to him in the past and it's always good to have a friend in law enforcement. Right?" She nudged Polly with her elbow.

"Right," Polly said with an exaggerated nod. "Because I have no friends in law enforcement. I was just asking Aaron if you guys had any news on those murders."

Tab frowned. "Nothing. We can't even get an identification on the second victim because his body was so badly damaged. There were no fingertips to print and DNA isn't useful if he's not in the database. We can't find any similar missing person reports. There was nothing on the trailer that he was found in.

Any fingerprints in Loeffler's truck were either his or there isn't a match in the system for them. I talked to Sandy's mother-in-law, but he didn't tell her where he was going after her house, so that was useless. I'm at a loss. You haven't heard anything new, have you, Sheriff?"

"I was just telling Polly that we didn't know anything because she hadn't gone to work on the murders yet. Once she puts her mind to solving them, we'll get our answers."

"Stop it." Polly blushed.

Henry was at the front door greeting a group of people that worked for him. She'd met many of them at their Christmas party, but this was a world that Henry and Heath inhabited every day. She sometimes forgot that they knew so many other people than were part of her everyday life. It was good to see the camaraderie.

Doug Shaffer, his wife and four kids came in, then Len and Andy Specek walked in the door with Beryl.

"Oh dear," Lydia said. "She's a rainbow."

Sure enough, Beryl was dressed in an ombre orange to red blouse, then a similar color-changing flowy skirt — green to blue. A bright purple scarf was wrapped around her neck and she was carrying, of all things, a yellow parasol. She grabbed Heath and pulled him into what had to be a highly embarrassing kiss, then handed him a small envelope before waving her yellow-gloved hands at Lydia and Polly.

"Hello, dears," she called across the room.

"I blame you for this friendship," Polly said to Lydia.

"I have to accept it," Lydia said. "But isn't she wonderful?"

"Poor Heath."

"Look at him," Tab whispered. "His friends think it's great. He might be embarrassed, but he's laughing and having a good time about it. She just never ceases to amaze us."

"What is this?" Lydia asked Beryl, gesturing to the woman's outfit.

"It's my spring there's-been-too-much-rain-I-need-a-rainbow outfit."

"But there's sunshine today."

"So that means I sparkle." Beryl wagged her finger at Polly. "Andy tells me that she and Lydia were here this morning helping you prepare the food. How come you didn't invite me?"

Polly opened her mouth to say something, but found that she had no words.

"That's right, Missy. Just because I'm the worst cook this side of the Mississippi doesn't mean that I can't mix cheese into potatoes."

"Rebecca said that you were trying to finish a commission today since she didn't have a lesson."

Beryl put her hands on her hip. "Well, that makes more sense than you believing I can't be helpful. Because I can, you know."

"Did you finish your work?" Lydia asked.

"Not yet. But I can do that tomorrow. The sun was shining and I needed a fresh dose."

"Excuse me," Polly said and headed for the front door just as Joss and Nate Mikkels came in.

Joss opened her arms and Polly rushed to hug her. "I can't believe you came."

"We got the littlest ones down for a nap after a busy morning. Mom said she could manage as long as most of them were sleeping." Joss patted her purse. "I told her to call and we'd come right home."

Nate took Henry's hand. "Good to see you, man." He put his hands out to embrace the room. "It's good to see people that are taller than three feet. We haven't left the house much."

"How's it going?" Polly asked.

"It's okay," Joss replied. "Sophie and Cooper are excited about it all. Lucas, Owen and Lillian are settling in. They had a rough time of it and I don't know if they believe this is the end of the chaos. But we are hanging in."

"Are you about ready for visitors? I want to meet them as soon as you tell me it's okay."

"Another week," Joss said. "Dad's coming in tomorrow. He and Mom are going to stay until the end of June unless we tell them it's okay to go home. I don't mind having the extra hands, that's for sure."

"You know we'll all be there the minute you cry 'uncle.' No questions asked."

"But I like that Mom is there in the middle of the night, too," Joss replied. "With three of us in the house, we take turns. I didn't expect to get any sleep this week, but ..." She looked up at her husband. "It's not that bad, is it?"

"No. It's been better than I hoped." He smiled. "I'm afraid that I'll be clinging to your parents' legs when they try to leave, though. Dealing with five little kids, three of whom are still shell-shocked, has been a bit of a surprise." He held out a white envelope to Henry. "Did you give Heath his present yet?"

Henry shook his head. "This goes with it?"

"I'm glad I asked first. This is for a day with that truck in my shop. We'll do some body work, change the oil, mess around. Generally get grease under his nails. If he can wait until August, that would be great. I think by then, life will be back to normal."

"So he doesn't know you're giving him the truck?" Joss asked.

"Not yet," Polly said. "I had to finally get to the point where I could look at it without thinking about what Joey and that creep did in it, but I've seen Heath in it so often that the bad memories are pretty much gone." She stepped back. "Come all the way in. You might as well talk to more real people than just us if this is your first trip out and about. Have you fallen in love with those kids yet?"

Joss smiled. "The minute I saw them. It will be better when they know that it's safe to love us, but for now, we'll carry it."

Tab, Lydia, Beryl, and Andy had made their way over and Polly stepped backward, nearly tripping over someone's feet.

"I'm sorry," she said, righting herself by grabbing the table.

"I've got you, love." Polly felt arms at her waist lift her back to a standing position.

She turned and found herself face to face with a strikingly good-looking man in his forties or fifties. "I'm sorry," she said. "I don't believe we've met. Are you a friend of Heath's?"

"I knew his mother quite well. Heath, old boy, come tell your guardian who I am."

Heath looked uncomfortable as he came to the table.

The man took Heath's arm possessively. "We go back a long way, Heath's mother and I. Surely you remember my visits."

"Polly, this is Jared Ellesworth. He knew Mom."

That was all Heath said. Polly wasn't sure what was going on. She looked around for Hayden, who was standing at the food table with Marie Sturtz.

"It's nice to meet you," Polly said. "Are you in Bellingwood long?"

"Just passing through on a business trip. I knew that the boy had to be graduating this year, so stopped by to see the boys at their aunt and uncle's home. They told me there was a celebration today and how to find it."

"I wish you would have called," Polly said, trying very hard not to grit her teeth and hiss at him. She wasn't sure if he set her on edge or the fact that Heath's aunt and uncle were willing to tell people how to get here made her angry.

He held tightly to Heath's arm. "I'm not staying long. I just wanted to see the boys and offer my condolences on the death of their parents. I heard about it, but haven't had time to get back to the Midwest. Thought they were staying with their aunt and uncle." With one hand, the man patted Heath's chest. "Sounds like the boy had some trouble with the law. Good of you to take him in. Too bad he couldn't stay with family, though."

"He is family," Polly said. "Excuse me, Heath. I think Sheriff Merritt would like to congratulate you." She reached across the man, took Heath's arm away from him and led him toward Aaron, who was talking to Bill Sturtz and Ken Wallers.

"Who is that man?" she whispered.

"I haven't seen him in years. He and Mom knew each other, but I don't know how. He'd show up every once in a while. Dad didn't like him. Mom was nice, but I could always tell she was glad when he left. That's all I know."

"Does Hayden know any more?"

Heath shrugged. "Thanks for getting me away. He asked a lot of questions about Mom and Dad and what happened to the house after they died. I didn't know what to tell him."

"Okay." Polly stopped in front of the three men. "Aaron, would you look at that stranger over there? Just stare at him for a minute."

Aaron obeyed and they all watched as the man finally flinched. He said something to one of the kids at the table and then left by the front door.

"What did I just do?" Aaron asked.

"You intimidated someone that Heath didn't invite." Polly chuckled. "We'll ask questions after this is all over. Thanks for that." She laughed to herself as she walked away from the group.

Ken Wallers tapped Polly's shoulder. "Got a minute?"

She nodded toward the kitchen and he walked through the door with her.

"What's up?" she asked.

"I just wanted to let you know that the girl you stopped last night has been through hell. I don't know what we're going to do with her. That's all up in the air. I called in a favor and she's got a good lawyer."

"She's talking to you?"

"Everything is coming out. She's been waiting fifteen years to tell her story. I can't go into all of the details with you, but I'll trust that you won't talk."

"You know I won't."

"After he killed the girl's mother, he tied the girl up. She's been his housekeeper, sex toy, punching bag, everything." He grimaced and closed his eyes. "You wouldn't have wanted to hear her story. I'm not going to get that out of my mind for a long time."

"How did she get away?"

Ken shook his head. "Her father fell down the steps and broke his leg three weeks ago. He dragged himself to her and untied her so she could take care of him. I don't believe he considered for a minute that she would retaliate. She drugged him with old painkillers every night and snuck out. Got the fuel from Jim Bevins' tanks across that beanfield. Every night she soaked a different room in the house and started testing fires around the city. Last night she put the last of the drugs in his scotch, waited for him to pass out, lit fire to the house, and took off. She'd have been long gone if you and Henry hadn't walked by at just the right time."

"That poor thing," Polly said. "I wish there was something I could have done for her."

"We'll do our best for her."

"Thank you for telling me what happened."

"You can't tell anyone, you know that, right?"

"Not even Henry?" She gave him a small smile.

Ken chuckled and looked up as Rebecca and Kayla came into the kitchen. "I trust him."

"Whew. I can't keep secrets from that man."

"What secrets?" Rebecca asked.

Polly and Ken headed back into the foyer. "That you're the best daughter a girl could ask for," Polly said.

# CHAPTER TWENTY-THREE

After the last guest left, Polly sat down, kicked her shoes off, and ran her fingers across one of the streamers. "That was a success," she announced. Kayla and Rebecca sat down beside her. "You two girls made this party what it was. Thank you."

Kayla smiled. "It was fun. I think it would be fun to work at Sycamore House. Do you think Stephanie would hire me?"

"She's *your* sister." Polly beckoned for Henry to join them and when he was in front of her, she put her hand out. "Can I have your wallet?"

He looked at the two girls. "Do you see how it is? She's always taking my money." He handed his wallet to Polly. "What's mine is yours, dear."

"I want to pay you for helping put this together," Polly said, flipping through the twenties Henry was carrying. She took out four and gave two each to Rebecca and Kayla. "I couldn't have done this without your help."

"Wow," Kayla said. "That's a lot of money."

Rebecca looked at Polly with wide eyes. "Thank you. I just did it because it was for Heath."

"I know that," Polly responded. She took another twenty out and put it on the table. "This is for the two of you to go up to Pizzazz for supper. I didn't see you eating much while you were working today. You can go for pizza."

"But the place is a mess," Kayla protested. "We should help."

Polly shook her head. "Nope. We'll take care of this. You've already put in your time."

If Rebecca's eyes could have grown wider, they would. "I don't believe it. We don't have to clean up?"

"You certainly can if you want," Henry said. "Otherwise, you might want to skedaddle. Anyone left in the room in five minutes will be put to work."

The two girls flashed a glance at each other, then ran for the stairs.

"You can let all of the animals out," Polly called after them. "Leave the doors open." She heaved herself back out of the chair and kicked her shoes further under the table. "I don't want to see those for a week or more. I need bare feet."

"Where do we start?" Hayden asked.

"Food into the kitchen, everything else that isn't a gift or a memory goes into a trash bag," Polly said. "If you want to supervise Noah and Elijah out here, they can help bundle up all of the streamers and tablecloths for trash. Any of the 2017 stuff Heath might want goes on the memory table. We'll sort through it later."

She walked to the food table and grimaced. They'd served up every dish of potatoes and green beans. While there were hefty scrapings left in each container removed from the table, they'd hit the amount close to the mark. She grabbed up two nearly empty trays of vegetables and a dish of potatoes, then headed into the kitchen. Henry came in behind her, carrying the last roaster of pulled pork.

Laughter burbled from him as he took in the horrific mess that had been left.

"I know," Polly said. "Do you want to start combining food or do you want to bring the rest in from the foyer?"

"I'll haul. You go to work in here. By the way, I think Hayden got the easier job."

The other thing Polly had done was purchase scads of plastic-ware containers. She took a deep breath, opened the pantry door and took down her favorite apron, then went on in and lifted out the largest containers she'd purchased. Thank goodness they'd decided to keep the old refrigerator on the back porch.

A knock at the back door brought her out of the pantry. She dumped the containers on the island and went out to find Mona and Rose Bright from across the street.

"Hello," Polly said. "Come in."

Mona smiled. "Thank you for inviting us to the party today. We had a good time. You have a very nice family. We're here to help."

"To help?" Polly was confused, but stepped back to invite them further in.

"With so many people here, there will be a lot of cleanup and you have to be exhausted. If we pitch in, it will go faster."

"Uhhh, thank you, but that's not necessary."

"I saw Heath take off with a few of his friends, right?"

Polly nodded. "They had some other parties they wanted to attend. Are you sure about this?"

"One day you told me that you worried about not being very neighborly. I've thought about that a lot. The other night when you invited us into your back yard and bought ice cream for everyone, I realized that you meant it. So here I am, trying to be a better neighbor."

"Okay," Polly said. "I won't turn down an offer of help. Rose, do you want to help Noah and Elijah in the foyer? They're tearing down all of the streamers."

Rose nodded. "I can do that."

"Hayden's supervising," Polly said to Mona. "I don't think he'll mind another helper."

Henry came in with a basket full of hamburger buns and an arm full of condiments. "Hello, Mona. I suspect you're glad to get all of those cars off the street."

"Mona came over to help me clean up," Polly said. She was standing behind the woman and gave him a look of complete confusion.

"Thank you," Henry said. He put things on the island. "You too, Rose?"

The little girl nodded.

"I'll bet you'd like to help my sons in the foyer. Come with me." Henry escorted the little girl through the doors.

Polly took another apron down from a hook inside the pantry and handed it to Mona. "I can't believe you're here."

"I talked to Chris. She would have come over, too, but the poor girl can hardly get around."

"This is so nice. I really didn't expect it."

"That's what makes it so fun," Mona said. She picked up a package of containers. "Potatoes in these?"

"Everything is going into plastic containers." Polly went back into the pantry and brought out a box of trash bags along with the large trash can. "There's no reason to save any of the used foil pans."

"Got it. I didn't realize you knew so many peace officers," Mona said. She began combining potatoes into one container.

Polly lifted the empty inner pan out of a roaster and took it to the sink. Turning on the hot water, she squirted dish soap in and let it fill. "It was a surprise to me, too. I just keep meeting more and more and then I realize that they're good people and pretty soon we become friends."

"Someone said you found Barney Loeffler's body out on Turnbull Road. That was you?"

"It's always me," Polly said with a sigh.

"I wasn't sure whether to believe that or not. When you found me in the basement last January, I was sure glad it wasn't always true."

"Me too. But yes, I found his body."

"He was down here, you know. The day before?"

Polly stopped moving and slowly turned to Mona. "Down here? Where?"

"I was talking to Carla and she says someone is buying Jim Bridger's house, so they are cleaning it out. He picked up a load from there."

Polly could barely function, her mind was moving so fast. "Jim Bridger's house?" Jim Bridger was the old man who had planted marijuana in the back yard of what used to be called the Springer House and then promoted the ghost-sightings to keep people away from purchasing it. He'd had quite a lucrative cash crop going there until everything fell apart for him.

"Yes. Right next to the house that burned down." She dropped a foil pan into the trash, pushed it down and came over to the island for another. "What's wrong?"

"Jim Bridger's house," Polly said, sitting down on a high stool.

Henry walked into the kitchen and looked at her. "What's up?"

"Barney Loeffler was at Jim Bridger's house before he died. Have you seen any activity going on there? Mona says someone is buying it."

"That's odd," Henry said.

She pointed at the kitchen table since he was carrying plates and silverware. "What's odd?"

"Well, Dad and I have been looking at properties in Bellingwood. I specifically asked about that house and Mary says that the property isn't on the market at all yet. In fact, she thought it was strange because a house like that usually has a trustee appointed to manage the property."

Polly tried to figure out what he meant. "Mary Mueller?" The real estate agent had helped them purchase the Bell House. Polly wasn't terribly fond of her, but she got the job done.

"Yeah," Henry said. "Jim Bridger died without a will and since he has no family, the state stepped in. Mary says this one somehow got lost in the paperwork. She's asking more questions, but I can almost guarantee that it isn't up for sale."

"Huh," Mona said. "I wonder what Carla heard, then?"

"Carla Wesley?" Henry asked.

Shawn and Carla Wesley lived on the corner. Polly had plenty of history with them and was more than a little surprised that

Mona talked to Shawn's wife on a regular basis. The woman wasn't terribly pleasant, but who would be with that loser for a husband.

"Yeah. You know her, don't you?" Mona asked.

Henry nodded.

"I haven't seen anything going on there either," Mona said. "That's just what I heard. His house is directly across from hers, so she would have seen it."

"I wonder if the Lynch's saw anything," Polly mused.

Henry chuckled. "They just haven't had a chance to tell you about it yet."

"Pat's a nice lady," Mona said. "But she sure can talk. When I hurt myself, she came over a few times. Always brought food for me and Rose, but she talked my ear off. I don't think her husband pays enough attention to her."

Henry winked at Polly. "Some women have a lot of words to say."

Polly rushed back to the sink and turned the water off. She'd gotten distracted, but it just flowed over the edge of the pan and into the sink. "I wonder what Barney Loeffler picked up in Jim Bridger's house that day."

"You know everything is still in there," Mona said. "Nobody's done nothing with it. He didn't have a family and there wasn't a will to be found. I suppose the state will come in here someday and take care of it. But he'd paid that house off a long time ago, so the bank doesn't care about it."

"It would probably go cheap, then," Henry said, looking at Polly.

"We don't want it," she scolded him.

"No, but ..." He shook his head. "Never mind. Tell me what to tackle next."

"Is there any cake left?"

"You want that in here now?"

Polly handed him a package of flat containers. "Fill these up — just one layer. Is there any punch left?"

"Nope. Pretty much just dregs."

"I have one carton of sherbet left and a couple of bottles of Seven-Up. That's perfect. Just bring the punch bowl in and I'll wash it up."

"On it, boss." Henry went back out into the foyer.

"Do you think that someone killed Barney because of what he picked up at Mr. Bridger's house?" Mona asked. Her voice was a whisper, almost conspiratorial.

"It makes me wonder," Polly replied. "Sometimes mysteries in this town never seem to be fully solved, even after everyone involved has died. What else could that man have been hiding?"

"We had no idea that he was growing marijuana in your yard." Mona chuckled. "I can't believe Shawn wasn't involved in it with him. That man can't stay out of trouble for anything. You know he's back in jail again."

"I didn't know that," Polly said. "What did he do this time?"

"Got caught selling meth down in Boone. I keep telling Carla that someday they'll put him away for a good long time and she should just divorce him and start over. Her kids don't need to have that lowlife as a role model."

"Why won't she leave him?"

"Says it's not right. She married him for better or worse. I don't think the person who wrote those vows knows what worse can really be sometimes. I had a girlfriend who wouldn't leave her husband, but he beat her black and blue all the time. Got so she couldn't ever leave the house she looked so bad."

"What happened?"

"He drove drunk one night and ran right up the back end of a gas tanker. It was all over for him. She got his insurance and left town. She deserved a new life. Haven't heard from her, though. Hope she didn't hook up with another loser." Mona shook her head as she pushed another empty pan down into the trash. "I don't know why we women put up with bullies. It's like we don't think we can live by ourselves and be okay. Me and Rose? We're okay. At least mine didn't hurt me that way. I wouldn't have taken it." She gave Polly a shy glance. "I'll bet you've never had to put up with someone like that. Have you?"

"Not exactly like that," Polly replied, scraping out the second pan of pork.

"Wait a minute," Mona said, turning around. "You got kidnapped by that serial killer guy, didn't you?"

"Yeah."

"If I remember right, it was an old boyfriend that brought him here. I guess it doesn't matter whether you have money or not, men and women are still the same. If they're bad men, they want to have power over a woman and if they're weak women, they let men." Mona stopped scraping. "I didn't mean that you were weak. You aren't."

"No she's not," Henry said. "Any man who thinks that about Polly is making a mistake that will cost him dearly. Here's the end of the cake." He put three stacked containers on the corner of the island. "And here's your punch bowl. What can I do now?"

Polly shot her eyes to the sink and he laughed out loud. "Time to roll up my sleeves and be manly, I guess. The dirty dishes are calling my name."

"How are things in the foyer?"

"Tables are cleared off, streamers are all down, lights are wound up again and everything Hayden thinks you should ask Heath about keeping is on one table. He's bringing in the rack for the chairs now and the kids are helping him stack those."

"That's faster than I expected." Polly set the other roasting pan beside the sink and opened the dishwasher. She gathered up all the serving spoons and ladles, surprised at how easy this cleanup was turning out to be.

"Can we really go down to Pizzazz?" Rebecca asked as she and Kayla came in from the back stairway. She pulled up short when she saw Mona at the counter. "Hi, Mrs. Bright."

Mona smiled. "Hi there. Rose and I just came over to offer our help."

Rebecca turned to Polly, who gave an imperceptible shake of her head. "That's really nice. Can we really go?"

"Go on. You two deserve it. Plan on being home before eight-thirty, okay?"

"Did I get it all?" Mona asked, looking around for another pan of food.

"I think that's it," Polly replied, dropping the last of the cut veggies into a plastic bag. She slid the zipper shut and dropped it on the counter, then headed back to the pantry. Taking out a shopping tote, she walked over to where Mona had been working. "We have too much food left over. Would you and Rose take home a container of each?"

"No, you have a big family to feed."

Polly pointed at the containers stacked on counters. "Before we could finish this, my family would kill me for making them eat the same thing over and over. Please take some with you."

"Rose did like those potatoes," Mona said. "But I didn't expect anything."

"Just like I didn't expect any help," Polly said, putting a container of each in the bag. She placed one of cake on top and grabbed an unopened bag of hamburger buns. "Just think. You don't have to worry about meals for a day or two. You can come home and relax after work."

"Thank you." Mona took the bag of food.

"Thank you so much for surprising me." Polly looked around the kitchen. There was still a lot to do, but at this point it was mostly just finding homes for things. She couldn't believe how fast this had gone.

Mona stepped to the doorway leading into the foyer. "Oh my," she said. "It's completely cleared up."

Polly joined her. "You did great, kids. Thank you."

Elijah ran over and hugged her. "Hayden said we were good workers."

"He's right," Polly said. "Rose, you and your mother were my surprise angels today. Did you know that?"

Rose beamed at Polly and then at her mother.

"We'll get out of your hair," Mona said. "Let me know if we can ever help with anything else."

Polly extricated herself from Elijah and went back into the kitchen. "We'll have some more impromptu block parties this summer. I've enjoyed getting to know you better." She walked the two to the back porch and watched as they left.

"Have you seen the dogs?" she asked Noah.

He shook his head.

"Would you two boys run upstairs and let them out of my bedroom? Just leave all the doors open. Make sure Rebecca's bedroom door is open, too. And while you're up there, change into your shorts and t-shirts."

As the boys ran for the back stairway, she called after them. "Fold up your vests and pants. You need those for tomorrow."

"A lot of good that will do," Henry said with a laugh.

"I can try. Okay, what am I supposed to do with the knowledge that Barney Loeffler was at old Jim Bridger's house? What did he find there?"

"Could be anything," Henry said. "That might not even be where he picked up his killers."

"I can't believe that I never saw his truck in there."

"Would you even know that's what you were looking at?"

"No. Probably not."

The dogs clattered down the back stairs, followed by Leia and Luke who flicked their tails in annoyance.

"Yeah, yeah, yeah," Polly said. "I don't lock you up very often and it was only for a few hours." She'd left them with water and a disposable litter box. They wouldn't eat again until later tonight, so all protests were mainly for show.

Luke jumped up onto the island and prowled around sniffing at anything he could find. She scooped him up, got another annoyed tail flick and put him on the floor.

"What do you want to do with the dogs?" Henry asked. "They're probably ready to go out."

"I want to walk down the block." Polly looked at his face and giggled. "But you knew that, didn't you?"

"I thought I'd ask, just to see if you'd admit it. Do you think they can wait while I change into something more comfortable?"

"Let's put food away and then we can test our luck and run upstairs." Polly grabbed up a stack of containers and headed for the back porch. She opened the refrigerator, set them inside and turned to take what Henry had carried out. "More?"

"Just one more stack," he said and disappeared around the corner. "Thank you for giving away some of the food. I didn't want to eat this for the next month."

"With Hayden and Heath working upstairs this week, it will only last a couple of days, but yeah, make it be gone." She shut the refrigerator door, pushed past him and grinned. "Race you for the bedroom."

"What?" He laughed. "You're a crazy woman."

Polly ran through the foyer and he raced to the back stairway.

She caught Hayden's look of surprise as she ran up the steps and flew through the double doors. Henry raced down the hallway after her, but she beat him to their bedroom. Trying to shut the door before he got there, she finally let him in.

Elijah came out of his bedroom. "We put our clothes on the chairs neat."

"That's great," Polly said. Henry stood behind her, tickling her waist. "You two can play for a while. Henry and I are going to take the dogs for a walk. We'll be back later."

"Can we come?" Elijah asked.

"No. You've had a big day." Polly giggled as she pushed her husband's hands away. "You play in your room or go downstairs and ask Hayden to play a video game with you."

His face drooped into a sad frown and he slunk back into his bedroom.

Polly shut her door.

"That's what we're calling it now?" Henry asked. "Taking the dogs for a walk?"

"Stop it. Be good. We are taking them out. Now change your clothes."

"Yes, ma'am, but only if you change yours first."

Polly shook her head. She turned around and said, "Unzip me, please?"

"I'll unzip you ..."

# CHAPTER TWENTY-FOUR

"Consider this," Henry said as he and Polly walked back downstairs.

"What?"

"I've been thinking that we need to move somewhere else."

Polly stopped on the third step from the bottom. "What in the hell did you just say?"

"This neighborhood is creepy."

She laughed. "I have no idea what you're talking about."

"Think about it. First, there was a ghost in this house. She turns out to be the long-lost granddaughter of a woman who hanged herself." He patted the banister. "From this banister, no less. Then there's the guy who profited from promoting this as a ghost house and planted marijuana in our back yard and has a creepy hidden gateway from his yard. Then, there's the man who lived next door to the old man who planted weed in our backyard. He's probably going to turn out to be some awful wife abuser, murderer, and child molester. Then there's Shawn Wesley, the guy who broke into the house while we were renovating it to steal copper pipe so he could buy drugs. Isn't that enough?"

Polly chuckled. "Don't you think we're starting to clean it up?"

"What if that poor Loeffler guy was killed in Bridger's house?"

"Yeah?"

"Oh Polly," Henry said, pulling her close. "I love you."

"The dogs have to be really antsy by now. We should head out."

"We need to bring back a couple of the vehicles anyway," Henry said. "We could walk them to the elementary school and drive back."

"That's a good idea."

They went into the kitchen and didn't see any of their kids or the dogs. "Hello? Anyone here?" Polly called. She giggled and whispered to Henry. "We weren't upstairs that long, were we?"

"In here, playing games," Hayden yelled back.

Polly found her boys snuggled together on the couch in the family room playing a racing game. The dogs were draped over the little ones and felines were perched everywhere, happy to be with people again. She supposed that in their short lifespans, three hours would seem like an eternity.

"We took the dogs on a short walk," Hayden said, turning to look at her. "The boys wanted to see the burned down house. I kept all of us on the other side of the street. That whole thing is a mess. The policeman said they won't be able to dig in until tomorrow at the earliest."

"Thank you," Polly said. "Well, if the dogs are good, Henry and I are going to walk to the elementary school and get a couple of the vehicles. We'll be back after a while. Kayla and Rebecca should be home by eight-thirty. I don't know what time Stephanie will be back."

"Heath texted me. He's going to be late, but he said he'd be home before we went to bed — eleven-thirty or so."

"Cool. Thanks." She went back to the kitchen, where Henry was putting plastic silverware into zipper bags. "The dogs are set and the kids are playing games. Let's just go get our trucks."

As they went out the side door, Henry took her hand. "It occurs to me that no matter where I move with you, trouble will find us. Maybe we *should* stay put. We'll be the good influence in the neighborhood."

"Good plan."

"Why doesn't anyone else find mysteries in their homes or thieves that stash treasures in their hay loft?"

"Maybe these things happen, but no one else thinks to look for them," she replied. "What about that? Huh? Huh?"

He waved at Cal Dexter's kids, playing in the yard across the street. "You've got me there."

"Did you talk to that creep that knew Hayden and Heath when they were kids?" she asked.

"No. He was gone by the time I heard about him. Hayden said something to me."

"Did Hayden talk to him?"

"Just for a minute," Henry said, stopping to look at her. "Their aunt and uncle told him how to find our house?"

Polly nodded in response. "What kind folks they are. What does Hayden think of him?"

"Not much. Said he hadn't been around in years. Some old friend of their mother's or maybe a shirt tail relation. I don't know that he really knew what the relationship was."

"Heath seemed uncomfortable around him."

"Hayden, too. Why didn't he stay longer?"

Polly laughed and sighed. "Ohhh, because I was mean. I told Aaron to stare at him after telling Heath in front of the man that the sheriff wanted to talk to him. Once he knew Aaron was law enforcement, I guess he decided to leave. That doesn't say much for his character, does it?"

"You're horrible."

They turned the corner and walked along in front of Jim Bridger's house. The sidewalk in front of the burned down home was roped off, so Polly stopped. "I remember the night I drove in here and chased that girl into Jim Bridger's back yard. The gate was just a latch." She walked down the driveway.

"Polly," Henry said under his breath, but he followed her. "That's Bert Bradford. What will you tell him we're doing?"

"We'll tell him that we've been interested in this house and now with the home next door burned down, we're thinking of buying all this property and doing something good with it."

"He's not going to believe that."

Polly turned on him. "Seriously? This is me and you we're talking about. We've done the weirdest things in town so far. Why wouldn't we do something crazy like that?" She flipped the latch up on the gate. "Look. That was easy."

The back yard hadn't been mowed this spring. With the intense rain they'd been getting, the grass was high and weeds were shooting up above it.

"Someone needs to get in and take care of this," Henry said. "I don't know who's maintaining his front yard. I should ask."

"We aren't going to find anything in that mess." Polly walked up the steps to the back porch and jiggled the handle, opening the door.

"Polly!" Henry shouted. "Stop it."

"But this shouldn't be unlocked."

"Then we tell Bert about it. Or if you think this is about Barney Loeffler, we call Aaron."

In the time it took him to spit out those words, Polly had pushed the door open, turned on her phone's flashlight, and was heading into the kitchen. She'd been in here before. "Henry, call Aaron," Polly said. "This is where it happened."

"I don't want to," he said, holding the back door open. He took out his phone anyway.

The sound of a man's guttural growl accompanied rushing feet and Polly was knocked to the floor.

"What in the hell?" she yelled, dropping her phone while scrabbling to get up. She opened the cabinet in front of her, hoping to find a weapon, knowing that this man might hurt her husband. Without looking at what was in her hand, she threw it as hard as she could and prayed that for the first time in her life, she might hit the target.

The man yelped and dropped. Polly grabbed her phone, stood up and rushed to Henry. "Are you okay?"

Henry nodded, his breaths coming in short bursts. "Are you?"

"I'm fine. I hit him. What did I hit him with?"

Henry pointed at a sauce pan that had landed two feet to the other side of the man on the ground.

"Oh," Polly said, sagging. "I didn't hit him."

"No, honey, I did." Henry held up a baseball bat. "Mr. Bridger must have been worried about prowlers."

"That was fast thinking."

"I hope I didn't hurt him too badly."

Polly saw the man stir and she pulled her foot back.

"Stop, honey. He's not going anywhere. You don't need to kick him, but you might check one of those drawers and see if Bridger had any rope."

"I'll just yell for Bert," she said. "He'll have handcuffs, unless you want to go get him."

He released a pained laugh. "I'm not leaving you alone with this man. I'm not sure which of you I'm more concerned for. Go get Bert."

Polly slipped past Henry and went back down the steps, out the gate, and down the driveway.

"Hi there, Polly," Bert said. "What are you doing back there?"

"I need you and your handcuffs. I think we found one of the murderers in Jim Bridger's house."

Bert picked up speed and they ran to the back door and inside. "What is this?" he asked. It took a few moments for him to take in the scene before him in the kitchen. "I take it things were this way before you got here?"

"This man rushed Polly and I hit him with the bat." Henry held it out to Bert. "He's starting to come around."

"Why is he in this house? It's been closed up for more than a year."

"Exactly," Polly said. "Can I call Aaron?"

"I should call Ken, too," Bert said, kneeling beside the man on the floor. "Do you want to confess to anything now or should I just put handcuffs on you and let these two beat it out of you?" He smirked up at Polly.

"There's another one around somewhere," Polly said. "There had to have been two of them. Am I right?"

The man snarled at her, but glanced behind her into the kitchen.

She jumped. "He's in the house?"

Bert snapped the cuffs on the man, leaving him face down on the floor. "Sit on him if you have to. Call Aaron, call Ken. When they get here, stay out of the way." He pulled out his gun and headed into the house.

Polly knew that Ken's people would get here the fastest. Rather than wait for dispatch to reach him, she dialed his personal cell phone.

"Polly, what is it?"

"I'm in Jim Bridger's old house. Henry knocked a guy down when he rushed me and Bert's going through the house looking for the other one. I think these guys murdered Barney Loeffler. Bert told me to call you."

"We're on the way." Ken hung up and Polly looked around, trying to find the best way to contain the man lying on the floor.

She finally grabbed one of the wooden kitchen chairs, situated it over his waist and buttocks, and sat down on it.

"Call Aaron," Henry said, shaking his head in amazement.

"I'm getting there. I just didn't want this guy to think he could move and run away."

"He's not going anywhere. Make the call."

She swiped the next call open.

"Polly, what did you find now?"

"Maybe the murderers. Bert Bradford's going through Jim Bridger's house right now looking for the second one. The first one is trapped under a kitchen chair on the back porch, but Bert handcuffed him. I called Ken. He's coming, too."

"I'm not sure what you've done, so we're on the way. I love you, but you scare the crap out of me. Bye."

Polly put the phone down and felt her hands and forearms shake. "I didn't think anyone was still inside the house," she said to Henry. "I swear. I didn't mean to do this."

He waggled the baseball bat in front of her. "I'm trying not to freak out. I don't know what's worse. Being here when you walk into the middle of something or hearing about it later."

"At least if you're here, you can help. Look what you did."

"Pure reaction and adrenaline. When he knocked you over, I didn't even think, I just did."

"That's exactly what I do."

"You're not helping the situation."

The man on the floor moaned and tried to move. He turned his head, confused at what was restraining him.

"Why did you kill Barney Loeffler?" Polly asked.

He didn't respond and she nudged him with her foot. "He was just a good guy. Everybody liked him. Why did you kill him?"

"Hnnh" was his only response.

"He's not going to talk to you." Henry said. He did take out his phone and snap a picture.

"Yes he is," Polly said, nudging him again. "Why did you kill that poor junk man?"

"Tried to steal from us."

Scuffling in the dining room and then the kitchen caused both of them to turn as Bert dragged a bleary-eyed man toward them.

"Drunk as a skunk," Bert said. "Passed out on one of the beds upstairs. All I had to do was put the zip-ties on and bring him downstairs. I had more trouble keeping him upright than anything else. Everyone on their way?"

"The troops have been mobilized," Polly said. "And idiot boy here just admitted that he killed Barney Loeffler. Said that he tried to steal from them."

"Well, that makes it easier." Bert looked at her sitting on the chair. "What have you done?"

"I didn't want him to move. Luckily he's skinny and the chair fit over him."

Bert started to laugh and before she knew it, she was laughing with him. They tried to stop, but it hit her how ridiculous the scene had to look and she let loose with uncontrollable laughter.

The back door opened and Ken stood there, taking it all in.

"What in the world?" he asked.

"Can we hire her, Chief?" Bert asked, through more laughter. "Look what she did!"

Ken just stared at them.

"Chief, I think these two men are responsible for Barney Loeffler's murder," Polly said. "If nothing else, you can arrest them for breaking and entering. I can't imagine they have a right to be in this house." She nudged the man on the floor again. "You don't, do you?"

"Hnnh," he said.

"He doesn't want to talk to me. But if you look at the kitchen, you'll see that is probably where the murder took place."

Ken gingerly stepped over the man lying on the floor and into the kitchen. "My god," he said. "What did you do to poor Barney in here? This looks awful." He turned back to Polly. "You called Aaron, right?"

She nodded.

"Good. He's got the forensics team. This looks like a slaughterhouse."

"It was a head wound," Polly said.

Ken nodded and stepped back onto the porch. "Let's get you all out of here so the sheriff and his people can get in and process the scene. We'll take these two in until Aaron is ready to move them. I don't want this collar, do you, Bert?"

"No sir," Bert said. "I have enough with the house next door."

More sirens tore through the quiet evening as emergency vehicles, police cars, and sheriff's vehicles pulled into the neighborhood.

As Polly and Henry walked back through to the driveway, Aaron was the first to greet them.

"Are you okay?" Aaron asked.

Henry put his hand out and Aaron shook it. "We're good. I beaned the bad guy after he knocked Polly down."

Aaron put his hand out to Polly and when she took it, he pulled her in tight. "Now you have Henry taking down bad guys?"

"He's my hero."

Ken and Bert came out next, escorting their two prisoners. The one who'd been lying on the floor under Polly's chair spat at the ground in front of her. Ken jerked his arm. "I'll be back in a minute to talk to you, Sheriff. This one is all yours. We're just glad to help."

"The kitchen is where the murder took place," Polly said. "Either that, or those two slaughtered a pig in there."

"How did you know to look for them here?"

Polly took a breath. "Mona Bright told me that Barney Loeffler had been here the evening before I found him because someone was buying the house. Then Henry said that the house wasn't for sale, that he and Bill had looked into it, so there shouldn't be anyone here. We were walking up to the elementary school to get our trucks and I snuck back here. The door was unlocked. It shouldn't have been unlocked. Right?"

Aaron nodded.

"When I went inside, I saw blood splattered around the kitchen. I was just getting ready to call you when that skinny guy that Ken brought out rushed me. Henry hit him with a ball bat and I came outside to get Bert."

Tab Hudson ran up to them and hugged Polly. "Are you okay?"

"I'm good."

"Deputy, you're in charge here. The murder scene is the kitchen. Get 'em suited up," Aaron said.

"Aye, aye," Tab said, giving him a crisp nod. She squeezed Polly's hand and headed for the back door.

Polly heard her barking orders as more and more people streamed in.

"Two nights, same neighborhood," Aaron said. "This is a new record for you, Polly."

She stepped back. "Hey. This is not my fault. I didn't set the fire and I didn't murder Barney Loeffler."

"It's a good thing. Otherwise, your neighbors would run you out of town."

Polly slumped her shoulders. "I know. Just about the time I'm starting to get to know them, this happens and I'm right in the middle of it."

"I just told Polly we're cleaning up the neighborhood," Henry said. "Anyone else we should know about around here?"

Aaron nodded his head toward the Wesley's house across the street. "You already know about him."

"I hear he's going to be gone for some time," Polly said. "Who picked him up in Boone?"

"The police have him. I hope his wife can make a go of it without him."

"Probably better than with him," Henry said. "So how do we slink home without people seeing us?"

Aaron laughed. "Good luck. Everyone is out on their porches again."

"Maybe we'll get our cars in the morning," he said. "I wish that gate in Bridger's back yard was still accessible. We could just slip through into our yard."

Polly swatted at him. "You just knocked a guy out with a baseball bat. You can handle a few curious neighbors."

"Go on home," Aaron said. He nodded at another deputy who was heading inside. "We'll talk tomorrow. You have graduation and then anything else?"

"Just graduation and then I'm collapsing," Polly said. "But I do want to know why they killed that poor guy. And who was the other man in the trailer?"

"As soon as I know something, I will tell you," Aaron replied.

"No you won't." She pursed her lips. "You never do."

Aaron gave her another quick hug. "You deserve to know after this escapade. I promise I will tell you as soon as possible."

For once, Polly was grateful for the large number of vehicles clogging the street. They stayed behind them as long as possible, hugging their shrubbery until they got to the driveway and entered the safety of their yard.

"I can't believe we got home without tons of questions," Henry said.

"The kids will have plenty, I'm sure."

"Those we can handle." He stopped at the bottom of the steps and took her into his arms. "I'm always proud of you and your fearless strength. You know that, right?"

"But," Polly said.

"No. I won't do any *buts* on this one. I am always proud of you. You scare the crap out of me, but even when I'm terrified, I don't really worry. I have confidence in you." He chuckled. "Except for that whole throwing thing. You thought you took him down?"

"I was so scared he was going to hurt you. I had to do something."

"And I love you for that." He kissed her nose, then pulled back and opened his phone to show her the picture he'd snapped of her sitting on a chair over the guy. "This one is making the rounds."

Polly started to laugh again. "I can't believe I did that. I was so scared he'd roll over and get up, then start hurting us. I had to come up with something. The chair was right there."

"For a girl who can't gauge the trajectory of a toss, you certainly managed to gauge the depth of those chair legs. Nice job."

They started up the steps and Polly laughed when she realized that their entire family, including Heath, was standing on the back porch waiting for them to come home. "It's time to face the music."

"We've faced worse tonight, right?"

"I'm not so sure."

# CHAPTER TWENTY-FIVE

Elijah bounced on his feet as he waited for Polly to hand him the bottles of ketchup and mustard. "This is going to be the best party ever."

She smiled as he ran for the door.

Kayla covered the bowl of slaw she'd made and Rebecca carried a pan of baked beans. She stopped at the door to the back porch. "I didn't get any spoons."

"I've got 'em," Polly said. "Go on."

"Anything else?" Stephanie asked, bags of hot dog buns in her hands.

"Just the chips and we're good to go."

Hayden was standing at the base of the steps when they went out. "Can I help?"

Polly shook her head. "We've got it all, I think."

"Okay, I just need to grab one more thing." He waited until she was outside before going in.

It felt like tonight was a turning point. When they woke up tomorrow, no one would be in a hurry ... well, except for Henry. Now that Heath's graduation ceremony was over, his life was about to take another course. Rebecca and Kayla were already looking forward to what high school might bring and the little boys were just happy to be alive. Every time Polly looked up from whatever she was doing, it felt as if the world was bending and changing, sending her family on a new course.

"Noah, could you bring a couple of those plates over here?" Henry asked.

The little boy jumped up from where he'd been playing with Obiwan in the grass and ran to the table in the gazebo. Polly handed two plates to him and he took off at a run for Henry and the grill. He waited patiently while Henry filled each plate with hot dogs and bratwursts. The two walked back much more slowly, Henry keeping an eye on every step Noah took.

"This is nice," Heath said. "Just us." He smiled at Stephanie. "I'm glad you're here too, you know."

Stephanie nodded. Skylar was seated beside her and took her hand, causing Rebecca and Kayla to whisper and giggle.

Polly glared at the two girls and they did their best to straighten up.

"Dig in," Henry said. "If we need more, I'll grill more."

Hayden returned and sat down beside Rebecca. She looked at him and he gave her a slight nod and a smile.

"Will we have a big party when I graduate from high school?" Elijah asked.

"You bet we will," Polly replied. "All of your friends will come to celebrate and so will this big family." She smiled at Hayden. "That's ten years from now. Who's to say what you'll be doing? And you, Heath, how many kids will you have?"

He looked at her in utter shock. "Me? Kids? I don't even have a girlfriend."

"That can change overnight," Henry said. "Trust me. All I was going to do was renovate an old schoolhouse. Now look what I've got. Five kids, more friends than I ever expected, a big old house and a wife who ..."

Polly interrupted. "Be careful there."

"Who always surprises me," he said.

282

Kayla put her sandwich on her plate. "I can't believe you hit that man over the head with a baseball bat."

"I can't believe Polly missed him with the saucepan," Henry replied. He put a scoop of beans on Elijah's plate.

Evidently, it wasn't enough, because Elijah gestured for more.

"Just a little more," Henry said. "If you finish everything, you can ask for seconds."

Elijah nodded and Henry turned to his other side and Noah.

"What about that man who was murdered?" Skylar asked.

"I talked to Aaron at the graduation ceremony," Polly said. "We didn't have much time, but it seems Barney Loeffler realized they weren't part of Jim Bridger's family and shouldn't have been cleaning the house out. They'd called to get rid of a sofa they slit apart when looking for cash that they believed was hidden in the house. Not the brightest men. They knew Bridger from the days he sold marijuana seeds, and apparently, there are stories out there about how he had millions of dollars stashed in his house. None of the neighbors knew any different, so when these two men said they were family, people accepted it. They acted like they owned the place, were nice to Pat and Al Lynch, and even asked questions about some of the other neighbors in the area, saying that old Jim had told them who were good people."

"I can't believe no one questioned it. What about the other guy you found?"

"Aaron isn't sure who that other man is that I found in the trailer. The two losers who killed Barney Loeffler didn't seem to know anything about him. That one's still a curiosity." Polly huffed a laugh. "As for the neighbors, why would anyone worry about a thief? Who would steal anything from that old house? Mr. Bridger didn't have anything nice in there. His television is so old, I can't believe it still worked, and it's not like he had fancy computer equipment or anything."

"What do you think he spent the money on?" Rebecca asked. "Maybe there *is* a fortune in cash hidden there."

"If there is, someone else is going to have to find it," Polly said. "It won't be us. The sheriff's department is going through that place with a fine-tooth comb now and the state is going to start proceedings to take the property so they can put it on the market. It was just one of those things that fell through the cracks."

"Maybe he buried it in our back yard," Rebecca whispered loudly. "We should get a metal detector."

"Trust me," Henry said. "When we went looking for tunnels, we would have found anything weird that was buried."

She drooped, turned to Kayla and stuck her lower lip out. "No fun." Then she perked up. "But the tunnel guy didn't look in Mr. Bridger's back yard. If we had a metal detector, we could check that out."

"Uh huh," Polly said. "Don't get your hopes up."

"That's two lots that will go up for sale," Hayden said. "And all because you ..."

Polly put her hand up. "Like I said, be careful."

He laughed. "I'm just saying."

"I know exactly what you're saying and stop it."

"What about that girl who set the fires?" Stephanie asked. "She must have been living in hell to go that far. I wish I would have known. I could have ..." She shook her head. "I don't know what I could have done, but she shouldn't have had to face that all by herself."

Skylar reached out and softly touched her arm. When she didn't respond, he took his hand back and draped it across the back of her chair.

"Ken brought in an advocate for her," Polly said. "Someone who's dealt with those types of situations."

"It's sick that you can say 'those types of situations,'" Heath said. "There just shouldn't be that many. People are sick."

He turned angry eyes toward Stephanie and then softened. "I'm sorry."

"It's okay," she said. "I understand. It is sick. Whatever it was he did to her in that house, nobody should be pushed to do what she did."

"I know it's all going to come out in the news," Hayden said, "but I really don't even want to know."

"Know what?" Elijah asked. "What did he do?"

Hayden took a long breath.

Polly nodded and sat forward. "The girl who started all of those fires in town lived with a bad man. He hurt her. All I saw were some bad bruises on her arms, but she was so mad at him that she burned the house down so she would never have to live there again."

Noah slid himself closer to Henry, who reached out to put an arm around the boy.

"Are you okay?" Henry asked.

"Bad people," Noah said, melting against Henry's side.

"You're safe here," Henry said. He put his other arm around Elijah. "Both of you are safe here. You have a whole lot of people who love you and will do everything they can to protect you from bad people. Do you believe that?"

Noah looked up, his big brown eyes swimming with tears.

Rebecca couldn't contain herself. She pushed back from the table and rushed around to Noah's side.

Henry moved his arm and Rebecca pulled the little boy into a hug. "That's the best thing about living with Polly and Henry. Even if bad people try to hurt you, they find you and make sure everything is okay. I promise."

With a small nod, Noah allowed himself to be held by Rebecca. He refused to let go and she picked him up and slid into his seat with the boy on her lap. Elijah, still holding half of a hot dog in his hand, reacted by finding his way into Henry's lap.

Polly looked around the table and said, "Anyone want to sit in my lap? I'm feeling a little left out here." Obiwan and Han, sitting politely on the floor of the gazebo, were waiting for food to drop. "Not even you two," she said. "That's sad. I think we've talked enough about bad people. Today we're celebrating Heath and Rebecca's graduations."

"Mostly Heath's," Rebecca said. "That was pretty cool today. I can't wait to be the one in the cap and gown."

"Thank you all for coming," Heath said. "Three years ago I didn't think I'd even finish high school. And now it's like I can leave all that in the past and move on to something new. Then you had a big party for me and all those people showed up. I can't believe I know that many people. It's crazy."

Henry nodded. "And they like you a lot. You worked hard to turn your life around and you've been successful at it. We're very proud of you."

"Mom and Dad would have been proud too," Hayden said. He took a small package out of his pocket. "I want you to have this now. Dad gave it to me the day I graduated from high school."

"Your watch?" Heath asked. "You love that watch."

"I love it because it came from Dad. If he'd been here today, he would have given you the exact same gift."

"But it's yours."

Hayden pushed the package toward his brother. "Let's make a deal. You take care of the watch. When one of us has a son who graduates from high school, the watch will go to him. Okay?"

Heath picked it up, took the paper off and cradled the silver watch in his hands. "I can't believe you're doing this. Thank you," he said in hushed tones. "I'll be careful with it."

"No," Hayden said. "Wear it. If something happens, we fix it. I took it downtown to the jeweler and he cleaned it up and it's working better than it has in a long time. You should wear it. These things aren't supposed to sit on a shelf."

"Okay," Heath said. "Thank you."

"I guess it's gift time," Rebecca said. "I'll be right back." She shifted out from under Noah and returned him to the chair beside Henry.

"It's by the door," Hayden called after her.

"She did all of that stuff for me yesterday," Heath protested. "What else?"

"Just wait," Kayla said with a smile.

Rebecca returned with an obvious frame, wrapped in gift paper and handed it to Heath.

He tore the paper away and stared at the painting in front of him. "You did this?" he asked, his words halting as he caught his breath.

"Beryl and I worked on it all spring," Rebecca said. "It was my big project."

Elijah attempted to bounce up, but Henry held him tight.

"This is me," Heath said in awe.

Rebecca nodded. "Well, it's you since I've known you. Who knows what you'll do next."

Heath turned the painting around. Polly had seen it before, but it still carried a strong impact. The left side of the canvas was made of small squares and rectangles of blacks and grays. The dark colors transformed across the painting, giving way to more whites and light grays. Color exploded at about the halfway mark, as if chasing the silhouetted figure who was standing in front of an open doorway glowing with the brightness of the sun. In the open palm of the figure's extended hand, he held a heart. Another hand reached through the doorway, their fingertips barely touching.

"You are amazing," he said. "This is as good as Ms. Watson."

"I don't think so," Rebecca replied, blushing. "She lets me create what I want, though."

"I'd buy this," he said. "I'd pay a lot of money for it."

"Well, luckily you don't have to. I didn't want to give this to you yesterday and have everybody see it. It's just between us, okay?" Rebecca said. She sat back down beside Kayla.

Polly reached around Kayla and rubbed Rebecca's back.

"Okay. Thank you."

"It's our turn," Henry said.

Heath groaned. "No. You've done so much. No more."

"Just one more," Polly said.

Henry put something into Elijah's hand. "Take that to your brother."

Elijah jumped down from Henry's lap and ran over to Heath and deposited a small white box with a red ribbon around it. "What is it?" he asked Henry.

"Let Heath open his gift," Henry replied.

Heath took the ribbon off and lifted the lid away. "What?" He held up the keys to his truck.

"The truck is yours. We'll go to Boone tomorrow and transfer ownership, but we want you to use the money you've been saving for a car on other things — like gas and insurance."

"You have books and other fees coming up too, bro," Hayden said. "You're going to need that money."

"It's mine?" Heath turned to Polly. "I thought you hated it."

"I'm getting over it. I've seen you in that truck enough that I can let go of the past and move on. It's all yours now."

"Wow. Thanks."

Henry handed over a white envelope. "That's from Nate Mikkels. Before you start going back and forth to school this August, we'll take the truck out to his shop and give it a good once over. I wouldn't let him give it to you yesterday because you didn't know about the truck yet."

"I don't know what to say." Heath's eyes filled. "You guys make me cry all the time."

Hayden chuckled. "I think that's Polly's favorite thing. Did you hear what she said earlier?"

Heath shook his head.

"They talk about having five kids. Count 'em up, bud."

"Oh. Wow," Heath said. "You, too."

"I feel like I'm one of their kids, too," Kayla said quietly.

Polly patted her shoulder. "You really are. My family is so big. When you two girls came into our lives, you brought me a lot of joy. I'm glad you're here." She grinned at Skylar. "And I love you too. Since Stephanie is my daughter, you'd better be good to her or I'll sic her brothers on you. She has a bunch these days."

"Free coffee on me anytime you guys show up at Sweet Beans," Skylar said. "Will that keep me in your good graces?"

Hayden smiled and wagged his index finger. "It's a start. But I'm keeping my eye on you." He sat back and put his hand on Heath's back. "Life's weird. You never know where it's going to take you. I didn't know what to think about this summer after Tess and I broke up, but that's okay. I can be ready for anything that comes along."

"You're going to be fine," Rebecca said.

He nodded. "We all are. We just have to go with the flow, right?"

Polly smiled across the table at Henry. She could hardly wait for what might come next.

"I think s'mores are in order," Henry said. He stood up. "Hayden and I dug a little pit for the branches and sticks you boys gathered yesterday. We'll light it up so we can melt marshmallows. Polly?"

"On it. The sticks are in the garage and I'll get the goodies. If the rest of you would help me carry food inside, we'll have ourselves a little bonfire." She walked past Henry. "Firepit is next on the wish list, you know."

"As soon as I scooped the first shovelful of dirt, I knew we'd be installing one soon." He took her hand. "Thank you."

She stopped on the second step.

"For this life."

"Even with the crazies?"

"As long as it's with you, even with the crazies."

Polly stepped back up onto the floor of the gazebo and kissed him. He wrapped his arms around her and she lost herself in the kiss.

"Would you puh-leeze," Rebecca said. "There are children around, you know."

Elijah poked Polly's leg. "It's okay. I like seeing you kiss."

Henry kissed her again, then whispered. "It's okay. Right?"

"Always."

# THANK YOU FOR READING!

I'm so glad you enjoy these stories about Polly Giller and her friends. There are many ways to stay in touch with Diane and the Bellingwood community.

You can find more details about Sycamore House and Bellingwood at the website: http://nammynools.com/. Be sure to sign up for the monthly newsletter so you don't miss anything.

Join the Bellingwood Facebook page:
https://www.facebook.com/pollygiller
for news about upcoming books, conversations while I'm writing and you're reading, and a continued look at life in a small town.

Diane Greenwood Muir's Amazon Author Page is a great place to watch for new releases.

Follow Diane on Twitter at twitter.com/nammynools for regular updates and notifications.

Recipes and decorating ideas found in the books can often be found on Pinterest at: http://pinterest.com/nammynools/

And, if you are looking for Sycamore House swag, check out Polly's CafePress store: http://www.cafepress.com/sycamorehouse